Jon Huer received his Ph.D. in sociology from UCLA in 1975 and is the author of 15 books on social criticism, art philosophy and political economy. TIME magazine called one of his books, *The Dead End,* "An important and brilliant book (about) America's national death wish." After teaching for the last 25 years of his career at U.S. military bases around the world, he retired to Greenfield, Massachusetts. Currently, he writes bi-weekly columns on U.S. politics and culture for the Greenfield Recorder.

To Terry and Jonathan, for their love and inspiration.

Jon Huer

Darwin's Progress

Austin Macauley Publishers
London * Cambridge * New York * Sharjah

Copyright © Jon Huer 2024

All rights reserved. No part of this publication may be reproduced, distributed, or transmitted in any form or by any means, including photocopying, recording, or other electronic or mechanical methods, without the prior written permission of the publisher, except in the case of brief quotations embodied in critical reviews and certain other non-commercial uses permitted by copyright law. For permission requests, write to the publisher.

Any person who commits any unauthorized act in relation to this publication may be liable to criminal prosecution and civil claims for damages.

This is a work of fiction. Names, characters, businesses, places, events, locales, and incidents are either the products of the author's imagination or used in a fictitious manner. Any resemblance to actual persons, living or dead, or actual events is purely coincidental.

Ordering Information
Quantity sales: Special discounts are available on quantity purchases by corporations, associations, and others. For details, contact the publisher at the address below.

Publisher's Cataloging-in-Publication data
Huer, Jon
Darwin's Progress

ISBN 9798889100829 (Paperback)
ISBN 9798889100836 (Hardback)
ISBN 9798889100973 (ePub e-book)

Library of Congress Control Number: 2024901838

www.austinmacauley.com/us

First Published 2024
Austin Macauley Publishers LLC
40 Wall Street, 33rd Floor, Suite 3302
New York, NY 10005
USA

mail-usa@austinmacauley.com
+1 (646) 5125767

Prologue

It was not too long after I had written *The Green Palmers Chronicle* for Miss Raynor that I received a letter from John Sabella. The last we had heard of him, actually a wild rumor, was that he might have become a merchant mariner sailing the oceans. In fact, I distinctly remember feeling envious of his adventurous and free life as a sailor when we first heard the rumor in Laurinville.

According to the letter postmarked 'The Republic of Moreland', but without his name on the envelope, John had indeed become a sailor, now having settled in Moreland. He first made me swear not to tell his parents or anyone else in Laurinville about his present location because, he said, he "would tell them in my own good time." In the letter, John detailed how he had joined the merchant marines as soon as he had come of age, adding a year or two on his own, and sailed all over the world. Then, he went on to describe Moreland as a 'living paradise' of wonder and sweetness.

Following that shocking first letter, we began to exchange letters more regularly, each time my curiosity rising higher about Moreland. The small island-nation was located somewhat in the middle of a triangle made up of Fiji, New Zealand and Australia. Its population consisted of the descendants of a mixture of retired English seamen and the natives, who eventually adopted the name Moreland in the 17th century in honor of Sir Thomas More who had written a book about 'Utopia'. The settlers and natives believed that their island-nation strongly resembled the utopia in Sir Thomas's fable. John sent me many photographs that seemed to confirm their claim, for they showed a place of uncommon beauty and wholesomeness.

Beginning in the fifth letter or so, John started to suggest that I should visit Moreland and, if I liked what I saw, become a schoolteacher there because, according to my friend, there was a critical shortage of teachers on the island-nation. For good measure, John enclosed a letter from the local school superintendent, apparently on good terms with John, who strongly urged me to consider the opportunity. The letter added that, from what the superintendent had heard from John, there was a good deal of similarities between Laurinville and Moreland and I should feel absolutely at home living there.

Life in Laurinville had become somewhat uneventful at the time as the memories of the Green Palmers and my own role in the affair had gradually faded. As a young man in his early twenties, and one great adventure already under his belt, I was strongly tempted to give in to this exotic overture. In fact, I soon did. Shortly after my twenty-third birthday, I left for the island on a small cargo ship that John had arranged for me, and subsequently discovered that the Republic of Moreland was every bit as wonderful as it had been described to me.

The full story of my life in Moreland is collected in the many letters I had written to my parents who then gave them to Miss Raynor, the town librarian, who, in turn, had edited them into a monograph somewhat romantically titled 'Letters from Paradise: Descriptions of Life in Moreland, by Michael Brown'. In those letters, I wrote about the fishing and farming island-nation and its people who were always peaceful and happy. I also wrote about my small adventures that I had experienced while in Moreland—among them, discovering pirate caves on the island, surviving the collapse of an old fort while I was studying it, attending John's big wedding to the superintendent's daughter. My life there, teaching, fishing, and exploring, was so agreeable to me that, as everyone in Laurinville now knows, I stayed nine years on that island.

Moreland resembles Laurinville in one very important historical fact. The modern world—including the United States—seemed to have bypassed Moreland completely, as it certainly did Laurinville. The simple life of fishing and farming on the island was self-sufficient, and predictably the Morelanders paid little attention to the outside world and, for all that they knew, the outside world paid them just as little attention in return. (The only exception was when the island's long-dormant volcano gave a false signal of coming back to life.) That suited me very well too.

Indeed, for nine years, I was content to be a school teacher for the eager children and was only vaguely aware of the tumultuous changes, including those in the United States, that were occurring elsewhere. John, who sailed with his merchant ship periodically, brought home enough news about what was going on whenever his ship came to port. These and other aspects of my life in the Republic of Moreland are recorded in greater detail in 'Letters from Paradise'.

I would have stayed in Moreland much longer if it hadn't been for Mr. LaGrange's retirement and his strong recommendation that I be appointed the next school principal in Laurinville. After some more letters from my parents that strongly urged me to come home, I finally decided to return to Laurinville and assume the role of a school principal. Now as a thirty-two-year-old teacher of some experience, I sailed back home once again on a cargo boat bound for an American port a few hours' bus ride from Laurinville. Finding that my hometown had remained virtually unchanged for over a decade, I began to settle down myself into a new routine life.

Indeed, my first year back home was wonderful, if uneventful, enjoying my parents once again, getting used to my job as principal, and telling stories about my life in Moreland to anyone who is interested. Now and then, Miss Raynor would tell me that my two 'books', the eyewitness account of the Green Palmers and the letters from Moreland, regularly found new readers at her library, many of them young. It is somewhat amusing to me that I am sitting down now at my desk once again to write another recollection of my recent adventures and discoveries, this time concerning my own country, the 'new' America, that I hardly knew.

How did it all begin?

It was in the late summer toward the end of my first year as principal, that I received a letter from one Professor Cecil McMiller at the University of Wilmington, North Carolina. It read:

Dear Mr. Michael Brown (so read the letter):

I have only recently read your autobiographical report entitled THE GREEN PALMERS CHRONICLE (I and my wife Carol have thoroughly enjoyed your resolute and honest account) and have been meaning to communicate with you. But my busy schedule at the university has kept me from writing to you sooner.

Since reading your account I have done some research on Laurinville and discovered that your town has been virtually isolated, now along with Atkinson and another small town within the county, from the rest of America following the dreadful encounter with the Green Palmers. I can understand the fear and foreboding that must have permeated all aspects of life in Laurinville and the terror that the Event, as you called it, has inspired in the hearts of its townspeople. It is no small wonder, then, that your town has completely withdrawn from 'us' and 'we' call you 'the new Amish people in America' for your tendency to dissociate yourselves from the rest of America. I have spoken several times on the telephone with my cousin Miriam Raynor, who earlier sent me a copy of your monograph, to get a better picture of the situation that surrounds the town of Laurinville in general and the author of the report in particular.

Considering all the information I have regarding the town and yourself, and especially considering your long stay in the Republic of Moreland, I have come to the conclusion, with the help of our academic dean at the University, that it would be to everyone's benefit that we invited you to visit the 'new' America and observe things yourself. The United States of America has changed a great deal in the last twenty years (that is, since the invasion of your town by the Green Palmers), and especially in the last decade or so while you were in Moreland. I am certain that you will find these changes highly satisfying to your intellectual curiosity and also enlightening to your personal knowledge in general. But unlike the Morelanders, I would not call our society a 'utopia' or anything like that as yet, although some proud Americans have been known to have declared it. But I and most of my social science colleagues at the University of Wilmington believe that we have achieved something no other society has ever done in human history in bringing about general happiness and consensus for so many people.

Observing the new way of life for American society yourself personally, you might get a rather different opinion concerning your own larger society about which you have had so little opportunity to learn. We would be happy if you could stay at our home with us during your visit. And carol is very enthusiastic about the idea.

I remain flexible as to what time period would best suit your schedule. What do you think? We would appreciate your response at your earliest convenience.

Sincerely,
(Signed) cecil mcmiller

PS. Cousin Miriam tells me that you are interested in studying old forts. We have a fine relic of a specimen in Fort Fisher near Wilmington, which is regarded by many experts as a prototype Civil War fort.

I read the letter several times and found myself in deep thought, with the letter still in my hand, at the sudden development. Visit the 'new' United States that I hardly know?

Professor McMiller (or mcmiller?) was essentially correct in assessing what Laurinville actually thought of itself and the rest of America. In the post-Green Palm isolation, the townspeople of Laurinville, not unlike the Amish perhaps, gradually began to think of the rest of America almost as a 'foreign' country. This habit of mind, I found, had become only strengthened and reinforced during the decade of my absence.

Under these peculiar historical and personal circumstances, as I thought more about it, the invitation from someone in 'America' was rather intriguing. As a bachelor of simple habits my private life at the time was uncomplicated. The role of school principal could be taken over by anyone for a few weeks (but not Mrs. Wilson, for she finally retired three years ago).

I talked the matter over with my father and stepmother, formerly Miss Casey, who were of the opinion that I should accept the invitation. Miss Raynor supplied further information about the McMillers, notably, that Cecil McMiller was a successful political science professor at the University and his wife Carol (carol?) a respected artist. The librarian reminded me that, for all practical purposes, I had become a foreigner concerning recent events and changes in the United States and I owed it to my students and townspeople to learn more about our larger society than was currently known. Much of what Laurinville feared about "the outside world," she said, could turn out to be groundless.

So, I made the decision to see the rest of my own country that I knew little about. I wrote back to Professor McMiller thanking him for his kindness and gratefully accepting his invitation. Immediately I received a delighted letter from him, in which he called me "Dear Michael" (I dropped Mikey when I became a teacher) as though we were old friends, quite different from the stiff formality of his first letter. He said he would make all the necessary arrangements, financial or otherwise, as soon as I told him the details of my schedule. Some more letters and telephone calls were exchanged, and I was on my way to a series of most unforgettable adventures in my own country.

Chapter One

The plane was large with rows and rows of seats and aisles longways and sideways. Attendants both male and female busied themselves helping passengers. They wore sharply pressed uniforms as well as friendly and dazzling smiles.

I had little time to enjoy the attendants, however, for my trouble began immediately. I did not have the 'HC', the Health Certificate, that every passenger apparently carried in person in America when they boarded a public transportation to show that one was disease free. The female attendant, hearing that I was from Laurinville (and long out of the country before that), was very sympathetic with me. She consulted with her captain and, with his permission, took me to the back of the plane and assigned me to what turned out to be one of the last seats. I expressed my gratitude to her and began to enjoy myself, looking at the panoramic view of the cabin from my good vantage point. Then as the engines revved up in preparation for takeoff a male attendant began his instruction to the passengers.

As he began his talk, pictures materialized on the many screens so that every passenger could have a clear view of at least one. First, he began describing how the plane was constructed, how much it cost, and so on. As he spoke detailed pictures synchronized with his speech, virtually one picture for each word. When he said 'this plane' it synchronized with the full view of the plane and when he said 'cost' it showed a huge stack of money. (Yes, I *did* think about the money-eating ritual at that precise moment.)

Then the female attendant took over and in her wonderfully friendly voice gave her instructions. All that was new to me, of course, but it seemed wholly routine to other passengers who hardly paid any attention to either the pictures or the attendant. She began to talk about some rules and regulations to be observed on the plane.

"On this plane," the attendance said, "every food item is individually and hygienically wrapped (showing how they were wrapped) to prevent the spread of any contaminations (showing germs moving from person to person). Please do not offer any of your food items, opened or unopened (showing a passenger offering an apple to another passenger and a large red X, apparently to mean 'do not', covering the whole picture). Please refrain from touching someone else (another appropriate picture prohibiting touching). You are liable to lawsuits according to Federal Regulations 32562C-DP-3594 (pictures of lawsuits served and of courtroom scenes)."

"If mutually agreed upon (two people nodding to each other), you may proceed to conversations with other passengers (they start talking) but only after presenting your HC's (both sides showing their HC's). At any rate, please maintain your personal distance of minimum three feet from the other person's face while carrying on a conversation (showing three feet in approximation) in order to avoid mutual transmission of diseases (some people getting sick) and to prevent lawsuit (again lawsuits and courtrooms)," etcetera, etcetera.

I could now understand why every American passenger carried the Health Certificate and how important it was for everyone's health and well-being. I was glad that there was no one in my immediate vicinity to transmit diseases to me. Now switching to the male attendant, some more instructions detailing other important matters were given out, with their appropriate pictures.

The last item mentioned was something called the TIW, and to show it to each other was 'optional'. But it was 'recommended as a matter of courtesy to each other' that they show their TIW's. Although I did not know what a TIW was, I was to find out almost immediately. A jovial looking man, sweating profusely as if he had run to the airport, joined me in the back to occupy one of the few remaining seats. As soon as he sat down, he smiled at me and pulled out something from the back pocket of his trousers.

"My drivers' license," he said smiling and holding it out close to my face so that I could see it. On his drivers' license was what appeared to be a picture of his face and other pertinent personal information. But what attracted my attention was a number '152' written in red across the whole license in large bold print. In fact, the number was the first thing I noticed.

Assuming it was some sort of classification number but, not knowing why the man was showing me his driver's license, I nodded politely and said, "Thank you. I am Michael Brown from Laurinville."

"What is *your* TIW?" the man said still smiling, but slightly confounded that I did not immediately respond in a like manner.

"I am sorry," I apologized, "I don't have a license and I have no idea what the TIW might be. You see, I only recently returned home to the United States from a long stay abroad."

His face darkened for a few seconds as if he had never seen anything like it before. When I repeated that I was from Laurinville and was out of the country for a long time, he seemed to understand me better. He relaxed and explained to me that the TIW number referred to 'the Total Individual Worth', the summary value of one's economic assets represented as a simple number. Looking at the man I judged that 152 was no small number.

"But why would you need to show it to other people?" I asked, puzzled.

The man explained that in America the TIW was thought to signify a person's place in society and identified the bearer of the number in the most straightforward manner. "It tells everybody who you are at a glance," he said. "It is the easiest way to identify people and to introduce yourself to others."

I was to learn more later about the meaning of TIW numbers and the clear and unforgiving ways in which the numbers cast a long and fatal shadow in American life. And it was through this ominous yet simplified method of human ranking that I encountered many of my adventures during my visit and met a woman who would eventually become my wife. But while I was sitting in the luxurious and somewhat overwhelming jet plane for the first time and learning about what amounted to a wholly new culture, my mind was too busy at the moment to fathom anything so dramatic and adventurous.

The plane finally took off, with a great roar that shook my whole body and deafened my ears. The airport soon disappeared from view and the plane broke through the clouds and came to a steady hum at the cruising altitude. As soon as I could hear I told the man, maintaining the three-feet rule all the while, that I was a schoolteacher and asked him what he did for a living.

"I am glad you asked," he said brightly. "I am glad you asked."

The man then proceeded to open a leather case the size of a small school lunchbox, which he carried with him. He pulled out a small machine with a screen that reminded me of an extremely small version of the tele-mindset that I had seen in my dream many years ago. The man put a small cartridge into the side of the machine and pushed a button to turn it on and adjusted a knob for sound. Immediately pictures materialized on the small screen. The man placed the machine in front of me on the coffee table. The screen showed the man, this time well-dressed and calmer, apparently speaking at his office.

"Hi, I am Ken Smith, and I am glad to tell you about my job," my fellow-passenger said on the screen. He then went on, with appropriate pictures, what he did for a living (he turned out to be a salesman). Naturally the pictures and his speech were mixed with background music, which was pleasant and unobtrusive. The program showed the product he sold and its importance to life and society in great detail. It was over in about five minutes. He said he had a 'longer version' for more professional occasions.

He told me that nowadays virtually everyone in America described their livelihood that way. It was more 'effective' in conveying the 'positive images' of one's 'occupational prestige', that is 'professionally and commercially staged'. The man was so enthusiastic and confident that I did not have the heart to ask him if everyone 'professionally and commercially staged' the program it would not eventually nullify the whole effect.

A little later, at my mention of family, he quickly put another cartridge into his machine to show his family, without waiting for my request. The screen showed a family—apparently his wife, and their two small children, a boy and a girl—happily frolicking in the yard. They were a picturesque and delightful family that anyone would be proud to show to other people. Now and then they waved at the camera, laughing and acting up. There was also music in the background that reminded me of a fairytale-like faraway place where everyone was always young and happy and pure at heart. I found myself being charmed by his family on the screen, smiling along with them. The 'shorter version' lasted about three minutes. He said he carried only the shorter version for his family when traveling.

"This family of mine," the man volunteered somewhat thoughtfully when I complimented him on his beautiful family, "is costing me an arm and a leg."

I nodded and agreed with him that raising a family in America, unlike in Laurinville or Moreland, must cost a lot of money. What I did not know at the time, and of course I could not have known, was that the man's innocent comment held the key to one of the best-known secrets of life in America. But this realization, of course, came much later during my visit.

As the flight maintained its cruising altitude the commotions died down and most passengers went into a restful long-term posture. My voluble salesman, too, started dozing off. The charming female attendant came to the back of the plane and, only three seats away from me, sat in one of the empty seats apparently to take her break. The light from above shone on her face, clearly illuminating it to my view. In contrast to her image only a few minutes earlier, she looked tired and suddenly old. Her smile that seemed so natural and ubiquitous had completely vanished from her face as she sat rigidly there staring at no particular point in the space in front of her.

I was surprised to discover that the world of dazzling smiles and energy could change so swiftly to a world of solitary void and loneliness. Feeling somewhat guilty as if I had intruded upon her private life, I turned away from her and looked out the window at the endless clouds. I listened to the hum of the powerful engines, thinking about the 'America' that I was about to visit. Some parts of it I felt I had already visited.

The flight took about three and half uneventful hours punctuated by food and drinks, and we finally landed at Wilmington International airport. My first day of bona fide visit was now under way.

Upon the salesman's advice to a virtual foreigner, I went to the airport bank to get what he called the 'cashing chip', the size of a folding matchbook, which was the substitute for cash for most Americans. One half of it was about as thin as the matchbook but its thickness increased gradually for the other half to accommodate a slit on its side which was large enough for another chip's thin side to be inserted. In other words, one side of the chip functioned as the 'inserter' as they called it, and the other side, the slit side, functioned as the 'receptor' as it was called, for another inserter to be inserted. A serial number, to identify the owner, was engraved at the bottom. Across one side was a dial that showed the total balance credited to my name. Its back had numbers from zero to ten and a plus and a minus sign, and also a small dial to ensure that you entered the right amount, just like the hand calculator.

"You don't need cash in America anymore," the woman at the window explained as she did to numerous 'real' foreign visitors to her country. "Everyone now carries this chip. When you pay someone, you use the inserter, by entering the amount of money you owe with these buttons. Then insert it into the receptor of the person you are paying. When someone pays you, the person does the same thing, except you will receive the amount with your receptor. The dial here always shows you how much money you have in your balance. All the necessary information for both parties is automatically transferred and registered in the chip at the same time. So simple, isn't it?"

She said all I had to do was to stop by one of the banks and have the chip 'cleaned' once in a while before it got overloaded.

"You mean no one uses cash anymore?" I asked, surprised and marveling at the famous American ingenuity and simplicity for convenience.

"I would say almost no one," the woman said. "Even children carry this too."

I told her that I had grown up in Laurinville and lived in another country for the better part of the last ten years, and this turn of event indeed was a surprise to me.

"Many other countries are thinking about adopting this system," the woman explained, assuming that Laurinville and Moreland were both foreign countries. She then went on to inform me that the chip could also be used on parking meters, newspaper stands, soda vendors, and other such machines that normally took small change. I thanked her and left her window.

No sooner had the gadget come into my possession than I had a chance to use it in a somewhat surprising transaction.

While I was waiting for Professor McMiller to materialize, I saw a small boy hanging about in the lounge, with no adult immediately around him. Just to be friendly and by my long-standing habit as a teacher of talking to children I tried my first casual conversation with a 'real' American child.

"How old are you, big fellow?" I asked, demonstrating all the friendly demeanor I was capable of producing.

"I ain't telling you," the boy said instantly.

"Then, can you tell me what your name is?" somewhat taken aback, I tried again.

"Nope," he said. "I ain't telling you that either."

"Why not?" I coaxed in some surprise.

The boy looked up at me directly and said in simple seriousness that only children can manage. "You haven't paid me."

"What?" I thought I hadn't heard him right. "Beg your pardon?"

"You gotta pay me," he said casually but quite businesslike.

"Pay you, uh?" I said somewhat like a fool. "How much?"

"A quarter for my age and another quarter for my name," he said.

I instinctively checked my pocket and was dismayed that I didn't have any small change with me. But while I was fumbling for change, the boy calmly took his chip out from his pocket and held it up. But I had to get some instructions from the boy in the proper way of using the chip. The boy showed me what buttons to push to enter the correct amount, which in his case was fifty cents, and then inserted it into his receptor. Instantly my dial showed a decrease of fifty cents and the boy's showed an increase by the same amount. It was so convenient and wondrous that I forgot the boy's odd refusal to talk to me unless he was paid. After the transfer of funds had duly been carried out, the boy then told me his name was Ryan and he was going to be six the next month.

"Tell me, Ryan," I said. "Who says you have to get paid to say those things?"

"My mom and dad," the boy said, putting the chip securely in his pocket.

Then I saw a youngish couple, apparently Ryan's parents, calling to him. The boy ran to them immediately. I stood there and watched them. The mother yanked the boy sharply at one of the wrists.

"I told you not to talk to strangers," she said with emphasis. The boy mumbled something and showed her his chip, now indicating a sum increased by fifty cents. The mother relented somewhat at that and briefly nodded in my direction. The family then walked away.

Standing there impressed, I was digesting my first use of the chip and my encounter with the budding entrepreneur when I heard the familiar booming voice of Cecil McMiller. He was a large man of well over six feet and perhaps close to two hundred pounds. I would describe him as an exceedingly generous man who smiled easily and, like most other 'typical' Americans, talked loudly and energetically with little or no self-consciousness about the reception by others around him. He seemed to be on the brink of disaster in proper manners, especially in ignoring the three-feet rule of communication.

"I'm sorry to be late, Michael," he said, picking up some of my luggage. "So, how do you feel, now that you are back on American soil?" he said laughing at his own reference to 'American soil'. I wasn't sure if he meant my stay in Laurinville or Moreland, or perhaps both.

I confessed my surprise at the chip and the experience with Ryan. Cecil broke up.

"Don't worry, Michael," he assured me as we walked toward the taxi area. "You will get used to it, I mean both the chip and people. You knew we love money in America, money and convenience, didn't you? That's the secret of our success and happiness. One must do in Rome as Romans do."

The line of the taxis moved slowly as passengers one by one engaged them. Our turn came and we moved toward one. The driver came out to meet us but he made no move to take our luggage. He was a short, stocky man with a mustache, wearing a baseball hat. His face was expressionless bordering on insolence.

"What's it going to be?" the driver asked without changing his expression.

"This is Mr. Brown from Laurinville and Moreland of late, visiting us for the first time," McMiller said with a flourish. "Let's go A-tip."

The change in the driver was remarkable following my friend's declaration of an A-tip offer, whatever it was. His hitherto expressionless face was transformed instantaneously into a wide grin that I had not suspected he was capable of producing. His body was likewise electrified into a bouncing ball, immediately taking our luggage to the trunk of the taxi. His insolent baseball hat had already departed from his head.

"What's an A-tip?" I asked the professor.

McMiller laughed again. "We have three categories of tips, A-tip, B-tip and C-tip. C-tips get the job done, minimum courtesy, you might say, no help from the driver with your luggage, nor any interesting conversations with him. He will take you to your place, but don't expect anything. An A-tip is the very best service you can get, as you are already seeing. The B-tip is somewhere in between."

"You mean you have to declare what kind tip you are going to give ahead of the service actually rendered?"

"Why not?" he said, pointing to the driver who was busy putting my luggage in the back of his cab, "so that he knows exactly how much service he should offer. It avoids all the uncertainty and confusion, for sure. This way, we know exactly what to expect from each other."

Before I could form my opinion, the driver finished his task and with lightning speed returned to us, opening the car door with elaborate courtesy. I could not believe that it was the same driver, expressionless a minute ago and now treating us as if we were royalties, his whole body animated with the desire to please his passengers. In the next few minutes, I learned the value of an A-tip. The cab driver was a study in perpetual motion. He talked incessantly, smiling without a break, offering descriptions of the history and significance of notable landmarks as we passed them. Still remembering what he had been like before my friend offered the generous tip that had changed his entire behavior, I remained unconvinced by his friendliness and ingratiation.

Obviously, the man was not sincere about the whole show. But McMiller seemed to be enjoying it all, broadly smiling and nodding at the driver's remarks. Sometimes my friend looked at me and, finding me impassive with the driver's commercial sweetness, laughed with great amusement. I almost told him that I would sooner endure a C-tip treatment than a wholly make-believe presentation of goodwill. I later realized that in America all business enterprises requiring personalized services, such as restaurants and hospitals, maintained the three-tip system.

As we entered the outer rim of the city McMiller ordered the jaunty taxi driver to stop at a nearby service station. The driver promptly obeyed. My friend paid the attendant with his cashing chip for the use of the restroom. I got out to stretch and to look around. The service station had various posters announcing the pleasures associated with the many goods and services that were being advertised. One particular poster for cigarettes stood out with a very attractive young couple, smiling radiantly into the blue sky as they puffed the 'Newperk' cigarettes, apparently at their happiest state of being.

Then there was another smaller poster, alongside the happy one, with the picture of a black, sinister-looking pistol and a caption below it: "MANDATORY 7 YEARS' PRISON TERM FOR ARMED ROBBERY." For a brief moment, I was confused about which poster represented the real America I was visiting.

Then I found myself watching the huge American flag fluttering in the gentle autumn breeze atop a tall flagpole in the middle of the service station. It was fresh and brilliant in color, but something was wrong with the flag. More specifically, as I squinted up at the flag to identify the problem, I noticed that what was wrong with it was the stars, presumably fifty of them. In place of the fifty stars, I saw fifty-dollar signs like these:

```
$ $ $ $ $ $ $ $ $ -----------------------------------------------
$ $ $ $ $ $ $ $ $ $-----------------------------------------------
$ $ $ $ $ $ $ $ $ $-----------------------------------------------
$ $ $ $ $ $ $ $ $ $-----------------------------------------------
------------------------------------------------------------------
------------------------------------------------------------------
------------------------------------------------------------------
------------------------------------------------------------------
```

"My god," finally recognizing the new symbol, I exclaimed to no one in particular, "since when?"

Then I turned to our driver. "Do you see that? The dollar signs?"

The driver trained his eyes to look up at the flag and, as he realized the source of my excitement, gave a good guffaw.

"I don't see anything wrong with it, sir," he said. He began to stare ahead while tapping his thumbs on the steering wheel. As I was mesmerized by the dollar signs, McMiller emerged from the restroom. He also looked up at the object of my intense gaze.

"I see you are a bit surprised," he said.

"Surprised? Since when our national flag has been redesigned?"

"Oh, it hasn't been redesigned, it's the same flag."

"But, but…" I pointed to the flag.

"I know what you mean," McMiller explained. "Merchants have been using the new signs instead of the old stars, to advertise their business more, you know. Still unofficial, but it has been fairly popular among businessmen for some time."

"Why, isn't that against the law," I said. "To alter the national flag like that?"

"No, Congress has already approved its provisional use for businesses," McMiller said. "Besides, we might eventually adopt the new design after all as our official flag. It is more in tune with our society than the old stars and stripes. As you may know from your Green Palm experience, we say the business of America is business. We worship the Almighty Dollar, which makes our national wealth and personal fortune possible. So why not symbolize our success clearly in our flag and bring our national symbolism closer to reality?"

I fell silent at his mention of 'wealth' and 'fortune', amazed and with nothing to say, hoping that he was partially joking. I had thought I had always kept up enough with the 'real' America during my life in Laurinville and Moreland to get by, but so much had changed that I could not have fathomed. Obviously, I had to learn everything from scratch. McMiller gave me that amused sidelong glance. The cab driver resumed his A-tip entertainment as he pulled out of the service station.

Then I saw a billboard that said, "the best feel-good church on god's green earth" and "the most popular preacher under heaven," apparently advertising a church. I then remembered that all the signs and notices and names I had seen on the plane, at the airport, and on the streets had no capital letters, all using the lower cases, including Cecil McMiller's name on his letterhead.

"Oh, that," McMiller answered my question, "we rarely use capital letters any more in America. We feel capital letters are not friendly because they tend to intimidate people. Small letters make people feel good and comfortable about themselves. Businesspeople first started it for their clients and now the rest of the country follows suit. You might also notice that salespeople of all capacities in America are also very small people. Research on consumer psychology has concluded that consumers are more inclined to buy if the salespeople are smaller than they are, so that they don't get intimidated. They do everything to make customers feel good about themselves."

While I was thinking that it was an amazing bit of psychological insight, we passed through several districts which showed different degrees of affluence, some better and some worse than the others. Most poor neighborhoods had signs in big capital letters: "THIS AREA WATCHED BY HEAVILY ARMED NEIGHBORS. WATCH OUT, CRIMINALS," where everyone could see and apparently with so little regard for the feel-good self-image of potential criminals.

One particular neighborhood even had the number, written next to the warning, of unfortunate intruders who were killed or injured by the vigilantes during the preceding month to emphasize their determination. McMiller explained that their use of capital letters in that case was one of the few exceptions. Considering the message, I understood the exception.

Soon coming into a fairly affluent-looking suburban district, the taxi came to a stop at a house upon McMiller's instruction.

The McMiller house was a medium size ranch-style with a horseshoe-shaped driveway as wide as the width of the house. Inside the horseshoe was a well-kept garden which, even in early October, had flowers still blooming nicely. I could see that it was a respectable neighborhood, quiet and spacious. The driver dashed out and opened our doors with the same elaborate courtesy. I pointedly ignored his gesture and, seeing this, McMiller laughed once again in amusement. The driver went about unloading my luggage.

As McMiller and I stretched ourselves after getting out of the cab, the front door to the house opened and out came a woman whom I instinctively identified as Cecil's wife Carol. I had heard her name mentioned several times before in our conversations and correspondence. She was in her mid-thirties, with short efficient hair almost like a boy's, curly and laid in all directions as if no particular style had been applied to it. She was not pretty in the conventional sense of the term, but had that easy, friendly manner often associated with the favorable image of confident women.

"Well, well," she approached me smiling and extended her hands.

I shook them.

"You are here finally," she said.

"Carol, this is Michael Brown, our man from Laurinville," McMiller said belatedly.

"Welcome back to America, Michael," Carol said, stressing 'back' and "America," and released my hands.

"This is Carol, my contract-wife," McMiller said. "Let's go inside, you need to wash up and rest some."

Apparently, I had not heard it right about McMiller's contract-wife for, at the time, I knew nothing about contract-marriages in America. His garden attracted my attention because gardening had been one of my more devoted hobbies. I excused myself and then walked over to the garden to appreciate its fine workmanship. There were still geraniums, marigolds, mums, carnations, and several varieties of flowers in good blooming condition all very tastefully arranged and maintained.

The cab driver in the meanwhile had unloaded the luggage and carried it inside where he was paid his well-deserved A-tip. I saw him bow profusely as he received the money with his cashing chip, murmuring, "thank you, sir" and "thank you, ma'am."

I stood up from my horticultural admiration and watched him drive by me. He was back to his C-tip expressionlessness and gave me that look of bored indifference that I had seen in him before. As soon as he got on the road, he sped away with gusto as if emphasizing the termination of our business contract.

I walked back to the house and joined the McMillers inside.

Chapter Two

After unpacking, I rested for a while in my room.

I was grateful for the McMillers' offer for me to stay with them, especially while I was in this area. The house was modest in size but comfortably furnished with a spacious backyard. On one corner of it stood an old model automobile that seemed to be still in good condition.

I changed and joined them for dinner. While waiting for dinner to be served, we engaged in casual conversation. I expressed my confusion about the extremely pecuniary American behavior that I had experienced with the boy at the airport and again with the cab driver.

"Either money or nothing," I muttered like a poor traveler in a foreign country quite different from his own.

"I understand why you should feel confused," Cecil said. "Even some of us real Americans are not quite reconciled with the changes." He then turned and pointed to the kitchen, "I don't think Carol is happy with that either."

"I was somewhat surprised," I said, "although I shouldn't have been, that everything is tied to money so much."

"Things have become more, shall we say, rational in our society in the last two decades or so," my friend said. "The result is that just about everything in America is clearly rationalized and identified with a price so that there is no confusion about anything."

When I was thinking about the confounding implications of what he had just said, he said: "Isn't that splendid, Michael? America is going to become the first perfectly rational society. It sure has solved a lot of problems."

"What kind of problems?"

"Well, for instance, the problems of emotion," McMiller said.

"How would rationality solve it?"

"Just think how many human problems in society have been caused by the uncertainties and unreliability associated with emotional reactions."

"Rather than—"

"Rather than rational decisions. Whether we like it or not, money represents the most rational of all human elements in society. I know you have a rather different perspective on money, especially after the Green Palm experience and living in Moreland for many years. But if you think about it carefully, you realize that there is no mistake in money."

At McMiller's comment about the Green Palmers, my thought returned to Laurinville and all that it represented, and Moreland, which, looking at them from this far, seemed like a dream already. Cecil looked at me with that amused understanding.

"I know what you are thinking, Michael," he said. "But look at it this way. Money is the most uniform, rational and predictable element in all social life. It is also highly standardized. One dollar is better than a dime, but ten dollars is better than one dollar; but a hundred dollars is still better than ten, all exactly at the rate of ten to one. An object valued at twenty dollars is exactly twice as important as an object valued at ten dollars, and so on so forth—"

Cecil had assumed a posture, I guessed, as if he was lecturing his students. "Handling money is impersonal. As its value remains exactly the same it doesn't matter whose money it is, whether an emperor's dollar or a pauper's. Wouldn't you agree, Michael?"

I had to agree.

Cecil resumed his discourse on the new, rationalized America: "Furthermore, since its value is absolute, those who have it control those who do not, to the extent of their money differences. And since everyone wants and needs money, it controls everyone. It certainly simplifies things, doesn't it?"

"I don't know," I said. "It all depends on how much value the society puts in money, I suppose."

"Do you know of any society that doesn't value money, or any people who don't need money?" he simply asked.

I could have protested his simplification by mentioning Laurinville or even Moreland but, taking his question as merely rhetorical, remained silent. Exclusive reliance on money was already a fact of life in America, as I knew, and Cecil was merely reiterating the fact. There was no point in arguing with either him or with the fact.

"Money is uniform and rational," he said. "Therefore, it knows of no religious differences, national boundaries, or, most importantly, emotional reactions in people. It is neither kind nor cruel in itself. It treats everyone equally."

"But it is not owned equally."

"Ah, that's a different question," my friend said. "We are having a small party tomorrow night in your honor, if you don't mind, and you will meet some very interesting people to rehash some of these issues with them, I am sure."

Then Carol informed us that dinner was ready. I was sure that she had been listening to our conversation from the kitchen. Somehow, I had the feeling that she was an exceedingly intelligent woman behind that easy smile and unhurried mannerism. Her dinner was delicious, and I complimented her on her cooking.

"Who cooks for you in Laurinville, Michael?" she asked.

I told her mostly I fixed a few simple meals myself or ate at my parents'.

"You should've gotten married," suggested Cecil.

I said I had not had the opportunity yet.

"We have simplified the marriage problem in America," Cecil said, kissing Carol on the cheek. "We solved it by contract-marriages." Then it reminded me that he had referred to Carol as a 'contract-wife'.

"What is a contract marriage?" I asked.

"It's our rational solution to all the marriage problems," Cecil explained. "Sure, we still have people who marry in the old-fashioned way, taking all the risks in their marriages. But most educated Americans, with respectable TIWs, prefer contract-marriages. Ours is a contract marriage, too."

"But what is it? How is it different from the old-fashioned kind?"

"Well," Cecil began.

"Why don't we wait until after dinner?" Carol suggested. "I want you two to enjoy the food while it is still hot."

We both agreed with her and concentrated on our food, while carrying on small talk.

After dinner we retired to the living room. Carol served us coffee and sat near her husband (or 'contract-husband'?).

"This is how a contract marriage works," Cecil resumed. "When a man (or woman) reaches a marriageable age, he compiles a complete profile of himself, that is, education, family background, religion, culture, hobbies, liabilities and assets, physical characteristics, aesthetic appearances, health history, mental state, special talents if any, and of course his TIW, you name it. Everything about the person goes on the profile."

"Wouldn't that be an enormous file, to have all that information on everybody?"

"It's not on everybody," Cecil answered. "Only those who agree to go the contract route, although the number is rapidly increasing because more and more people are becoming convinced of the benefits of contract-marriages. Besides, the computer does all the compiling and storing. Once the formula is set up, it's fairly simple. All you have to do is plug in the pertinent data. The computer takes care of the rest."

"Does the government do all that?"

"No, the government hardly does anything nowadays, it's become greatly reduced in importance. There are corporations which specialize in the contract-marriage business. A lot of insurance companies are in that business because they have the most experience with that sort of thing. The company we choose to do business with maintains the file for a fee. It makes the information available to other companies, of course, for a fee."

"Is that how you two—?" I gestured with my fingers putting Cecil and Carol together.

"Yes," answered Carol. She was remarkably matter of fact. There was no expression on her face that indicated anything associated with her matrimonial background. Her indifference seemed such a contrast with most married women in Laurinville who had their romanticized versions of how they had met their husbands and how they had proposed, among other highlights.

"The most important element in the file, of course," Cecil continued. "Is one's TIW number."

I told him about the salesman I had encountered on the plane and his TIW.

"Yes, Michael, you understood it correctly. It stands for Total Individual Worth, as computed by the involved company, it is also popularly known as the 'bottom-number'."

I asked him why it was necessary for people to tell everyone about one's own economic worth.

"TIW is simply the total value of a person converted into monetary terms," McMiller said, "so that everyone's value can be compared to everyone else's in numbers. What's the point of doing all that? That avoids a lot of confusion because now everyone has one simple number to refer to. It simplifies everything in our dealings with each other. Every item that goes into the file is converted into an asset if positive, a liability if negative. The company makes all the files available to anyone who pays a fee. Those who wish to find a marriage partner can go through the files and see if there is anyone that suits his predetermined criteria or fancy the best."

"That sounds all very good, Cecil," I said. "But what about the small inconvenience called love. Where does that fit in? Or does it fit in at all?"

"Oh, love—yes," mused my friend. "It is indeed an inconvenience, isn't it? Except it's a *big* inconvenience, not a small one as you put it."

Cecil lifted his coffee, took a sip, and contemplated for a moment or two. Carol got up and poured us some more coffee. She remained friendly and impassive while our discussion centered on the subject of love in their marriage.

"Love," Cecil mused again. "Is damned inconvenient because it is the source of the most regrettable human errors. Do you know how many faulty human decisions have been made because of this thing called love?"

"How can you say that, Cecil?" I objected. "It's the most beautiful thing a human being can—"

"I know, I know," he motioned as if to calm me down with my defense of love. "That's precisely my point. Let me ask you a simple question: Should one make the decision whether to marry one's partner when one is *in* love or *not* in love? Which way do you think one can arrive at a more rational decision regarding the marriage issue? When you buy a car, my dear Michael, do you go by your *love* for the car or by cool-headed, cold-eyed rational judgment as to which vehicle best suits your situation?"

"Getting a partner for life is not like getting a car," I protested.

"Exactly," Cecil said triumphantly as if he had waited this turn in our discussion. "One's marriage partner is perhaps the most important selection one would ever make in one's lifetime. Shouldn't that be, then, absolutely free of all emotional errors? Shouldn't it be done with utmost respect for rational judgment? Or, should one go blindly, fully charged with nothing but emotion and all the follies of a man in love? Have you seen a bigger fool than a man, or a woman for that matter, who is in love, have you?"

"Still—" I persisted. Somehow, I was losing the argument.

"Let me ask you another question, Michael," Cecil said, knowing that he had me cornered. "Do you know the current divorce rate in America?"

"Slightly over fifty percent?" I guessed.

"See? That's exactly the figure for those Americans who marry the traditional way. They fall in love, decide to get married, and then more than a half of them divorce. That speaks rather poorly for this great thing called love, doesn't it?"

"How about divorce among contract-marriages?"

"There is no divorce in contract-marriages, just dissolved contracts, and there is a world of difference between the two," said Cecil smiling at Carol. "At any rate, going back to my earlier description of contract-marriages before love interfered with us, the computer picks out a certain number of candidates who come closest to one's own criteria. In fact, we believe it's the best way of matching two people."

"What if their—what do you call it—don't match?"

"You mean, TIW's? That's where the contract comes in. If two parties have an identical TIW or close enough, which is not uncommon, then there is no need to speak of contracts. They can marry each other purely on the basis of love, emotion, whatever they like. It is when one's TIW's is at variance with the other's that some adjustment has to be made if the agreement is to be made."

"What kind of adjustment?"

"Money," said Cecil without hesitation. "When two people whose files match except the TIW's, then one partner can compensate the other according to the deficiencies or assets of the other, which could be so much a month or a lump sum paid at one time."

Carol picked up the coffee pot and retreated to the kitchen. Cecil motioned with his head toward the kitchen and said, "Carol's TIW happened to be considerably lower than mine at the time, but because of her artistic talent, which I value rather highly according to my own agreed assessment, I pay her for the difference. In short, one pays for what one likes to get. In my case I happen to like artists, that's all."

So, Cecil was paying Carol for being his wife! Which meant that theirs was not a union of love and romance. It was a union of convenience, as people used to whisper about such marriages, except this was no hush-hush affair. Cecil seemed to be perfectly comfortable in talking about his own arrangement. But did I notice any sign of discomfort in Carol in the way she had swept out of the living room into the kitchen?

"How long is the contract supposed to last, I mean, normally?"

"Oh, anywhere from one year to ten years, depending on the agreement. In our case, it's five years. This is the third year of our contract. Contracts can be renewed after that if both parties agree. There may be slight changes in the agreement, however. After all, people do change."

I wanted to ask why Carol had agreed to the contract but refrained from asking. Instead, I said. "What if one party violates the contract?"

"How, for instance?"

"For instance, personality changes, bodily shape changes, skin gets wrinkled, or in general one is not as sharp on the uptake, and so on. What happens then?"

"The company determines first whether the change or violation as you call it is a deliberate act or a natural process. If it is determined to be willful or negligent, then the payment involved is readjusted or in some cases reversed because their TIW's would be adversely affected. If neither is feasible, then the contract is dissolved. If it's a natural phenomenon, such as added wrinkles, why, then nothing can be done about it."

"Isn't that somewhat callous? We are talking about marriages between two human beings, not just a business transaction."

"All marriages, even in your town, Michael, are civil contracts," my friend dismissed my observation with a sweep of his hand. "We just recognize that fact in America more openly and conduct it more rationally than in Laurinville or probably in Moreland, for that matter. Besides, contractual obligations keep us all on our toes, so to speak, so that we'd better try hard to live up to our initial conditions. You know how some people, after they get married, let their hair down and let themselves go to pot, now that they don't have to worry about the marriage game anymore. Contract-marriages have the advantage of keeping the partners alert to their mutual contractual obligations."

I was briefly persuaded that contract-marriages, after all, had their advantages until Cecil added: "—No one likes to pay for violations."

Then Carol returned with fresh coffee and some cookies.

"Enough for all that lecture on Michael's first day, don't you think, Cecil?" she said. "Why don't we watch some TV? After all, Michael has never seen American television."

It was true. I had never watched American television before (other than the Green Palmers' version, called tele-mind, briefly in Laurinville).

"Good idea," Cecil and I said at the same time and turned our attention to the coffee and cookies and television.

Carol switched on the TV set.

Chapter Three

In progress on TV was what appeared to be a police drama. It was hard to tell because I was not used to its dramatic twists. As I watched it a little longer it turned out to be a comedy of sorts between the police and what they called the 'Mafia' in a large city.

The story (which McMiller told me was based on a recent, controversial issue hotly debated among some) involved a frustrated police department which was trying to upgrade its bullet-proof vests in order to withstand the Mafia hitmen's ever-increasing firepower. Whenever the department purchased new bullet-proof vests from a manufacturer who, in the classic commercial bravado, 'guaranteed' that no known bullet in the world could penetrate the vest, the same manufacturer produced a bullet powerful enough to 'penetrate' any known bullet-proof vest in the world, which the manufacturer sold to the Mafia. It was really comical to watch the police chief getting frustrated with the turn of events. The built-in laugh machine was uproarious in parts where the newly vested policemen were soon riddled with bullet holes on their vests, many of them dead. In the meantime, the Mafia and manufacturer were slapping each other's hand in triumph.

"Why do you allow the manufacturer to play both sides against each other?" I finally asked Cecil who was laughing just as uproariously with the show. "Police can't do their job that way."

"Free enterprise, my friend, free enterprise," he said, still concentrating on TV. "It's good business. Well-off Americans don't need the police anymore. They get it from private companies. Our neighborhood, for example, is patrolled by the private police we hire. Only the extremely poor who can't afford the private service get so-called police protection or arm themselves as you saw from some of the signs on the way here."

Although the show's premise was scandalous for law enforcement, I must admit that it was funny. The general quality of American TV as a means of entertainment was superbly effective. American TV was a science, a perfection, a pinnacle of human ingenuity. Even their commercials were superb, highly believable with good actors and situations. Virtually every commercial seemed to be based on real life, real love, situations indistinguishable from reality.

Most of them were expertly crafted to elicit emotional reactions from the audience in just a few seconds, perhaps less than 20 seconds or so, and what a job! Even knowing they were just commercials, many of them moved me almost to tears. They were short, graphic and to the point, maximizing their punching power right on the viewer's emotional guts. Some aimed at children were extremely frightening and horrible, obviously intended to scare wayward children to death.

One of the apparently more popular commercials, judging from the McMillers' reaction, had a character known as 'Hairy Harry' for a hair-grower. Longer commercial episodes were produced like a minor regular show. The present segment had to do with a beach scene in which Hairy Harry, covered with hair all over his body, was repelling his competitor-suitors at a beach in a variety of ways to protect his woman. It was obvious that his hairy body was presented as a desirable thing to have. At the end of the commercial, like Popeye eating his spinach, Hairy Harry smeared the hair-growing lotion all over his body to grow some more hair. The voice in the background left no doubt about the potency and desirability of a hairy body.

"You know, the invention of hair-tonic in the eighties got rid of much of baldness in America by the early nineties," said Cecil who himself had a full head of hair. "There are few baldies left anymore."

"So, they are selling it as a body-hair grower, now?"

"Well, that's free enterprise again," Cecil said. "If you are the businessman selling the hair-growing tonic and there are so few bald heads left, what do you do with all your bottles of tonic?"

"I suppose you encourage people to grow body hair," I said.

"Exactly," said Cecil amused, "that's the point of the commercial, to make people think that body hair is a wonderful thing. And Hairy Harry is doing a good job promoting the idea. I understand the sales are brisk and Americans, especially males, are becoming all hairy animals again. There are enough insecure males in America who want to look like Hairy Harry and impress their mates. In fact, you go to the beach any time now, although this is October, you will see quite a few hairy males showing off the effect of the hair-tonic. Hairy bodies are becoming extremely popular nowadays. Thanks to the commercials, and that's good for the razor industry, too."

There were commercials specifically designed to appeal to teenagers not to take drugs, not to lie, not to kill other teenagers, not to forget to use contraceptives, and so on. The commercials, although produced to appeal to children, were packing intense punches with their effects and some were so intensely dramatized that even I was affected by them.

A thought occurred to me. "What are the parents doing with their teenagers," I turned to Carol and asked. "Aren't they supposed to teach those things to their children, not TV?"

"Parents have their busy schedules," Carol said noncommittally. "Besides, we spend so much time with TV that it has become the most effective communicator in American society. Nothing gets across unless it's on TV."

Then Carol described what was currently the most popular video for children. They were called 'veggie videos' which had actors dressed as various vegetables, like carrots, celery, broccoli, spinach, who sang and danced and told funny stories as a way of encouraging children to eat these vegetables. The manufacturer quoted their research scientists who found that children increased their vegetarian intake by 24 percent if they watched the video entertainment while eating the vegetables.

"Kids don't listen to their parents anymore," volunteered Cecil. "They listen to TV better than anything our society can offer by way of communicating with them. TV is a lot more entertaining and a lot easier to relate to, they say."

"Besides," Carol said, "American kids are weaned on thirty-second messages. They don't have enough attention spans to listen or reason anymore. It has to be straight to the point, in explicit language and pictures with a lot of power packed into few short seconds to communicate with them. Or else, you lose them in another few seconds. Even our college classes do not last longer than twenty-five minutes. For grade school and high school, the legal length is fifteen minutes. Kids have to have breaks every fifteen minutes or so. No speech from a politician, no sermon from a preacher can last longer than that. Adults can't sustain their attention; it's shorter for the kids. Parents have become obsolete in America. For that matter, everything else has become obsolete. All you need are those thirty-second spots and good TIW, and everybody is happy."

Well, I had to learn more about my own country.

"I read somewhere," I said, "that most Americans now choose TV over their own families as, quote 'the most meaningful thing in their lives,' unquote."

"You read it right, Michael," said Cecil. "Up until the eighties, family used to top the list of preference, TV following closely at second. But in the early nineties it finally caught up and became, as you say, the most meaningful element in American life."

"I've seen a survey recently," Carol volunteered, "which says an average American spends close to three thousand hours a year watching TV, up from two thousand hours in the late eighties."

"Three thousand hours a year," I said, doing some quick mental calculating. "That's almost as much as we spend on sleeping in Laurinville."

"Oh, maybe," said Cecil. "At any rate, we don't sleep that much anymore. From what I read in a sleep magazine, researchers have found that an average American spends less than six hours a day sleeping, down from seven hours in the eighties. Since we spend less than thirty hours a week working, that's about six hours a day, I suppose the increased TV-watching hours can be explainable. We sleep less and work less and watch TV more. That makes perfect sense to me."

"I sometimes wonder what would happen to America without TV," Carol observed.

"I can't imagine," Cecil said. "It's like asking, what can we do without air?"

"Now that we no longer have nuclear missiles aimed at each other," said Carol cautiously. "Can you imagine what would happen if the Russians could perfect a new weapon to disrupt American television, the whole American way of life? Can you imagine the havoc it would create?"

"True," agreed Cecil with her. "It would be hard to imagine."

We then watched the evening news. The most amazing thing about the news program was that every news item was dramatized with actors portraying the events on the news. There was an item, for example, about an eye doctor who was accused of fondling the women's certain anatomical parts while he was examining their eyes. The news showed a male actor playing the eye doctor actually fondling some actresses playing the victims. In another news item, a toddler who climbed onto the back of a moving van before her father pulled out of the driveway clung there for five miles as the van drove along at about 60 miles an hour. For that item, a child actor actually played the toddler for a thrilling few minutes of re-enactment for the viewer.

In another, a woman claimed she had sex with a man, whose wife she eventually shot and killed while the man denied he even knew her. The re-enacted dramatization was so intense that it had to be played twice upon popular demand. There were some war scenes in which actual footage of dead soldiers was shown with the caption that said, "These are real pictures." But the studio audience, who was there watching the news and reacting for the psychologists, cheered at the pictures anyway for their 'realism'. Because of re-enactment, the news program seemed long but very entertaining.

Then with a great deal of fanfare and colorful background, the station announced the night's special, the 'Gospel Academy Awards'.

"I prefer the real Oscar anytime," murmured Cecil indifferently. "The preachers never get it right."

Carol explained to me that the Gospel Academy Awards were the religious version of the more prestigious Oscar, which was given to good actors and creators. But like the other award, the Gospel Academy had its own statuettes that vaguely resembled Jesus to be given to the categories of Best Acting, Best Supporting Acting, Best Music, and so on just like the real Oscar, Carol explained. As the show progressed, I realized that there were other categories of their own in this show such as Best Rated Gospel Show on TV, Best Performance by a Faith-Healer, Most Successful Fund-Raising Performance, Best Emotional Performance Live and Best Emotional Performance on Video, Best Comic Performance While Preaching, and so on. Cecil, apparently uninterested in this program, started snoring on his sofa.

In between presentations of the award ceremony, there were the usual commercials. Churches of different denominations had prepared wonderful video commercials to advertise their houses of worship. Many showed, generally guided by an attractive man or a woman, ornate sanctuaries, new air-conditioners for comfort, powerful stereo speaker systems, and teary testimonials of those who had benefited from their respective churches. The commercials urged everyone to come to their churches. Some even had graphics showing the quarterly growth in investment based on offerings. One particularly moving commercial showed a woman, named Mary, suffering 'deep depression' who 'church shopped' and tried many different churches, without success. But when she finally tried Church X (which showed the wonderful decor inside and the friendly staff members applying therapy) she recovered fully from her depression. She was telling happily to the camera that she enthusiastically recommended Church X.

Interspersed with the church commercials were also those urging to buy what they called 'Instant Prayers', which turned out to be cassette tapes and video tapes. They were not only messages taped by preachers but also those by other celebrities in entertainment and sports who were selling religious messages. These tapes were offered, personalized to order, on weddings, birthdays, funerals, and so on. Many such commercials showed a family sitting around the kitchen table watching a videotaped message on a TV screen in profound reverie.

Some not-so-famous celebrities were offering discount messages as well. Still some others offered all-purpose messages by well-known personalities to be used on any occasion. Apparently, those were popular items, judged by the zeal with which the items were pushed. I thought how irresistible it would be for a little boy to get a videotaped message for his birthday from a famous celebrity, calling him by his own name no less.

One particular commercial that got my attention had a preacher, who looked like Jesus, advertising what he called 'my special Bible' that he himself had translated specially for American consumers. He said, for example, "Love of money is the root of all evil" was now translated in his new version as "Love of money is the root of all happiness." He quoted many other such changes in his Bible as good for the 'positive self-image' of American churchgoers and guaranteed that his version had nothing but good things in it. He said it was the first and only Bible in the world in which God said 'only good things' about people, a true Gospel, eliminating all the sayings that might make people feel bad about themselves.

He was very energetic and persuasive in preaching that "We *can* serve two masters, and we *can* have it both ways." The extended commercial ended with a caption that said, "All dialogues, props, scenes are the property of The Gospels of Jesus Corporation. Unauthorized uses prosecuted."

The Best Male Acting award went to a beefy preacher representing an organization called Freedom College, accompanied by a beautiful young woman who, he said, "has never been kissed by a man" and who was studying 'swimsuit cosmetology' at his college. Best Female Acting was won by a buxom blonde woman with a low-neck dress whose winning caused an avalanche of catcalls from the audience, to which she responded by waving her hand and giving a knowing smile. Another preacher with impeccable hair and a demeanor of great urgency received Best Performance by a Faith-Healer, reminding everyone not to forget his faith medicine commercials. A good-looking preacher couple, whose woman was fairly bedecked with jewelry and heavy eye makeup won Best Emotional Performance Live, while a young man from Oklahoma received Best Emotional Performance on Video, whose announcement was greeted with a thunderous ovation.

A preacher with a short neck and an obvious southern drawl was named for Best Comic Performance While Preaching, and as his name was announced and he walked onto the stage to receive the statuette, a howl of laughter burst forth from the audience, which was responded to by the winner's smiling face. Each time the nominees were announced, highlights of their performance were shown on the large screen on stage and the band struck and the crowd went wild. To close the show, half a dozen naked men and women did a Salome-like dance, which was received by an excited crowd with great enthusiasm.

About two hours or so later the program finally ended, and we suddenly realized that Cecil had been snoring with a loudness matching the audience on TV.

"My goodness," Carol said with a good-natured start, "you must be awfully tired, Michael. You have to forgive us. We should've offered you to retire earlier. With all that flying and new experience—"

"Nothing to apologize for, Carol," I said. "In fact, it has been the most interesting day of my life, or at least since I was twelve, to say the least. I haven't been tired at all."

"You have a busy day tomorrow," she said. "Cecil plans to take you to the university. And don't forget we have a party tomorrow night in your honor. As Cecil already told you, you would meet some very interesting people."

"I would be delighted to meet them," I said. Then an urge to yawn came over me. "I suppose I ought to retire then," I said suddenly feeling tired. "Apparently I didn't realize that, after all, I *was* tired."

Carol gently shook Cecil awake.

"Is the show over already?" said Cecil shaking his head.

"Michael is ready to retire," said Carol. "So are you, Cecil."

"Of course, of course," he said half-asleep. "I will see you in the morning then. Good night, buddy."

We bade good night and retired to our rooms. Thus, the first and fairly eventful day of my life in real America came to an end.

Chapter Four

The University of Wilmington was a medium-sized campus spaciously situated with a lot of trees among what were described as the early-Georgian style buildings. There was a huge sign posted next to the name of the university that said, "Where student-customer satisfaction is our number one educational goal," with no capital letters. All buildings, old and new, were designed also to reflect the 'South' motif blended with an air of the medieval academy, which gave their architecture a subtle emphasis of the elitism for which it had generally been known. Located so close to the beach, sand was everywhere on the grounds and the grass was obviously having a tough time taking root. Barren spots could be seen here and there all over the campus ground in spite of its otherwise meticulous gardens and yards.

I immediately liked the physical setting of the university. It could have been any nice liberal arts college in the United States, I was told. Cecil McMiller explained the functions of each building as we drove by, and a little bit about the history of the campus. The Social Science building, where Cecil's political science was housed along with other social science departments, was on the western edge of the campus, somehow older and appearing less well-kept than the others. It was also smaller than the other buildings we had passed.

"I know what you are thinking," Cecil said. "Social science is not a very popular subject on campus, as you will soon discover. So, we get the second-rate treatment. What can you say? It's free enterprise."

What made the Social Science building look punier was the huge, spanking-new building right next to it which towered over its lesser brother on the side. It looked affluent and exuded a sense of positive power and importance.

"Oh, it's our Business Administration building," said Cecil noticing that I was impressed with it. "Imposing, isn't it?"

He then went on to explain that business had become one single dominant field of study on American college campuses. Not only was business chosen by more college students as their career field, but also was the basis upon which the whole university operated.

"Our market approach to education is only natural, I would think," McMiller said. "But our academic dean will explain it to you better. We have an appointment with him this morning. Be nice to him, he is partly responsible for your expense account."

I was introduced to a small staff of the Department of Social Science in which Cecil's political science occupied a section. There were smatterings of other social scientists, such as sociologists, psychologists, historians, and even one philosopher named Robert I. Lee. At the introduction, someone joked about his middle name which stood for Isaiah, thanks to his apparently religious father who gave his four sons a middle name from the old prophets. "And Robert really takes his middle name seriously," at which the whole crowd of social scientists broke into a good-natured laugh.

All of the social science professors seemed well-dressed and fairly delightful as company, but the philosopher struck me immediately as an oddball in the crowd. He was wiry-looking and his long, dark beard and his deep-set eyes glowing with intensity cut a brooding figure of discontent. Somehow, his wiriness seemed to hide the physical strength that could spring out of him at any moment.

"I am just a token philosopher," the professor with a prophet's middle name confided to me, his eyes shining and his dark beard slightly trembling with emphasis. "And our students hate philosophy and philosophers." While we were exchanging small talk, McMiller materialized and announced that it was time for us to go see the dean. He told me that we would have lunch with them later.

"What do you think?" my friend asked as we got out of the building.

"The professors?"

"Yes."

"A delightful and humorous lot," I said as the idea easily came to mind, forgetting Robert Isaiah Lee. "I am sure they hold the students' attention."

"The 'caring skill', as we call it," said McMiller, "is the number one criterion for faculty employment and salary on this campus, or for that matter on any campus. You can't survive without it on any campus. As you have noticed, the ability to convince students that we care, mostly by demonstrating respect and love, is a cardinal virtue in our survival and prosperity. Our salary is practically determined, after the volume of student business we produce, by the way students rate us on the item, 'Do you feel the professor respects and loves you?' All other attributes are absolutely secondary."

"What about knowledge and competence, and so on?" I asked more boldly since I knew a little about teaching. "Anybody can show false respect and love to students, but can anybody be knowledgeable about the subject and be a serious teacher?"

McMiller dismissed my question as if it was irrelevant by muttering something about "those lazy and spoiled students who wouldn't know the difference," which somewhat surprised me. Then ignoring my reaction, he pointed to the building which contained the dean's office, just ahead of us. We walked through the Business Administration building where students seemed to be much more animated than those in the social sciences, talking to each other about the latest 'stock quotes' and 'dividend indexes'.

Some other students were looking through a thick catalog that contained pictures of automobiles, television sets, electronic game items, and other things of interest. On display was a new University of Wilmington brochure which featured a bright red convertible on the cover with students ready to hit the nearby beach. In one of the classrooms nearby a lecture titled 'Jargon Convergence as a Measure of Alignment in Understanding Between Management and Information Systems Professionals' was in progress, given by a business professor named Anson.

Once outside, McMiller proceeded to tell me about the Dean of Academic Affairs as the man responsible for the college curriculum and operation.

"Of course, his background is business," McMiller said. "B.A. in business, master's degree in business, doctorate in business. His whole life has been in business; he talks, breathes, and sleeps business. How about that? A quintessential American of the coming century, you might describe him as."

"Is he considered a good academic dean?"

"An excellent one, no doubt," my friend sounded enthusiastic. "We have produced more graduates to order in the last five years than in any comparable time in our history."

"Graduates to order?"

"Well, he will explain it to you. Here we are."

We then entered what was marked as the administration building and the difference was obvious. The spacious and well-illuminated main lounge for that building was freshly painted and well decorated with plants, flowerpots, and wall paintings. Directly below the transparent sunroof that allowed the generous amount of daylight was a small but exquisitely crafted waterfalls that announced its presence without much noise. There were two large chandeliers hung from the ceiling as if confirming the air of opulence, almost reminding me more of the airport than a college building—not that I had seen many.

The secretary, a well-dressed woman in her early fifties, recognizing McMiller, rose to meet us. She was full of propriety and sincerity, which seemed, at least to me, very polished.

"Dr. McMiller, how good to see you," she extended her hand which McMiller shook.

"This is Mr. Brown, from Laurinville," he introduced me, and we shook hands. Her fingers were thin and felt cold.

"He has an appointment with Dean Nettor."

"Of course, I know all about it. I processed the papers for Mr. Brown," the woman said, smiling profusely. "The Dean has been expecting you. I will go in and announce your arrival."

She excused herself and went into the inner office. Within a few seconds, she came out and held the door open. "You can go right in, gentlemen."

As we entered a well-furnished office, the academic dean rose from his seat and stood up to greet us. A beautiful mahogany coffee table sat in the middle of the office, flanked on its long sides by two splendid-looking sofas. On one side of the office was the imposing desk which was the dean's workplace. There were meticulously kept boxes for 'In' and 'Out' memos. In one corner, I saw a tastefully arranged bouquet of cut flowers. Several discreet landscaping paintings were hung on the walls.

A small bookshelf was placed against a wall on which a selective number of volumes on Business Administration, obviously more for their aesthetic value than practical use, were carefully displayed. A large grandfather clock, bearing the donor's plate as 'Business Class of '96', hung decorously on the opposite wall from the desk. The impression of the office was nothing short of magnificent, if only too artificial and arid, nevertheless representative of success and affluence and comfort.

The man who occupied this successful, affluent and comfortable office, however, didn't look at all like one who was enjoying his success, affluence or comfort. The dean was a short, stocky man of perhaps sixty or so in a dark business suit, with searching eyes behind his horn-rimmed spectacles, thinning hair combed back (apparently unaffected by Hairy Harry), and a small smile managed uncomfortably on his pale round face.

The image the man generated, even with an impressive office in the background to demonstrate the level of his achievement, was that of intense unhappiness. He might have felt more at home in the Complaint Office of a department store than in the office of the academic dean at an opulent university.

McMiller introduced me to the dean and we had an appropriate round of handshakes. The dean said he was happy to have me at the university as Visiting Scholar and all the university's facilities, such the library, the secretarial pool, office space, etcetera, would be at my disposal.

"Dean Nettor," said McMiller after we had exchanged the perfunctory small talk, "Mr. Brown is rather unfamiliar with our university system in America, particular at the University of Wilmington. He would be grateful if you could give him some pertinent information as to—"

"I shall, I shall," the dean said, gesturing wildly with both his hands. "I had prepared a small speech for that purpose already."

McMiller and I acknowledged his feeble joke by giving a discreet smile. He may be a great business administrator, I thought, but not a very jovial academic like the social science faculty I had met earlier. Entrusting me in the dean's hand and instructing me to return to his office afterward, McMiller then left the office.

"The crucial difference between the universities of the past and those of today in America, for example our own university, I think," the dean began as we sat opposite each other in the sofas, "is that today's American university operates almost wholly on the basis of business rationality. We avoid educating anyone who is not clearly useful in society."

He paused and I waited.

"I am proud to say," the dean continued. "That only the most extremely wealthy can now afford to study poetry, philosophy, or classic languages. What can a poet, philosopher, or a classic linguist produce that's beneficial to our society? Only the idle rich don't mind wasting their time and money in such subjects that have always been nothing but a drain in the society's resources. Don't you agree, Mr. Brown?"

Somehow, thinking about Robert I. Lee, I politely reminded him that I was just a small-school principal from Laurinville.

The academic dean chuckled. "Sure, I understand," he said, in a patient tone of sympathy. "The absolute majority of our students at the University of Wilmington, I would put it at about eighty-five percent, are trained on order from government and corporate employers, mostly the latter."

I said I didn't understand what he meant by 'on order'.

"This is how it works," the dean explained. "A government agency or a corporation makes its own estimate of how many workers they would need in the coming years, say, how many bureaucratic functionaries, accountants, lawyers, office workers of all kinds, advertising specialists, image makers, copy writers, and so on so forth. Based on their long-term needs and projections that are scientifically calculated, this estimate is not as difficult to obtain accurately as it might first seem."

I said I understood it, somewhat fascinated by his explanation.

"Then the agency or the corporation puts in an order at an appropriate university in its district. The University of Wilmington covers the southeastern corner of North Carolina, which is a rapidly expanding area in this region. After the orders have been received, the University announces these fields of specialization to prospective students and then screens the applicants. Each field has its own attrition rate. For example, Accounting seems to have a higher drop-out rate than other fields, perhaps because of the mathematical rigor it demands from its students."

"The University then anticipates the drop-out rate in each field and admits an appropriate number of candidates into each subject area so that the number that graduates is the same as that on order from the employer. If ten accountants are on order and the drop-out rate is fifty percent, we simply admit fifteen students to the program to produce the required ten accountants. It's fairly simple."

"What if the student doesn't know, say, at the time of contemplating a college education, what he wants for his career?"

"That, Mr. Brown," he said with indulgence, "does not exist in American universities today, certainly not at this university, with the exception, of course, of those who are extremely rich. The problem in our own country until ten years or so ago was that people wasted too much time and money trying to decide what they should study in college. School counselors might advise their students to go into certain fields, but by the time they finished their four years, why, the fields were already too crowded."

"Or conversely, there was a field not many people knew to be a good field of employment at the time the decision was made, and four years later the government and industry employers were caught short of necessary workers for that field. The first case caused waste for the student; the second case for the employer. Education-to-order eliminates both these wastes. Every student entering our university is assured of a job upon graduation. What better prospect is there, Mr. Brown?"

"But Dean Nettor," I said, "are there still those students in American universities who go to college just for the pleasure of learning?"

"We used to have those students," the dean said. "And we used to pay a great deal of lip service to a thing called a liberal arts education. Which, thank god, no one nowadays talks about anymore. The career-minded middle-class individuals don't see any value in liberal arts, nor do their employers, incidentally, and the idle rich don't care if they waste their money on liberal arts, so they indulge in it without comments. Intellectuals used to think our society would fall apart if there were no liberal arts education."

I fell silent, reflecting on his insightful remarks.

"What about the faculty? The teachers?"

"Professors get paid exactly according to their productivity. The greater their market demand, meaning their contribution to producing and satisfying students, the greater their income. Incidentally, your friend Dr. McMiller is one of the more popular ones on campus."

The reference to McMiller's success again reminded me of the dark, brooding philosopher, who somehow seemed to stand apart from this affluent university.

"We used to have a system that paid every professor regardless of the productivity difference," the dean continued breaking my silent thought. "We now recognize that it was an irrational, and even an unfair, system. A professor is extremely productive by teaching many students, say in Stock Management, while another one teaches just a few, say in the Philosophy of Ethics, and they used to draw roughly equal incomes!"

As the dean explained it, however, the market principle of higher incomes for higher productivity, for instance, a stock professor making much more than a philosopher, made perfect sense within the context of business model in America.

"We are just more rational about it, more businesslike, if you will," the dean said as if he knew what was on my mind. "There is no reason to pretend that the worth of an accountant and that of a philosopher are the same, is there?"

I said I understood.

"For all intents and purposes," the dean continued. "Our university, like all the others in America, might as well be a private company. We are completely self-sufficient so as not to require any public monies to support its operation. In step with the rest of the country, as a matter of fact, we have been considering its transfer to a private company entirely. It might as well be a private corporation for profit also on paper as it is in reality."

There was a knock on the door and soon the secretary walked in with a pot of coffee and some pastries. While she was pouring the coffee, I was mulling over what I considered an important question to ask the academic dean.

The secretary left and we faced each other once again.

Chapter Five

"Since your liberal arts education is virtually non-existent," I said carefully, "wouldn't that produce fairly inadequate graduates for their employers, without some general notion of life and its principles?"

"Not at all, Mr. Brown," the dean said, obviously enjoying the chance to describe the virtues of his university to a country school principal. "In fact, the opposite is true. The employers don't *want* the liberal arts education at all."

"Why wouldn't they? After all, I was always taught, and we still teach our children that it is the foundation of Western civilization."

"True," Dean Nettor chuckled in obvious reference to our educational system in the town of Laurinville. "But what you would call Western civilization hasn't seen anything like American civilization at the threshold of a new century, the scale of which the world has never seen before."

I told him that, from what I had seen, I could only vaguely understand what he was saying.

"Take philosophy, for example," the dean said, sipping his coffee. "What does it really contribute to our business civilization of production, promotion, and consumption, and its endless repetition of this cycle with more products? A typical philosopher causes nothing but headaches for business executives and managers, not to mention government bureaucrats, by raising all those questions that make little or no sense to the leaders or to their balance sheets. So, what if the greatest philosopher in the name of Socrates says, 'the unexamined life is not worth living?'"

"We say, 'the unconsuming life is not worth living.' It's all very wonderful for him to say so, but did Socrates ever run a business corporation or a government bureaucracy? Or a modern university, if I may add in all modesty? How is examining your life going to help raise quarterly earnings and get paperwork done in time, or produce students in satisfactory condition?"

"Still—"

"Look, Mr. Brown," the dean was beginning to have fun. "While I understand that Laurinville is no modern America, wouldn't you agree that so-called Western civilization itself would have been impossible without all the toils of tradesmen, merchants, government bureaucrats, inventors, bankers, and so on? In America today we have simply raised the obvious to the visible. We merely practice what has always been true throughout history."

I then inquired about the importance of the brilliance and excellence of the creative few, including perhaps a few moral prophets. A society that ignored this fact would be in deep trouble sooner or later.

"Perhaps, perhaps not. Perhaps later than sooner," the dean said, not protesting too strenuously to my comment. "But I would submit to you that in our present circumstance, the employers in business and government don't want brilliant or creative minds who would carry the torch of our civilization. They want workers who can follow directions without asking a lot of unnecessary questions or wasting a lot of company time examining their souls."

"What good would this really do for the purpose at hand? Our University, like any other university in the United States, follows the same principle of survival and prosperity, survival and prosperity. To do that, we must produce what would satisfy the market, and the market is the employers. Employers don't want philosophical excellence or creativity from their employees. They want obedience from their workers, nothing else."

Being reminded of the university's motto that I had seen earlier, I asked him about the meaning of 'student-customers'.

"That simply is another way of saying that this university follows the business model," the dean explained. "After all, the students are our customers who butter our bread and pay our salaries. They have every right to demand satisfaction for their investment. That's why at this university, as elsewhere, students have a great deal to say about what is to be taught, how it is to be taught, by whom, when and where. Every instructor must submit the content of one's course to the students for their approval at the beginning of every term. After all, as our motto clearly says, they are our customers. In fact, our faculty salaries are determined by how well professors satisfy their students."

I briefly wondered if Robert I. Lee was seeing the handwriting on the wall that declared that his days at the University of Wilmington were numbered.

"You don't mean that," I said. "Wouldn't that merely encourage mediocrity in education? You wouldn't want your students to leave your college with that as their achievement?"

"That's exactly what the employers want and that's exactly what we aim to do with our students," the dean said, emphasizing the point by putting his coffee cup down on the table. "'Educational Mediocracy', a term that is gaining momentum in our country, is the guidepost of all things in society. The employers want average people, not brilliant people, not creative people, just average people. Mediocracy is the rule, not the exception."

"What about advanced learning, like master's degrees and doctorates?"

"They are advanced mediocrities," the dean said. "Master's degrees are given to those who advance beyond the mediocrity of bachelor's degree, the doctorate is given to those who advance beyond that of master's degree. As the graduates advance, they become better workers by becoming more mediocre or more average. Employers in business and government love advanced mediocrity. The advanced graduates are more willing to follow directions simply because they have invested more and have more at stake with their careers."

"How can you possibly suppress all tendencies toward individual excellence and creativity? I mean—"

"It's not as difficult to do as it may seem to you," Dean Nettor said. "Of course, we have certain cultural advantages in our recent history in that we have been stressing mediocrity in our culture a lot longer than people realize. We are now well prepared, shall I say, for a life and culture of total mediocrity. Our television has been excellent in popularizing the idea that mediocrity is nothing to be ashamed of. Hours and hours of mediocrity on television eventually dull any remnants of creative urges or brilliant ideas in people. Plus, our philosophy of mediocrity begins early in kindergarten where children learn the value of not becoming troublemakers by raising questions and being different from the other children. Did you know that the American public, after nearly half a century of mediocre cultural practices, is perhaps the easiest people to train or condition in the world?"

I said I didn't know that because I had always thought of Americans, that is, those who live outside Laurinville, as ruggedly individualist and fiercely nonconformist.

"Maybe in its early history, but not today. Besides, in a business society, who can resist employers who demand mediocrity and conformity? Either you follow directions and obey, or you starve. It's not terribly difficulty to impress our students with that simple principle, is it, Mr. Brown?"

"How do the teachers react to medi—mediocracy?"

"We rely on them to carry out the policy and we are not disappointed with the results. They are by and large cooperative with the university's effort because in the end it is beneficial to them too. We all share in the benefits in this business endeavor."

"How about their lectures, books, and thoughts, and so on that must contain some notion of creative quality?"

"We encourage our faculty members to be entertaining, caring, and most importantly, optimistic with their lectures. Don't use big words or big concepts. Don't get complaints from students. Their book-writing follows the same advice. So does their activity concerning new thoughts. No one deviates from the rules of mediocracy and expects to survive and prosper. They produce, their income goes up; they stagnate, their income goes down."

"No certainty in anything. Of course, there is no tenure here or anywhere else. It was abolished a long time ago as unbusinesslike and counterproductive. It's a viciously competitive world out there and the university business is no exception. Our faculty has been on the whole very cooperative in maintaining the policy of mediocracy. Likewise, they generally weed out the troublesome students quickly from their classes."

"How?"

"Oh, there are ways," the dean said pensively. "The professor can discourage brilliant or creative students in classrooms. You know there are many subtle ways to accomplish that. You can ridicule them in class, you can ignore them, you can discourage them in many different ways. Or simply fail them if nothing else works. Eventually they get the message that being too smart hurts. On the other hand, you can give a lot of Cs in class by making your exams fairly easy so that every student does a similar job on the test."

"Which, of course, results in a massive number of C's. Some students call this university 'The University by the C', a takeoff on our logo, 'The University by the Sea' in reference to the beach. At any rate, the Admissions Office can do its part, by weeding out students who seem to have certain qualities that are at odds with our mediocre requirement, those who have extremely high IQ scores or creative talent, and anyone whose behavior pattern tends to deviate from the expected norms of mediocracy, and so on. Our campaign of mediocracy has been extremely successful in the last few years or so, and in no small measure thanks to faculty cooperation."

"You've convinced me that, under the given circumstances of American society, mediocrity in workers is essential," I said. "But what I don't understand is, even in America there should be some excellent and creative individuals who are the driving force of this society and the mastermind of its planning and management in the long run. Where do they come from if not from universities? I mean, wouldn't you need those oddballs and creative minorities who keep things going in society? From what you have described to me, Dean Nettor, there won't be any of those people in America. Is it possible?"

"I can appreciate your puzzlement," the dean responded. "Because no society can survive much less prosper without the top-notch managers and scientists and brain trusts. One thing is certain, however. They are not produced by the universities, for mediocracy and top-notch minds are incompatible."

"Then, where do they—"

"Mainly from two sources," the dean counted with his fingers. "Number one, from the sources outside the university community. Those who are excellent cannot survive our university system so that, even if they try, they have to drop out sooner or later. These individuals succeed in their specific fields of endeavor largely on their own without any help from formal education. They are brilliant and strong enough to do that, so that university education means nothing to them; they do it on their own. If you looked at all of our leading men and women of industry and government, you would find that indeed very few of them are university products. Unless, of course, the position is so routine and mindless that anyone can handle it."

The dean poured himself more coffee. "Number two, they are also imported from foreign countries, mainly from Europe and Asia. From Europe we get brilliant scientists and artists; from Asia we get excellent quality technicians and innovators. To them America is still the land of opportunity, and we pay them well, too. In the last ten years or so, most of the research laboratories have been increasingly staffed by foreign scientists, mainly German and Japanese, and now a few from India and China."

"What about Americans," I said. "Are they content to be mediocre?"

"Well, it's supposed to be a big secret," Dean Nettor said with a smile. "We never tell our students outright that their lives are destined to be mediocre, by glorifying mediocrity in the media. For the short term, which is America's popular model of thinking, I would say, yes. A decade or two ago, I might have said no. They have become so used to the ways of mediocrity that they cannot think about their lives or society in any other way. Customers who demand satisfaction in all things tend to be quite mindless, unable to think in long terms. Being mindless and unable to think in the long terms, they are quite happy being the total consumers, which they have always wanted to be. There is no feeling greater among the masses than the feeling of being a total consumer, courted by business, waited on by others, pampered by—"

Dean Nettor seemed to have caught himself from going too far in the discourse on American consumers.

"At any rate," he said, slowly, "we have been preparing ourselves for this role for a long time and our society is quite content with the times, I am sure. Scientific or artistic excellence can be purchased easily, so why bother with all the trouble of producing it on our own native soil? What difference does it make if it comes from another country, and not produced in America? After all, we are a nation of immigrants."

"I don't know," I mumbled more or less to myself. "This business model of university operation, like a lot of other things I have seen here so far, is quite new to me and I don't know what to make of it."

It was my honest state of mind.

"The business model is as it should be, Mr. Brown," the dean said, perhaps feeling that the visitor from Laurinville was hopelessly undereducated about the American way of life. "Because it is based on the laws of demand and supply, there is no waste to speak of. It is impeccably rational and logical. For example, four years of Elizabethan literature just so that you can recite some poems, that's a waste. In our current system, moreover, because there is no waste between demand and supply there is no emotional trauma involved. One gets exactly what one expects to get. Thus, all human suffering is eliminated in contemporary America. Every aspect of American society follows the productivity model so that if you don't produce, you get nothing. It's as simple as that and there is nothing to suffer from."

"What about those who don't get it, not being part of society's rewards? Wouldn't they suffer?"

"We suffer only if we expect something and don't get it, don't you think? When the rules are clear and everybody knows what to expect, why would not getting it bother anyone as long as one understands the rules of the game ahead of the time, and as long as the game is played fairly?"

"But is it played fairly?"

"Absolutely," Dean Nettor said with emphasis. "Everyone knows how the game is played. It is the rules of the marketplace, demand and supply. Is there anything in the world simpler than the rules of the marketplace? Take, for example, the way we get much of our revenues."

"Revenues? You mean taxes?"

"Yes. A great portion of our revenues comes from lotteries, now played in every state. Every lottery game is played with its rules clearly publicized, such as the odds for each ticket, etcetera, so that each player knows exactly what the odds are and what his chances of winning would be before he decides to play the game."

"What are the average odds?"

"Oh, I would say about three million to one that you would win."

"Three million to one? Isn't that a bit insurmountable?"

"Of course," the dean said, "I wouldn't play the game myself because the chances of my winning are virtually non-existent. But many Americans, especially the poor ones, cannot think that far and the government doesn't tell them anything about the odds. Television only announces the winners and shows people how happy the winners are. But it is absolutely fair as a game of winning and losing because they understand that everyone has the equal chance of winning. That's all people care about and that's what the game of the marketplace is all about. In the meantime, government is happy to get the revenues somewhat painlessly from lotteries."

Our discussion went on some more, covering other similarly fascinating aspects of life in American society. Obviously, Dean Nettor was mostly the speaker and I the listener, for I was learning and absorbing all about this fascinating society of ours, so to speak, which I knew so little about. The impression I received about American society, as described in the optimistic and robust terms of the academic dean, was that most Americans were happy with their social system and an air of contentment was everywhere.

When I left his office to return to the social science building after our audience finally ended, my head was bulging with information and reflection.

What little I had known of my own society had to be radically altered in light of the new knowledge. I met the academic dean again soon, much sooner than I would have imagined, but under a circumstance that I could have never imagined possible.

But that part of my story must wait for its proper turn.

Chapter Six

"Did you learn enough about how our university operates, Michael?" McMiller asked as we drove out to a restaurant on the outskirts of Wilmington where we were to have lunch with the social science professors.

"Dean Nettor gave me a pretty good background," I said. "Not just about the university but about other things too."

"He's good in what he does," said my friend.

Traffic was fairly heavy with the lunch crowd but McMiller negotiated his vehicle with ease and skill. I told him that the dean had repeated a similar defense of the business model as McMiller himself had done the night before.

"You think we are going too far with it?"

"In some ways, yes, I think so." Then I relayed the conversation I had with the dean regarding the values of liberal arts as opposed to purely career training. McMiller chuckled.

"You have to admit, though," he said. "Our business model has produced certain side-benefits that could have taken much longer to accomplish under different circumstances."

"For instance?"

"For instance, take racism and sexism. As you well know, because America was notorious for those things one time, our discrimination against blacks and women was such that no decent American could hold his head up."

"You don't have that anymore?"

"Of course, we still do, but nothing like what we used to have."

"How was that accomplished by money or the business model?"

"Money interest has simply replaced all other cultural values in America. A black man or a woman can be a corporate president as long as he or she can produce profits for the company. No corporation would ever reject a black man or a woman only because they are not white males, that is, as long as they produce beneficial results for the company. After all, profit is profit, no matter who brings it in."

"Would shareholders care who made the profit for their shares? All economic positions are therefore completely open, as they should be, to anyone who can bring in money. I am not sure even a monkey can be discriminated against nowadays if he can make more money for the company than a human being. I would hate to think that one day I could be replaced as a professor by a more entertaining monkey professor. Wouldn't you, if you were me? I don't think Dean Nettor would think twice doing just that."

McMiller laughed uproariously at his own joke. I had to laugh too. He was laughing so hard that he had to recover just in time to avoid hitting the curb.

"What about those political positions?" I asked. "Can blacks and women join the top political ranks as easily as they can climb up the economic ladder?"

"Certainly," he said. "As a matter of historical fact, Michael, we no longer have what you might call political positions any more in America. All political positions are economic positions."

I waited for his explanation.

"Before our time," my friend the political scientist said. "Presidents, governors, mayors, and so on were paid pittance for their salaries, compared to corporate executives and others in economic positions. So, naturally everyone in a political position either cheated the government and the public to make up for the difference or couldn't leave the political position soon enough to write memoirs, sell government information as a consultant, or join a prestigious law-firm or a lucrative corporate board. Well, by and large, those days are gone. Every political position is now comparably paid with its equivalent in an economic position, which is only fair. So, the result is that every political position has become an economic position. Now, you have two ways to make money: You either become a politician or join a corporation."

"Or teach college."

"You are right," McMiller chuckled. "I haven't been doing too badly myself, but I know some professors whose income is easily in seven figures. Those great entrepreneurial professors—"

He did not get to finish his sentence. What happened next was like slow motion, which, in real life, took no more than two seconds.

We were driving south on what appeared to be a main highway, bisected by cross streets at regular intervals. As we were approaching that one particular interval I saw, and apparently so did McMiller, a smaller car approaching the same intersection from our right. I distinctly remember looking up at the traffic lights and we had the green. But our right-of-way mattered little at the moment because the other vehicle came straight into the same intersection we were about to enter. McMiller slammed on the brakes hard but it was too late.

Our vehicle, much bigger than the other, rammed the rear half of the other car with such force that the smaller vehicle made a one-hundred-and-eighty degree turn more or less on the same spot in the intersection, now pointing the other way. If McMiller hadn't reacted with the alertness with which he had, our vehicle would have driven straight into the other driver, a youngish woman perhaps in her late twenties. Both vehicles came to a noisy halt in the middle of the intersection and my slow-motion world came to an abrupt end.

Apparently neither of us, although shaken, was hurt. We looked at each other and, after being assured that both of us were all right, got out of the car. It was obvious at first inspection that the other car was hopelessly mangled. Its side was pushed in long ways by our front bumper beyond repair, perhaps even beyond my stepmother's great mechanical skill. Miraculously ours had sustained only one broken headlight, the one on the driver's side. The young woman looked ashen white, her forehead showing a couple of scratches. Her passenger, an older woman who turned out to be the young woman's mother, was doubling over on her seat moaning. Several bystanders converged on the scene out of curiosity.

"Have somebody call an ambulance, Cecil," I hollered.

"No use, they won't do it," he said. "Besides, the police will be here in a minute. All our vehicles are hooked onto their central monitoring post. They know that a collision has occurred and are probably on their way here right now."

"Are you all right?" I asked the young woman.

Recovering her senses somewhat, she made a feeble attempt at a smile. She had a face that suggested a life of woes and sorrows. In spite of the shock in which she presented herself to me, and the cuts on her forehead that added a none too favorable appearance, I was instantly impressed by her innate innocence and dignity.

"I am all right," she said. "But I am not sure about my mother." Then she turned her attention to the older woman.

After some inquiry from her daughter, the older woman managed to sit up, still holding her head with both hands. I judged from the sight that my worst fears were unjustified. McMiller was now inspecting his vehicle front, walking back and forth, looking for any other damage.

"I'm terribly sorry it happened," I apologized. "My friend was driving the car and it is only my second day of visiting here. I am from Laurinville."

The woman managed a better smile this time, which made her look much more attractive.

"I knew you were from somewhere else," she said, frowning and smiling at the same time.

"You did?"

"Yes, because most people here wouldn't think of apologizing."

I realized that McMiller had been showing little or no concern about the woman's car or its passengers. He was preoccupied with his own damage assessment.

"My friend says the police will be here any minute," I said.

"I know. Thanks."

Although I wanted to talk to her some more, it was rather too awkward a situation in which to carry on a normal conversation. While I was fretting about, the police car arrived with its usual lights and siren. Two officers got out of their patrol car and approached us. None of the participants made any move to redress their grievances against the other party. One officer approached McMiller, and the other the young woman. Upon request, McMiller produced his driver's license. I saw the young woman do likewise to the other officer.

"Where is your Highway Identifier, sir?" the officer asked.

"Under the hood," my friend answered.

"May I see it?"

"Of course," and with that McMiller opened the hood. Near the engine bloc there was a black box the size of a house telephone. The officer flipped open the top and under it were several well protected meters with numbers and codes. The officer wrote down the numbers and codes on his clipboard and waited for the other officer to finish his inspection of the other vehicle. The other officer walked back to ours and told him that the women didn't seem hurt badly. Nevertheless, an ambulance was on the way to take the women to a nearby emergency medical station. The two officers walked back to their patrol car with their respective clipboards.

"What's a Highway Identifier?" I asked McMiller who sat in his seat looking out the windshield.

"It tells you how many miles you traveled and on what kind of roads."

"Why?"

"Because we pay road taxes according to how much we travel on what kinds of roads, so that if we travel on good roads, we pay higher taxes and less if we use mainly low-grade roads."

"The machine records all that?"

"Yes, by the car's vibration, and more. It also records all the pertinent data in case of a collision, like this one. It tells you who is at fault by analyzing the raw data. That's what the officers are doing right now. They are feeding the information into a computer at the central office. We used to waste a lot of time and money arguing who is at fault in traffic accidents. No more, all is settled instantly now. That also applies to traffic tickets. No more arguing with the officer or appearing in court."

"That's all very marvelous," I said in genuine admiration although that sort of thing was unnecessary in Laurinville. "But isn't that a little bit too much to pay highway taxes according to how much you travel? I mean—"

"It's a wonderful system, Michael," he said. "We pay the post office only if you use its services, don't we? Why not the same principle for the uses of highways? Why pay when you get no service from it? We've extended the toll concept a little further, to be fair to everyone. You pay as you use it."

I was trying to see what the women were doing. Mother and daughter were now talking to each other in a more reasonable state of mind, it seemed, and I was relieved to see their apparent recovery. Then an ambulance materialized with its lights blazing. It parked near the stricken vehicle and two men in white uniform jumped out of the front seats and approached the women. Within a minute, they were helped out of the car and were loaded onto the ambulance. The older woman hobbled a little, leaning against the men.

"They don't seem to be too badly hurt," I said.

Then the two officers returned to the scene of accident. McMiller got out of the car and I followed suit. We followed the officers to the ambulance in which the two women were secured on stretchers. The young woman looked at us as if anticipating bad news. Her struggle with her woes and sorrows in life seemed to register more visibly in her face this time. There was, I thought briefly, a sense of resignation in her. A searing wave of pathos ran through my mind.

"Miss Baker, Dr. McMiller," the officer who took care of our end of the business addressed both parties. "We just completed our investigation and this is what the central office computer tells us."

The officer consulted his clipboard in which was stuck what looked like a computer printout sheet. "Miss Baker, you have been found to be at fault. You owe Dr. McMiller for his left headlight and whatever other damages he finds, and also two negative points would be assessed against you because you violated the traffic regulation by running the red light."

The officer then gave both parties some more minor instructions and told us we could leave. A tow truck would arrive shortly to take the crippled vehicle away, the officer said. By then, at least two dozen spectators had gathered, some of them gesturing to one another how the accident took place. McMiller walked back to our car, but I lingered a little so that I could talk to the unhappy woman. The officers finally left and I rushed to the woman on the stretcher.

"I hope everything turns out all right, Miss Baker," I said.

She smiled and said she was sure everything would turn out all right. Her mother, more miserable looking than her daughter, complained mildly on the stretcher placed next to her daughter's. I wanted very much to say more but didn't know what to say. One of the ambulance men came to close the door and I had to step back. Just before the door was closed, however, the woman managed a brief smile for my benefit. I stood there and watched the ambulance take off.

"Well, we are going to be about thirty minutes late to our lunch," McMiller said. "And one headlight short."

He was putting his driver's license back in his wallet and I saw "164" printed across it. McMiller noticed that I was looking at it.

"Well, American society got rid of much of the racial and sexist bases of discrimination," he said as if reading my mind. "In their place we now have TIW numbers in order to identify social standings."

"Isn't it just as bad?"

"No, not at all," McMiller said. "In racism and sexism, one was born into a certain color or gender, there was nothing one could do to change the fact. Identifying everyone's total economic worth is absolutely fair. Black or white, man or woman, anyone in America can now achieve any TIW value he or she is capable of achieving."

McMiller mused for a while and said with mock smugness, "one-sixty-four isn't a bad number at all for TIW."

"Did you see the woman's?" I said, hiding my anxiety.

"Yes, it's all here." McMiller showed me a copy of the computer printout that the officer had given him. He pointed to a number which said "48."

"Not a very good number, is it?" I said, dismayed.

"That means she is extremely poor and possibly uneducated," Cecil said.

"Where do you think they took them?"

"There is a medical station for all those with TIW under 50," McMiller said. "Let's see if we can get this machine cranked up."

The engine came alive easily and McMiller negotiated his car out of the intersection, carefully avoiding the debris from our headlight and from the unfortunate Miss Baker's crippled vehicle.

We fell silent, still reeling from the event.

"The other driver said Americans don't apologize," I said, breaking our silence.

"True," McMiller said. "In America, we don't apologize for anything because that means we admit our own fault. That we cannot afford to do, especially if one is charged with some wrongdoing or involved in a traffic accident. Even those corrupt politicians, dishonest businessmen, erring military leaders, outright criminals, and what have you, all live by one motto—Never admit that you are wrong or say you are sorry. You have to wait for the matter to be settled in court, but not before."

"Well, how could you then have any moral standing in society?" I asked what I felt was a fairly irrelevant question.

"All moral standing in America, whatever it is, is decided in a court of law," said my friend the political science professor. "In some ways, Michael, if you want to put it that way, we have become a *shameless* society. We do not feel any shame as a society or guilt as individuals, especially on matters that have grave moral or legal implications."

"But if you never feel compelled to apologize—"

"I know what you mean," McMiller said thoughtfully. "Most Americans feel they are infallible. Remember not too long ago? We had a president who publicly vowed, 'I will never apologize for America.' Since then, apologizing for anything, other than for trivial things, has been unfashionable as well as unprofitable in American life."

While I was mulling over his explanation, we came upon a lively scene that seemed to prove what he just said. The traffic slowed to a virtual halt when we saw a small group of people apparently protesting something in front of a fresh-looking office building. A large, multi-colored sign on its front said, 'Wilmington seahawks franchise' with no capital letters. McMiller explained that the sports franchise, a professional hockey team that had come to Wilmington promising 'community love', 'brothers and sisters of Wilmington getting together', 'the spirit of solidarity', and so on, had decided to move the team to another city for a more lucrative contract. That apparently had triggered the protest from the unhappy fans. From the signs and looks of the protesters, they were angry about the betrayal and the pain that it had caused in their hearts.

"We demand an apology," a man hollered, holding up his sign.

"You said you loved us," one woman hollered toward the office.

"You said you cared for our feelings," another said.

"You promised to love us and stay in Wilmington," another said.

The protest made our car come to a complete stop now and I watched the people and read their signs that reflected their hurt feelings.

"They are not going to get an apology from the franchise," commented McMiller.

"Didn't they know," I said somewhat puzzled at their hard reactions, using a logic learned from my friend himself the night before. "That the franchise was just a commercial organization, here to make money, not love?"

My friend chuckled at the obvious contradiction and said nothing. Soon a policeman emerged and started directing the traffic to clear the bottleneck. Thus, leaving the protesters, we drove the rest of the way uneventfully.

As we entered the restaurant, we were met with questions from the impatient social science crowd about the cause of our delay. Somewhat subdued by the experience, McMiller was less than his usual jubilant self when he described what had happened.

While my friend was describing the accident, I kept thinking about the poor woman who tried to smile. It was a smile of great pathos. For a brief moment, I thought I understood her after all.

Chapter Seven

"It's a shame, it's a shame," someone mumbled as McMiller finished his narrative.

Everyone looked at the source of that comment. It was Robert I. Lee, the philosopher, who had been quiet during the whole uproar over our adventure.

"What's a shame, Robert?" asked McMiller. The others gave that oh-you-again look at the philosopher.

"Have you been to the medical station reserved for those with TIW less than 50?" Lee's question was directed at no one in particular.

Everyone was silent. Some murmured, "not me."

"Well, I have," the philosopher said. "Two years ago, my TIW was 43 and I had diabetes, compounded by viral pneumonia. Not that I am doing much better now."

"Your TIW or your health?" David Granger the sociologist said. He was a youngish man with glasses, and his unassuming air made the question a serious one. Nevertheless, some chuckles were heard.

"Both," Lee said without flinching. "The place is a madhouse and combat field hospital. Sometimes you can't see a doctor for several hours unless you are dying. They didn't think my situation was critical enough and I had to wait from one o'clock till four before I could see a doctor."

"So, what about it, Robert?" McMiller said with surprising kindness.

"I just hope that the woman and her mother got decent medical attention at that horrible place, that's all."

"But you don't have to go there anymore, Robert I. Lee," a heavyset man with a great deal of formality about him, whom I had remembered as Jim Bardeaux, an industrial psychologist, said with his emphasis on the middle initial. "Your TIW entitles you to a good medical standing now, doesn't it?"

"That's not the point," the philosopher said as if he was used to that sort of experience. "It's simply criminal."

Somehow Bardeaux's stress on his middle name seemed to have evoked a response in him, because he suddenly went into a trance-like rigidity with his whole body and slowly recited the following: "'I have trodden the winepress alone; and of the people there was none with me: For I will tread them in mine anger, and trample them in my fury; and their blood shall be sprinkled upon my garments, and I will stain all my raiment. For the day of vengeance is in my heart, and the year of my redeemed is come.'"

I guessed that as from the Bible (Isaiah?). The effect was palpable even with the irreverent group of college professors. Although they must have been familiar with the philosopher's oddities there was a definite sense of uneasiness in the crowd.

"Speaking of crime," I said, breaking the ice, "would someone tell me how criminals are punished in America, what kind of crimes, and so on."

The mention of crime made everyone turn instantly to Dale Flynn.

"Well, Dale, isn't that your eminent domain?" McMiller said.

"Horsefeathers," Flynn snorted.

"Come on, Dale," McMiller coaxed him as if he was familiar with Flynn's usual procedures. "We know you are an eminent criminologist and expert in virtually every field of human endeavor, especially in crime and punishment in America, don't we, fellows?"

Everyone murmured their assent.

With those preliminary theatrics out of the way, Flynn, who was more scholarly looking than anyone present wiped his mouth carefully to begin his lecture.

"As you all know, with the exception of Mr. Brown, the criminal justice system in America, is based on the fundamental principle that the offender must pay." The term 'pay' had many connotations, and Flynn waited for a second or two for that ambiguity to sink in.

"Pay with money, that is," he finally said it with significance. "In America, everything is based on the economic law of the marketplace. Why should crime and punishment be an exception? America has always been, even long before our own generation, a nation of money justice. We pay our fines as punishment, that's money justice. We can stay free on bail, that's money justice. We get the very best or the very worst, depending on our ability to buy, uh, hire lawyers, and that's money justice. Today, we simply recognize the principle in a more open, systematic way than before. Let me summarize the motto of criminal justice in America, and the motto is: pay for your crime. If you can pay for it, fine; if not you go to jail."

Someone let out a loud burp that interrupted Flynn who looked at the offender disdainfully before resuming his talk amid chuckles. "We have basically one court system, which is for criminal cases. Almost all civil suits go to commercial courts, popularly known as 'People's Court'. Big corporations either added a court division to their operation or started this business of settling civil cases."

"For example, Sears, Wal-Mart, JC Penney, and Kmart are among the more popular people's courts in America. Let's say you have a complaint against a fellow American or an organization, which requires redressing. The complainer's lawyer chooses, in cooperation with the opposite number for the other side, a people's court whose decision both sides would agree to abide by."

"Wasn't that copied after a popular television program called 'Country Court'?" someone asked.

"Well, true," Flynn said with dignity. "In fact, our current designation of those civil courts is an extension of the same concept. Except it is no longer for minor entertainment, it's for real."

He then took a drink from his glass carefully.

"That leaves," he resumed. "mostly criminal cases to go to regular court. If one is found guilty of a crime but cannot pay the penalty, we send him to what is euphemistically known as 'criminals' paradise', which is a string of islands from which no one can escape, not unlike the old 'Devil's Island'. It is economical because you don't waste money on heavy security and feeding and clothing the criminals while they presumably suffer in the jail cell. It also keeps the criminal element out of sight so that everyone is happy."

"How do they survive on the islands?" I asked.

"Well, a survey of all those uninhabited and possibly uninhabitable islands determines the degree of difficulty for human survival based on indigenous resources alone. In other words, if no help from the outside is added, how difficult is it for a human being to survive in that environment? Based on these survey results, heavy criminals like murderers and rapists and thieves are sent to those islands with a higher difficulty for survival. Likewise, the lesser criminals are sent to easier ones. But mind you, no island is self-sufficient without outside help."

"You mean thieves are considered in the same category with murderers and rapists?" I asked.

"Of course, the law is rather harsh on stealing. The philosophy is that no civilization can exist unless its property is respected and protected. We respect and protect our property in America, against all enemies, domestic or foreign. The government determines the difficulty of survival for the prisoners and subsidizes a certain percentage of the needed but unavailable resources. The percentage, of course, depends on the severity of the crime. For example, murderers and rapists and thieves get less than fifty percent so that their life is a constant misery of hunger and discomfort. Lesser criminals get a better subsidy so that their survival is made a little less miserable. All this is handled by private companies."

"Why private companies?" I inquired. "Isn't that the business of the government?"

"For the reason of economics, mind you. The government has found it cheaper to contract it out to private companies. Just about everything else is being privatized in America. Why not criminal justice? At any rate, to continue, if it's a white-collar criminal paradise for those embezzlers who for some reason could not pay their way out, the subsidy comes close to being one hundred percent, their only punishment being isolation from the rest of humanity. Which is not bad."

"Not very fair to the common thieves, is it?" shouted the philosopher who, in spite of his slight frame, had consumed an enormous amount of food. That, however, seemed to have alleviated his intense unhappiness somewhat.

"Well, Robert," the criminologist said looking back at the philosopher with the same mock condescension. "It is a matter of principle. Our society needs businessmen, especially those who are active with their imagination, they are the lifeblood of the American economic system. Every day they think about how to increase their profits, thereby contributing to society's well-being, using a lot of active imagination. Now, occasionally some of them would let their imagination run wild and step outside the boundaries of the law. But is it really that bad that they sometimes forget the line between imagination and reality? Besides, who can tell for sure in this world of all-out business competition what is legal and what is illegal, for heaven's sake? The businessman is the pillar of our society and the moral foundations for our children. They make up the membership of Lions International, Kiwanis Club, the Boy Scout leadership, and so on. Should we punish them severely just because they were a bit too active with their contribution to society?"

"No such benefit of the doubt extended to thieves," complained Robert I. Lee.

"But the thieves on the other hand," said Flynn unaffected, "have absolutely no socially redeeming value. They steal things, property that belongs to someone else by the law of the state and in some instances by the grace of God—"

"The grace of God?" the philosopher inquired, as if ready to go into another trance.

"Well, I was thinking of those religious thieves," the criminologist commented quickly, as if to appease Lee. "The thieves who steal things from churches."

"You mean the evangelists and preachers?" shot back the unrepentant philosopher.

There was a smattering of chuckles.

"No, Robert, I mean the common thieves who steal from churches," Flynn said impatiently. "Be that as it may, the thieving criminals are the greatest menace to our business civilization in America. Now for example, just think, gentlemen, what if every American became a thief, what kind of society do you think that would make ours?"

"Not any worse than if all Americans became embezzlers, I should think." It was the philosopher again. More chuckles.

"Don't forget this discourse is for the benefit of Michael Brown who knows virtually nothing about America," reminded McMiller to his quarrelsome colleagues.

"Good point, Cecil," said Flynn and turned to me once again. "American society has introduced perhaps the most far-reaching innovation in the annals of criminal justice in order to ensure justice for all, and it is this."

He then proceeded to bring out a small metal object from his coat pocket the size and shape of a pack of cigarettes. He put it on the table in front of me for the benefit of my close inspection. At first glance, it appeared to be a rather sophisticated recording device as I carefully weighed it in my hand. Flynn allowed me to examine the object and, when I showed an expression of incomprehension, he took it away from my hand with a dramatic flourish.

"This little device, popularly known as the 'logger', gives us a twenty-four-hour recording of our activities, both auditory and visual. Virtually every self-respecting American middle-class and educated segments of the population, carries this in his person. We can lie to and fool other people as to what we have been up to, but we can never lie to or fool this machine. It has been proven absolutely fool-proof. It is a combination of a tape recorder, a lie-detector, a VCR, a diary, a camera, the repository of all that is honest and decent in America."

"What if you don't have one?" I asked timidly, much awed by what the little gadget could do.

"It began basically as a business expense logger for tax purposes," Flynn said somewhat descending from his lectern. "Obviously many Americans, especially those in the ranks below TIW 50, don't make use of this wonderful mechanism. This is still somewhat expensive."

"What happens to those who don't carry it?"

"Well, they just have to take their chances with the law since they have no record of their whereabouts. The law respects those who respect themselves, especially in the issue of the logger. A man who doesn't respect himself enough to carry a logger with him is obviously not a very good citizen, and very likely to be guilty of the crime he is accused of."

"Wouldn't it be a little too rash," I ventured. "To equate one's economic inability with one's moral inadequacy?"

"For heaven's sake, Michael, how else would you judge a man's character?" Flynn roared. "Unless you do it by the most accurate measurement there is in the world, that is, the level of one's economic success?"

"How about privacy, Dale?" I persisted. "With all these round-the-clock revelations you don't have any privacy left any more, do you?"

"Who needs privacy when you are talking about self-defense, self-protection, self-vindication, and above all, self-interest?" emphasized the criminologist with conviction.

"And self-destruction," added the Bible-quoting philosopher, whom everyone ignored.

"Now, Michael," Dale Flynn said. "Some people in America used to carry tape recorders and Polaroid cameras in their cars just in case they got in an accident and needed an accurate record of the event. Who were these people?"

"Basically lawyers, insurance agents, and some people who were slightly paranoid," someone responded.

"I don't know about the paranoid types," said Flynn. "But lawyers and insurance agents, along with accountants and businessmen, are some of the moral paragons of society. They are smart individuals who protect themselves with an instant record of the event. Today in America, we do it a few steps better with this logger, much more comprehensive and accurate than our clumsy tape recorders and Polaroid cameras because it produces a continuous record of your comings and goings, and those of others around you. Only the criminal types would be reckless enough to disregard the paramount need for keeping legal records of themselves. Most of them get convicted of the crime they are accused of when they fail to produce the logger. Judges are rather unanimous on this point and render merciless verdicts against those logger-less scum."

"Are there other preventive measures for the not-so-successful citizens?" I inquired.

"Two things you can do," said the criminologist. "In fact, most Americans, that is, good, law-abiding Americans I mean, carry two protective agents with them."

With that, he produced two more items from his coat pockets. One was a plastic card the size of a business card and the other that looked like a small memo pad. Dale Flynn held them up to me so that I could see them more closely.

"This is an insurance card," he said as he held up the first item. "It is perhaps the most expensive insurance card there is. No one below a TIW number of 150 can obtain it."

"What does it do?"

"It protects you from all legal punishment, both criminal and civil, other than murder, rape and thievery, by paying the necessary penalty for you. One must have an impeccable record of past conduct, almost wholly unblemished, to qualify for this one."

"And darn expensive too," said David Granger rather unnecessarily, but demonstrating the fact that he had one also.

"That's right," Flynn heartily confirmed. "This second item is an added measure of protection from civil suits basically, popularly called the 'bill of satisfaction'. Years ago, this sort of document was used only in some legal settlements, like divorce cases. But as the struggle for money got a little rougher in our society, lawsuits became too common. Therefore, lawyers now advise that everyone carry this pad and collect signatures from anyone they suspect to be lawsuit happy. I even collect the signatures of satisfaction from my students after each lecture. I don't want them to turn around and sue me for a poor lecture. Michael, you may be signing a lot of memos as you use commercial or bureaucratic services in this country."

Several faculty members nodded in agreement with the criminologist, proving that they also carried the memo pad.

"It seems to me," I said carefully. "That, while trying to protect oneself from everyone else, a good deal of mutual trust has been lost in our American society."

"Trust?" Flynn said the word with great reflection. "Trust. Oh, yes, it's not completely gone out of American life, mind you. But today only basically two segments of society ever rely on trust simply because other forms of protection are not available to them."

"Two segments?"

"Yes, Michael," Flynn declared solemnly. "They are the poor Americans because they can't afford all the devices of protection, and the criminal element because that's how they always conduct their business anyway. The poor must trust each other because they have no other way of conducting business; they can't hire lawyers to sign and witness all the legally sound documents so that they have to do with a handshake or trust if you prefer to call it. Criminals, like the Mafia, must trust each other because they cannot use the long arm of courts and police and society; so, they have to pledge their word to each other."

"Trust seems to have fallen on hard times," I mumbled politely.

"No," the criminologist flatly denied my observation. "We've discovered that, in the evolution of civilization, trust is the least reliable measure of human conduct."

"War of all against all," our unhappy philosopher said.

"You must admit, Robert," said the criminologist to the philosopher. "That it's a lot more reliable than trust. Don't you think?"

"From what I've learned in my conversations with Cecil and Dean Nettor," I said, "it seems there is too much commercialization in America. Just about everything, justice, education, national defense, marriage, you name it, has been turned over to the private sector, that is, the commercial institutions. Don't you think it's a little bit too much?"

"Not really," David Granger responded with the air that it was his domain of expertise. "The commercialization process began with President Reagan's Commission on Privatization in 1987, which recommended that many of government services be turned over to the commercial sector, for cost consideration, and it has been working just fine."

"But do they produce the same results?" I asked.

"The private sector only does a better job," Granger observed.

"How? The commercial sector is interested only in profit, nothing else."

"That's precisely the reason why the commercial government, if you would call it, does a better job than the traditional government," the sociologist emphasized. "We no longer have a 'public' in America. Good or bad, it disappeared a long time ago. In its place, we now have customers, customers who have to be satisfied. Who can satisfy customers better and more eagerly than the seller of goods and services that can best respond to consumer demand as his sole purpose of existence?"

"But," I wondered, "can the commercial government serve better?"

"Of course," Granger said. "Would you choose to eat at a government-run cafeteria or at a private restaurant like this one, tell me, Michael. Which one would serve your demand better? There is no comparison, is there? Consumers in America demand to be satisfied, and there is no better way to satisfy them than through commercial services. The Communists tried the other way, and look what happened to them?"

"I don't know," I had to admit. "But what's the point of having a president or a government at all, if—"

"Our president is also a commercial president," Granger said.

When I looked surprised at this comment everyone laughed.

"What I mean is," Granger said when the laughter had died down. "The president of the United States is kicked out of office if he fails to satisfy his custo—constituents even before his term is up."

"Oh, how?"

"If polls show that his approval rating falls below fifty percent, he has to leave the office of the presidency. He stays on the job as long as he keeps voters satisfied."

"Wouldn't that cause terrible chaos? I mean, the uncertainties of the office, not knowing how long he is going to be president, and so on?"

"Well," said Granger, "that's precisely the point of commercial presidency. He must always satisfy his people if he wants to stay on his job. But not to worry. No president has ever been kicked out of office before his term. He has all sorts of media advisors and ways to keep his popularity up above the fifty percent level. He simply does what the majority wants him to do, that's all he has to do. It's not as difficult as it first seems to a 'foreigner' like you."

The reference to foreigner prompted Jim Bardeaux the industrial psychologist to comment on the way the American government made money from foreigners coming into the United States.

"We don't need foreign workers anymore," he explained. "Aside from artists and scientists we import, we only encourage wealthy foreigners to come to the United States by charging them a sizable citizenship fee."

"Selling citizenships?" I said, surprised.

"Yes, and in large quantities," Bardeaux said. "We sell our citizenship only to those foreigners who are wealthy enough to afford it. That way, we increase our national income and at the same time keep out those poor teeming humanities who used to come to our shores."

"Citizenship for sale," murmured Robert I. Lee, "most disgusting."

"Well, there is another side-benefit," said Bardeaux as if responding to the philosopher. "The wealthy new citizens replenish our declining native population in America. All in all, selling citizenship to wealthy foreigners was one of the bright ideas that came out in the early nineties."

Somehow, I sensed that Bardeaux and Lee didn't get along well at all. But, of course, I had no idea then that the next time the two scholars met in my presence it would be over a life-and-death matter.

"And most importantly," chimed in McMiller who had been rather quiet. "It helped reduce the horrendous national deficit that had been piling up in America through the eighties."

Speaking of reducing the national deficit took us to other success stories in American using the method unique to American society, namely, financial inducement. From their report, America had solved many of the social problems—drug addiction, juvenile delinquency, teenage pregnancies, and so on which used to divide the nation in debate. When I mentioned my admiration for this fact, all the social scientists present beamed with pride as if they were personally responsible for the accomplishment. Everyone started speaking at once, explaining how they succeeded in eliminating those social problems typically the "American Way."

"That was a stroke of genius, and luck too, at least in the beginning of the program," said David Granger to whose authority on such matters the others seemed to defer. "We paid the parents whose children stayed out of trouble until the age of eighteen."

"Paid the parents?"

"Yes, Michael," said Granger. "According to their economic standing. So, for example, if the youth from a poor family avoided getting in trouble, we paid the parents a little more than, say, middle-class or upper-class parents because of the obvious difficulty involved. As long as their kids stayed out of trouble, the parents received a certain amount of money each month. For the money they were getting, if nothing else, the parents were compelled to get on their kids to behave themselves, to stay away from drugs, to avoid pregnancies, and so on, and it worked."

"It must've been expensive," I observed. "I mean, paying all those parents for their kids' good behavior."

I almost added, "which we in Laurinville take for granted."

"Not at all," Granger said. "It turned out much cheaper than all the expenses of rehabilitation and therapy the wayward kids had been costing our society. Only a small portion of the money spent on drugs annually, for example, was enough to finance this what you might call Pay-Off-the-Parents Plan. It was also the American way simply because the reason it worked is that we value money here as the only motive for doing anything. I am sure it would work in Laurinville, too, not to mention Moreland. Perhaps not as well as the rest of America."

My thought briefly returned to the Green Palmers.

Dale Flynn mentioned the violence the plan caused between some parents and children in the beginning, both attacking each other out of sheer frustration, parents to keep their children in line and children to get free from their parents. But eventually the money factor won out, and children learned the lessons.

Then the conversation drifted to other things, including the new phenomenon on the rise called 'rotational marriages'. As David Granger volunteered to address the issue again, rotational marriages, which lasted only about a month or so, kept every marriage in a constant state of honeymoon.

"Research shows," the bespectacled sociologist pronounced, "that a month is the maximum length of time that two partners in a marriage can remain satisfied with each other. Hence the idea of rotational marriage, which is just beginning to be offered by some corporations. I saw their ads appearing in national magazines."

I mentioned the fact that advertisements seemed to be everywhere, on private automobiles, on the sides of school buses, and even on some houses, not to mention billboards.

"I saw quite a few on church pews," Dale Flynn said. "They were advertising places like 'Heavenly Gate Restaurant', 'Salvation Auto Repair Shop', 'Faith Medical Clinic', and so on."

"Everyone hustling everyone," the ubiquitous philosopher complained. "'What's a man profited if he shall gain the whole world and lose his own soul?' And what is this world coming to?"

On that philosophical note, our luncheon finally broke up. Several from the crowd, led by Dale Flynn, signed the 'bill of satisfaction' as presented by the restaurant as we paid our bills.

But just before we left, I visited the restroom and Robert I. Lee followed me. He just hung around there fussing with his hair and shirt buttons while I was attending my business. He waited patiently until I finished washing my hands.

"I want to see you tomorrow, Michael," he whispered to me, looking around as if suspecting eavesdroppers. "I will show you something very interesting. But don't tell anyone about it."

"What is it about, Robert?"

"I can't tell you now," he whispered fiercely, although obviously there was no one else but us there.

I was overcome by curiosity but thought better of it. He handed me a note with his address scribbled on it.

"Of course," I said. "I will see you tomorrow."

We agreed on ten o'clock in the morning. I would take a cab. McMiller was waiting for me by the car.

"It has been a very interesting day," I said as McMiller and I drove back home. "All sorts of things and facts."

"It's a shame, it's a shame," said McMiller rather suddenly, reminding me of the philosopher's utterances earlier.

I looked at him questioningly.

"It's a shame about Robert Isaiah Lee," my friend said as if that thought had been on his mind all along. "One hour of lecture by him is worth more than a hundred hours of mediocrity with these so-called professors of social science. He is perhaps the only true professor among us, but it's a shame that his days are numbered at the University."

"Why?"

"He gets low ratings from his students on the issue of 'respect and love for students'. While other professors worry about high ratings, he worries about the students, their education and their future life in American society. So, he is honest about their follies: Their laziness, selfishness, lack of spiritual values and so on, and students hate him for it. They don't want their own faults exposed and criticized although it may be for their own good."

"How do other professors get such high marks for respect and love toward students who are obviously so lazy and spoiled?" I said, wondering about McMiller's own remark about the students that he had made earlier today.

But my friend offered silence as his answer, and I did not press further.

We stopped on the way home at an auto repair shop for the broken headlight. There McMiller signed another bill of satisfaction.

There was still a party in my honor ahead, but my mind mostly was on the Bible-quoting philosopher and our little secret.

Chapter Eight

When we arrived home the house was quiet.

"She must be in her studio," said Cecil. "You haven't seen her studio yet, Michael."

I followed him around the house to the backyard. There was a small barn-like structure the size of a two-car garage built against the back fence that I hadn't noticed before. Apparently, it served as Carol's studio.

We entered the studio quietly and saw her back turned to us. She was working furiously on a canvas. She turned around with a start and saw us.

"My goodness," she said, breaking into a smile. "I didn't hear your car coming up the driveway."

Cecil kissed his contract-wife on the cheek.

"Don't let us interrupt," I protested.

"No interruption," she said. "I was about to take a break."

Then she proceeded to take her smock off and hung it over a stool.

"How was your day, Michael?" she asked.

"Oh, a fairly uneventful day," I said, and Cecil and I burst out into laughter.

"What's so funny?" Carol inquired. She knew something had happened.

"We'll tell you all about it later," Cecil said. "What have you been working on?"

The three of us gathered around Carol's canvas. On it was the sketch of an old man with a long, flowing beard like someone from the Greek mythology seated behind the steering wheel of a modern car. His hands were placed on the steering wheel as if he was driving but his eyes were closed. The sketch looked altogether incongruous to my unpracticed eyes but somehow it touched me with a sense of deep sensibilities.

"What would you call this painting," I asked her. "When it's finished?"

"'God Driving the World,'" Carol said.

"'God Driving the World,'" I repeated it. I was too impressed by the creative artist at work, so closely observed, that I didn't dare ask any more questions. I would've liked to ask her what it meant. But somehow under the circumstances, it would have sounded improper. Cecil, apparently used to his wife's artistic imaginings, urged her to continue with her work. "You don't have to stop for us," he told his wife.

"I was about ready to quit," she said putting the box of pastel colors away.

I looked around at the studio. There were all sorts of sketches and paintings hung on the walls, some oil, some pastel, and some ink and pencil. They were the usual array of works in different stages and styles expected of an art studio. Other materials and instruments of art, such as paper, canvas, paint, frames, books, and the likes, were strewn all over the place. A half dozen or so pastel drawings of a nude male posed in various stages in and around the bathtub were placed at random against walls. Carol laughed, seeing that my attention was fixed on those works.

"That's my imitation of Degas' 'At the Bath' series," she explained. "I had a tough time persuading Cecil to pose for me."

"They are all Cecil?"

"I think she idealized me a little," he said, a bit embarrassed to be showing his behind in our collective appraisal.

"I'm art-illiterate," I confessed. "But there is a strong likeness, I think."

The remark produced a mild chorus of chuckles from us. She brought out her portfolio which contained photographs of her paintings that had been sold previously. They were a mixture of portraits and impressionistic human drawings. There were several folding screens with distorted human figures. Even her portraits avoided naturalness in them.

"I don't see any landscapes," I observed. "Don't you do any landscapes? Wilmington seems to be such a beautiful place to—"

"I hate doing landscapes," she confessed. "I can't get interested in them and I have never done any."

"So many people do seascapes around Wilmington, it seems," I volunteered.

"I know," she said. "But natural settings have never interested me for some reason. I like doing portraits."

"What would you call your style?" I asked.

"I don't know if I am good enough to have a style," she said modestly. "But I would call it, if I had to, figurative-expressionistic realism. Perhaps a combination of symbolism and realism, like the 'God Driving the World' sketch."

"I think I will go fix some drinks," said Cecil and, getting our preferences, left the studio. I ordered a glass of lemonade.

"Wait a minute," Carol said suddenly looking at my face with renewed interest, and I knew her artistic impulse had been awakened and I was the object of her awakening.

"Let me do a portrait of you, Michael. We have enough time before the guests get here for the party."

She set me down by the window, my left arm loosely resting on a small desk. She positioned me this way and that until, finally, she was satisfied. Then she set to work. I had never sat for an artist to do my portrait and squirmed uncomfortably. It was like being under a microscopic examination by a biologist. Carol began to work with the same fury in which I had earlier observed her upon entering the studio, her lips tightly pursed in concentration. Now and then she stopped to reflect, then resumed her work.

Cecil McMiller returned and, seeing his wife at work, entered quietly and placed a glass by her side and one by me.

"You can drink, Michael," she said, taking a sip herself.

I murmured thanks and took a drink. Cecil stood next to her and inspected her work.

"What do you think?" Carol asked her contract-husband. "Something is not quite right, don't you think?"

Cecil, apparently well trained by his artist wife, took a few steps back, and concentrated on it again. "I think it's the hairline," Cecil said after a while. "It's too straight. It should come down here this way."

"Can I see it?" I asked while the couple was discussing my portrait.

"Not now, Michael," Carol denied my request. Then she resumed her work.

After a few minutes or so, she announced her work was finished. I got up, stretched myself, and walked over to her easel with some apprehension. The three of us stood there looking at her work.

What I saw took my breath away. The face in the portrait, ostensibly the most familiar face known to me, shattered my previous self-image. The features were familiar enough, but the expression they created was a portrait in deep anguish. The 'unnatural' colors of mostly green and blue gave the image a startling and unsettling quality. The total effect was devastating. I stood there speechless. I had been expecting a more traditional exercise in realism that one watches at a county art fair, not a staggering blow to my smug self-expectations.

"Well," I said, finally. "It's very different."

"Nothing like what you expected, uh?" Carol said with the obvious delight of an artist who had just upset someone's confidence in conventional wisdom. She took the portrait from the easel and hung it on the wall.

"It's in a way shocking, isn't it?" I told Cecil who stood there looking amused.

"It might look a little bit different in natural light," Carol said, adjusting the portrait. "Maybe we'll look at it again tomorrow."

We turned the lights out, closed the studio, and then walked back to the house. Then Cecil proceeded to tell his wife about the day's events.

"My goodness," Carol declared after hearing Cecil relay our auto accident. Then she said, "the poor women, I hope they came out all right. What a terrible thing to have happened."

Cecil retired to shower and change. I asked Carol for the name of the medical station where the Baker women had been taken. When I called the station to inquire into the situations of the two women, the ward clerk said they had been discharged immediately, apparently without any serious injuries sustained from the accident. I felt relieved but somewhat disappointed that I could not speak to the younger woman.

"They left the station," I told Carol. "Apparently, they were all right. At least there was nothing serious from the accident."

"She just doesn't have a car anymore," Carol said ironically. "That's all."

"Perhaps she is fully insured," I said hopefully. "I wish I could've talked to her."

Carol looked up at me in that odd way that sometimes only women can manage with their wonderful insights into a man's head, and sometimes heart as well. I found myself blushing and turned away.

"Just to make sure everything was all right with them," I mumbled casually. "I mean, after all, it was a severe accident."

"Of course, Michael," Carol said with a slight trace of smile, "of course, it was." Then she added, "I am not saying you are smitten by this Miss Baker, am I?"

"I would like to change too," I said and hurriedly retreated to my room with a feeling of embarrassment that somehow Carol had seen my more than goodwill interest in one Miss Baker.

When I showered, changed and returned to the living room, Cecil and Carol were talking and, seeing me coming in, tried to act normal.

"I hear you called the medical station," Cecil said, deadpanning.

"Yes, I did," I said. "Just to make sure they were all right."

"Of course," Cecil said. "How were they?"

"They seemed to be all right, from what the woman at the station told me on the phone. They left the station immediately."

"That's good news," Cecil said. "Did they tell you drove them home?"

I said they didn't and I hadn't asked.

"Hmmm—" Cecil reacted mildly and returned to the kitchen.

I was looking out the window at the horseshoe-shaped driveway, thinking about the woman who was suddenly without her transportation, when I saw the accident report placed on the windowsill, apparently left there by Cecil. Her first name was Jeanne, aged 27, and was listed as unmarried. I looked for and found her home address; she didn't have a telephone number.

I was still memorizing her address when I saw the first guests arrive, pulling into the driveway.

"It's the commissioner and his wife," said Cecil coming out of the kitchen.

Carol and I followed Cecil to the door. Soon the bell rang and, when Cecil opened the door, there stood a man in his late fifties with gray hair and a woman with a blue dress with white polka dots. They were introduced as County Commissioner Steven Warrick and his wife Evelyn. The commissioner had the shrewd look of an intelligent survivor, but his wife seemed a little pushy and left no doubt who was in charge in the Warrick household. The commissioner took his wife's pushiness good-naturedly. He inquired about Cecil's university and Carol's artwork.

Another couple arrived, almost at the heels of the Warricks, whose distinction was immediately apparent by coming in a chauffeur-driven limousine. After disgorging the couple, the uniformed chauffeur left smartly. They were Circuit Court Judge Martin Roberts and his wife Sibyl who occupied a lofty position in the Better Business Bureau of greater Wilmington. The Roberts and the Warricks were old friends.

The judge looked to me like a quintessential country judge, with nothing distinguished about him. He was about the same age as the commissioner, but his hair was still dark, parted in the middle, which got the major credit for making him look so nondescript. His wife Sibyl (who was particular about the spelling of her name) was a nervous looking woman, pale and uncertain behind her glasses, although she was surrounded mostly by old friends. The judge was interested in my impressions of the changes in the United States, but I managed to remain noncommittal.

The third and last couple arrived not too long after the Roberts. The man was in his forties, short but powerfully built with broad shoulders. His wife, much taller than her husband, had the ease of movement like a good athlete. She had short light brown hair with a much natural, efficient look about it. Cecil introduced them as Richard Davis, the university's athletic director, and his wife Kim who coached women's tennis and volleyball also at the university.

All three couples were basically well schooled in public relations, but the Davises were the most relaxed of the three. Richard, who was familiar with the others, was blunt and to the point with his statements. But this facade of bluntness, I felt, hid a fine intelligence rare in athletics. Kim, who also taught English during the off-season, was more elegant and reserved than her husband.

Although the Davises were from the university, I was struck by the fact that there were none invited from among the faculty members in social science. These guests were friends of the McMillers, not Cecil's or Carol's, I guessed. I thought it interesting, also, that in a society of extreme business and money consciousness there still existed circles of friends and parties to attend. From the ease of the interaction among them that I observed, it was evident that they met often with one another.

"Complaints, complaints," Sibyl was speaking to Carol when I approached them. "Complaints about babies are the fastest-rising items at the triple-B right now."

"Sibyl," said Carol. "Michael would be interested in hearing about it. Would you please tell him all about your work again?"

"Nothing exciting, really," Sibyl said in a nervously high voice. "I was telling Carol about the rising complaints in the baby market."

"The baby market?"

"The customers who purchase babies are sometimes not happy with the delivery," she said. "If it's not one thing, it's another. We at the bureau try to tell them that babies are not like other commodities; they are not produced from the same mold, and every baby is different. But to no avail."

"What kind of complaints, for instance?" I inquired.

"Oh, most commonly about the baby not having the talent that the producer promised or in some instances guaranteed. For example, this man we had today at the office was furious that the two-year-old child he got showed no talent with the piano, which the producer had apparently guaranteed."

"What did you suggest for a solution?"

"Well, I called the producer," said the judge's wife with a nervous laugh. "A woman who is a professional surrogate, to see if some form of refund could be arranged. She said no, in no uncertain terms. In fact, she insisted she should've charged the man more because it was a direct pregnancy, not test-tube or artificial, and he was not an attractive sperm-donor, she said, which raises the fees. It was her opinion that the man should be grateful that she wasn't charging him any more than what he already paid her."

"So, what happened to the case?"

"I persuaded the man not to file a formal complaint, which he accepted. He knew after all he had no other choice and went home very upset, however."

The judge's wife promised to take me to a 'baby market' as soon as she and I could coordinate our time.

After some more talk with the judge's wife, I excused myself to make my rounds with the other guests and was about to discuss something with the county commissioner when Carol and Cecil together announced that dinner was ready.

Upon the announcement, we milled slowly toward the dining room.

Chapter Nine

"I hear, Richard, that you've been out of town for a few days," said the judge to the athletic director. "Where did you go?"

"Oh, we were looking over some athletes at one of the AFs," said the A.D. "The coach found a good prospect, but I think the price is too high."

"How much are they asking?" Cecil, who was known to be an avid sports fan, inquired.

"One-seventy-five," Davis said.

"That much for a free safety?" said Cecil. "A hundred-seventy-five thousand is a lot of money for that position."

"This kid," the A.D. said. "is being put on the block for a bid from several other colleges too. Our coaching staff thinks he is going to be an outstanding player. Now remember, how many games did we lose last year because of the poor free safety?"

"True," the county commissioner chimed in. "But I don't know if we can afford that much for him."

"Richard," Cecil called the A.D.'s attention. "Michael here doesn't know anything about the AFs and such. Would you be good enough to explain all that to him?"

"I was getting the general drift," I said when everyone's attention turned to me. "But not quite. I should be grateful to hear if you could explain it to me a bit."

The athletic director agreed.

"An AF stands for Athletic Farm," Davis began. "There is at least dozen or so of these corporations whose main business is selecting and training athletes."

"For the Olympics?" I asked.

"No, for high schools, colleges and professional ranks," the athletic director said. "These corporations consolidated and commercialized all the operations of hodge-podge fly-by-night individuals and organizations into more streamlined and scientific operations. Sports became such a big business in the late eighties that educational institutions simply couldn't coordinate all the recruiting and training on their own. So, naturally the corporations took over. I must say it is now one of the fastest growing industries in America."

"I've invested some money in one of the AFs," growled the county commissioner. "It'd better be a fast-growing business."

There was a mild recognition of the commissioner's joke.

"Before the AF system, as you must have known about our country a little," the A.D. continued when the chuckle died down, "a college coach or, for that matter, a professional scout, would scour the countryside, very often on someone's tips and opinions alone, looking for good athletes. Toward the mid-eighties a lot of enterprising amateurs started the business of selling athletic information to the colleges and professional teams. They published and sold lists of blue chippers, sleepers, potential All-Americans, and so on. But they were all individual small timers, obviously, because it was basically a one-man show, operating out of a suitcase. Not only was there a lot of confusion in knowing which tips and opinions to believe, but also it got to be extremely expensive. Many colleges and professional teams lost money on players because they made a bad choice on the basis of inaccurate forecasts."

"Richard had his share of that too," said Kim.

"She is right," the athletic director said. "But not anymore. Beginning in the early nineties, some big corporations in the health and sports equipment business began to see the possibilities, in fact gigantic possibilities, in it because America was becoming enormously interested in sports."

"Mostly as spectator entertainment?" I ventured.

"Basically," agreed the A.D. "because most Americans are armchair athletes. Sports are good on TV."

I said sports on TV seemed to have always been popular in America.

"Nothing like what it is today," said the circuit court judge. "It's the national religion of the 90s and beyond."

"Well," Davis resumed, "so, as one corporation got into the business another followed, and now it has been stabilized into about a dozen of them operating practically all athletic businesses in the United States."

"How does that actually work," I asked. "I mean these athletic farms?"

"When the corporation finds a good prospect, after much rigorous scientific testing and so on, obviously," continued the A.D. "It pays either the prospect or his parents, if he is underage, a certain amount of contract money depending on the ability and the stage of development. Some good ones can make enough money up front before they reach fifteen to send their parents into comfortable retirement. Then the prospect is sent to this athletic farm, which is a marvel of modern science and technology in athletic training, where he spends all his time in athletic development, nothing else."

"What kind of family background do these, uh, prospects have?" I asked.

"Many of them blacks from poor families," said the athletic director. "The training is physically too rigorous for some WASPish kids to handle. Besides, the middle-class kids would prefer to go to college so that they can work for business or government where mediocrity is the norm. Athletic competition requires physical excellence and WASPs can't handle that as well. At any rate, while they are at the athletic farm the trainees are monitored by the most scientifically accurate methods of selection and training. The best among them are eventually sold to colleges and professional ranks."

"What about the not-so-good ones?"

"The best among the not-so-good ones are selected for the Olympics and other local amateur competitions. But big-time college and professional athletics get the cream of the crop."

"At big-time money," chimed in the county commissioner.

"That's right," said the athletic director. "The prospect we saw the other day is not really one of the tops. We can't afford it because the University of Wilmington is not one of the big-time majors. But we bring in good revenues from our sports programs. To continue, I said they are sold off to colleges and professional ranks, but actually they are auctioned off, to be more accurate."

"The auctions have been on TV too," said Kim, the off-season English teacher. "People like to watch those splendid specimens parading on the screen, buyers competing for them, calling out their prices."

"I saw them too," volunteered Sibyl giggling nervously. "And some of the buyers' wives were feeling the prospects all over, even the private parts. One woman in particular insisted, when a handsome black specimen objected to her feeling him, that she had every right as a potential bidder to inspect the object of her bidding."

"I suppose she was advising her husband," interrupted Cecil. "on certain technicalities for which only women are qualified to judge."

"The woman quit only when told by the auctioneer, a Major Something."

Chuckles went up.

"Could a buyer put the speci—I mean the athlete, to any use he or she sees fit?" I inquired. "Since one is 'buying' him—"

They, even Davis, seemed uncertain on that issue. The judge raised his voice to claim his authority on matters judiciary. "There was a case a while ago in one of the circuit courts when a wealthy woman wanted to buy a particular prospect, a magnificent athlete trained as a running back, for her personal service. The objection raised by the farm people was that the service was non-athletic so she could not bid. Thereupon she proceeded to buy enough athletes to form a team so that she could buy the one she wanted. The judge had to agree to this new version of personal service and ordered the athlete to perform any service his buyer demanded."

"Of course, when the prospects are selected at a young age it's a lifetime contract," resumed the athletic director, "because there is simply too much money involved. You can get out of it by becoming sick or performing poorly. But nobody would think of getting out of the contract by failing because there is nothing else the athlete can do for a living. It is a multi-billion-dollar no-nonsense business, and fairly harsh in economic consequences. The corporations mean business."

"Doesn't it amount to a new form of slavery, then?" I suggested cautiously.

The athletic director looked around at the room as if saying that there should be someone better qualified to answer that question.

"In a very general sense, yes," the judge said, still warm from his recent remark about the wealthy woman and her muscle man. "But technically all contracts are voluntarily signed. People can sign their lives over to a medical research center; women can bear children for other people on a strictly commercial basis. If a prospective athlete signs his ability over to a commercial agent, the law has nothing to say except the contract be upheld. Of course, we enforce these contract laws strictly because, without them, our business civilization is impossible to maintain. As long as it is voluntarily agreed upon, any contract is valid, as it should be."

"Besides," the athletic director resumed, "they are well fed, well taken care of in every way, and good medical care is always available, and so on, and fairly good money goes to them or their guardians."

"If it's slavery," said the judge, "I say it's good slavery. But as in all contractual situations some prospects try to escape."

"What happens to them?" I asked.

"Well," the judge said, "our effective private bounty-hunters bring most of them back to the farm. Most of them, however, realize that escape is a wrong thing to do to themselves and their society. Still, an unhappy athlete is better than no athlete."

"There is a question I've been meaning to ask," I said. "Weren't the rules of amateurism rather strictly enforced by an organization called the NC-something?"

"Yes, by the NCAA," said Davis.

"What's the NCAA?" Evelyn, the county commissioner's wife who had been quiet, inquired.

"The NCAA," Davis answered, "stood for the National Collegiate Athletic Association, a loose organization to administer amateur college sports."

"What happened to this, uh, NC—whatever?" Evelyn followed.

"It got disbanded in the early nineties," said the A.D. "I should say it disappeared because so many violations occurred in college athletics, money under the table, point-shaving scandals, drugs, and so on, that it became impossible to control college sports and individual athletes. So, colleges, very unhappy with NCAA control of their business to begin with, formed their own leagues, pretty much like the professional teams, and started their own business. First there was CFA, then CAA, then MAC. We belong to a lesser league called the NEA, the Northeast Athletics. Gradually, therefore, the NCAA became useless and consequently powerless."

"With that organization out of the way, colleges were basically free to do anything they wanted to do without fear of NCAA sanctions. As they say, the rest is history. It was only logical that sports would soon become completely commercialized, as it should be. It's like TV, movies, rock music, pure entertainment. Why should it be anything but a commercial product like the rest of the commercial products? People watch sports as long as it is enjoyable and drop it the minute it isn't. It's that simple."

"What about the alma mater," I said. "You know, cheering for your alma mater?"

"Oh, I can tell you something about that too," said Davis with assurance from his years of experience in athletics. "Alma mater, I can tell you, is the biggest phantom there is. Do you know any losing alma mater that can retain fan support? If the beloved alma mater doesn't win often enough to keep the fans going, the alumni members stop coming. And there goes your home team. People can drop their teams like dirty socks and just as easily and just as frequently."

"What about amateurism, then?"

"Sure, we do maintain some of that element just for appearance's sake. For example, international competitions like the Olympics pretend to be amateur sports. We send some of our lesser ones to those. But, admit it, there is no money in amateur sports, and people have little interest in it unless it entertains. All the big monies, however, are in commercial sports and we have the very best in the world, colleges or pros."

I expressed the desire to see one of the athletic farms and Davis promised that he could arrange it for me in the next day or two.

The conversations then drifted to investment in sports stocks and bonds.

"Judge Roberts," Cecil said loudly enough to quiet the crowd, "you've been to Washington D.C. recently on some committee. What was it about?"

Everyone's attention was now focused on the hitherto quiet circuit court judge.

"I was extremely honored, of course," the judge said, combing his hair with his fingers, "to have been asked by the American Way Committee on Pecuniocracy."

"Pecuniocracy?" I said, having a difficult time pronouncing the word, with accent on the 'o'.

"I didn't know there was such a word in the English language."

"Not so far," the judge said, "We only have democracy for government by people, theocracy for government by church, plutocracy for government by the few, and so on but not pecuniocracy. However, it will be a household word if our committee has its way. It will soon replace the word democracy in America, and not one minute too soon I might add. It's much more accurate in describing our system than democracy, and certainly more advanced."

"But what is pecuniocracy?" I asked the judge, this time managing it better.

Chapter Ten

"Pecuniocracy," said the judge, pronouncing the word slowly to increase its significance, "is literally 'government by money'. Pecuniocracy is derived from the Latin word 'pecunia', meaning money. We add 'cracy', meaning government, to pecunia and we have the word pecuniocracy. Yes, it is a new word that has never been uttered before, much less used in practical reality—until now. The American Way Committee on which I had the honor of serving has formally adopted the term to be a designation for the form of government in the United States of America beginning in the new millennium."

"Would that be in the form of a constitutional amendment?" I asked.

"Yes," the judge said. "And all the sweeping changes in school textbooks as well as all general references. The old term, democracy, will no longer be used."

"What happens to democracy, then?"

"Nothing," Judge Roberts said. "Pecuniocracy does not contradict democracy. It merely extends it."

"How is it so?"

"Well," said the judge, showing flashes of scholarliness under his country judge demeanor, "pecuniocracy is the last stage of development in democracy. When a society becomes a true democracy, I emphasize 'true', it is inevitably pecuniocratic, and I emphasize 'inevitably'. Hence it is the most advanced form of democratic government. Let me put it this way. In the very beginning of democracy, society opens up politics to everyone, which is popularly known as universal franchise, as everyone knows."

"What happens to democracy after the universal franchise in which everyone can exercise his political rights like everyone else, allowing no one to enjoy any particular privileges? The end result of democracy in universal franchise is that, since competition is open to all, it naturally leads to meritocracy, meaning success for those who are talented, which is the second stage of democracy. Children from the lower class can compete against, and actually succeed over, the children from the upper class. The cream of the crop rises to the top, so to speak, in the meritocracy."

"What happens after that?" I was fascinated by his analysis.

"The meritocracy is impossible for everyone, you understand, Michael," the judge continued. "Because there is so little room at the top. If there is one beneficiary of meritocracy, there are at least a hundred mediocre individuals who make meritocracy possible by doing all the mediocre things that are necessary to sustain the few successful individuals. Take government and industry, for example. How many mediocre individuals are there for each brilliant, meritorious person at the top? Too many to count."

"So, naturally, after a while it dawns on everyone that the world consists of mediocrity, not meritocracy. The meritocrats, those who are the cream of the crop, also recognize that it is necessary to emphasize, for their own security, that being mediocre is in fact a wonderful thing. After all, what would the meritocrats do without the multitudes of the mediocre? Slowly but surely, the idea catches on."

"What idea, Judge?" I interrupted.

"The idea that mediocrity is beautiful, as they used to say in the sixties in another context. Thus, democracy is transformed from its early phase of may-the-best-man-win into our present phase of may-the-mediocre-live, or more technically known as mediocracy, which is glorified in entertainment, public education and simple cultural propaganda until everybody believes that it is normal to be satisfied in his own station of life."

"How would that lead to pecuniocracy?"

"What happens after that, and this is what was discussed extensively the committee meeting in D.C., is the conflict between meritocracy and mediocracy, or to put it in another way, conflict between the few powerful and wealthy and the many mediocre and average. Both are, mind you, very much at the heart of modern America and, having been established as the very soul of democracy, both are as American as anything. The important point is that neither side gains any dominance of the other, ultimately reaching and maintaining a stalemate, meaning live-and-let-live. So, what happens then?"

"So, what happens then?" I echoed him, and some chuckles broke out.

"What happens then is the status quo in America. We are going neither up to meritocracy nor down to mediocracy. That simply means, ladies and gentlemen, whatever one *has* at the moment is whatever one *is* at the moment. Hence the importance of money in our society, because what one has is money if one has it, and that determines one's standing in society, depending on the size of one's TIW."

"What stage of pecuniocracy do you think American society is in now, Judge?"

"I would say the early phase of pecuniocracy," said the scholarly judge. "According to the committee's somewhat rhetorical documentation, pecuniocracy is described as the 'final flowering of modern democracy in America'. Ours henceforth shall be known as GOVERNMENT BY MONEY, OF MONEY, AND FOR MONEY."

"And it shall never perish from this earth," atoned the commissioner.

"Might as well call a spade a spade," McMiller, hitherto quiet, said. "Remember, Michael, what we discussed last night? American society has been operating on the principles of pecuniocracy for some time, a classic case of government by money. Gambling is not only legal but now children can enjoy the full fun of all sorts of state-run lotteries and horse-and-dog races promoted specially for them; sex is freely available through the four biggies, Sears, Wal-Mart, JC Penney, and Kmart—"

"Going back to pecuniocracy, judge," I said, "you mentioned pecuniocracy as the most advanced form of democracy. Why do you think it is?"

"Because it gives each individual his or her complete freedom," the judge said. "Each individual does exactly what he wants to do and doesn't do exactly what he doesn't want to do. What better system is there in the world? Isn't it the most advanced system of society anywhere ever dreamed of? In America we no longer dream about it, we *do* it in reality. Take, for instance, defense. Remember the dark days of national defense in America before our time? Young men were drafted into the army or were persuaded to 'volunteer' for the army, where they went through the most degrading mind-and-body control to become soldiers? Remember during Vietnam how hated the military became? All that existed because people didn't recognize the value of individual freedom, the principle that each individual is entitled to his own decisions in life."

"So, what is the situation with national defense now?"

"We pay for defense," the judge said. "All defense has been completely commercialized. Some large corporations, which used to make weapons for the Pentagon and know all about national defense, have divided up the nation into different regions and are responsible for defending their particular regions."

"What if they don't do their job right?" I asked, somewhat worried.

"Why wouldn't they do their job right, Michael?" the judge asked back confidently.

"Because they are interested only in profit-making, not—"

"That's precisely the reason why they *would* do their job right. They are there only to make a profit. The last thing they want is to lose their profits. Is there a better motive than that to do one's job right? That's why we can always trust the corporate defenders, not because they love us, but because they love their money."

"Who mans the military functions?"

"It's mostly mechanized now, but they have some foreigners to man certain weapons. There is no need for a large standing army any more, anyway."

"How are the corporate defenders paid?"

"Oh, there is a small defense tax we pay, some of us pay more and some of us less. Younger Americans live longer than others and hence they pay more because they have more to lose should there be a war. Older Americans, because they have lived long and don't have much more to go, pay less. We have a chart that tells us how much we pay every year."

"That also goes for the different TIW rankings," volunteered Cecil. "The higher your TIW the higher your defense tax because you have more to protect."

"That seems fair enough," I agreed. "But I am still not convinced that pecuniocracy is the most advanced form of democracy."

"Look at it this way," the judge counted his right-hand fingers with his left-hand fingers. "Number one, pecuniocracy or government by money is the most open system there is because anybody can be somebody in it if he has the money. Number two, it is the most just-and-fair system because money never discriminates against anybody—"

"Except the poor," I ventured.

The judge waited for the chuckles to die down, and then continued, "—and everybody has a chance at it. Number three, it is absolutely rational because there is no emotionalism involved in arguing whose money is better; everybody's money is the same, only the amount is different and all you have to do is to count it. Number four, it is the most efficient system because the law of market demand and supply eliminates all waste; you can't make money unless you do something somebody else wants you to do for him or conversely you are not going to give anybody your money unless he does something for you. Number five, it is the most effective system because you don't have to motivate people to make money, everybody being driven by one's self-interest, and what's more powerful and persistent than self-interest, can you tell me? Number six, it is the most democratic of all systems because only the largest number speaks, which is the fundamental principle of democracy, isn't it? The largest number or amount is *always* right."

"And, finally, it is the most perfect and certain system, I would submit, because, where money is concerned, there are no two interpretations possible and everything is absolute and final. Now, can you think of any better system than pecuniocracy? Defense rests."

After the effect of the judge's dramatic ending faded, Cecil McMiller, like a good host, turned to the county commissioner who had been quietly listening much of the time.

"Now, Commissioner, it's your turn to enlighten our guest of honor from Laurinville," Cecil prodded him elaborately.

"I am not as eloquent as our friend, the judge," the commissioner said modestly. "I don't know what I can tell him that would be so enlightening, as you put it."

"Well, you are an old hand in politics, aren't you, Commissioner?" Cecil suggested, then turned to me. "Commissioner Warrick has been recently elected to the post of county commissioner."

"I couldn't have been elected without the merit votes," the commissioner said. "At least five thousand votes."

"Merit votes?" I was puzzled.

"It is a vote a political candidate is allowed to purchase," explained the country commissioner.

"You mean buying votes?" I asked, greatly surprised. "I thought everyone had only one vote in America."

"There used to be the one man, one vote policy," said the recently elected commissioner. "But now a candidate can buy as many votes as he wants to, by paying into the public funds, and that's why we call them merit votes. If you have enough money to pay the government, that's your merit."

"You mean you don't campaign to get elected to political office?" I was naive and incredulous. Apparently, there was more to the changes in America than I had ever imagined.

"Not anymore," said the commissioner undisturbed with my excitement. "We *buy* political offices."

"Commissioner Warrick," Cecil called to him. "before you puzzle my friend anymore, don't you think we ought to explain our basic political process? My knowledge after all is confined to theory, not reality. Since you are most experienced with practical politics, I think you should take on the task, Commissioner."

The others nodded their heads vigorously in agreement.

With some more prodding, and shaking his head a couple of times to dramatize his duty, the commissioner began. "Unlike one man, one vote in politics, we have always practiced one man, *many dollars* in the United States of America. Translated into politics, it has to be one man, *many votes.* Since Americans cannot and do not tolerate the idea of one man, one dollar, in which we all make the same income, the only way we could resolve the conflict was making politics conform to economics, not the other way around."

"So, in the early nineties, we simply said to ourselves: All right, let economics rule! Let economics be economics! From this day on, no more one man, one vote. It shall be one man, many votes, as many as one is capable of getting, in the same way one makes as many dollars as one is capable of making. So, you get votes exactly the same way you get dollars: You *earn* them!"

"But is it fair for one man to have so many votes?" I inquired.

"Of course, it's fair," the commissioner said. "If it's fair for one man to have so much more money, why not so many more votes? Why should I be stuck with one vote when I am far more successful than Joe Six-Pack down the street who is no good?"

"Is that the rationale for merit votes?" I asked.

"Exactly," said the commissioner. "When the commissioner's post was up for grabs, I simply bought more votes than my competitor."

"But," I said, "what I can't understand is, what's there in politics for you to gain? I mean, unless you steal or take bribes. If you are well off already, what more can politics give you?"

"That's a good question," agreed the commissioner. "In our own state of North Carolina in the early eighties, a U.S. senate seat was won by Jesse Holmes who spent over ten million for his campaign expenditure. His competitor spent something fairly close to that himself. So, you have combined expenses coming close to twenty million dollars, and what was the annual salary of a U.S. senator? A miserly one hundred-thousand dollars! You spend close to twenty million dollars to get a job that pays you just one hundred thousand dollars? Isn't something obviously wrong in this? Yes, what is wrong is that the value of an office is not equal to its *market* value. That's what is wrong. If you spend twenty million dollars to get elected for a political office, the office had better generate market value better than twenty million to make it all worthwhile, wouldn't you say?"

"So, you equalized the two."

"Exactly, that's what we did. We made the value of the office equal to its actual market value."

"Of course, its actual market value wasn't anything like twenty million dollars, was it?"

"Definitely not," the commissioner said. "It's considered market value is about six hundred-thousand dollars. Anyone who spends more than one hundred-thousand dollars annually to get elected to the U.S. senate would be a fool, because there is no more value than that in the job. No matter what you do, just short of stealing and taking bribes, as you suggest, a U.S. senate job doesn't pay you any more than one hundred-thousand dollars a year. That's where you draw the line."

"What is the value associated with your commissioner's post," I said. "If you don't mind telling me?"

"Of course, I don't mind," the commissioner said. "It's no more than thirty thousand dollars a year, that's the sum most observers would agree is its market value."

"How much did you spend to buy the merit votes?"

The commissioner smiled. "You would have to guess that it is less than that amount, wouldn't you?"

I said yes.

"I spent twenty-five thousand dollars for it," he said. "My competitor didn't think spending any more than that was worth it and quit. So, I got the job of county commissioner."

"I suppose that's how you can check someone from buying up every vote and win every election," I observed.

"Exactly," the commissioner said. "You are right in wondering what if some rich man bought every vote and got himself elected president of the United States? But this principle of equality between political value and economic value stops that. The principle that operates here is the same principle that operates at an auction. Many bidders may like a certain item, but the bidding would go only so far, and not one step further than the object's presumed market value. Political offices, although you can purchase them if you have enough money, are not any more attractive than their presumed market value. Not one bit more."

"Even the president's office has a finite value associated with it, and no one but a wealthy person who can afford to spend an amount close to the value can get elected president. Besides, your own self-interest can expand through your office only to the extent that the self-interests of others would allow it. It's a wonderfully rational system."

"But you realized a small margin of profit in your election?"

"I did, although the margin of profit isn't large. I could have invested the same amount in something else, like a venture stock or money market that would give me greater returns, perhaps. Yet, after all, there is some satisfaction of calling yourself county commissioner, isn't there? The same reason goes for the president of the United States even if he gets very little profit from the office, I suppose. You get to have dinner with queens and kings, sometimes."

"Since all important matters are decided by economic institutions, like corporations, the political machinery in this country as a purely 'political' process has become much less important than even ten years ago. Remember, our social system practices pecuniocracy, the real power is in money. Money, not politicians, runs the system. It is entirely possible for the Russians to buy enough votes to have one of their men be president of the United States, but they would soon realize that there is no value in the presidency larger than their investment."

"So, there are no elections and election campaigns in American anymore?" I inquired, fascinated.

"Oh, there are some elections left where candidates still make grand speeches and promise a lot of nothings," the commissioner answered. "But they are largely honorary or ceremonial positions with no real compensations, such as Chairman of the Wilmington Art Society, Director of Environmental Advice, President of the Boy Scout Council, and so on. In reality, all successful politicians who hold any positions of any significance, by which I mean a position that pays money, are also successful businessmen, for the former is impossible without the latter first. You've got to make money first to be a big politician."

"Wasn't it always the case in America?"

"True, but it has now become open, more rationalized, and publicly accepted and recognized. There are no more shadowy politicians anymore. Everything is done out in the open. In some ways, we have become more honest than before when we did a lot of pretending, such as pretending to keep your own money and campaign money separate. Of course, it was impossible, so the candidates either pretended to keep them separate, or got embarrassed when caught. Now politics is completely commercialized."

There was vigorous agreement with the commissioner, and everyone was talking with everyone else at once, the subject of conversation generally being money or their recent investments in particular. The political discourse had apparently come to an end and I decided to change the subject to one that had just occurred to me while the crowd was buzzing with random conversation.

"One of the social scientists at the university that I met today," I said after the buzzing had run its natural course, "showed me an insurance card that insures him against any kind of criminal penalty that involves payment. What about other types of insurance?"

It seemed as if the subject of insurance was one in which everyone felt knowledgeable, and hence they all offered information. Sibyl gave me some names of insurance companies that she recommended. I said I was reasonably well covered, courtesy of Cecil and the University of Wilmington.

"But you have never had this coverage," Sibyl said, naming one of the companies she had just listed. "No company outside the United States has ever offered this type of coverage before, ever."

"What kind of coverage is it?" I said. "It can't be insuring your reincarnation, can it?"

"No, better than that," Sibyl said with excitement from teaching someone who was practically a foreigner one of her society's better features, which made her forget about her nervousness. "It is insurance against 'alienation of affection'."

"Alienation of affection?" I repeated after her. "Insurance against divorce?"

"Part of it, in non-contractual marriages." she said. "It guarantees that you will never lose your loved ones. Of course, it is expensive and gets more expensive as the number of your loved ones increase that you want to ensure against."

"How could you ensure against that?" I said, disbelieving. "People die, leave you, or no longer care about you. What can you do about that? No insurance policy has enough power to stop that."

"Suppose you have a child who is insured," Sibyl said, almost whispering, "and the child suddenly dies. The insurance company guarantees to replace the child with one who is almost exactly like the lost one, detail for detail."

"What?" I nearly shouted and jumped at the same time. It had to be a fairy tale in which witches and wizards did strange things. "How?"

"The insurance company keeps a minute computerized record of the insured in every detail," said the judge's wife. "If nothing happens, everything is fine. If something happens, say the person dies, becomes crippled or no longer acts interested in you, whatever, the insurance company will substitute someone, normally a trained actor or actress, to replace the insured. The quality in the replacement is so superb that, in many instances where the original person recovered or returned to normal, the policyholder actually prefers the replacement. I know some such cases among my friends. There was this friend of mine in particular whose husband had a stroke, became disabled, and required long-term hospitalization. Her insurance company then provided a substitute, but the substitute husband being a trained actor, superior in many ways than her real husband, she became really attached to her substitute husband. When her real husband recovered and wanted to come home, she said no. She said she no longer wanted the real husband. She liked the actor better."

The other two women sympathized with the woman under consideration.

"You mean," I said, gasping, "if my lover leaves me, the insurance company will send me someone exactly like her in every detail or better? For how long?"

"Yes, and as long as your policy specifies. You pay more for longer periods, of course, lifetime being the most expensive option. But most people who know the value of the policy prefer it for life. You wouldn't want to let go of a good thing in the middle of it, would you?"

"But, why?" I said, still incredulous. "Aren't sorrows and pains supposed to be part of normal life?"

"Oh, Michael Brown, you are a romantic. Who wants sorrows and pains of life?" said Kim Davis who knew something of human emotion through her literature study. "American society has been getting rid of all kinds of emotional problems in the last three decades, thanks to TV which is the Great Simplifier. Remember how many people used to suffer depression? No more. They are cured now easily with TV, religion, psychology, and even therapeutic surgery. The insurance policy that Sibyl is talking about, which I have on one particular person I won't mention, is the ultimate protection against emotional trauma. Aside from our own grievous illnesses or death, society provides all sorts of defense against emotional and social pains, as long as you can afford to pay for the services."

"People nowadays don't have to visit their old folks at nursing homes anymore," Sibyl said. "They can hire professional visitors to visit their old folks once a week, once a month, once a year, or on major holidays, whatever, depending on the coverage they are willing to pay for. That eliminates all the guilt people used to feel about their loved ones in nursing homes that they cannot visit often enough because they are too busy or live too far away."

"It's a wonderful solution, of course," agreed Kim.

"I wouldn't know if I should feel blessed or cursed if I were a true American like you," I said, somewhat recovering my wits but still feeling confounded in general.

Then the crowd, inspired by my reference to true Americans, began discussing truly American TV programs. Carol, who had been almost invisible all that time, emerged with refreshments. The party lasted almost two more hours after this point.

When I finally retired late that night, I was beat, both mentally and physically, from the extraordinary events of the day. Within a few seconds, I fell into a deep dreamless slumber.

Chapter Eleven

The address that Robert I. Lee had given me was not too far from where the McMillers lived. I did not tell either of them where I was going and they didn't ask.

Just to be safe from cultural misunderstanding, I gave the cabdriver a B-tip and received what I thought was a performance appropriate for the medium level of gratuity. Soon we were driving by a large cemetery and then into rows of condominiums, one of which turned out to be Lee's. The buildings were all painted gray and, especially being located right next to a vast cemetery, looked desolate and depressing. The way they were kept, as we got closer, told me that the condominiums were somewhat in a state of neglect.

The cabdriver dropped me off and I found myself standing in front of a door bearing his house number. As I was about to press the bell the door suddenly opened and Robert I. Lee, as if he had been watching through the peephole, motioned me to come in quickly. He looked around to see if anyone else was there before closing the door. His secretive manner led me to believe that a great conspiracy was being hatched between us.

"Come in, come in," he said, leading me into what appeared to be a living room. "Have a seat."

I sat where he indicated, still uncertain about the purpose of the meeting. The house seemed to be kept clean and orderly. A large bookcase against the far wall, befitting a philosopher's residence, occupied the most prominent place in the obviously Spartan household. Although I hadn't been told, I could guess that Lee was a bachelor.

"Did you have trouble finding the house?"

I said no, feeling that our conversation was highly irrelevant. But I sensed that Lee was just getting around to the subject of our meeting and there was no doubt he knew that I was anxious to get going. He fussed some more with offering me coffee which I declined.

"I know you are curious as to the meaning of all this," he said in an apologetic tone, but he seemed to be waiting for the right dramatic moment. After a couple of other inconsequential inquiries, he swallowed hard to indicate that the moment had come. I waited.

"Michael," he said, looking at me intensely, "did you ever hear about the Hockers?"

"Hockers?" I thought for a moment or two and shook my head saying no. I had never heard of the Hockers.

Because Lee lapsed into his dramatic silence, I had to ask: "Hockers? Who are they, or shall I say, what are they?"

I looked at him, indicating that I was waiting for his explanation. He sighed deeply as if thinking that he had a lot of educating to do to bring this ignorant foreigner from Laurinville fully up to date on the subject of 'Hockers', or whatever they were.

"You know American society pays those who take their lives voluntarily, for reasons of ill health, old age, being tired of living, or whatever," Lee said. "Compensations being determined by their TIW standings at the time of their departure."

I said I didn't know that. But I wasn't altogether surprised that euthanasia was actively encouraged in America.

"Who takes advantage of this, uh, early departure?"

"Mostly poor, old, and disadvantaged types," he said. "Abortion is also administered freely with payment, the length of the pregnancy determining the amount of payment. The sooner the abortion takes place, the less expensive it is. If the fetus is determined to be deformed beyond any redeeming economic value, then it is done free of charge, as it is considered a contribution to society."

I sat there listening, thinking about what all that was leading to.

"There is also this life-for-sale program, similar to euthanasia except this program applies to a healthier population," Lee said.

I sat up. "Life for sale?"

"I know you are surprised," he said. "But the principle is really simple. Philosophically speaking, it is now universally acknowledged in America that each individual life belongs to each individual, and to no one and nothing else. The basic premise is that one can do anything with his life, and whatever he does with his life is his own business. If he wants to take his own life, that's his business—"

"If he wants to sell it, that's his—"

"—Business, of course," Lee said. "Medical institutes normally buy lives for research purposes, although I've heard that some wealthy people are offering good money to buy live targets for their shooting sports."

Many people seemed to think that hunting animals for sport was bad enough, but using human lives for experiments seemed a bit too much. But I also understood that the scientific desire to use live human subjects was irresistible and overwhelming in the research community. I also knew from history that only under highly immoral circumstances and much moral condemnation, like the Nazi doctors, however, that live subjects had been tried. But what does one make of the fact that these American subjects were *volunteers* in exchange for a considerable sum of money? The question was simply beyond my limited mind.

"Who gets the money if the volunteer gives up his life for it?"

"Sometimes his family, but mostly the person himself. He can spend it any way he wants to before the day of appointment at the research center where he surrenders himself."

"But why? Who would want such a terrible deal, giving away his life for money?"

"Mostly for the reason of poverty, what else?" said the philosopher.

"But why?" I asked again.

"It's not really too difficult to imagine," Lee said. "Suppose someone offers you a large sum of money in exchange for your life. Suppose you are destitute, long unemployed, can't support yourself or your family. Suppose you have fantasized all the things you have always wanted to do but couldn't because you never had enough money. Suppose you have been a failure all your life in general. You can suppose many other reasons for taking that one fateful step. The temptation is great and terrible, knowing that in the end you can always sell your own life for a relatively large sum. I know it's a ghastly alternative, but it's still an alternative, isn't it, to redeem yourself in the eye of the rest of humanity?"

He reached out and picked up a newspaper lying near him.

"It goes both ways," he said, looking for a particular page. "Some individuals advertise themselves as research subjects. Let me see—Here they are. Listen to this one: Male, mid-fifties, good health, prefers painless surgical experiment. TIW 37. For contact call—"

He read several others and then some columns put out by the research institutes advertising for volunteers. One such column offered an unusually large sum for a subject who would endure a two-week long experiment on the effect of third-degree burns compounded by terminal pneumonia.

Then the philosopher put down the paper.

"Those who have already signed their lives away, waiting to be experimented on, are popularly known as the Hockers," Lee said, slowly rising from his seat to stretch to his full height as a measure of emphasis on what he was about to say, reminiscent of the time when he quoted the Bible passage to the faculty.

"I have a Hocker right here with me."

My jaws dropped as if he had said that a ghost was hiding in his house and I found myself looking around for that ghostly or, more precisely, ghastly soul.

"Randy," he turned to the direction of what appeared to be a bedroom and called out, "Randy, you can come out now."

Into my mortified presence walked out a man who was simply the most miserable looking man I had ever seen in my life. He looked like an old man, at least in the late sixties, but I instinctively knew he could be much younger in reality. He was so skinny that he made Robert I. Lee look positively obese. His face was pale as if he had been hiding indoors all summer (which I later learned had actually been the case) and limbs hung loosely from his shoulders with no apparent purpose. Even the clothes he was wearing, obviously borrowed from the host, were too big for him. It was his total lack of vitality in the way he presented himself, however, that was most striking. Obviously, the poor man, as a hocker, had been on death row too long and suffered terribly.

I had never before met anyone on death row, nor anyone terminally ill whose days were numbered. But the man made me think about death row inmates and the terminally ill and I shuddered involuntarily.

"Michael," Robert I. Lee turned back to me and said with touching affection, "meet my mentor and friend, Professor Randy Parrish."

Professor Randy Parrish smiled feebly and sat on the sofa next to Lee.

"Randy was my professor at the university where I took my doctorate in philosophy and taught at the University of Wilmington with me until he was fired four years ago for being unproductive," Lee explained.

We shook hands and I was surprised that his grip was much stronger than I had suspected.

"But his actual crime was that he didn't believe in mediocrity," Lee said. "He tried to teach excellence and creative thinking. The University didn't appreciate what he was trying to do and fired him."

I recalled my conversation with Dean Nettor.

"He is a fugitive from the law now," Robert I. Lee said. "He did not report to the medical research institute on the day he was supposed to, which was in early June."

I did not have enough nerve to ask him why he hadn't.

"What happens," I said finally, my voice hoarse. "If one changes one's mind like—?"

"—Like me?" Parrish said, managing a courageous smile. "Certainly, we can change our minds as long as we can pay back the money with interest. In my case, by the time I changed my mind, most of the money had already been spent. I have been on the run ever since."

In the next hour or so, I heard Randy Parrish's story of how he had struggled to survive with his wife, finally making the dreadful decision to sign up for a life-for-sale deal. His wife, whose illness had consumed most of his hard-earned money, had died a month before his appointed time. He had been hiding in one of the abandoned beach houses all summer and had recently contacted Lee only because he was near starvation.

He explained that he had left the beach house just in the nick of time because, when he returned after a food-scavenging foray at the beach one night, he saw that the house was being searched by two bounty hunters. After three more days without food, he finally contacted Lee. The former philosophy professor was reasonably certain that they might have tracked him down, and it was a matter of time before he would be caught.

"I changed my mind about surrendering on my appointed day," the professor said, responding to my question that I had not asked, "after my wife died a lonely death at our miserable house without medical care. I was so angry that I decided to live for a while and not let them have the pleasure of cutting me up for an experiment. But I think I made a poor decision. My time is up anyway."

On impulse, I offered all of my own money in the bank, and I was sure Cecil McMiller would help toward repaying the money Parrish had owed the infernal research institute.

"Very kind of you," the doomed philosopher said. "But it is no use. It's too late for any restitution. It's too late for me to get out of the contract and the law is very strict in such matters. No one has ever successfully broken a contract after the appointed time. Besides, I am just too old to be on the run anymore."

"You can stay here as long as you want, Randy," the younger philosopher said kindly to his mentor and friend. "We'll figure out something."

The older philosopher smiled and thanked us again for our kindness.

I had lunch with them and stayed there for another hour before I returned home, considerably shaken with the new experience and by the uncertain fate that awaited the hocker.

When I got home, there was a message from Sibyl Roberts saying that she could take me to the baby market at three in the afternoon if I was free. Carol looked at me as if asking for an explanation for my dark countenance. But I could not talk about life-for-sale without mentioning Robert I. Lee's unhappy fugitive.

"Could you go?" she asked.

"I would be delighted to," I said, brightening up. "She promised to take me there, but I didn't think it would be so soon."

I called the number and Sibyl said she would come over right away to pick me up.

"You are the most wanted man, Michael," Carol said. "Do you remember Richard Davis?"

"The athletic director at the University?"

"Yes, that Davis. He called while you were gone too. He wants to visit the athletic farm he mentioned last night. He wanted to know if you would go with him tomorrow. Tomorrow is his son's big day, he has just been told, and he wants to go see it."

"Is his son graduating?"

"Well, he will tell you all about it himself. Shall I tell him you would be going with him tomorrow? It would take all day to get there and come back, though. You don't have anything planned, I hope?"

Ever since the accident I had been planning to visit Jeanne Baker at her home. However, I had been uncertain about its justification and bashful about its purpose. I decided I could use the athletic director's invitation as an excuse to postpone the decision at least one more day.

Carol, acting as my caretaker, called the athletic director's office and left word that Mr. Michael Brown would be ready for the trip the next day.

Sibyl showed up in the next few minutes and we set out on our way to one of the baby markets. But we were not gone more than two minutes when Sibyl suddenly remembered something. "My goodness, I've almost forgotten about it," she said. "I hope you are not in a hurry."

I said I had all the time in the world.

"I would like to talk to Martha Jo at McDonald's," Sibyl said, already changing her direction. "She died yesterday of a heart failure."

I looked at her in obvious puzzlement. Sibyl laughed.

"Her funeral service has been scheduled at McDonald's Center downtown," she said, still laughing. "We might be able to catch the last part of it if we rush."

"But you said you would like to 'talk' to Martha Jo," I said, "and she died yesterday?"

Sibyl gave one of her nervous giggles, as if amused by my incomprehension of her joke. "McDonald's is now what they call a 'complete center for human services,'" Sibyl explained. "Of course, they still sell hamburgers."

As she was continuing her explanation of the expanded functions at one of America's most beloved institutions, we pulled into the parking lot of a huge brown building. From where I stood, I could see only one wing of what later turned out to be a four-wing structure, roughly in the shape of a cross. If I hadn't spotted the familiar yellow arch, I would have never thought I was standing in front of a McDonald's restaurant.

As we walked into a large office in the wing that faced us, a handsome woman in an impeccable business suit rushed out to meet us. Sibyl introduced the woman as Jean Bacall, the director of commercial operation. Her name reminded me of Jeanne Baker although circumstances were quite different, and, while Sibyl explained the purpose of my being there, my mind shamelessly drifted to Jeanne Baker.

"Michael, Jean here will take you on a brief tour of this McDonald's Center," Sibyl said. "Then you can join me at the tail-end of the funeral service. Would that be all right with you?"

I said it would be fine.

Sibyl left us for her departed friend's funeral and the director of commercial operation described the center with practiced ease. One wing, according to Jean Bacall, was devoted to physical fitness. Another wing was used primarily for family counseling and therapy. The third wing, the one in which Bacall's office was located, contained similar offices for financial advice and planning services. The last wing, toward whose direction Sibyl had walked, served the function as a restaurant and as a series of halls for the various parties, including funerals, which Sibyl had mentioned.

"We are a total service center," Jean Bacall said proudly. "From birth to death, and all the needs in between we can take care of completely."

I told her that I was indeed impressed by its immensity and comprehensiveness of operation.

"I suppose people don't need their family anymore," I said, "McDonald's is their family, isn't it?"

Beaming with pride, she said: "Who needs family, indeed? We *are* their family."

The large hall that was the traditional hamburger place was busy with customers. One of the more popular items, the director of commercial operation told me, was a new hamburger called "McAir," a new synthetic sandwich which contained absolutely no calories. She offered me one but I had to decline.

The hamburger restaurant occupied roughly one half of the wing and the other half was divided into several smaller halls for parties. My tour guide said Martha Jo's funeral was being held in the middle hall.

"Would you like to attend the service?" the woman asked.

I hesitated for a moment with indecision. I had toured the building and there was nothing else for me to do. On the other hand, I didn't know the deceased and funeral was such a personal affair, not open to total strangers.

"I bet you never attended a funeral service at one of our centers," she suggested helpfully. "It might be interesting."

I made my decision. "You are right," I said.

When I opened the door to the middle hall, it led to a small foyer from which I could hear the muffled sounds from the room inside. An elderly woman in mournful appearance standing at the door directed me inside, opening the door herself. The scene inside was nothing like any funeral service I had ever attended or imagined. It indeed was a party. People wore bright party dresses, and drinks and food were being freely served, everyone talking to everyone all at once. Sibyl spotted me immediately and rushed over, slithering through the crowd.

"Come," she said, pulling me by my hand. "I want you to see Martha Jo." We moved with some difficulty back to the other corner where Sibyl had been. There was a small roped-off area, but we climbed over it and walked closer to the casket.

Martha Jo was reposed in a splendidly ornate coffin the top half of which was open under a bright light so that people could view the deceased. Sibyl said Martha Jo had been sixty-five years old, but she looked much younger and life-like. I still hesitated on the account that I hadn't known the deceased and, out of my respect for her, I would keep a respectable distance from her.

"Come on, Michael," Sibyl said, motioning with her hand. "Come, take a closer look at Martha Jo."

Reluctantly and with much reservation I edged up a little, giving in only at Sibyl's repeated urgings. Some alcoholic consumption had apparently eased her normal nervousness somewhat.

"Look at her face closely," Sibyl said. "Isn't she lovely?"

For no other reason than that I was being urged on, I found myself standing directly over Martha Jo, only a few inches from her face. I had to marvel at the skill of the mortician, for her face was almost ruddy like that of a healthy beachgoer and had the natural tone as if she had never died. Flowers had been crowded into the small area in the corner and their combined presence gave out a rather strong smell. Admiring the deceased woman's face which I had never seen before, and being overwhelmed by the strong-smelling flowers surrounding me, I was beginning to feel somewhat stupid.

Then, suddenly, Martha Jo's face moved. Her eyes opened and, seeing me right above her, she smiled at me. Then, slowly, she raised her head, turning it around as if to look at everyone in the room. I let out a small shriek. One by one the guests realized what was happening and stopped talking. In a few seconds, the room was silent. Soon Martha Jo managed to raise her whole upper body and rest her arms on both edges of her coffin. She then let out a sigh of relief. That broke the spell.

"Martha Jo," said Sibyl to her once-deceased friend, "you look so wonderful. I am glad we will remember you as a young beautiful woman."

"Thank you, Sibyl," Martha Jo said. "I'm glad you could come to my funeral."

Then the two women began to reminisce about their past together. They even laughed when they came to some private jokes. After a few minutes of their reminiscence, Sibyl helped Martha Jo climb out of her coffin and get on the floor. Other guests converged on the once-deceased and began their own reminiscences with her. Martha Jo went around the room spending some time with most of the guests.

They seemed to agree with Sibyl on the splendid appearance of Martha Jo, for virtually all of them mentioned how happy they were to remember her in such a wonderful state. Martha Jo, on her part, said she was also happy to be remembered in her younger age. Everyone, including Sibyl, exchanged goodbyes with Martha Jo who was soon helped by a man back into her coffin. Thereupon the guests began to leave the room.

I remained virtually in a stupor throughout the whole ritual and Sibyl had to forcibly drag me out of the room, and into the parking lot. The bright afternoon sun returned some of my lost sanity.

"She was the best stand-in I have ever seen at a funeral," Sibyl said as we got back into our car. "She had memorized everything I had told her about the real Martha Jo and me."

"Stand-in?" I croaked.

Those were the first words I managed to speak since Martha Jo had opened her eyes and smiled at me.

"Yes, an actress who was made up to look like Martha Jo and studied her relationships with the invited guests who had been her close friends. Of course, the stand-ins are much better trained today, and the idea of making the stand-ins younger and more attractive than the deceased would revolutionize the funeral business. At least that's what the McDonald's brochure claims."

"But where is the real body, I mean the real Martha Jo?"

"Oh, she is somewhere being cremated. All her family members are here, however."

"But why? Why this substitute?"

"To remember her as a healthy, beautiful young woman as she once was," Sibyl said. "Stand-ins nowadays are so well trained. It's a wonderful experience especially for those parents whose children died. They overcome their grief quickly when they can see their dead children come alive and talk to them. I remember when I saw my grandma at her funeral service last year—"

"You mean her stand-in," I corrected her.

"Yes, of course, her stand-in," Sibyl said. "I was so thrilled to see her alive again. I will never forget that moment. She was so much like the real one, her voice, manners, and everything exactly as we had remembered her."

"Don't you want to remember the deceased in some discomfort or pain?" I suggested. "After all, death is never a pleasant thing."

"Precisely," Sibyl said. "That's why we want to preserve only good memories. No decent American is supposed to suffer from anxiety, shame or guilt, or, for that matter, bad memories. Remember what Kim said last night? We worked hard for many years to rid us of all those mental pains. Why should a funeral be a source of such unpleasant memories, you tell me?"

I feebly responded that pain in life was frequently the source of great art and philosophy in human history. Without pain, especially that associated with the death of loved ones, I ventured, what could we say about life? I had buried my mother when I was seven, I told her.

"Isn't it also true," Sibyl said, "that human history is also a history of trying to eliminate all that pain? What's Western civilization if it isn't a long process of getting rid of pain? As we replaced pain with pleasure in our society, we also replaced art and philosophy with entertainment. Who needs pain and sorrow, just to enjoy art and philosophy?"

"I suppose you've been successful with your effort," I said not without some bitterness.

But that note of bitterness entirely escaped Sibyl.

"Of course, we have been," she said pleasantly. "You just saw an example. We are about to make funerals as much fun as birthday parties."

We had spent less than thirty minutes at the McDonald's compound. But I felt we had been there for all eternity. She drove in silence after that, obviously in reverie about her friend Martha Jo. I remained silent also but for a difference reason.

Chapter Twelve

"Lee, did you know we have two children?" Sibyl asked, breaking our silence.

I said I didn't know.

"One was purchased, and the other one was awarded," she said. "We purchased the boy, now eight, three years ago and the girl, who is now six, was awarded only last summer."

"Purchased and awarded—" I said, still trying to recover from the earlier surprise.

"Of course, you can buy children in America as you would buy anything else on the market. And that's what the baby market is all about. If you don't have your own children, you can have one through surrogacy, either by direct pregnancy or artificial insemination, as I told you last night. Or you can go to the baby market if you don't mind getting one that's not biologically related to you."

"I can see that's selling and buying babies," I observed. "But what's this awarded child?"

"The court may award a child to someone on the basis of better qualifications as a parent," Sibyl said.

"Better qualifications?"

"Judged mainly on the basis of one's TIW, of course," Sibyl explained.

"How do you do that?"

"This is what you do," Sibyl said with confidence because this child business was her familiar territory. "If you are a person with a reasonably high TIW rank, say over 150, you can challenge any parent who has a relatively low TIW standing, maybe below 50. Fifty is generally regarded as the absolute minimum for decent citizenship."

"You mean you can challenge a mother and say you want her baby?" I asked, slightly puzzled. "Only because you have more money than she does?"

"Well, in a nutshell, yes, that's the way it's done," Sibyl said. "You will have to ask my husband about all the legal and moral implications. Incidentally he is going to stop by the McMillers this evening to look at one of Carol's paintings. All I know is how it's done, because we did it last year ourselves. My husband being a judge and our TIW being so high, the couple gave up the child without a fight."

"Go on, tell me, Sibyl, how is it done?"

"First, you pick out a child you like. Could be in your neighborhood, at your workplace, at an educational center, somebody you know, or maybe a total stranger that you saw only once at a park, whatever. Then you file a paper in court stating that you would make a better parent than the current one. Your lawyer does all your paperwork, of course. He documents your economic ranking in society, your claim that you can provide a better environment for the child, better educational opportunities, better cultural upbringing, better mental health, and so on."

"Your lawyer can also show, perhaps during the trial, how miserable the child has been, how meager the parents' TIW is, how poor their living environment is, what little chance the child has for any respectable career, and so on. If the lawyer can find out that the parents have been behind on payments or other such financial misdeeds, all the better. It costs money, but if you can afford it, you can go after any child whose parents' TIW is below 50. I have seen a lot of challenge trials in my husband's court."

"How often does the court decide for the wealthy, I mean the challenger?"

"I don't know the exact figure," Sibyl said in consternation. "But I would say in the majority of the cases. But the chances seem to be improving for the challenger still, all things being equal. Poverty generally makes anybody look bad in a court of law and most of the time it acts against the poor. You can lose your case simply because you are poor. I know I've seen it many times myself."

I was slightly impressed by her astute observation, for she was the first person with a high TIW ranking that I had met in America who recognized poverty as the cause of many social inconveniences. But I also remembered she had shown no qualms about challenging someone's baby herself.

"What if the poor parents win," I asked, "is it the end of trouble for them?"

"Only in that particular instance. The challenger can come back again later with a better TIW standing and challenge again."

"It seems terribly unfair to the poor, doesn't it?"

"There is some consolation, however," Sibyl said. "The challenger has to pay all the court costs if he loses the case. So, there is some element of risk, but if money is no object to you, it's worth the try. After all, you only lose money. The parent loses the child."

"That's no consolation, it seems to me," I said.

"Why, Michael," Sibyl emphasized, "even if the parent loses, it's not a total loss. After all, the child gets to live in a better house, goes to a better school, wears better clothes, eats better food, and enjoys a better environment all around. That's no small consolation for a lot of poor folks. Look at Amy, my little girl, for example. It would be a crime to send her back to her original parents. After all that she has been used to in our household—"

"Is that all there is to it?" I objected. "What about love?"

"O, yes, love," Sibyl said pensively. "Parents don't have a monopoly of love, you know that. Not all parents always love their children, do they? If a parent can give love, so can a stranger. Besides, parents hardly raise their children in America anymore."

"They don't? Who does, then?"

"Experts," Sibyl said as she pointed to a large modern building to indicate that the baby market was inside that building. "Parents first decide what kind of children they want. When they know what they want from their children and they simply engage the specialists and experts to do the job. School, along with television, nowadays only does the routine caregiving. All the real education is done by the paid professionals. Of course, these professionals get paid by the results they produce."

"I have never been a parent," I admitted, "but I've always enjoyed dealing with children. Why do American parents avoid the joys of child-rearing?"

"I can tell that you are not a parent, Michael," Sibyl chided. We were now driving into the underground parking lot directly under the building. "The real joy of parenting is in enjoying the results, not the trouble of getting the results. If you can enjoy the results without trouble, why not? Speaking for myself, I never have to deal with any of the child-rearing problems that other poor parents do. We pay the professionals to do all the work so that we can just enjoy the results. That's what makes children such a wonderful thing to have around. That's why I love my children."

Her reasons for avoiding the chores of child-rearing left me speechless. Although I disagreed with them, I had to admit she had points.

The main office of the baby market, whose formal name was the Parental Fulfillment Center, one of the largest such markets in the southeast, was located on the third floor.

Once again, Sibyl carried much weight at the place and we were immediately ushered into a large office where a half dozen or so clerks were working at full capacity. As we entered, a pleasant short young man stood up and greeted us. He was introduced as director of marketing named Bill Sanders. Sibyl told Sanders that I had come to see how the center operated.

"This has been a rather busy month," the young man said, pointing to his clerks and the computer printouts that he had been holding in his hands. "Demand and supply have gone up by at least 35 percent. We have never had so many babies in stock and another shipment is coming in tomorrow."

The man took us along a fairly long hallway with glass walls on both sides. A dozen or so couples and quite a few single people were looking inside, comparing the babies with their folders that they held in their hands, opening and closing them as they went from one baby to the next. Four or five saleswomen in their smart uniforms, vaguely resembling the governesses and nannies seen in some pictures, were helping the customers. I was surprised that most of the prospective baby-buyers were in their fifties and sixties. One woman was holding her magnifying glass close to a chubby but happily laughing baby girl of about nine months.

Inside the walls were babies in a wide-ranging variety of ages and colors and shapes, playing, crying or sleeping in their small cubicles, which reminded me of the puppies and kittens at a pet shop in Laurinville. Some older babies were lazily responding to the prospective buyers outside. Half a dozen nurses were busily moving about, feeding, changing diapers, and generally taking care of their charges.

On the outer side of each cubicle facing the hallway was posted a chart which contained all the necessary biological and biographical information for its young occupant. At the bottom, each chart had the baby's serial number and price code for more detailed information available from the central file. One particular baby of less than a year, named 'Johnny', gurgling happily had a chart that told the story of how he got to be there. His young parents, both in their late twenties, decided to commit suicide after a severe business failure and left the baby with his grandparents.

They wrote a long letter, expressing their agonies and apologizing to little Johnny for their terrible act, to be opened when he was of age. The chart said the letter, described as a 'heart-breaking true story' was 'on file' and was part of the package. Johnny's grandparents, with good intentions but a modest TIW standing, could not afford the expenses involved in raising the baby any longer and tearfully offered him for a quick sale. Indeed, his chart was labeled in large block letters 'CLEARANCE SALE'. Some others, perhaps in similar predicaments as Johnny said, "MUST SELL. MAKE OFFER." Two black children who looked like twins had 'TWO FOR PRICE OF ONE' written across their charts.

I saw an elderly gentleman, perhaps retired but with an air of life-long authority, move away from his wife and take one of the saleswomen aside.

"Listen," the man said to the saleswoman. "My wife's birthday is next week. I am looking for something special, a surprise gift, for my wife on the anniversary, you understand."

The saleswoman, a pretty young woman of about twenty-five with her yellow hair tightly pulled back, and animated in her small-framed body, nodded and said encouragingly, "do you have anything in mind, sir?"

"I was thinking maybe an Oriental baby with natural red hair," the man said, lowering his voice so that his wife wouldn't hear him. "You know, with slanted eyes on a moon face and flaming red hair, it would really go well with my wife. She likes a lot of red and yellow in everything."

"I am sorry, sir," the smallish saleswoman said, after thinking over her inventory for a couple of seconds. "We don't have any Oriental baby with natural red hair in stock at present. How about an Oriental baby with natural blue eyes? I believe we have one available. We are not getting a lot of Oriental babies. They are just not available in good varieties."

The man said, "Oh, I'll have to think about that." Then he mumbled to himself as he returned to his wife, "Oriental babies with blue eyes, uh?"

Sanders took us to a corner where about ten babies, all strikingly blond-haired and blue-eyed, were specially marked with "HIGH I.Q. GUARANTEED. CERTIFICATE ON FILE" on their charts in capital letters.

"These babies are our special of the month," the young director of marketing said, gleefully pointing to the special lot.

He tapped the glass and some babies responded happily.

"See how alert they are?" he said with genuine affection like a proud father. "They are such wonderful creatures."

The marketing director explained that older children were displayed on another floor. Sibyl volunteered that it was here that she and the judge had purchased their boy. I didn't ask if the boy had been on sale.

Sanders then invited us to see the video room, a large hall almost resembling a library reading room, where at least two dozen people were engaged in viewing videotapes. The marketing director said the video tapes contained information on those babies whose parents wanted the prospective buyers screened first by the Parental Fulfillment Center before they could see the babies.

"These video babies are all very specially selected by our center," Bill Sanders said. "Their IQ must be at least 130."

He quoted sample prices on some of the babies, and I was impressed with the prices that the babies commanded. I mentioned this to Sanders.

"Well, Mr. Brown," the young man said, "it's a booming market, and the sky is the limit."

"What about those babies who are not so bright?" I asked.

"They sell fast too," the marketing director of babies said. "In fact, we are having a blue-light sale today at four-thirty. Would you like to stay on for that?"

I said, "No thank you, I was not in the market for a baby."

"Whose babies are these?" I asked. "Do poor parents sell their babies?"

"Sometimes," Sanders said. "But most of our stock comes from the baby factories where they employ young healthy women to produce babies conceived from equally healthy young men. We buy them wholesale from those factories."

Sibyl offered to take me to one of the baby factories any time I wanted. She said one of her nieces worked as a baby producer.

We spent ten or fifteen more minutes at the baby market touring its various functions before we decided to leave.

Once we were on the road, Sibyl asked if it would be all right for us to visit her pet resort-and-cemetery community not too far from the baby center since we had still a good bit of afternoon left. I said it would be fine for me. After a day of surprising events—hockers, a funeral at McDonald's, and a baby market—I told her about a visit with pet animals would be greatly relaxing.

The pet resort-and-cemetery community was actually a large compound consisting of two modern buildings on one side and a luxuriously stretched out cemetery on the other. Sibyl's business was with the cemetery where her cat was buried only a while ago. I immediately noticed that the pet cemetery was much better decorated and kept than the human cemetery in Laurinville where my mother was buried. And much more artistic, too.

There were a variety of tombstones beautifully carved in the shape of the deceased, from the most common household pets like cats and dogs to some uncommon ones as well, including a long, thick python delicately and languidly coiled up and so life-like that it looked as if ready to strike any moment. The craftsmanship and material employed were first rate and exquisite, indicating a good deal of expenses to keep one's beloved pet memories.

There was an older couple sitting in front of what appeared to be a poodle's grave, judging by the tombstone, two graves away from Sibyl's own pet. The woman was sobbing while talking to her deceased pet and the man was silent but dabbed his eyes with a handkerchief once in a while. The sobbing woman called her poodle 'my dear Charlie'.

"My dear Charlie," she was saying between sobs, "well, Uncle Bill—you remember that obstinate uncle who refused to recognize his own son?—finally gave in and did recognize his son as his own before he died. Aunt Angelina is still suffering with arthritis but insists on making the Carnegie Hall debut she has always wanted. Young Lucas and Lillian are still in love. Recently they announced their engagement, and it was about time. We were all delighted about that. Rick is now out of prison for the murder he did not commit, we all knew that, and is looking for the real murderer. The gardener, the real murderer, is of course still at large…"

The man broke his silence one time and corrected his wife's recitation with correct facts about somebody's impending trial. The woman went on some more with the details of her family tales to what must have been a very close family dog. I was beginning to imagine the close-knit happy family in which everything was shared with their pet dog while the latter was still alive.

"Charlie must have really liked the program," Sibyl whispered to me. "I know a lot of dogs watch soap operas, too. The stories she is telling come from last week's episodes of 'As the Earth Stands Still', a popular soap opera on TV."

Sibyl herself kneeled down in front of her cat's grave and sat there in silence for a few minutes in remembrance of the departed. Not personally involved in her sorrows for the moment, I looked around the compound, being easily impressed by its immensity and opulence. Flower gardens were everywhere covering the whole ground not occupied by the pet graves and sidewalks. A small but well-crafted pond with an artificial waterfall supplying it with fresh water decorated the center of the cemetery. Immaculately groomed hedges, marking the boundaries of the pet cemetery, formed a vast semi-circle around this part of the compound.

Unlike the other couple who were still there, apparently Sibyl had no soap operas to summarize for her departed. After a while, she got up from her reverie and, wiping off the mist from her face, suggested that we visit the pet bereavement clinic which was located in one of the two modern buildings. As we got near the first one, she explained that the bereavement clinic was housed within that building and asked me if I minded joining it briefly. I said no.

The bereavement clinic was in full session when we entered the classroom. The man who was giving a lecture to a full audience on how to overcome the pains of pet bereavement instantly recognized Sibyl and stopped his talk. He called to her in familiarity and walked over to meet us.

"Here is one of our most experienced veterans in pet bereavement," he introduced Sibyl to the audience, some of whom knew her already. Then turning to her, he said, "Since you are here, would you care to tell the class a few points about pet bereavement from your personal experience? I think they would benefit much from your insights into how to handle the heartbreaks of losing your closest companion in life."

Overcoming her usual nervousness, the veteran pet mourner soon warmed to her subject and emphasized that the most important secret was to "keep your perspective, your *human* perspective."

"Always try to think of them as human beings, not pets," she stressed her point. "As long as you keep remembering them as animals your mourning will never end, and your sorrows will never be comforted. Forget their sweetness and obedience, their loyalty and honesty. You must think of them as *human beings* with specific economic values associated with them, such as their TIW's and contract values, and so on, so that you can become more objective and rational as to their worth to your life. I know I have not been very successful myself at times, because once I refused to have a stand-in for my cat while I welcomed one for my own grandmother. Why didn't I treat the cat the way I treated my grandmother? I don't know, but it was my human error, and I won't repeat it again—(turning to the instructor)—thanks to what this clinic has taught me."

The audience warmly appreciated her heartfelt advice and applauded the insights. Several members asked some questions on how actually to 'transfer' pets to 'human images', for they seemed to be having trouble with that point. Sibyl's concept of thinking of pets 'as human beings' as a way of overcoming bereavement so that one might not attach oneself too much to them was somewhat difficult for me to understand. Her answers to the questions did not completely satisfy me then. However, what we saw in the next few minutes more or less clarified that question.

Following her impromptu lecture, we walked to the other building at her suggestion, which, being its 'resort' center, had its own good-size playground with various structures for pets, mostly household animals, to play in. What caught my eyes was the number of smartly uniformed human employees working with pets, trying all sorts of tricks and playfulness to please their pets. One group was having fun playing fetch, only in this case it was the employees who fetched the ball to their pet monkey who jumped up and down in delight every time he threw the ball for his employees to fetch. The monkey was clever, for he varied the direction of his throws to keep the employees breathless.

One particular dog seemed to have four male employees, the most that I could see there, who were at the moment involved in some serious coaxing with the dog. They were having a tough time, it appeared, trying to get the dog to cooperate with their purpose, which he was apparently refusing to do.

While I was fairly amused and diverted by the scene, an older woman wearing efficient overalls and rubber gloves for handling animals came out of the building and greeted Sibyl like an old friend. Sibyl introduced her as the director of pet satisfaction at the community. Her job, Sibyl explained, was to keep the inheritance pets as happy as possible.

"Inheritance pets?" I was puzzled.

"Oh, they are the animals, generally household pets, who inherited large sums of money, many times more than we can imagine, from their wealthy owners who died," the director of pet satisfaction explained. "We try to keep them as happy as possible according to the owners' instructions. Of course, we also have temporary custodial pets too, like that monkey there playing fetch."

"Is that one of the inheritance dogs?" I asked, pointing to the dog that was giving the male employees a hard time.

"Oh, that's Bingo, the famous Texas millionaire dog," the director said, breaking into a smile and with obvious affection. "A Texas oil billionaire left a good portion of his fortunes to his dog when he died. Of course, needless to say, he felt very deeply attached to his pet dog, Bingo."

"What were his instructions?"

"They were very specific," the woman said in genuine admiration. "Everything about Bingo's daily life. What time Bingo should get up and go to bed, what to eat for breakfast, lunch and dinner, what kind of meat, vegetable, and fruit for his balanced diet, regular checkups and daily health care. Also, meticulous provisions for entertainment, and many other details."

"That's more than what a lot of people get, I know," Sibyl volunteered.

Sibyl's comment made the director look suddenly proud at the quality of service she was providing her charges. "Well, Bingo is a rich dog, richer than most people obviously. He is rich enough to hire three teams of four-man staff around the clock."

"You mean the men *work for* the dog?" I asked in fair amazement.

"Yes," the director said, still proud. "both in fact and by contract. They work for Bingo, and he is their legal employer."

Then she recognized that the employees were having trouble with their employer over some vital issue, because they were now on their knees in a supplicating posture.

"I know what their trouble is," the director said, showing her experience and competence. "The dog has to 'sign' their pay vouchers, so to speak, for them to get paid. That's one of the instructions. But he is as usual refusing to cooperate. He hates to put his paw on the ink pad."

She hurried to the scene of the employee-employer relations in trouble and we followed.

"Hey, fellows," the director called to the four male employees who were sweating and panting in their variously prostrate positions. "Why don't you try singing again? You know he likes it and it worked before."

The men got up and scratched their heads in some consternation and, apparently deciding that there was no better solution, made a formation as if they were getting ready for family picture-taking. The director of pet satisfaction admonished them to straighten their uniform and look more professional and show more respect for their employer. Bingo's men, knowing their job, alertly straightened their hair and uniform and dusted the debris of grass and dirt off one another. I then realized that the men were forming a barbershop quartet getting ready to do their singing.

On signal from their leader, the four male employees began a surprisingly well-harmonized rendition of a song that was obviously their employer's favorite.

There was a farmer had a dog,
and Bigo was his name-o.
B-I-N-G-O, B-I-N-G-O, B-I-N-G-O,
and Bingo was his name-o.

Bingo apparently liked the singing, because he gave three delighted barks. That was a message that the men understood as 'one more time'. (The director whispered to us that the dog taught the men at least 35 different messages. "He took almost two years to train them with sign language," she added.) Bingo's barbershop quartet sang again.

There was a farmer had a dog,
and Bingo was his name-o.
B-I-N-G-O, B-I-N-G-O, B-I-N-G-O,
and Bingo was his name-o.

Their singing rang out so beautifully and sweetly in the melancholy air of late afternoon, with birds nearby chirping their own notes in approval. I wanted to hear it sung one more time myself. But, unfortunately for me, Bingo was satisfied enough with the performance and eagerness of his employees to please him, for he allowed them to use his paw to sign their pay vouchers.

"Thank you, Mr. Bingo. Thank you, Mr. Bingo," the youngest of the four, profoundly grateful, bowed several times in the dog's direction as he was pulled away by his colleagues, presumably toward the payroll office. A new team of four men, fresh from their rest, now replaced the departed crew.

"Why do you think some people in America get so attached to animals?" I asked Sibyl as we finally left the compound.

"Because—" she said hesitantly. "Who else in America would love you so unconditionally and so absolutely?"

For the rest of the way home, I found myself mulling over her simple comment.

When we returned to the McMillers, Judge Roberts, flanked by Carol and Cecil, was critically examining Carol's painting titled 'God Driving the World'. The painting, which had been a mere sketch when I had last seen it, was now in finished form.

"I came here to buy this," he said when he saw us come in. "What do you think, Michael, Sibyl?" I said I would reserve my judgment on the ground that I was art-illiterate. Sibyl, however, offered her opinion which was favorable. The deal was struck upon which the judge handed over his cashing chip to the artist.

"Thank you, Judge," Carol said in mock gravity. "It's not every day that people buy artworks in Wilmington."

Our conversation then drifted to what I had experienced that afternoon with Sibyl's help. What had rankled me the most, I told the judge, was the fact that wealthy people could challenge any parents to take over their children.

"Don't you think it unfair?" I asked. "What's your opinion from the bench's point of view?"

"I think I have a case in the docket coming up pretty soon," the judge said. "You should come down to my court and watch it. It should be interesting for you. To answer your question, the cardinal issue is, What is in the best interest of the child? Whether one set of parents are in the better interest of the child as opposed to another set of parents is a difficult or almost impossible question to settle, isn't it? The only reasonable answer we can consider feasible, all things being equal and absent any overriding evidence to the contrary, is, who has more money? Or, to put it in another way, who can do *better* and *more* for the child?"

"Money is always the best answer because it is always money in America that can get anything done if it is important enough. How else could you define what's in the best interest of the child? As a judge presiding over many of these cases I find it difficult to decide otherwise, at least in the majority of the cases."

"Why, Judge," I persisted. "wouldn't then all children belong to the upper class first, because they have the most money? No poor people can keep their children because there is always a wealthier couple who would challenge them and take their children away from them."

"Theoretically speaking, yes, of course," the judge said. "But only theoretically. Thank God, there are enough children to go around, rich and poor. Besides, not all wealthy couples want children, you understand. But speaking of the issue theoretically, awarding all children to the upper class first, and then giving leftovers to the lower-class families, is not a bad idea altogether. Some parents are so poor they can't do anything good for their children even if they want to. Why should children suffer because of the luck of their draw? Did Sibyl tell you we have a girl that we were awarded? It has been a great change of fortune for the little girl to be with us rather than with her biological parents. It's simply the most traditional way not only in America but everywhere in human history."

"Could you explain that, Judge?"

"I would say it this way," the judge said, stroking his prize painting and then putting it away. "You look at anything in the world that's precious, namely, jewelry, good artworks, food, good education, good health care, easy living, sometimes beautiful bodies, or whatever. Don't they always go first to those who can afford them? If there is so little or few of them, naturally they go to the upper class first, don't you agree? It is only after the upper class has been satisfied, and not before, that the lower class gets the bread-crumbs thrown by the upper class. Suppose, just for the sake of argument, babies are considered precious, just like those precious metals, shouldn't they go to the wealthy class first? In a pecuniocratic society, money pays for everything. Why shouldn't babies go money's way, you tell me?"

"But, Judge—"

"Good thing," the judge declared, rising to leave, "the majority of the upper class doesn't think babies are precious, not as yet. But if and when it does decide that having babies around is just as pleasurable as being bedecked with fine jewelry or enjoying expensive wines, then the babies in America will have to go to the upper class like everything else that's precious. The poor will have to wait for the leftovers, as they have no way of defending their interests against the money class, no way. More money is always more money, and less is always less. The poor produce and the wealthy people consume. Don't forget to come to the trial. I will have you notified as soon as it comes up on my calendar."

I promised the judge that I would attend the trial. With that, the judge and his wife left the McMiller household.

Chapter Thirteen

Richard Davis, the athletic director, was punctual with his time as he was precise with his movement. He came to pick me up at nine on the dot in his university-issued vehicle, which was large and comfortable, specially equipped for the business needs of its occupant.

As soon as we drove out of the McMillers' driveway, Davis punched several buttons in rows and columns on the dashboard, pretty much like the average tape recorder I had seen in Laurinville, except it was much more complex-looking.

"This is my 'Mood Enhancer', a message synthesizer," the athletic director said as he finished his programming. "Today is my son's big day and I want to be all ready for it."

Even before I could ask what the Mood Enhancer was all about, the synthesizer started playing its message. Stirring music, very much like a military march, was heard in the background.

The synthesizer began its message in a seductive but powerful voice: "TODAY IS YOUR DAY, AND NOBODY ELSE'S. IT'S YOURS, NOBODY ELSE'S. YOU ARE THE MOST IMPORTANT PERSON IN YOUR LIFE. ANYTHING YOU WANT YOU CAN HAVE. WHAT CAN STOP YOU? NOTHING! NOTHING! ABSOLUTELY NOTHING! ARE YOU, RICHARD DAVIS, ARE YOU GOING TO LET ANYBODY OR ANYTHING GET IN YOUR WAY OF YOUR HARDWORK AND SUCCESS?—"

"No!" Davis shouted. "No!"

Davis's face had been turning gradually tighter since the message had started, and as the synthesizer called out his name repeatedly, I could see tears glistening in his eyes.

The message on the whole was repetitious and nonsensical, but it was this very repetitiousness and nonsensical simplicity that created its mesmerizing pepping effect. It lasted less than two minutes, but its effect was obviously galvanizing on the athletic director. He was sweating and breathing hard even after the message had ended. It took another five minutes or so before he returned to normal. I sat there silently, slightly disturbed by its resemblance to the exhortations of the Green Palmers a long time ago.

"You can arrange different strengths by combining these buttons," he said pointing to the machine and breaking up my recollection. "The synthesizer can then produce the message just right for your mood and need. For example, you can ask for a simple 'Inspirational', which is the mildest level. 'Battle-Ready' is the next if you want a stronger dosage, which is what I just had. My usual message is the medium one called 'Another Tough Day'. I needed something tougher than usual this morning. If it is an extreme case, you can get an 'Annihilation', but I don't use that unless it's a do-or-die championship game."

"What's happening with your son, today?" I asked. "Is he competing in a sporting event?"

"No, much more important than that," the athletic director said. "He is going to be auctioned off today."

"Auctioned off?"

"Yes," the athletic director's jaws tightened again and I thought he was fighting off the temptation to turn on the synthesizer again. "You know it takes a nerve of steel at those auctions. His whole career is determined there. He has been training for a long time for this opportunity."

I vaguely remembered Davis's talk at the party about how athletes were trained and bought, but the auction was something new.

We arrived at the Never-Punt Athletic Corporation located on the southern tip of South Carolina, a sprawling complex of three large modern buildings and several smaller auxiliary ones besides, by lunch time. We noticed that a crowd had already begun to gather for the auction to take place in the afternoon.

The compound, occupying at least a thousand acres in a secluded rural area, was heavily fenced in with barbed wire which I suspected was electrified. A guardhouse at the gate examined the invitation issued to the athletic director, which also served as our pass.

"Why all this hush-hush, barbed wire and all?" I inquired.

"Oh, mainly to keep the industrial spies away," Davis said. "You know, this is a highly competitive business. Their technological innovations are fiercely coveted by everybody. Some people would do anything do get their hands on some of the training secrets."

The barbed wire obviously had more to do with keeping the athletes in than with keeping anybody out.

The first and the largest of the three buildings, Davis explained, was used for training, the second for players and employees' quarters, and the last for offices, cafeterias, and research and development.

The first building indeed contained all the state-of-the-art modern equipment that had been developed in the previous two decades. Every bodily movement was dissected and analyzed to the most minute degree of perfection. I watched what they called a blue-chip prospect for a football quarterback practice his throws over and over again while a researcher timed him with a complex stopwatch until his timing was perfected.

The researcher fussed over one-tenth of a second difference in the quarterback's repetitious moves, which were recorded and analyzed on the computer. To a sedate school principal from Laurinville who had no stomach for rough sports, it was amazing indeed to see how silly little games could command all the modern technology and the human devotion that bordered on religious missions.

Richard Davis found his son, who was indeed a handsome young lad of about eighteen, and they went through an elaborate eight-step high-five which they had apparently been perfecting for a long time. Davis was still all pumped up, thanks to his early morning Mood Enhancer to get him 'Battle-Ready'.

It was in the third building, however, that I became party to a strange incident.

As we were walking through the main part of the structure, which contained rows and rows of offices and laboratories, we came upon a large hall that had no label on the door. The door was unlocked. We pushed the door open and innocently walked into the hall. There on one side of the room huddled a group, perhaps a dozen or so, of boys and young men, many of them black, sitting or lying down in various postures under the bright florescent light. Their postures, I noticed, were determined primarily by the lengths of the chains they had on their ankles that were all connected.

Five uniformed men stood on guard in strategic points around their chained captives. Some prisoners moved about laboriously, carrying the chain in their hands. Obviously because all of them were superb athletes with brute strength, the chain was of special heavy-duty quality.

"Oh, they are some of the escapees brought in by the bounty hunters," Davis explained without waiting for my question.

None of the bounty hunters (more professionally called 'skip tracers') carried guns, but they brandished different sorts of instruments that I had never seen before. They poked the prisoners with their instruments to keep them in line.

"At least they are not using any guns," I said, impressed with their humanitarian impulse. "They could kill their prisoners."

"No bounty hunter carries guns anymore," Davis observed. "They use high-powered stun guns, cattle prods, whips and sticks. They are a lot more effective."

"I would say it's more humane too," I said.

"I don't know about that," Davis said. "They don't want to damage the merchandise."

We walked toward the chain gang to take a better look. Some youngsters raised their tired heads to see who we were and dropped back. One of the boys with short dirty hair and a dirty face, perhaps no more than thirteen, who had been hidden behind the heap of human bodies, managed to crawl toward me from his place about three to four bodies away. He lifted his tear-streaked face with the purpose of speaking to me.

"Mister, mister," the boy said in a pathetic voice. "My name is Alvin Clemmons, from Huntsville, Alabama."

"I am Michael Brown," I said, responding to him. "And I am from Laurinville."

"Would you call my mom and dad?" the boy said as if in a daze. "I wanna go home, mister, I just wanna go home. Would you call my mom and dad for me, please, mister?"

Encouraged by an embarrassed and soft look on my face, the boy crawled some more and wrapped his arms around my legs and pleaded in a deeply affecting posture of prayer. Moved and confounded, I just stood there not knowing what to do or say. The bounty hunters, seemingly more amused than annoyed or moved, let the boy continue his pleading.

Finally, I took out my pen and paper and asked him: "What's their telephone number, Alvin? Or, can you give me their names?"

"Alice and Tom Clemmons, sir," the boy said. "Their number is 516-3420, the area code is 305. They don't know I am here. Would you please call them?"

I promised I would do my best.

"No use," one of the bounty hunters, a powerfully built man of perhaps in his late twenties, who had been watching our small transaction, walked over to me and said, "It's his own parents, Mr. and Mrs. Clemmons of Huntsville, Alabama, who sold the boy in the first place. They then moved to Florida with the contract money. They don't want the boy back. They got too much money for him."

The boy, hearing the bounty hunter, started crying.

"That's a lie, that's a lie," he protested, holding my legs even tighter in the effort. "My parents would never do that—"

The boy's protest and pleading reminded me of some event very familiar to my own experience, but I could not quite recall it there and then. Only later did I realize that it was from my dream about the Green Palmers in which I pleaded for more tele-mind.

Confounded, I looked at Richard Davis for his judgment.

Davis shook his head in agreement with the bounty hunter's report. He moved closer to us and gently but firmly removed the boy's arms from my legs.

"Too late, boy," Davis said consolingly as the boy slumped back, weeping and protesting. "Too late."

This minor drama seemed to have stirred some other athletes in custody, however. A young black man in his late teens, who had been watching the whole scene intently, stood up slowly. His chain clanged noisily as he stretched his large and powerful frame to full height. He picked up the chain that was tied to his ankle and inspected it closely and dramatically.

"This chain," he said in his booming voice. "Why this chain?"

Other prisoners, black and white, stirred by these sudden theatrics, bolted up and watched him with some interest.

"Why this chain?" he boomed again in his fine cadence as if he was in his Sunday pulpit. "All men are created equal. But why this chain?"

"Because you sold your body," the bounty hunter said. "It now belongs to this corporation."

"It may own my body," the young man said in response. "But it doesn't own my soul."

"They are not interested in your soul," the bounty hunter responded and several of his colleagues chuckled. "They only want your body, that's all. You signed it away, didn't you? Did anybody force it on you? You did it all on your own."

The former escapee was not interested in the finer points of legality. His predicament was apparently more philosophical than legal.

"I have a dream," he raised his voice to a new height, and the bounty hunter rolled his eyes and said, "another radical."

"I have a dream," the young man repeated in his fine cadence. "One day our children will be judged by their character, not by the size of their TIW's."

Several of the black prisoners chimed in: "Amen, brother."

"Don't pay any attention," Davis told me as we left the scene of the remarkable prisoners to go to the more palatable and happier scene of auctioning. "They tend to be more melodramatic when there are visitors around. Of course, part of their athletic training is mental conditioning. By the time they are ready for the auction, none of that radical element would be left in their attitude."

The auction was divided into two sessions. The first consisted of displaying the auctionees so that prospective buyers could examine the merchandise more closely. The auction itself was scheduled to follow the first.

The crowd gathered around an oval platform which was raised a foot or so from the floor. The athletes, including the young Davis, marched into the hall to a band of musicians playing 'Pomp and Circumstance' and climbed gracefully onto the platform. A group of young women dressed as Grecian maidens spaced in a larger circle behind the crowd played violin music in harmony with the band. It was a magnificent sight. Every one of them, ages ranging from about fifteen to twenty-five or so, was a combination of power and control. Their muscles, bulging yet all in proper proportion and developed for specific purposes in athletic prowess, glistened under the bright light above. Black and white, young and very young, graceful and powerful, they stood on the edge of the platform side by side.

They were the physical cream of the crop that represented all that was wonderful about American sports. I could feel the changing atmosphere in the room. Electricity was in the air. The buyers, mostly older former jocks and team owners, smiled at the auctionees with obvious pride and anticipation.

After a short but sparkling sales pitch by the master of ceremonies about the group of fine young men, the customers were invited to examine the merchandise-auctionees. All sorts of examinations and conferences followed in animated but hushed conversations, punctuated by feeling the muscles and postures of the athletes. Some buyers were so picky that they demanded that their athletes bend their knees at least fifty times to show that they were durable. The athletes, ever eager to please the buyers, obliged all the requests. More inquisitive than most were the women, some of them wives of the buyers and some others independent customers.

They gave the auctionees more thoroughgoing examinations than a doctor with an accident victim. They felt the legs, the thighs (especially long), the genitals (although their athletic connections were questionable), and the buttocks with the care of a sculptor selecting the next block of stone to chisel a sacred monument. I then learned that the buyer had absolute control over the merchandise once it was sold, and the purpose to which the athlete was put needed not be sports-related at all.

"It's a private service contract," Davis told me, recalling the conversation we had at the party. "The athlete must perform almost any duty related to his physical capacity."

There was this particular woman, in her late fifties and heavily bedecked with fine jewelry, who was more thorough than the other women. She inserted her hand inside the athletic support of some athletes and felt their genitals with great concentration almost bordering on glee. Because this woman was obviously one of the wealthier customers, officials and athletes both tried to look pleased with her thoroughness.

She finally came to the young Davis, who struck a fine pose with his long yellow hair flowing over the back of his neck and found the young man to be of special interest. There her exploration began to go deeper and longer. She moved her hand this way and that, eyes closed in concentrated appreciation of her task at hand. It went a bit too long for the young man's father.

"If she continues one more minute," Davis said to himself. "I will have to tell her to stop it. I don't think she is really interested in buying him."

But unfortunately, the examination went on longer than a minute. Then the athletic director made up his mind.

"Lady," he hollered to her. "You touch him! You buy him!"

The woman suddenly awoke as if from a trance and slowly removed her hand from the merchandise. The boy looked relieved and gave his father a high-five.

There was a small break between the two sessions. We were served refreshments by the Grecian maidens who had stopped their violin playing. But the band kept playing its music. For the auction the crowd was invited to the next room which looked more like an elegant theater with rows of seats and a giant screen above the stage. We took our seats facing the screen to the left of the center aisle. I noticed that the thorough-examining woman occupied one of the seats closer to the screen, which were obviously reserved for the elite buyers.

Unlike the auctions I had been familiar with on some Sundays in Laurinville, the athletic auction had no auctioneer with his usual podium. Instead, a voice through the public address system reminded the rules and protocols. Everyone seemed to be old hands at the business.

With each auctionee introduced, the screen showed various postures of the athlete in enlarged details. After an appropriate amount of time elapsed, the screen flickered 'FIRST BID' across the bottom with the minimum amount deemed appropriate for the merchandise. Davis showed me a small button just in front of him. "You push this button if you want to bid," he explained.

A number immediately appeared on the screen, just below the amount, indicating the identity of the bidder. Then it went on to SECOND BID, and onto THIRD BID, and so on until the auction on that particular merchandise was completed.

When the young Davis's turn came, about two-thirds through the proceedings, the thorough-examining lady outbid all her competitors, to everyone's surprise, by bidding close to four-hundred thousand dollars. Many, even including Richard Davis himself, seemed to think it was a bit unexpected. The athletic director was obviously pleased. He sought the lady out after the auction was over to thank her personally.

"I touched him, and I bought him," the thorough-examining woman said, with the young Davis standing next to her, beaming.

"He is a good athlete," the proud father said.

"I know," the woman said. "And I intend to explore his full athletic potential."

As we left the athletic farm, Davis told me that he and his son had signed an agreement to split all the latter's athletic income with him.

"Two hundred thousand dollars for my share," he said almost to himself. "It's not bad, is it? That will boost my TIW at least by ten."

The senior Davis was so excited that he couldn't resist after all, calling up an 'Annihilation' on his Mood Enhancer, which he played over and over on the way back to Wilmington. His exuberance, strengthened by the message, was so infectious that even I was affected by his good mood.

But this good mood was shattered immediately when Davis dropped me off at the McMillers after dark.

"I don't know what's the matter with him," Cecil said when he saw me. "But Robert I. Lee wanted you to call him as soon as you returned from the athletic farm. He sounded awfully agitated, for sure."

I knew instantly what it was about.

"Michael," the philosopher said without a preamble when I telephoned him. "They got him."

"When?"

"This afternoon."

"I'll be right over," I said and hung up. To Cecil, I said, "a small philosophical problem to resolve."

Cecil snorted to confirm the worst about philosophers, and I dashed out.

Chapter Fourteen

"They picked him up clean," Lee said as soon as he saw me. "I came back from the store around noon, and he was gone."

Three bounty hunters from the Evergreen Medical Research Center had quietly surrounded the house and asked Randy Parrish to come out. According to the neighbors who had witnessed the scene, the philosopher did not offer any resistance. The neighbors told Lee that the fugitive came out with his hands high up as if he thought someone was going to shoot him. One of the bounty hunters subdued him with a high-power stun gun although he had shown every sign of submission.

One neighbor, an old lady in her house robe who subsisted mostly on a modest income like the rest of her neighbors, had actually attacked the bounty hunter but she was handily beaten down by his stick. The brave woman, still with a lump on her forehead from the scuffle, swore to Lee that she had seen a trace of smile on Parrish's lips as he went down into a heap upon the stun gun attack. The fugitive philosopher was so light, the witness said, that a bounty hunter picked him up like a bag of groceries.

"Is there anything that can be done to save him?" I suggested, feeling almost fatal about the affair.

Lee became thoughtful. "There is one slim possibility," he said. "That's why I wanted to wait for your return from the athletic farm."

He asked me about the trip with Davis. I gave him a hurried account, elaborating a little on the scene of the captured escapees. With that, we went back to our present situation.

"What's the one possibility?"

"Jim Bardeaux of our psychology department at the University (Remember him at the lunch the other day?) also works there as a shift director," Lee said. "He is our one last hope."

From what little I could recall, Bardeaux the industrial psychologist and Robert Isaiah Lee the philosopher did not seem to be on the best of terms. The impression that I had retained of Jim Bardeaux was not one of kindness or generosity. In fact, he had struck me as a hard man of science, not given to an easy understanding of human shortcomings. But Lee had obviously known him as his colleague longer than I did and was following his instinct.

Besides, Lee told me he felt that the two of us could combine our strength to persuade the seemingly unyielding scientist. After all, I was a special visitor from Laurinville, and he might be moved by his patriotic sentiment to show that mercy did exist in America. Fortunately for us, Bardeaux's shift was three-to-eleven, which, Lee told me, was not as hectic as the day-shift. A slow evening could restore a reasonable frame of mind even in a hard man. We considered even that little as a good omen which might work in our favor.

We immediately drove to Evergreen, about ten miles or so outside the city limits of Wilmington. The guard at the gate waved us in when Lee showed him his university faculty ID and told him we were visiting Dr. Jim Bardeaux. We drove on for another mile or so on a well-paved road when we suddenly came upon the main compound of the Evergreen Medical Research Center. The lights were blazing everywhere on the outside of the three-story building. There was much blue in the lights that gave the whole atmosphere an eerie effect.

I had lived virtually all of my life in a small town where bright illumination was rare, and the blazing lights at Evergreen were a sight that made me almost jump. There were two more smaller buildings, one on each side of the main compound, which seemed to make up the whole of Evergreen. The sight impressed me with its sense of importance more than its size or power. It occurred to me then that I really didn't know what the medical research center was all about.

We parked our car in a slot marked 'Visitor' and walked to the reception hall. The receptionist, a woman perhaps in her early thirties who seemed new to her job, almost fumbled when a Dr. Robert Isaiah Lee and Mr. Michael Brown wanted to see Dr. Bardeaux.

"Yes, sir, right away," she said as she punched the buttons on her intercom. In a second or two, Bardeaux's voice came on. "Two gentlemen, Dr. Lee and Mr. Brown, would like to see you, Dr. Bardeaux," the woman said breathlessly.

There seemed to be a split-second silence on the phone, but his voice came back pleasantly. "Of course, I will be right there."

For the next minute or so, while waiting for the appearance of Bardeaux, I looked around the interior of the building as much as I could see. From the center of the building where the reception hall was located two large marble hallways extended into the four corners, forming an X, and two smaller ones crossed each other dividing the building roughly into four rectangles. Each section was further divided into offices and laboratories whose interior was brightly lit with a fair amount of activity in progress.

Occasionally men and women in laboratory smocks passed us, paying no attention to the two strangers who were obviously feeling uncomfortable. To add to our discomfort, everything in sight was immaculately clean. Somewhere in the building, however, was the misguided former philosopher who had sold his life. But the two strangers were there on a mission to save him. There was always hope.

But my hope was dealt a severe jolt when I saw Jim Bardeaux suddenly materializing from the elevator not far from us. What disappointed me was his white coat. I had been imagining him the way I had seen him at our lunch, which had presented him in a good deal more humane light. But seeing him in that impersonal white coat and in a setting that was quite alien to us but elementary to the man suddenly affected my view of the whole thing as hopeless. He waved and smiled at us but obviously he was in control. Although he was polite, he now looked much more authoritative and powerful and I found little in his gesture or appearance that was charitable.

After shaking our hands, he led us to his office on the second floor. He pointed to this and that office, this and that lab, describing their functions as we passed them, but we paid little attention to what he was saying. His office was neat but comfortable, in contrast to the ornate orderliness that characterized Dean Nettor's. I thought it might be reflective of the difference between an administrator and an academic man.

Neither Lee nor I felt encouraged to mention Parrish. The simple fact that Bardeaux had not asked us about the purpose of our nocturnal visit made it clear that he knew why we came to see him.

I told the night-shift director that I was impressed by the center and asked him what its main research activity consisted of. The subject was effective in easing the awkwardness of our presence.

"Our primary activity is research and development in 'Biological Age'," he said. "It's a medical product we pioneered here."

"Biological age?" I had never heard of it before, but Lee's expression said he knew all about it.

"Well, biological age has to do with the process of reducing our aging," the shift director said.

"You mean like the fountain of youth?"

"In a way, yes," Bardeaux was now within his own element. "People used to try to become younger with cosmetics and haphazard plastic surgery, as they still do in other parts of the world, I am sure. But Evergreen developed the first comprehensive medical process that reduces the total biological age of the body. Naturally, the Biological Age program has been our biggest money-maker."

"How do you do it; I mean reducing biological age?"

"I am not involved in the actual research," Bardeaux said. "As much as the administrative side of the operation—"

"Such as purchasing experimental subjects?" Lee interjected with remarkable neutrality in his tone.

"Yes," the industrial psychologist said in the same matter-of-fact manner. "But the actual process consists of organ transplant, readjustment of body chemistry, muscle re-processing, etcetera, that is ultra-high technology. It reduces the biological age of a person up to twenty years from his chronological age. In other words, we can make someone up to twenty years younger than he actually is. Our lab scientists have been assuring the stockholders that it is possible to reduce biological age by thirty years if all our current research is successful."

"How wide-spread is the use of, uh, Biological Age?"

"We are proud to say," the shift-director said, smiling in obvious pride, "that in the past five years we have lowered the biological age of over ten thousand American senior citizens at least by ten years. And there is greater demand than all the practicing plastic surgeons in America can handle at the moment. We are trying to simplify the procedures so that it's much easier to implement with little or no side-effects."

Forgetting briefly why we were there; I was fascinated by this development in the reduction of biological age. I thought it wonderful that so many older people could become young again and prolong their active life through the process developed and marketed by Evergreen. Both my father and my stepmother were in their fifties. It could help them too.

"What do you have to do," I asked. "To benefit from this extraordinary procedure?"

"It costs money," Bardeaux said simply. "In fact, a lot of money, so that only the extremely well-to-do can afford it, at least for the time being. After the process is completed, we issue them a Biological Age Certificate to make their rejuvenation official. We are trying to persuade the legislature to allow us to alter their birth certificates so that once a client has reduced ten years his or her birth certificate would actually show the new reduced age. If we could alter their age on birth certificates, we believe our Evergreen stock would sky-rocket."

"That would be nothing short of a revolution, practically everyone's dream," I observed.

"Absolutely," Bardeaux agreed. "Except it would be a reality, not fantasy or daydream. Just think, the possibility is unlimited. Parents can become younger than their children, and when their children get old, why, they can become younger than their parents once again, so that the two generations can have parent-child relationships twice in their lifetime. Or, they can reverse their parent-child roles for a better understanding, parents becoming the children of their children, and children the parents of their parents. Just think."

"I would say that opens up a fascinating possibility," I agreed.

"I would say it is a nightmare," Lee interjected.

"That's why," Bardeaux said, ignoring the philosopher's objection. "The current phase of our research project is so extremely important."

His last remark brought us back to our unhappy reality. Bardeaux seemed to sense that himself.

"Well, gentlemen," he said pensively. "What can I do for you?"

Lee, hitherto relatively quiet, stepped forward. "Bardeaux," he said, jutting his small face up to Bardeaux's enormous head. "You know why we are here."

Bardeaux remained expressionless.

"We came here to ask you to help us with Professor Parrish," I said reasonably. "I understand you are in a position to save his life."

"Save his life?" the shift director responded. "How can I save his life? Only Parrish can save Parrish's life. But he gave up his life voluntarily, didn't he?"

"He was poor and desperate, you know that," hissed Robert I. Lee. "His wife was sick and he was unemployed."

"I know all that," Bardeaux said. "I know how you feel, Robert. He was your close friend."

"He was my close friend, all right," Lee said. "But he was your professional colleague one time."

"I wear a different hat here, Robert," Bardeaux said, pointing to the floor of his office. "I have to answer to some people."

"What people? Stock-holders, money-mongers, you mean?" Lee insisted.

"Don't forget Evergreen is a self-sustaining corporation for profit and I am merely an employee of that institution," said the shift director, then he went into what seemed to be the pattern of speech common among many American social scientists and educators: "Central to the marketing orientation is the notion of exchange, Robert. Organizations obtain the resources they need by offering something of value to resource owners. We must analyze a process of identifying and choosing among service alternatives for which target populations are willing to trade something the agency values. Needs are wants. We must select the target population. We must choose a competitive position in the market. We must develop an effective market mix of strategy. We must serve our clientele's needs—"

"Cut out your social science nonsense," Lee said impatiently, indicting his familiarity with such strange styles of speech. "We don't care about your stock-holders or clientele. We are here to save Professor Parrish."

"Jim," I intervened. "What's one experimental subject? Don't you have others to experiment on? Can't you help with just one subject?"

"No, not really," Bardeaux said, thankfully returning to his normal speech. "It is especially difficult with Parrish because he broke the contract and we had to spend an enormous amount of money to get him back. We can't do anything about it."

"We'll pay back the money," I pleaded, although I didn't think I or anyone else I knew had that much money anyway. "If the expense is the issue."

"It's only a part of the problem," Bardeaux said, picking up a stack of computer printouts from his desk and theatrically throwing it on the floor. "The real problem is that we *need* Randy Parrish."

"What do you mean, you need him?" Lee inquired. "He's just an old man who is too weak to serve any of your research purposes."

"You are wrong, Robert," said the industrial psychologist. "Look at those printouts. We are conducting a very delicate research right now on the rejuvenation process of the human brain. We need a highly intelligent human brain to see if it can be rejuvenated a lot better than what we have been getting so far."

"You don't mean to use Professor Parrish for—" I said, stammering at the enormity of what I was hearing.

"Yes, Michael, we mean to use his brain for that purpose," Bardeaux said. "In fact, the reason we put such a high premium on his recapturing was because he is the most intelligent subject we have ever had among our volunteers."

"You are a heartless monster; do you know that?" Lee argued hotly. "All of you, you and your great so-called research center."

"It's out of my hand, or anybody's hand, Robert," Bardeaux said and I believed him. Evergreen was just too big for anyone. Or, was it the whole of American *society* we were dealing with?

"When do you plan to, uh, use the professor's brain?" I asked.

"Tomorrow," Bardeaux said. "We have no time to lose."

"Where is he now?"

"He is in the pre-op ward," Bardeaux said. "Getting ready for tomorrow."

"Can we see him?" I asked. "Just for a few minutes?"

The shift director stared at us hard, thinking. "I suppose you can, as long as you promise not to disrupt our procedures," he said finally. "I suppose there will be no harm, although this is against our company rules."

"Your company rules can go to hell, Bardeaux," Lee said ungratefully even as he was leaving the office to see his friend and mentor.

Considering the circumstances, Bardeaux apparently decided to ignore the philosopher's rudeness. I promised him that we would observe his company rules.

The pre-op ward was located on the first floor, close to the Operating Room, which we were not allowed to see.

Randy Parrish was lying motionless on a hospital bed. He was wired to all sorts of monitoring devices a few of which were flashing red numbers at highly confusing intervals. Two station nurses were efficiently watching the monitors. To make sure that we would not attempt anything, a guard was posted at the door. Bardeaux remained at the door near the guard and signaled to the nurses not to interfere with our visit.

As Lee and I walked closer to the bed, mindful of the wires everywhere, we were surprised that Parrish had been fully awake, watching us. He smiled as he saw us.

Lee and I pulled up two small chairs close to the bed. We wanted to touch his hands but they were tied to the bed because of all the intravenous tubes connected to them.

"I told you," the doomed philosopher said. "They would get me sooner or later."

"How are you?" Lee said as he could find not much else to say. "Are they treating you all right?"

"The best treatment anybody can get," Parrish said with a trace of irony. "You wouldn't believe the things they have been doing for me to make sure I am in the best of health until tomorrow."

"I am sorry, Professor," I said. "We've tried."

"Nothing to be sorry about," the philosopher said. "It was I who caused all this, remember?"

"Randy," Lee whispered. "All is not lost. You can still escape."

"How, my dear boy?" asked the old man, more amused than curious.

"I can overpower the guard. Michael can handle Bardeaux. We'll then take care of the nurses together."

Randy Parrish let out a chuckle, and I had to laugh too. Lee's plan was so outlandish that we found it humorous. The mild commotion about escape died down and the doomed philosopher became serious again.

"You are right," he said with surprising clarity and strength. "Perhaps you two can overpower them, and perhaps I can live a few more years. But what is the point? I am too old to enjoy the preciousness of freedom anymore. There comes a time in your life when you welcome the end. I believe my time has come and I can honestly tell you that my heart is glad that the end has finally come. Who knows, my old, tired brain might contribute something to lowering the biological age of our future generations."

Bardeaux signaled to let us know that our time was up. When we didn't respond immediately, he sent the guard to us to make sure that we ended our audience.

"Is there anything we can do, Randy?" Lee asked as we were about to leave. "Anything?"

The philosopher smiled and said, "I would like to sleep just one more night at the beach house. But you couldn't help me with that, could you?"

Bardeaux, who had walked over to us, gave an indulgent smile.

"There is one thing you can do, however," the condemned man said. "Find that woman among your neighbors who courageously attacked the bounty hunter. I was fully conscious and saw her courage. It was remarkable simply because she risked her life to help a stranger. Tell her, my good friends, that I was a happy man when I died because I was thinking about that courageous woman—"

"We know her," Robert I. Lee solemnly promised that he would tell the woman.

"—And you, too. I will be thinking about you. Goodbye, Robert. Goodbye, Michael. Now, go."

In the semi-darkness of the pre-op room, I could see a broad smile on the former fugitive's face as we left.

Jim Bardeaux hardly said a word as he led us back to the reception hall. Nor were we in any mood for words.

"Michael Brown," he said, extending his hand as we parted, which I shook. "This is America. Don't think anything of it."

As Lee drove me home my mind raced back to the past few days. I tried to put all my experiences into some sort of orderly catalog.

In an effort to do so, I was thinking about Jeanne Baker. I resolved to visit her the next day, and then my mind drifted into a state, largely occupied by her, which was at once optimistic and apprehensive.

"I was in a mental hospital once," Lee said suddenly, ending our silence as if he deliberately wanted to disturb my private thought.

I turned to look at him, fairly startled by the sudden revelation. The philosopher broke into a grin to ease my surprise and fear.

"It was my son," Lee said, looking straight ahead with a deliberate indifference. I nevertheless noticed that he had tensed up as he spoke of his son. He swallowed hard apparently to keep his emotion under control.

I said I didn't know he had a family.

"Oh, yes," Lee said. "A son and a wife—Both are gone now."

"I am sorry," I said.

We were once again silent for a while. Although I was curious to know the circumstances under which he no longer had his family, I felt I couldn't push him for the revelation. It wasn't too long, however, before Lee spoke again.

Chapter Fifteen

"Robert Isaiah Lee, Jr., that's my son—at least it was his name then. I was challenged and lost," he said. "My wife left me right after Bobby's birth—I guess for someone with a higher TIW rank. I had to raise Bobby by myself while struggling to get through graduate school. It was during these difficult times that Bobby and I grew extremely close. As close as two human beings can possibly be. We were like hand and glove. Everywhere I went he went. We were always together, father and son, practically day and night. He was a sweet, wonderful boy, never causing any trouble."

Lee wore the expression of a man recalling an event both sad and affectionate, which alternately prompted him into grimace and smile. He described some anecdotes in Bobby's early life, which portrayed a boy of fetching sweetness. He reached into his pocket and pulled out from his wallet the photograph of a handsome boy of about three, smiling confidently into the camera. He had his father's dark hair and dark eyes, which the proud father pointed out.

"There was this woman at the university where I was a graduate student, a faculty member married to a wealthy businessman," Lee said as he was putting the photograph back in the wallet. "She had seen Bobby on campus with me and, like the many others who saw Bobby, fell in love with him, and decided to challenge me. I fought hard to keep him, but with my poor philosophy student's TIW it was really no contest, as I knew it would be. She won it rather handily. In fact, she didn't even have to use her husband's TIW to make her case. Her income was enough to impress the judge by making me look like an incompetent parent."

"When was this?" I had to ask something, even if trivial.

"About four years ago," Lee said.

His eyes were moist with the sadness and resignation that were his lot.

"I will never forget the night I left him at the woman's house, as ordered by the court," Lee said with deep feelings. "I had been telling Bobby that I had to go away for business but would be back soon, and that in the meantime he should stay with the good couple and behave himself. He was such a good boy and accepted my explanation for our separation, but he must have known that something was happening to him and his father. He was teary and weepy but did not cry out when I left him. 'Yes, Daddy,' he said as the woman took him into the living room and closed the screen door. 'But, how long?' he wanted to know. 'Not very long, darling,' I said, by then unable to control my sobbing."

Lee was now openly crying; the pain of recollection was too much. He wiped his eyes and blew his nose.

"I repeated that I would be back soon. 'Daddy,' he said, now tearier and weepier, 'finish your business in five minutes and come home.' He said that through the screen door and that was the last thing I heard him say. 'Finish your business in five minutes and come home,' he said, and I will never forget those words as long as I live. A mouthful for a three-year old, but five minutes used to be his way of saying hurry."

Lee repeated 'five minutes' several times as if those were the most significant words in his life.

"Is that when you—?"

"That's right," he said dreamily. "That's when I broke down. I was hospitalized for nearly the whole semester."

"You haven't seen him since then?"

"Yes, I have, one more time," Lee said, somewhat recovering from his traumatic reminiscence. "The woman made sure, after she took Bobby, that I wouldn't run into him even by accident. But two years later, I saw them together, the woman and Bobby, at a park quite by chance. He had grown up so much, I couldn't believe it was Bobby. He was big enough to ride a bicycle and was showing off his riding skill to his mother. He rode it straight to where I was standing. My heart pounded at the sight of him, and I rushed out and grabbed his bicycle and held his arm."

Lee stopped his talk and went into a faraway look for a few seconds. A bitter, resigned smile appeared on his mouth.

"You know what, Michael?" he said, turning toward me briefly for emphasis. "He didn't recognize me. He didn't recognize his father. I had grown a beard by then. Bobby simply let out a cry and ran back to his mother. I took the bicycle to them as Bobby was gesturing wildly about the stranger who had grabbed him, and the woman became alert as she saw me walk over to them. I apologized to her for the intrusion. I said I was sorry to have frightened the boy and, before she could say anything in protest, left them quickly. It's illegal for the original parents to bother their children or the new parents once they transfer their children either in commercial sale or through court challenge."

"Then, what happened?"

"The following year I finished my doctorate and found a post here at the University of Wilmington. I never saw Bobby again."

"You must miss him terribly," I said needlessly.

"I did," he said, giving me a sidelong glance, then let out a deep sigh as if the burden had finally been lifted. "But, you know, human beings are resilient. They can live through anything, just about anything. Look at the Jews in concentration camps, they survived through even the most barbaric and painful human tortures. For a while, I thought I could never live without Bobby, but I did. During my hospitalization I did nothing but sit up in my room and cry. You know crying, crying with a total abandon, crying your heart out like an animal, is the best mental therapy there is? It certainly helped me. The doctors didn't know what to do and gave up on me. There was really nothing wrong with me except that I missed my son, and there was nothing they could do for me. They suggested a precision operation to remove my memory of him, but I refused."

I did not ask why.

"I guess I wanted to suffer," the philosopher with a prophet's middle name said at last. "I guess I wanted to remember him even if the memory was so painful for me. I guess I wanted to live with my anger and with my terrible longing for my Bobby, even if it killed me. I guess I survived it although it nearly did kill me. The pain made me stronger in the end, and I survived. Yes, I survived, but how I survived—"

I didn't know what to say. His story was deeply touching, contradicting the general impression of American society as incapable of experiencing basic human emotion. However, I must confess that I wasn't quite sure about father-son relationships, especially from the father's point of view. I supposed that it was entirely possible for a man to be so terribly in love with his son that he would suffer a mental breakdown when he lost the boy.

It occurred to me that his wife, who had deserted him, must not have caused him nearly the same heartache, for my friend mentioned nothing of his faithless wife. Obviously, a man's love for his child and his relationship with another adult were two quite different kinds of human affection. I wondered briefly whether the second kind was much easier to endure and forget than the first. In my simple mind, I found the issue too complex to ponder intelligently.

This quick chain of thought took me once again to the image of Jeanne Baker, especially that pitiful face which attempted a smile while in terrible shock and pain. Her courage and dignity had left a profound and lasting impression on my mind that I could not understand or obliterate.

"I still see him in my dreams," Robert Isaiah Lee said.

I looked at him, somewhat startled out of my thoughts. I had forgotten about Lee and his son.

"Bobby," he said in a hushed tone. "I still see him almost every night. Sometimes he is with me in our old house, which puzzles me terribly even in the dream. I wonder why he is with me when he should be with his new parents. Sometimes he is the way I remembered him, about three years old or so, sometimes he is older. In other dreams, I am frantically searching for him at a grocery store or some other public place where I had just lost him. It's almost always one or the other kind of dream. Once these dreams wake me up the sleep is gone for the rest of the night, of course. The terrible reality of the morning is something I haven't quite overcome yet. Sometimes, especially after a sweet dream, I find myself crying."

"Do you keep things around the house that remind you of Bobby?"

"Yes, I do. Everything. I keep everything in the house that reminds me of him. I even have things in my office as well. I am not afraid of being reminded of him, after all."

"But your dreams—"

"That doesn't bother me," the forlorn father said with obvious defiance. "I just miss the boy, that's all. What can anyone do about it?"

"I see your point," I said. "I suppose there is nothing that can be done, is there?"

"No," he said. "There is nothing that can be done."

At that point during my stay in America, Lee seemed to be the only person openly unhappy with America's pecuniocratic way of life. Since I had not previously known any philosopher, it was difficult to tell whether it was his philosophical learning which made him so violently unhappy with the system, or it was his private pain as a victim which turned him against his own society. It was not very pleasant altogether for me to hear this man's sad story and observe his suffering, however, because I rather liked him.

I expected to maintain our friendship for the remainder of my stay in the United States. But because of the extraordinary events that followed, I never saw him again.

We drove in silence the rest of the way home, each occupied with his own affairs of the heart.

Next morning, I was so relieved when Cecil McMiller informed me at breakfast that the day was free. I could roam anywhere I wanted to. The university, per its original offer, would make one of its official vehicles available to me for the duration of my stay in the Wilmington area.

"I want you to get the bearings of the city on your own, Michael," announced my friend. "Driving around by yourself gets you quickly acquainted with the geography. Just do whatever you want. You don't even have to do anything, in fact."

"Michael might want to rest for a while," Carol suggested. "After all the hectic schedule he has had lately."

I assured them that I felt fine and would be delighted to wander around the city and its vicinity to get oriented. Besides, I told them, the sooner I got my bearings, the sooner I could be independent of their guidance.

McMiller took me to the University's motor-pool where I collected my assigned car, which was a medium-sized gas-efficient model (so the motor-pool director told me). It had, however, all the conveniences of the bigger models. The motor-pool director pointed out that the vehicle was equipped with both heat and air.

"You know, Wilmington this time of the year is slightly unpredictable," the man said, making the final checks. "You need both heat and air, just to be sure. In fact, this morning I needed heat, and I am sure right now you would have to use air."

McMiller gave me a map of the city and showed me the main arteries in relation to the University and his house as reference points. Wilmington occupied a large section of an up-side-down triangle known as Cape Fear, bordered by the Cape Fear River on one side and the Atlantic on the other. My friend marked on the map a few landmarks and places to visit and, giving me cautionary words on the 'crazy Wilmington drivers', left for his classes.

As both the motor-pool director and McMiller disappeared from view, I immediately studied the map in search of 31 Sutton Drive, the home address of Jeanne Baker that I had found on the computer printout. The relatively short street was not too far from the campus and, getting my bearings, I set out to find the house.

I followed College Road, which was one of the two main thoroughfares until I came to Waltmore, where I turned left as the map showed. On my left on Waltmore was a large, new fenced-in building with a sign on the front that said, "Southeast Youth Reconditioning Center," which I assumed to be some kind of educational institution. Waltmore stretched for another mile or so and I noticed that the neighborhood began to look less prosperous on both sides of the road. By the time I came to a T which was Sutton, the houses looked smaller and poorer, with children playing outside on the street. In contrast with the area in which the McMillers lived, Jeanne Baker's neighborhood was almost a shocking revelation.

As I turned right on Sutton according to the map, the street became more crowded. The children playing seemed so reckless and abandoned that I had to slow down to avoid them. A woman came out of a house and hollered at the children, presumably hers included, to watch out for the cars on the road, then gave me a dirty look as if it was all my fault. But before I reached the block, I suddenly realized that the road was cut off by a railroad. Consulting the map once again showed me that 31 Sutton was on the other side of the railroad. I doubled back to Waltmore, went two more blocks toward college, then returned to Sutton.

The house that presumably was the home of Jeanne Baker was somewhat more respectable than the others around it. It had the neatness of a house whose owner made a great deal of effort to make it look respectable. But the overwhelming decline around it made that effort seem awfully close to irrelevant. The house obviously had been painted recently, but it showed age in spite or perhaps because of that recent paint job. Some of them were painted over so many times to look decent that the effort itself became prima facie evidence of its age and decay. Jeanne Baker's house appeared to fall under the weight of that fate.

As I parked my car a couple of children on the block stopped their playing and eyed me suspiciously as if they welcomed no strangers. I was sure there were adults around who were watching me but I didn't look around to face them. After all, I told myself as I was feeling slightly embarrassed, I was on an entirely noble mission of inquiring into the health of a woman and her mother who had unfortunately collided with a vehicle in which I was a passenger. There was nothing wrong for the passenger to feel responsible for the event and inquire into its aftermath.

I approached the house slowly. Looking for a bell but not finding one, I uncertainly knocked on the door. Somehow, I was afraid of alerting the neighbors any more than necessary. No response came from the inside although I thought I had heard some signs of life in the house. I applied some more force with my knocks in the second attempt. Then I heard a shuffling of feet apparently on a hardwood floor and saw a figure approaching the door.

"Who's there?" A woman's voice came through the door, which I judged to be the mother's.

"I am sorry to bother you," I said, regretting that I hadn't brought some flowers for the occasion. "But I was in the other car when we collided the other day."

There was a hostile silence as if the woman was deliberating if it was to her benefit to respond. I said through the crack in the door that I just came by to see if the ladies were doing all right and to express my regrets about the terrible mishap.

Then I heard what I judged to be Jeanne's voice asking her mother who the visitor was. Her mother said something about the accident.

"Is he from their insurance company?" Jeanne asked.

Her mother said no, and then, getting her daughter's instruction, opened the door slightly.

"Would you wait a moment, please?" the woman said through the opening with greater civility. "My daughter will come out and see you."

"Are you doing all right yourself, ma'am?" I asked. "I called you at the medical station that evening and they told me you had been discharged. I am terribly sorry about the whole thing."

"We are all right, sir," the woman responded. "It was entirely her fault, or our fault. She was not watching the lights. She was under so much stress. It was her fault."

She didn't sound as if she was specifically blaming her daughter, but was stating some vaguely generalized notions of their lives and fate. I said again that I was very sorry and hoped that it didn't cause them too much inconvenience.

"There is no inconvenience, sir," she said. "We just don't have a car, that's all."

"He can come in now, Mother," the young woman said and her mother opened the door wide enough for me to pass through.

"I am sorry to have bothered you like this," I said as I entered the house and saw Jeanne Baker standing there on the floor. It was a small living room furnished with what I considered unmatching pieces of furniture, some contemporary, some old enough to be antique. There was a moderate size aquarium by the window with several gold fish swimming lazily in the morning light coming through the water. It was a tidy household with the excessive cleanliness with which sometimes poor families try to make up for their poor standing in society. Jeanne was dressed respectably but not as formally as the first time I saw her. The two scratches, darker now, remained on her forehead. The mother quietly disappeared into one of the rooms.

"It's no bother," she said. "But you shouldn't have taken the trouble of coming here yourself."

"I called the medical station that afternoon but you had been discharged," I explained. "And I found your address on the police report because you didn't have a telephone that I could have—"

"Won't you sit down?" she asked, pointing to a chair.

She got herself seated facing me as I sat down in the chair she had indicated. The morning's bright light made the two cuts on her forehead more visible. Apparently, they had received no special medical attention despite their cosmetic significance for a reasonably attractive young woman. Not oddly, Jeanne herself seemed totally oblivious to their presence on her face.

"Yes, they didn't find anything terribly wrong with us," she said with a forced smile. "No broken bones or severe internal damages. Mother got some bruises on her arms but nothing serious. She has been complaining of soreness but there is nothing to worry about. So, we were sent home without further ado."

"Your car was damaged beyond repair?"

"Yes, it was. Beyond repair. We were brought home by one of the emergency medics although it was against their rule."

"I hope you had adequate insurance coverage for the automobile," I suggested hopefully.

She gave out a resigned smile to say the contrary, but she said nothing. I told her that it was only my second day there from Laurinville (which she had remembered) and something about my purpose as a visitor.

"So, you are a school principal," she said as if it were a strange occupation. "I work for a small construction company as a secretary."

Then she said more about her job and that she had called in sick for the day since it was a Friday so that she could recover from her accident and find a new means of transportation. As I had guessed, she had no insurance. She said she was thankful that no one had been seriously injured from it.

As we exchanged small talk my first impression of her gathered at the scene of the accident was confirmed more strongly. In spite of her obvious poverty and vague personal unhappiness, she showed no discomfort with the fact and she didn't even seem conscious of it at all. She displayed that strong sense of innocence and spiritual strength that is often observed in children and exalted religious teachers.

The stated purpose of my visit to her home had thus been terminated with the confirmation that neither she nor her mother was seriously hurt. But I lingered on with further inquiries of her life in general, about which I knew little beyond the superficial. She too seemed to become aware of my personal interest in her beyond the simple state of their health. We hadn't said much about our personal lives, and I was dying to know more about her.

The transition from a simple goodwill health inquiry to the true nature of the visit had not materialized, and that fact became acutely embarrassing for me. However, I had not detected any sign that Jeanne Baker was thinking our audience over.

"Would you like to have some coffee?" Jeanne offered, relieving me of my enormous discomfort.

"Yes, please, if I could have some tea?" I said, thankful for her rescue. "If it is no trouble to you, Miss Baker."

"It's no trouble at all, and call me Jeanne and I will call you Michael," she said as she rose to go to the kitchen.

"Splendid," I said.

"—then I want you to tell me a little bit about Laurinville," she said. As I was looking around and thinking about nothing in particular because my mind could not focus on anything, Jeanne reappeared with a tray. She poured me a cup and then poured herself one.

"What is it like in Laurinville?" she said. "I always wanted to travel but I haven't even been out of North Carolina."

"Sure, I am not detaining you from any urgent business, Jeanne?"

"No, I am not going anywhere, Michael. I am staying right here."

I had to laugh self-consciously at her obvious reference to the total destruction of her vehicle. It was also a good-humored reference to her inadequate insurance protection and equally inadequate TIW rank. But at that precise moment I felt our relationship took a gigantic step forward. She had confessed her relative economic helplessness to me without feeling embarrassed, and we had just called each other by our first names. In these seemingly insignificant tea-leaf readings, my own silly heart leaped wildly at the prospect of trying to gain a tiny foothold in the heart of this attractive young woman.

"Tell me," I said, regaining my calm. "Why did you miss the traffic light yesterday?"

For a brief moment, her face was clouded and then she recovered quickly.

"I suppose I was not concentrating on the road, my mind sometimes wanders away," she said casually.

I was not satisfied with her explanation, but somehow didn't feel right to press the inquiry any further.

We changed the subject to Laurinville. I described some of the highlights of life in Laurinville that I felt would be of interest to her, but without mentioning the Green Palmers. I told her, in conclusion, that Laurinville could be thought of as a frozen moment of America's past, frozen from its normal historical and cultural development.

"Do you think Laurinville could become like the rest of America?" she asked.

"I hope not, but I don't really know," I admitted. "So far we have been successful in protecting our town."

The word 'protecting' somehow sounded too harsh.

"That means you are not wholly happy with what you have seen," she said in what was obviously an astute analysis of my reaction to America.

I had to agree with her assessment. She was interested in knowing more about my life and my family in Laurinville. I told her about my father the bakery man and my stepmother the semi-retired mechanic; all the while my memories rushed to Laurinville as if it was another world and in another life that had no connection to my present time and place. I also told her about my experience in Moreland.

Jeanne seemed interested in the history and geography of the island-nation, which was as exotic to America as America was to Moreland, and asked many sensible questions about the people that I knew. The more we talked, the more I became aware of her native intelligence uncluttered by education. And she was so unconscious of her own intellectual powers.

After some more small talk, I felt I had finally come to the most critical point of my visit, and it was also the most awkward moment.

"I know this is fairly out of line and perhaps obnoxious," I managed enough courage to say this much. "We don't know each other well enough for me to suggest this—"

My heart was pushing through the throat and I had to stand up so that I wouldn't choke.

"—but would you be good enough to accept my invitation to a dinner tonight?"

Jeanne smiled at my gallant effort to speak. Her face expressed the easy comprehension and sympathy of a wonderful heart, which had been my first impression of her at the scene of the accident that had brought us together. Then her face changed to one of regret.

"It's nice of you to invite me out to dinner," she said reluctantly, "but—"

Interrupting her was the voice of a child from one of the rooms down the hallway.

"That's Mary Sue," she said. "My two-year-old girl. She was taking her early morning nap."

I stood up as if I were going to receive the child.

"Would you bring her out here, Mother, please," Jeanne Baker called to her mother.

Almost instantly grandmother and granddaughter materialized. Jeanne walked over to them and took the girl from her grandmother. She held her in her arms expertly and comfortably, and walked back to where I was standing. The girl, like her mother, had light brown hair and deep blue eyes, cheeks rosy from her sleep. She showed her natural reluctance with a stranger, but her mother patted her to ease her. The child finally smiled an uncertain smile. That magically broke the spell.

"Mary Sue," Jeanne Baker said. "This is Mr. Michael Brown, Mom's friend, who came to see us."

"How do you do, Mary Sue?" I said, extending my hand.

Chapter Sixteen

I had always prided myself as a child-pleaser. Rarely did I fail in impressing a child of any age with my funny tricks and playing around. Ryan, the boy I had met at the airport who rudely destroyed my confidence, even as a pecuniocratic American child, was a rare case of failure in my annals of child-pleasing. There was hardly a small child in Laurinville or in Moreland, for that matter, to whom I was not a popular figure.

Mary Sue turned out to be an easy child to delight, and a bright one too. She brought out some cards with animals and objects of different sizes, shapes, and colors, and, to my surprise and her mother's and grandmother's pride, named all of them correctly. In the next half hour or so, I found myself having a wonderful time playing with her. I had taken my jacket off and was on my fours all over the hardwood floor sometimes with her on my back, her mother steadying her from the side. Mary Sue giggled and wanted to play more when I stood up and declared beat.

Upon Jeanne's suggestion the grandmother took the child back to her room. I wiped my brows, and said, "I'm beat. Too old to play that hard anymore."

Jeanne and I looked at the direction of Mary Sue's room, then we looked at each other, and we burst out laughing. The child had broken the ice and we knew it and felt it.

"Now," I said, taking her by the hand back to her chair and sitting down myself, "would you tell me all about Mary Sue?"

Jeanne Baker said, with neither hesitation nor dramatics, that she had been all set for her wedding, a conventional marriage between two people with similar TIW's. The day before the wedding, however, her husband-to-be got killed in a freak accident related to his occupation as an electrician. It was not long after his funeral that she discovered that she was pregnant with Mary Sue.

"Nothing much else to tell you," she said. "Since then, Mother, who had just been widowed herself a year before, moved in with me and we have been struggling to survive ever since. She takes care of my daughter when I go to work. But the three of us spend our time together when I am not working."

"Must have been rough on you," I said, meaning economically as well as emotionally.

"My TIW has almost always remained below 50," Jeanne said. "In fact, my current TIW is the highest it has ever been. When Calvin, that's Mary Sue's father, got killed, of course, I was devastated beyond belief. But I survived because of Mary Sue. The other day, in fact, Mother and I were talking about Calvin when—"

"You missed the light and we rammed you from the side?"

She nodded, managing a feeble smile.

"What are you going to do about your transportation?"

"I don't know," she said. "But I will try to borrow a car from the construction company I am working for."

Having seen the other America, the wealthier and the more elegant part of America ever since I arrived, Jeanne Baker's troubles seemed almost refreshingly real. A somewhat more complete picture of the new America began to form in my mind.

"If I can help in any way," I said, picking up my jacket, "I would be delighted to lend a hand, although I am a stranger in paradise myself."

"You've been very nice," Jeanne said simply. "I should be grateful for your kindness."

"Well," I fumbled for words, walking toward the door.

"Michael," she called. I turned around and faced her. "Is the dinner invitation for tonight still good?" she asked.

I got busy that afternoon with visits to two museums and one historical society. Wilmington had maintained a wonderful array of historical documents and artifacts from the Civil War era and I was absorbed in them for a good portion of the afternoon. I had a nice lunch at a restaurant overlooking the river, and I gladly signed the bill of satisfaction.

It was close to five o'clock when I got back home. Cecil was working in his prize garden.

"Where have you been, Michael?" Cecil inquired without stopping his work. "You look tired, must've had a busy day."

In the next few minutes, I described what I had accomplished that day, but without including the visit with Jeanne Baker. Somehow, I felt bashful about it.

"That gives you a little better idea about Wilmington's layout, doesn't it?"

I told him that I was getting better oriented with the city. In a week or so, I should be fairly independent.

"Guess what happened today at the University?" he suddenly remarked.

I looked at him quizzically.

"A student by the name of Hugh Seago got killed in the university diving pool."

"Oh," I said, not knowing how to respond to this seemingly accidental death of a college student. "What about it? How did he die?"

"Apparently, he hit the diving board with his head, which is one of the more common diving accidents, I hear. And it is presenting a problem for the University."

"Is it the university's fault?" I asked. "Wasn't the student responsible for the accident?"

"It would seem it was the student's fault, although it hardly matters," Cecil said.

"What do you mean, it would seem?" I said.

"You see, the student was not given the pre-dive psychological counseling. At least there is no record of it at the Aquatic Director's office."

"Pre-dive what?"

"It was the student's first dive ever from that height," Cecil said. "It is our university policy, for that matter the policy of most universities in America, to give students proper advice about the emotional trauma of first-time dive. Of course, we have similar counseling for first-time exams, first-time dating, first-time driving, first-time this and first-time that. We keep psychologists busy. We try to eliminate any kind of emotional difficulty involved in individual life. At any rate, there is no record at the pool office that it was ever given to that student, which complicates the matter, as far as the university is concerned."

"What kind of complications?"

"The point is that," my friend said. "His father—his mother is dead—is claiming that the university is responsible for his son's death because he had died in its diving pool while presumably diving under its guidance. See the point? I am chairman of the Student Affairs Committee which is charged with taking care of this sort of thing. But this student's death is the biggest thing we have ever had to take care of. It has been on TV already all afternoon. The president is very upset that this could ruin our image, and the student's father is counting on that pressure, obviously, because image is everything. If it is ruined, everything is ruined. The pressure is really on the committee, meaning, one Cecil McMiller."

"Hmmm—" I contemplated my friend's situation. "What can you do?"

"The most important thing right now is to correct the impression that the university has neglected its responsibilities. We must demonstrate that we are very much together as a community, as a team, as a family—the administration, the faculty, the student body—"

"How?"

"I've organized a memorial service for the student tomorrow afternoon at the courtyard of the union building. It's going to be a first-class memorial service. All the representatives of the community and the media will be there tomorrow. It will be packed with TV cameras to telecast it live to every household in Wilmington."

"Should I go to the service? After all, I don't know the—"

"Of course, you should go. You may never see another memorial service in America if you miss this one. There will be a couple of experts from Authentic Life to help us produce a good show at the service."

"Authentic Life?"

"It's a media consultant firm which advises people on image making in public. We have them on our university's payroll for half-time staff and they are good with their expertise. They will take charge of the service tomorrow, because it's going to be for the media people."

"Then I shall go."

"We will go in around ten o'clock for the Authentic Life fellows, and get things organized until the service begins at one o'clock."

"Does Carol know about that too?"

"Yes, I already told her. She might come to the service, but not the rehearsal."

"Where is she?"

"She is working in her studio."

"Would she mind if I interrupted her? I want to look at my portrait one more time."

"No, she wouldn't mind, I am sure. Go ahead, I interrupt her all the time," Cecil assured me.

I walked to the studio behind the house and knocked on the door.

"Who is it?"

"Michael."

There was hesitation for a split second, then she said to come in. I walked in and looked around.

"Where is your painting, Carol?"

"Which painting?"

"Cecil said you were working at the studio, so I naturally assumed you were working on a new painting."

She laughed uneasily. "No, I wasn't painting. I was reading."

"Oh, I see. I hope I wasn't interrupting your reading. I just wanted to see my great portrait one more time."

"I moved it over there," she pointed to a wall directly opposite from the window. "I thought it would look better with more light coming through the window."

I was ambivalent once again with my face, looking at me somewhat somberly, even menacingly, through much green and blue. Carol watched my reaction.

"What do you think? Does it look any different today?"

"I don't know," I said, sighing helplessly. "I guess I wasn't born to be an artist or even an art connoisseur. I can't make up my mind about it."

"You know ambiguity is one of the essences of art," she said, hopefully. "Sometimes I don't even understand my own paintings."

I smiled at her modest reference to her art.

"Did you have a productive day, out alone?" she asked.

"I did," then I briefly told her what I had done. I hesitated whether to tell her about Jeanne Baker and our dinner tonight. I decided Carol had to know because I wouldn't be home for dinner. Besides, I felt much more comfortable about discussing with Carol my unauthorized visit to Jeanne.

"That's wonderful," Carol was genuinely surprised and delighted when I told her about it.

"That's great. Come to think of it, it's going to be great for Cecil and me. There is a play in town that I've been wanting to see. Tonight is good as any other night."

"I hope I am not ruining your plans."

"Absolutely not," Carol said, getting off her artist's stool. "In fact, I'd better tell Cecil to get ready."

Carol walked toward the door, then stopped and turned around. "Would you want to look at your portrait some more, Michael?"

I said I would like to if she didn't mind.

"Not at all," she said as she went out the door. "Just turn the lights out and close the door when you leave. Sometimes night animals get inside if it's not closed."

I went back to my portrait, trying to comprehend the true significance of that artwork as a window to my soul, so to speak, as seen by an artist. For some reason, I wasn't flattered by what I saw in myself. There was too much conflict, too much agony, much more than I would have liked to contain within my soul. Or was it Carol's own soul that I was looking at in front of me? It was inconceivable to me that Carol, the quintessential all-American housewife, could contain within her so much brooding darkness. I got closer and stepped back, changing the distance from the portrait to see if that altered anything.

Remembering that it was always proper to stay at least several feet away from any artwork, I took one more step back from where I was standing. As I stepped back, I stumbled over Carol's stool and found myself sitting on the floor with one leg wrapping around the stool. Mildly embarrassed with my own clumsiness, I hurriedly tried to get up. But when I tried to get up by pushing myself up, I found that my right hand was laying on a piece of paper which I must have, while falling, knocked down from the desk on which Carol had kept some of her painting material. I picked it up with the idea of putting it back on the desk where several of other pieces of paper were lying about.

But something on the paper caught my eyes. It was a hand-written letter addressed to Carol, thanking her for her recent visit and for the support she had shown, all in just three lines or so.

But what caught my attention was the letterhead. It said, "ANTHROPOLIS, U.S.A." Below, it was signed, "YOURS TRULY, ANTHROPOLITANS."

Anthropolitans? I had never heard anyone speak of either Anthropolis as a place or an organization, or Anthropolitans as a group or members of a group.

Anthropolis. Anthropolitans.

As I thought about these enigmatic words, suddenly it occurred to me that they were an art organization and Carol was a supporting member of that organization. My curiosity thus satisfied; I returned my attention back to the disturbing portrait on the wall. Within a few moments, I had forgotten all about Anthropolis and Anthropolitans.

"I hear you have a dinner engagement with one Miss Baker," Cecil roared as I went back to the house. "Watch out for these women, Michael. They will get you in the end one way or another."

I confessed that I was somewhat uncertain as to how to approach it. "Since Miss Baker's TIW is under 50," Cecil said matter-of-factly. "You and she will get along fine."

I said I didn't understand him. I even felt somewhat offended by his cavalier reference to Jeanne's low economic standing which had been clear even from the beginning, and he didn't have to rub it in. Cecil saw my stiffening face and roared with laughter.

"Don't you get upset, Michael. I didn't mean to upset you," he said. "What I meant is this. In America, people whose TIW is below 50, which there are quite a few of, more than most of us would like to admit, have not changed that much with the flow of things in American life. They remain, in their lifestyles, cultural outlooks, political views, and what have you, more or less the way they were many decades ago. They marry the conventional way, they cannot afford to carry insurance, they don't believe in the logger, and so on. They are what sociologists would call deviant types, people who are different from the majority. They are Americans all right, but they don't act or think like contemporary Americans. They act and think more like, shall I say, your townspeople in Laurinville, Michael. That's what I meant when I said you and Miss Baker would get along fine."

I didn't appreciate his calling Jeanne a deviant, because, unlike Cecil's and some sociologists' thinking, poverty was not deviance although it had become so in American life in 1998. But I understood his reasons for feeling optimistic about our introduction to each other. I decided to ignore the first part of Cecil's comment, and magnify the second. Once I came to that conclusion, I found myself eagerly looking forward to seeing Jeanne that evening.

Indeed, she and I had what I can only call a wonderful time. The more I got to know her the more I became aware of the sources of my fascination with her. They were essentially anchored in her simple honesty within herself and acceptance of her lot in life with much dignity, and her innate desire to survive in a harshly unsympathetic society.

Besides, in spite of her excruciating poverty, I noticed a certain sense of genuine happiness in her household, which was affecting and contagious. Mary Sue was a bundle of joy and, having been completely won over from the morning experience, she easily claimed her proprietary domination of my time when I was at her home, and insisted that I play with her all the time. Even Jeanne's mother somewhat relaxed her normally severe countenance with me.

Jeanne Baker was a tonic that, like a thorn in the side, pricked my sometimes-confused vision in this strange paradise to a sharper focus.

Chapter Seventeen

When we arrived at the courtyard the two media experts from Authentic Life were already at work, directing the arrangement of seats, flowers, podium, and other paraphernalia for the memorial.

The courtyard was an open quadrangle, the size of a small playing field, located within the university union with imitation cobblestones on the ground. There were several small flowerbeds and shrubs along the three walls that had windows, and several trees planted near the center. The antiquarian design of the four two-story brick walls gave the quadrangle a sense of being inside a medieval university, which was obviously the intended effect.

The podium was arranged near the main entrance and the folding chairs, about fifty or so, were placed in two groups facing the podium. The rest of the quadrangle was left unoccupied for the comings and goings of the general public. Extension cords from the wall outlets were coiled in bundles for the operation of TV cameras and microphones and speakers.

Two men, radically different from each other, one tall and thin and the other short and heavy, waved at us as McMiller and I entered the courtyard, and we approached them.

McMiller introduced the men to me. "Michael, this is Alan Jefferies and this is Don Munson." He then introduced me to the duo.

"We are generally known as Mutt and Jeff," the tall man said pleasantly. "It would be easier if you followed the convention and just called us Mutt and Jeff."

Dean Nettor, who was to be the main speaker as the dean of student affairs, representing the administration, spotted us and swiftly made his way. He took McMiller aside. "Good news, Cecil," the dean said, speaking aloud to be heard above the workmen. "The father agreed to settle for one million."

"Oh," my friend was delighted. "When did that happen?"

"Early this morning. It will be announced at the service to cap it all." The dean then whispered something to McMiller's ear at which my friend looked surprised and then pleased. The dean gave a satisfied smile and hurried off to attend to other matters. McMiller returned to where I was standing with Mutt and Jeff. He repeated the story to us, the one-million-dollar settlement, which was no secret because it was going to be announced at the end of the service as its climactic event.

Exchanges of some small talk out of the way, Jeff suddenly became all business.

"In a few minutes," he said looking at his watch, "all the main participants from the administration, the faculty, and the student body should be coming in for rehearsal."

"Did you get the preacher too?" McMiller asked.

"Yes, we did," Mutt said. "He will be here later, close to the service time because he said he didn't need the rehearsal."

"I don't blame him," McMiller said. "He is a professional."

"Now, I am going to have the family sit over here," said Jeff, pointing to the first row of the seats on the left from the podium. "Better camera angle and lighting. I am going to see if I can coax the cameras to concentrate on them for a while when they sob. We put the flowers in the background to enhance the effect. Let me see if we can change the colors of the flowers. We want more pastel there."

McMiller and the Mutt-and-Jeff team were going over many details of the operation when the main participants began to pour into the courtyard for their appointed task of rehearsal. Mutt and Jeff directed the crowd into a nicely balanced group of administrators, professors, and students for the two clusters of folding chairs.

The seating arrangement itself took some time because late participants kept coming in, forcing a constant reshuffling. McMiller was one of the main participants so that he was assigned a seat close to the podium, and I took up my position in a corner near one of the flowerbeds to watch the whole scene. In about half an hour or so, the team pronounced the arrangement satisfactory.

"Now, ladies and gentlemen," Mutt announced. "Where you are seated right now will be your final assigned seats when the service begins at one o'clock this afternoon. Please do not change your seats. The present arrangement has been made for the best effect we can create. Now, speaking of the effect, I will let my colleague Jeff handle the matter."

"We are going to have a first-class show of emotion," said Jeff with the polish of a professional handler. "Many of you have been to some other occasions like this one before so that emotion comes easy. For some of you, it is a new experience. At any rate, let's try it. First, let's emote sorrow. It's sorrow. Okay. Get set! Ready! Go!"

At Jeff's signal, the mourners started sobbing, grimacing and covering their eyes with great emotion. Jeff watched them intensely. Something was not right.

"Hold it, hold it," he hollered and instantly everyone stopped. "There is too much on this end and not enough in the middle."

He then proceeded to rearrange a dozen or so people until he was satisfied. After that, he ran the group through at least five walk-throughs of sorrow. Then he gave them a finger signal to watch for upon which the emotion of sorrow, at a strategic point during the service as determined by the expert team, was to be displayed.

"Now, this is a little more difficult," Jeff said. "Let's emote rapture. It's rapture, now. Okay. Get set! Ready! Go!"

The participants all looked up at Jeff with the eyes of the faithful at the scene of a Second Coming. There was some technical adjustment in that scene to be made, but not as extensive as the first emotion. Nevertheless, Jeff consulted with Mutt and repeated the emotion three more times. The crowd responded wonderfully, I thought, almost as well as any group of professional actors and actresses I had seen on TV at the McMillers. I was impressed with the acting ability of ordinary Americans to manufacture intense emotion on such short notice. Jeff again identified the finger signal to be given for rapture's proper moments.

The third emotion was what Jeff called 'constant solemnness' as the all-purpose expression when the specific signals were absent. From my evaluation, this constant solemnness, as it went through several repeats, seemed to be a lower-energy level of sorrow that was rehearsed first. Jeff skillfully randomized slightly varying expressions throughout the crowd to maximize the effect. It was wonderful to see the way he mixed the mourners, so that the more effective ones were seated among the less effective to make their conduct stand out on TV. Obviously, Jeff knew that everyone doing the same mourning act all at once lessened the dramatic effect.

Jeff had two more, what seemed like highly technical, emotional displays aimed at two specific points of the service. One was when the student's name was announced and the other when the father was presented with a check from the University. Certain participants, perhaps old hands in this game, were selected to lead the first scene of great emotional trauma (some went too far, and Jeff had to tone them down) and also the second scene of final resolution.

Jeff suggested to the rest of the participants that sobbing was appropriate at any time during the service, and demonstrated the proper techniques of effective sobbing, after which they practiced the techniques several times. I learned from watching them that sobbing with the TV camera on required a very different set of techniques, which I had not realized, and marveled at the advancement of this industry in America.

Some loose ends having been tied up; the crowd was excused to the dining hall of the union building for their early lunch. But the speakers, Dean Nettor, McMiller and the preacher who had just joined, remained for a final strategy session. Mutt applied some makeup on the three participants.

"Do something about the bag under my left eye," the dean requested, to which Mutt responded with expert touching up until both were satisfied.

"Does anyone of you need an artificial tear-maker?" Jeff inquired and everyone said no. "How about a sinus-congester?"

They all said no again. Then their skull session lasted for at least thirty more minutes. Finally, they were released from the rehearsal to have their lunch.

"They know their business, don't they?" I ventured my opinion, referring to the Mutt and Jeff team, in genuine admiration.

"They sure do," McMiller said. "They are making a bundle by selling videotapes on how to emote properly. They have all sorts of tapes showing appropriate emotions for all occasions. Some of them, like how to emote at birthday parties of your superiors, at funerals for your pets, how to look sincere and advance in life, and so on, have become bestsellers. In fact, these emotional techniques have become so popular that we Americans now are probably the greatest acting population in the world. Bureaucrats, waiters and waitresses, teachers, salespeople, even housewives and kids maintain a good library of those emotion videotapes."

"Why?" I inquired in some puzzlement, however. "What happened to real emotion?"

"Who can tell what's real and what's not real?" McMiller said, chewing on his food in earnest. "In the last two, three decades of television, Americans have learned how to behave under what circumstances. They learned to express joy and rapture from the game shows where the winner is supposed to jump up and down in ecstasy. They learned the proper expressions of sorrow and tragedy by watching the families of terrorist hostages and the president of the United States at funerals. They learned the somber, serious manners of importance from politicians at press conferences. They also learned the proper ways of expressing and making love from TV commercials and expert testimonials. How does a parent know the proper techniques of hugging a child? Why, from television, of course."

"Then, how does anyone know what's proper behavior in America?"

"The best way to know if anything is proper is if the behavior under consideration reminds you of a scene from television. Remember, of course you don't, in the seventies and eighties how Americans used to judge if anything was real and authentic?"

"How?"

"They used to say, 'Why, it was just like on TV!' as a measure of realness and authenticity. Unless it reminded them of a scene from a TV show, people generally didn't think it was true. You know, toward the eighties, it got so that most Americans thought only the ballplayers and actors and preachers were real because they were always seen on TV and believed in them, while ignoring their own kids and spouses as inconsequential."

"But what they are doing now, I mean Mutt and Jeff—"

"What they are doing is, which is incidentally done all over the United States, really a natural development of our past. And a good service to people too. If you are not properly brought up by your parents or guardians, which most Americans nowadays aren't, how are you going to know what to do under what circumstances?"

"Is there anybody left in America who is real and whose emotion is not faked or coached?"

"I don't know," McMiller said with consternation. "Perhaps some of those under TIW 50 maybe. And—"

"And who else?"

Before he could say more, Dean Nettor appeared from the crowd. "The rehearsal went really well, don't you think?" the dean said.

"I think it did," McMiller agreed. "I think it will be a first-class production, no doubt."

"I called the president and told him about it. He is very happy with the preparation."

With that assessment, the dean left us in a hurry to talk to someone else in the crowd.

"You were saying," I reminded McMiller when we faced each other again, "some of those under TIW 50 and—"

"Oh," he concentrated on his thought. "I was going to say, perhaps the Anthropolitans."

"Anthropolitans?"

The mysterious letter-writers from Anthropolis whom Carol McMiller apparently "supported."

"Who are these Anthropolitans?"

McMiller took a sip of his coffee with an air of strong disinterest.

"There is a small area, actually the size of a fair city, about half a day's drive from here, called Anthropolis and the residents of that place are generally known as Anthropolitans."

"Who are they? Are they Americans?"

"They are Americans all right," he said. "But from the way they live and think, you wouldn't believe they are Americans at all."

"Why?"

"They don't believe in the American way of life, for one thing. They object to virtually everything that America stands for. They are in a way extreme social deviants, much more so, if you forgive me, than those under TIW 50. At least these people accept the American way of life, they are just poor. But the Anthropolitans are much more extreme than the poor."

"To what do they object, more specifically?"

"Everything. The business model, the laws of demand and supply. The principle of the marketplace. American individualism. You name it. Anything that has made America great they object to and disdain, if you can believe it. You would think the sole purpose of their existence is to do exactly opposite of the American Way of Life. They reject everything and withdraw into their little tiny hole. Dale Flynn did a study and wrote a paper about them one time.

He called them Bohemian derelicts, hippies, decadents, drop-outs, and other assortments of undesirable characters. Many Americans are delighted that they congregate there, and were relieved when that parcel of land was set aside for them some years ago, just like an Indian reservation."

"How do they live, the Anthropolitans?"

"That's one interesting thing about them, though. They claim to have founded a utopia there in Anthropolis, if you can believe it. Incidentally, Anthropolis means the City of Humanity. A lot of social scientists, like Flynn for example, are openly skeptical about them, if not outright hostile. But understandably so, wouldn't you say? I don't care for them too much one way or another. They don't bother me and I don't bother them. But you can see why some people would be nervous about the Anthropolitan claim of a perfect community."

I was waiting for him to say that his contract-wife was a supporter of Anthropolitans, but McMiller did not mention Carol's connection.

"Are there any Anthropolitan-sympathizers among your social circle?" I asked tactfully. "I mean, the judge, the commissioner, for example. Or the faculty at the university?"

"Maybe Robert I. Lee, who may very well be a closet Anthropolitan because he is very unhappy about American society as it is now. The others on the faculty, I would doubt very much any one of them would be sympathetic. Among my social friends outside the university, absolutely none."

"Would the Anthropolitans be equivalent to the former Communists? I mean the stigma, the community antagonism, the social ostracism, and so on. You know, even in the seventies and eighties no respectable American ever admitted being a Communist or being a Communist-sympathizer. From what I understand, it was thought to be an awful thing in those days to be known as—"

"I would say it's fairly close," McMiller said uncertainly. "Perhaps more stigmatized than the Communists in those days, bless them they are our best trading partners now, or perhaps less. Fairly close, I should say."

Did he know about Carol? Would he have mentioned it if he had known that? Perhaps he didn't know. Perhaps he didn't think it significant enough to mention the fact. Perhaps, perhaps not. I wanted to know more about the Anthropolitans. Would Carol tell me about them?

Then McMiller told me a few things about Lee from the viewpoint of a colleague. I was surprised to hear a tone of personal affection and professional admiration coming from him for the unhappy philosopher. McMiller described some of Lee's 'outrageously original' books on America, which, despite their 'critical' and 'damning' nature or perhaps because of it, were completely ignored by most people, including his own colleagues. His comments reminded me of the way Cecil had compared one hour of Lee's teaching to a hundred hours by his colleagues.

"That sort of thinking went out of style years ago," McMiller said of his colleague, not without sympathy. "People don't want criticisms. They want everything sweetened with much praise and flattery. Robert Isaiah Lee sounds at times almost like his namesake in the Old Testament—prophetic, relentless, and yes, absolutely true. Few can stand any part of reality in America today, and that's why Lee's days at the University are numbered. Either you play it their way, or you are destroyed."

Then, somewhat departing from his usual indifferent look, he said: "One thing Americans have always detested and, shall I say, more accurately, *feared*, is being criticized by someone, especially by someone who is morally superior to them. I doubt if Jesus Christ himself could do any better."

I was going to mention Randy Parrish to my friend when, as the hour of the service approached, Mutt and Jeff re-emerged into the dining hall and announced that within the next minute or so we should finish our lunch and return to the courtyard. In fact, there were not many left in the dining hall. The majority had already finished their lunch and returned to their assigned seats. McMiller and I rose from our table and returned to the scene of impending emotion.

The TV people were already there fully operational and ready to go. The empty space between the folding chairs and the walls were now filled with people, mostly secretaries and lesser faculty members, standing in a three-row or so thick circle. The family, apparently two sisters and three brothers, but no mother, led by the father, sat in the front row that Mutt and Jeff had arranged for them. They were sniffling, especially the two sisters, which I judged to be a mild level of sobbing. Jeff watched them with a professional eye and, after offering a couple of minor adjustments and being satisfied with their improved level of performance, turned his attention to the others.

Dean Nettor, McMiller and the preacher with a fine beard sat close to the family. I stood near a window where I could see the secretaries from the nearby offices who peered through the second-floor windows. The stage was set for the memorial for one Hugh Seago.

Chapter Eighteen

Dean Nettor, the main speaker, also acted as the master of ceremonies.

"Hugh Seago was an excellent student, an exemplary young man of his generation," the dean spoke slowly and deliberately. "Everything he did as a member of this University he did in wonderfully average form. He never asked difficult questions, never confronted difficult issues, and never called for difficult tasks. He was our model student that we should all be proud of."

Then the dean proceeded with a list of his academic courses in which he had obtained a 'C' average, and started reading the list. Business 101. Business 103. Business 108. Business 200. Business 202. Business 208. Business 251. Business 298. Business 301. Business 305. Business 310. Business 338. Business 351. Business 371. Business 380. Business 399. Business 401. Business 405. Business 410. Business 414. Business 420 incomplete due to death, but maintaining a C average at the time. Business 425 incomplete due to death, but maintaining a C average at the time. Business 475...

The dean read off the Stocks and Bonds courses Hugh Seago had taken at the University. Stocks and Bonds 101. Stocks and Bonds 103, and so on. There were also courses on Effective Emoting and Business Evolution in which the student received C's.

Dean Nettor would have read some more if it hadn't been a signal received from Jeff that it was getting close to the limit of the crowd's attention span. He had been speaking for almost six minutes.

"Hugh was a wonderful member of the University in which all administrators, faculty and students form a large family, a true, loving family," he resumed his speech after putting down the list of the deceased's academic mediocrity.

At that precise moment, Jeff gave a hand signal to the main participants on the folding chairs, upon which they went into a magnificent re-enactment of sorrow that they had perfected a while ago. The TV cameras zoomed on the sorrowful crowd and the scene lasted for about thirty seconds, which, I learned later, was equivalent to thirty minutes in real life.

"I remember..." The dean then went into a personal reverie of his own college days, which had little to do with the matter at hand.

Jeff recognized the crisis and gave a frantic hand signal for rapture. The crowd immediately responded by producing the most effective performance of the faithful gathered at their leader's resurrection. Their eyes shone with light, faces looking up for meaning in life, hands clasped in the knowledge of higher spirits, mouths gaping open for the breath of truth and destiny. The TV cameras got busy again.

Through all this McMiller managed to give me a smile once in a while as if saying that everything was going all right. But the crowd was becoming edgy, for the dean had been speaking now for close to nine minutes. Finally, Dean Nettor brought his reverie to a conclusion and realized the purpose of the service at hand.

"The university family is truly sad at the untimely death of Hugh Seago," the dean said. "But there is a silver-lining behind every dark cloud."

With that dramatic and portentous remark, he searched inside his breast pocket and brought out an envelope. He opened the envelope carefully in the manner of a prize announcer on television and pulled out what appeared to be a check.

"This is a million-dollar check," the master of ceremonies told the crowd while holding up the check for everyone to see. There were hoots and whistles, upon which Dean Nettor gave a benign smile of acknowledgement. "Yes, it is a lot of money, no doubt. And—(pregnant pause)—we are very proud to present this check in the amount of one million dollars for the death of Hugh Seago to his loving father Mr. Adam Seago."

As Mr. Seago rose to accept the check the whole family started sobbing. Taking advantage of this situation, Jeff signaled the main participants to start sobbing too. There arose a chorus of sobbing, some mixed with wailing from the general crowd, which echoed with melancholia within the walls of the quadrangle. The techniques had been perfectly executed as taught by the Mutt and Jeff team of experts. TV cameras got busy again. Mr. Seago carefully folded the check and put it in his wallet and placed the wallet in his inside coat pocket. He felt it a couple of times to make sure it was secure, and sat down among his family to join the crowd in sobbing.

When McMiller's turn came, he walked to the podium and simply announced that the whole faculty of the University bemoaned the passing of such an outstanding average student, and he was asked by the faculty to read a poem for the deceased. He held in his hand a sheet of paper upon which the poem was written.

Calling it 'a poem by an anonymous poet', his booming voice began to fill the quadrangle:

Do not stand at my grave and weep:
I am not there; I do not sleep.
I am a thousand winds that blow,
I am the diamond glints on snow.
I am the sunlight on ripened grain. I am the gentle autumn rain.
When you awaken in the morning's hush, I am the swift uplifting rush.
Of quiet birds in circled flight, I am the soft stars that shine at night.
Do not stand at my grave and cry: I am not there; I did not die.

McMiller's voice was resonant and his poem deeply moving. I watched Mutt and Jeff and they looked quite uncertain as to the effect of this old-fashioned rendition. In an age of graphic television and visual images, the effects of poetic words were apparently difficult to judge.

Then the bereaved family did an unexpected thing. The two girls and three boys stood up and clapped wildly at McMiller who was putting the poem back in his pocket. There is nothing like the spontaneity of applause to ignite an uncertain crowd. The whole inner section and the general public lining up against the four walls erupted and joined the family in the cheering. Even Adam Seago, feeling his coat pocket one more time, stood up with his children and cheered. The TV cameras of course recorded it all. It was a wonderful moment for the service. McMiller, at the moment of his unexpected triumph, looked somewhat embarrassed, which I believed was absolutely unrehearsed.

The appearance of the preacher was anticlimactic after McMiller. He gave a standard speech about life and death, and Mutt and Jeff had to use the hand signals frequently to get the crowd responses going. The main emoting section did well, missing the signal only once, upon which one section sobbed and the other did rapture. Within the next few seconds, both sections realized the mistake and got their acts together by synchronizing their performances.

When we thought, and certainly the preacher thought because he was about to offer his final prayer, that the service was over, Dean Nettor, who had disappeared through the main door, dashed back in and whispered something into the preacher's ear. The preacher rolled his eyes to heaven and said, "Hallelujah!" and stepped aside to make room for the dean.

"Ladies and gentlemen," the dean said in his most dramatic manner possible. "I can honestly say that we are a complete family because no member has been lost."

Everyone, even the Seagos, looked around, puzzled.

"Ladies and gentlemen," the dean said loudly to be heard above the buzzing crowd and, flinging his arm toward the main entrance, declared: "I am proud to introduce to you one and only—Hugh Seago!"

A deathly silence came upon the crowd, which seemed to last into eternity. Into this utter silence of the courtyard a young man made his appearance through the entrance. He walked to the dean and stood next to him. The family gasped. "HUGH!"

The young man smiled as the family rushed toward him and hugged him wildly. Realizing the meaning of this new epiphany, the crowd cheered happily.

"Isn't he a splitting image of the real Hugh?" a woman standing next to me turned and said. She looked like a secretary who knew the university business fairly well.

I said I wouldn't know; I had never met the deceased.

"He must have been delivered just now," the secretary said in amazement. "Because they contacted the insurance company only yesterday afternoon. Great job they did. In less than twenty-four hours, they trained somebody so fast. Marvelous."

The dean, beaming with pride, calmed the crowd down. The family and the substitute Hugh Seago all sat in the family row. Quiet returned to the quadrangle once again.

"Given such a short time we had to work with," Dean Nettor said. "We are so lucky to have been delivered this young man who is every bit as real as the real Hugh Seago was only two days ago."

The dean allowed the family some more fussing with the stand-in before resuming. "The University is also proud to announce that the president has authorized a period of six months for the young man to stay with his Seago family. We hope that six months will be enough for the family to put the grief and shock of losing Hugh behind and get back to their normal lives."

The crowd rose to cheer once again and the preacher had a tough time putting in his benediction. All the while Mr. Seago kept touching his coat pocket. For the TV cameras, the whole show was a smashing hit. The knowledgeable woman next to me cried uncontrollably.

"Wasn't it a beautiful service?" she said through her tears. "Wasn't it a wonderful service? Oh, it was so real, so real, so wonderful."

I drove home alone, feeling somewhat exhausted from the experience. Although I hadn't been directly involved in the event, their various turns of emotion had impressed me as so authentic that I couldn't help but share the wave of affecting joy, almost agreeing with the secretary. McMiller had to stay over at the university to discuss some administrative matters with the dean and the Mutt and Jeff team.

When I got home, I found Carol in her studio. Even before I reached the studio, I heard the chattering of a typewriter inside. While debating whether I should interrupt or not, the typewriter stopped for a while, so I decided to knock.

"Cecil?" she called out.

"No, me, Michael. Cecil had to remain on campus for some more business to take care of. Am I interrupting something?"

She said, no, and opened the door for me to come in. She had been typing something on her small desk. There were sheets of typing paper strewn nearby.

"I hope I didn't interrupt," I said again.

"I was about to have a break, anyway," Carol said. "How was the memorial service? Sorry I didn't attend."

I briefly summarized the happenings of the day at the courtyard. She nodded in comprehension. Then I asked her what she had been up to.

"I was trying to finish up a novel that I had started some time ago," she said modestly.

"A novel?"

"A small story, actually, perhaps a novella rather than a novel."

"What's the title? What is it about?"

"It's called *God's Honest Truth*," she said. "It's about whether God could get elected God in the United States if the election were held today."

I looked at her quizzically. I hadn't known that Carol was also a writer, much less on a subject as potent and ambivalent with meaning as that. Carol explained that she had written many short stories before and *God's Honest Truth*, the longest one yet she had ever attempted, was inspired while reading Henry David Thoreau.

"Thoreau wrote somewhere," she explained. "That if the devil were elected God in America, the majority of people would go along with the election. I thought it was an interesting idea and tried to develop a story along that idea."

She showed me a fairly thick folder with typewritten sheets in it indicating that it was her manuscript. She had only one chapter to go, she said.

"It's an interesting question, isn't it?" Carol said when I remained silent, trying to digest the significance of my new discovery, and as if to herself: "Could God get elected God in America if the election were held today?"

"Who is running against him?"

"The Devil," she said.

Whenever they couldn't understand something, my students in Laurinville used to say that it was way over their heads. I must confess I was tempted to say that the subject seemed way over my head. God and the Devil running against each other to get elected God of the United States? It was too fascinating and too fraught with pitfalls that my mind, basically framed in the limited simplicity of life in Laurinville and its history, could not easily grasp.

"Could He?" I finally asked. "Could He get elected?"

"Of course, that depends on what He does to get elected, such as campaign strategies, advertising slogans, political promises, whether they would choose to use the merit-vote option, and so on."

"I would imagine so. If He would use all his mighty powers, no one could beat Him, right? After all, He is God already."

"But," said Carol, showing an increasing interest in talking about her ideas with someone, "God cannot use tricks or money or false promises with which to impress people, simply because He is God."

"What else can a God use then to persuade people to vote for Him?"

"Well, I would think the only thing that He has that is His essence: Truth. Hence the title of the book," Carol said. "Truth, the whole truth, nothing but the truth, so help me God."

The weighty issue of God and man was briefly interrupted by Carol's lighthearted joke.

"Can He get elected just by telling the truth, promising nothing and giving away nothing?" I wondered aloud.

"Well, that's what the book is about," the modest author said.

I asked if she would permit me to read the manuscript. She was reluctant at first, on the ground that it was unfinished. But, fatal to all writers and artists, her curiosity about my reaction won her over and she agreed to show me the unfinished manuscript. Then she handed me the folder that contained the manuscript.

"By the way," I said, changing the subject. "What can you tell me about the Anthropolitans?"

"Anthropolitans?" she repeated the word as if she was hearing it for the first time. She looked at me uncertainly without responding further.

I told her that I had accidentally seen the letter from Anthropolis addressed to her and heard from Cecil a brief description of that strange city and its inhabitants.

"From what I heard," I assured her. "They seem to be an interesting lot."

"Did you mention to Cecil about my association with the Anthropolitans?"

I said no.

"Not that it would have any earth-shaking consequences," Carol said quietly. "But I would want to be the person to tell him that. I don't know how he would react when he heard it, though."

"Basically, live and let live?" I suggested.

"I don't know."

"Could you tell me a little about them?" I prodded.

With a sigh she opened a drawer of her work desk and pulled out a small document the size of a weekly magazine. On the cover it said, "ALL ABOUT ANTHROPOLIS."

"The Anthropolitans publish this magazine once in a while, but most Americans wouldn't get caught dead reading this. It tells you what's going on in Anthropolis and what the Anthropolitans are all about from their point of view."

"Were you reading this yesterday when I entered here?"

She nodded.

"Can I borrow this magazine too?" I asked. "I won't show it to any single soul, I promise."

She thought about it for a long moment. "Not even Jeanne Baker," she said it as a statement, "at least for now."

"Not even Jeanne Baker," I repeated solemnly.

So, our conspiracy was hatched. Carol relaxed with me more visibly from that moment on as if she had decided that I was a trustworthy character.

"Tell me, Carol," I said. "How often do you visit Anthropolis?"

"About once every month or so," she said. "Otherwise, I communicate with them through a special system of couriers."

"Are there a lot of Anthropolitan-sympathizers in Wilmington?"

"I don't know what would be considered a lot," she said. "But enough to keep an underground network going in this area."

I stood up with the materials I borrowed from her securely tucked under my arm, anxious to get started with them.

I stopped at the door and turned around.

"Can I visit the place?" I inquired.

She took a few seconds before responding.

"Perhaps," she said.

Chapter Nineteen

'ALL ABOUT ANTHROPOLIS' served as an introduction and an outline of the basic philosophy of Anthropolis. It began as an idea among a small group of unhappy Americans, unhappy with what they regarded as dehumanizing possibilities of a pecuniocratic society. As it gathered momentum and more followers, it had eventually grown to be the semi-autonomous state of existence that it was currently maintaining.

According to the magazine, the Anthropolitans claimed that self-interest was the basis of all social evil, and happiness was doing things for others, which ended up with and the everyone doing things for one another. To put this philosophy into effect, they practiced strict community ownership of all property. They insisted that all Anthropolitans work no more than three hours a day and still enjoy all the material freedoms one needed for civilized and comfortable living among fellowmen. A communal warehouse, of which the literature showed a photograph, contained all daily necessities and was located virtually within easy reaches of all Anthropolitans.

They claimed that no one got wealthy in Anthropolis, but no one was ever fired from his job or went hungry. Family life was also communal, children being raised by the whole community and the task being shared by all Anthropolitan adults. More incredibly, the Anthropolitans had no particular school curriculum, every child learning at his own pace by the guidance of an adult rather than a teacher.

Their 'university' had no professors, no students, no administrators, and most amazing of all, no classes: Everyone learned and studied at all times without these organizational structures. The magazine claimed, however, that Anthropolis contained thirty-five times as many scientists, artists and writers per capita as the population of the rest of the United States.

My inquiry into their marriage system was met with the strange fact that they had no marriages. They insisted that marriage was nothing but a way to subjugate women by men, in the same way the strong subjugate the weak in politics, and the rich controlling the poor in economics, therefore worked against human nature and happiness. Since marriage neither elevated nor lowered the standing of all Anthropolitans, they saw no reason to tie two individuals in love to a shackle called marriage. What was important, they said, was love, not marriage. I wondered if Jeanne Baker would agree to this idea.

Some photographs showed the Anthropolitans enjoying their leisure activities. All leisure and play activities in Anthropolis, the literature emphasized, had to be in group activities. There was no TV in the house. But frequent concerts and sports events encouraged everyone to participate. Even within each 'household' of about fifteen to twenty persons, there were constant musical performances and poetry readings.

The Anthropolitans strongly discouraged solitary enjoyment of life because, the magazine explained, solitary life was always the basis of corruption of the mind. All human beings, they emphasized, could live only as 'social' beings in a human 'community'.

What was interesting to me particularly was the way they elected their community leaders. Only the highly learned people were allowed to select from among the scholars the ones they deemed most virtuous and wisest. Since no one ever gained any material or political advantage over anyone else, the elections always resulted in choosing the very best among them as leaders of all Anthropolitans. They rejected the vote-buying practices in the United States where only the wealthy and ambitious could occupy political office, and claimed their own system was more democratic.

Reading 'ALL ABOUT ANTHROPOLIS' I wasn't sure if I would like this City of Humanity. But it did not seem as terrible as most American critics maintained. Some of their ideas aroused my curiosity and I very much wanted to visit the place myself. I was resolved to make the trip, either alone or with Jeanne, as soon as possible.

God's Honest Truth, as Carol had described it, was a small but interesting cautionary tale on America. As I read it, I was surprised to find that it was a veiled criticism of contemporary American society. Her points seemed to be that, given the social, economic and cultural conditions of the United States, Americans were not likely to elect God as their universal god if the election between Him and the Devil were held today. It was written in simple fable-like prose that seemed to have been favored by traditional writers of such stories.

The story began with the Devil challenging the Lord God of the Universe to a democratic election, and this is how the first two chapters went.

Chapter One

"Dr. George Dunlap is here to see you, Master," the servant announced, bending low with his courteous bow.

The servant was good at it because he had always been a servant in his other life. The Master, Lord of Hell, sitting majestically in his customary throne on the shiny hot marble floor, looked at the servant. He was a young man, one of the new additions to the place. He was always wearing a three-piece suit, the same one he had worn the day he died, carrying a briefcase which he used to carry for his employer in his former life. He was the kind of man who served any master without complaining and this new assignment suited him just fine.

In Hell, people remain exactly the way they looked when they died and, seeing the servant always with the briefcase, the Devil sometimes wondered what was in the briefcase which he carried so devotedly.

"Oh, yes," the Devil remembered. "Send him in."

The Devil started twisting his mustache and humming a tune when a man of perhaps late sixties, the age at which he had died, walked through the gate.

But, instead of coming straight to the Master of Hell, the doctor stopped at the gate and put some questions to the gatekeeper and, getting answers, scribbled them down to his data book, nodding as he did so. Dr. George Dunlap used to be a poll-taker in his other life and could not resist asking questions anytime he had a chance to. He finally walked over to the Devil and bowed.

"The results of your latest poll are in, Master," the former poll-taker said. "For the most part, they are exactly as we anticipated, with a margin of error of three percent."

Dr. George Dunlap had been made the Devil's official pollster and used his expertise with professional efficiency, which pleased his master.

"Tell me what your poll says, Doctor," the Devil said and stopped twisting his mustache to concentrate on what the doctor had to say. He had stopped humming some time ago. After all, it was important for him to know what the inhabitants of Hell wanted. The polls were taken frequently to better serve their wishes. The Devil believed in giving them what they wanted, that made living in Hell a lot more fun.

Dr. Dunlap consulted his data book.

"The demand for violence is up by fifteen percent," the polltaker said.

"I have taken the liberty of notifying the Entertainment Department to increase the dosage of violence by that much."

"Good job, Dr. Dunlap," the Devil said, shifting in his throne with satisfaction. "After all, what's Hell without violence? They shall get what they want, I've always said. No one shall be unhappy in my kingdom. Go on."

The good doctor continued his report on the wishes of Hell inhabitants. Generally, it appeared that the actual results had confirmed what the poll-taker had predicted. Demand for certain items, such as alcohol and blood, were up and certain other items, such as paint brushes and books, were down. Loud music and junk food, the doctor noticed, remained fairly steady. From time to time, the doctor reported what actions he had taken to give the inhabitants what they wanted, and the Devil approved them heartily.

"Give them anything they want," the Master of Hell declared. "More violence, more blood, anything else they demand, they shall get. This is a place where all demand is supplied, isn't it, doctor?"

"Yes, Master," agreed the poll-taker, bowing. "But there is something else in the results that I had not anticipated at all."

"Oh?" the Devil became serious. "A demand not anticipated?"

"Yes, Master."

"Well, doctor, what is it?"

The doctor hesitated a moment, then consulted his data book before speaking. "A new question was put to them," said the doctor.

"What new question?"

"The question, in the spirit of your democratic kingdom. Master. was: Do you approve the master, Lord of Hell, as your absolute master of the underworld?"

The Devil eyed the doctor critically for a long moment. "All right," he said finally. "What does the poll say?"

"An overwhelming majority of those polled, over ninety-five percent, answered yes," Dr. Dunlap said consulting his data book. "But there is something else in it."

"What?" the Devil asked impatiently. One of the many virtues he lacked was his patience, which often made him act like a spoiled child.

Dr. Dunlap was more hesitant this time. "The same majority wants you," he said very carefully. "To be God of all of the Universe, God of Everything, not just Hell."

"Are you sure about that, Doctor," the Devil inquired. "I mean the percentage?"

"Yes, Master. I am absolutely sure," the doctor said, bowing slightly.

The Devil went back to his mustache-twisting and humming, but added tapping his fingers on the sides of his throne. Doing all three meant he was thinking very seriously, which he seldom did.

He finally came to a conclusion. "I can't do that," he said modestly. He was somewhat shy about the idea even though the inhabitants of his kingdom wanted it. "I can't challenge the Lord God directly, how can I? God knows, if you pardon my pun, I have done enough mischief to last my lifetime in this Hell. Proclaiming myself as God of the Universe would be too much, I am sure of it."

"Master," said the pollster. "I am not a politician. I only report what people say, and they have almost unanimously demanded that you should be God. Besides, you are forever condemned to Hell, what have you got to lose by trying?"

The Devil continued his three acts simultaneously, only doing them more thoughtfully than before. "Hmmmmm—" he contemplated deeply on the wishes of his kingdom. "I guess they are somewhat tired of their master being the second banana, with all the abuses heaped on him, relegated to this Hell. You know those who live in Heaven have no respect for our place down here at all."

"I wouldn't be sure about that, Master," the doctor said humbly. "I haven't taken any polls in Heaven and I don't know what their attitude toward us might be."

The Devil ignored the poll-taker's comment as irrelevant.

"People seem to think it's about time you stood up to those high above, Master," Dr. Dunlap volunteered, peering at his data book as if the data book were speaking to him.

"If I ever decided to do that," the Devil said with considerable interest now. "How do you think I should go about it, Doctor? I mean, challenging the Lord

God for the title of God of the Universe? You helped many politicians before, didn't you?"

"Yes, Master," the poll-taker bowed again. "I helped many candidates get elected using my strategies."

"Can you help me now?" the Devil demanded.

"If I were you, Master, I would argue one point in which the Lord God is somewhat weak," Dr. Dunlap said as if he had already given the subject a lot of thought.

"But He is the Lord God. He has no weakness," the Devil insisted.

"There is one, Master," the poll-taker said, and he paused dramatically. "His weakness is His inability to lie. The Lord God must tell the truth at all times. *You* can lie, cheat and steal, Master, and bend the truth to suit your purpose if you forgive me for saying so, but He cannot. That, my Master, is His weakness."

"I would agree with you on that, doctor," the Devil said, feeling somewhat optimistic. "But how would that help my career?"

"This is what you do, Master." The doctor moved closer to his master and whispered the strategy.

As he listened to his poll-taker, the Devil's face, already as red as fire in Hell, got redder, which was a sign that he was excited. Mischief always excited him, and this time it was the biggest mischief he or anyone else ever dreamed of before. He nodded and nodded, and his face became redder and redder as he listened to his strategist for challenging the Lord God. The Master of Hell lost no time once the decision was made, for he was not the brooding type. He made an appointment to see the Lord God in Heaven, at once.

Chapter Two

"What does the Devil want this time?" The Lord God asked no one in particular.

A young girl near Him playing her harp shrugged as if saying, "No idea, Lord." She had worked as a harpist at a fancy restaurant in New York, and she loved to play the harp which happened to be the most common instrument in Heaven. Just about everyone in Heaven played the harp.

The Devil did not ask for an audience with Him too often, but, when he did, it was always about some complaints from Hell. The inhabitants of Hell wanted this, that and the other. The list was often endless. Even for the Lord God whose patience was infinite it was sometimes hard to listen to it all.

The Lord God looked around at his Heaven. Its inhabitants, aside from playing the harp, were engaged in all sorts of activities at the moment. Some were testing their wings, perhaps new ones, by flapping them against each other. Others were taking a leisurely walk on the clouds. Everything was fairly peaceful and quiet as Heaven normally is. Not much else ever happened here.

"What does the Devil want this time?" He asked again. When no one around him volunteered anything about the intended visit by the Master of Hell, the Lord God decided to leave the scene.

"Well," He said to Himself. "I guess I will go and see the Devil, although I don't want to." With that, the Lord God walked to His office in Heaven where the Devil was waiting to see Him.

"My Lord," said the Devil as he bowed with a flourish, which always irritated the Lord God who did not like elaborate curtsies. Although the Master of Hell was in his best red suit, shiny and well pressed and appearing extremely respectable, the Lord God knew that the Devil was never sincere about matters of courtesy. In fact, he was never sincere about anything. After all, the Lord God told Himself, what do you expect from the Devil but clever insincerity?

"Yes, what is it this time?" the Lord God asked, looking down from His throne.

The Devil looked up and smiled. He was uglier when he was smiling, showing his crooked teeth, made sharper from years of tearing into the flesh of his victims. The Lord God sometimes regretted that He had ever created the Devil, although he performed a certain function with efficiency.

"My Lord," the Devil bowed in his ingratiating best. "It is about you that I came here to see you." He was still smiling. The Devil was up to something devilish.

"About me?" the Lord God was puzzled. Even He didn't always know what was on the Devil's mind.

"Yes, my Lord," the Devil said, standing erect on his legs as if showing his full resolve. Of course, it took a lot of nerve and gusto to challenge the Lord God of the Universe.

"Tell me about it," the Lord God said, curious. He had heard many complaints from the Devil before, but it was absolutely the first time that He Himself was the subject of the Devil's complaint.

"My Lord," the Devil said. "You are the Lord God of Everything. The whole world below worships and adores you. They do everything in your name.

You appear on everything including American money, which says, 'In God We Trust.' So many things are done in the name of your wishes."

"Well, I suppose so," the Lord God said matter-of-factly. What is this Devil driving at? "What about it? I can't do anything about people worshipping and adoring me. After all, I am their God, aren't I?"

"That's precisely the point, my Lord," the Devil said. "All that is wonderful, my Lord. But have you ever been officially elected to the position of the Lord God by the people who worship you and adore you?"

The Lord God thought about it for a while. To be truthful, the principle of democracy had never occurred to Him as far as His position was concerned. Come to think of it, He had rather taken it for granted that He was the Lord God of the Universe. Certainly no one had ever challenged Him on that. Until today.

"I guess not," the Lord God said after giving it some more thought. "But what is your point, you Devil?"

"My Lord," the Devil took his deepest bow yet. "Considering the progress of the Universe, all the wonderful things you have created between Heaven and Earth, all the learning that has been made possible, and all the happiness man has been able to enjoy with your blessings, don't you think it is about time that the office of the Lord God of the Universe were put to the test of a democratic election so that your supremacy can be reaffirmed by the electoral process and legitimated once and for all?"

So, the story began. God and the Devil stipulated that they would come down to the United States as the testing ground because it was the most godly nation of all, according to the number of churches per capita and people who identified themselves as 'believers of God'.

They were disguised in human form as Mr. Smith and Mr. Jones to begin their electoral process. Further stipulated, rather in favor of the Devil on grounds that the Lord God had enjoyed a certain advantage over the Devil, was that God would materialize as a highly unattractive man whereas the Devil would be an appealingly handsome devil. Their contest was announced by some heavenly edict in all newspapers and television networks of the world.

The most significant element of the story was the fact that God could not lie. His only campaign weapon, as He promised the Devil, was that he would be telling the truth while the Devil, being a devil, was allowed to use any tricks in the book to win popularity. Thus, severely handicapped by truth and ugly appearance, however, God confidently consented to test His acceptance by the American electorate.

Their celestial contest, of course, became the greatest news since the Creation, and every God-fearing American, from both the left and the right, was gearing up for the greatest reception of all time for the descending God. The federal government, with the help of Hollywood and Disney Corporation, provided an elaborate stage upon which God was to materialize.

With the whole world watching, the president of the United States rushed to the handsome one, naturally assuming that the hero had to be good-looking, and prostrated himself mistakenly at the grinning Devil. The president kept calling the Devil 'my lord' and assured him that the God-fearing nation of America was at his disposal and that its godly citizens would show the world for all eternity its unequivocal devotion to the Lord God.

The ugly unassuming man, who had been standing quietly in the corner, then stepped forward and told the president that *He* was the Lord God of the Universe. Thereupon the president shamefacedly rushed over to the real God, profusely apologizing for his mistake.

During the seven days in which God and the Devil had agreed to hold their campaigns across the United States, God was constantly handicapped by His promise to tell the truth. People, who had come out in droves to see him, gradually got tired of hearing the truth because it was not what they wanted to hear. The Devil, on the other hand, handsome liar that he was, was telling a lot of sweet nothings and promises that people always wanted to hear.

The public opinion polls, which had been ninety-nine point nine-nine-nine-nine percent pro-God (there were always some cranks), gradually shifted as time and time again God refused to make miracles to satisfy the crowd's largely selfish demands. At one such rally, the crowd unabashedly demanded that all of them be made instant millionaires. God's crowd, enormous in the beginning, gradually dwindled while the Devil was enthralling his followers with tricks, flatteries, spectacles, and all sorts of promises for greater pleasures of life and everything else that Dr. Dunlap had told him as favorites of American voters.

There was a particularly moving scene in the story. God and the Devil were holding a rally on the fifth day or so at a park not too far from each other. Both campaigners were drawing large crowds. Suddenly rain started falling. Both crowds, not having anticipated rain that day, were caught unprepared and immediately demanded that their respective candidates stop the rain. The Devil obliged, turning rain instantly into beautiful sunshine on his side, along with a rainbow for good measure. God, holding fast to His promises with the Devil, refused to heed the popular demand to stop the rain. The result was disastrous for His rally.

One by one, the crowd drifted over to the Devil's sunny side. At the end, only a prostitute, a cripple, and an old beggar remained at God's campaign site. It was a touching moment, as Carol described it, when God spoke the Truth to His now pitifully reduced crowd.

One of the Devil's crowds, a heavyset man with an unruly beard, was interviewed on TV and said, when asked why he had switched over to the Devil instead of getting wet on God's side, "I don't know. I am just trying to go with the winner. It's the American way, isn't it?"

The story went on some more, with the predictable decline of God's popularity with Americans. But to my dismay, forgetting briefly that Carol had already told me, the last chapter was not there. Unhappily, I found myself reduced to raising many questions and getting no answers. Did God after all win the election? Was the Devil the new Lord God of the Universe, at least declared by the American electorate? Or, did the American electorate recover its godly sense in time to recognize the peril of their democratic election?

It was early morning when I finally finished the manuscript.

For another hour or so, however, I could not sleep although I was extremely tired. I stared at the dim early morning images outside my window, thinking about what I had just read.

Chapter Twenty

The novel was a simple fable, which reminded me of George Orwell's *Animal Farm* that I had read as a child. Just like Orwell's, Carol's book meticulously chronicled how a people changed their minds, from enthusiasm to gradual disillusionment at the inability or unwillingness of their savior to satisfy their private demands or fulfill their self-rewarding expectations. Also, like Orwell's, Carol's Americans seemed to demonstrate how precarious, under adverse conditions, human devotions to an idea could be. But above all, to me, it revealed Carol McMiller in a radically different light.

I knew, or sensed it, that she had never wholeheartedly approved the pecuniocratic way of life in America simply because she had never shown any signs or uttered any words that reflected such a frame of mind. In fact, I had always thought she could just as well fit in my own town of Laurinville, or American society before its pecuniocratic transformation.

But, as simple in the telling and uncluttered in the premises as it was, the book was a devastating critique of her society which, in her gentle satire, was ready to desert God and embrace the Devil as their new god. Coupled with the knowledge of her association with the Anthropolitans, Carol now appeared to me as a woman of uncommon courage and critical faculty.

Did Cecil know about *this* Carol? I wondered. I remember his remark that he had admired her artistic ability as a factor in their contract marriage. Did that include her 'critical' disapproval of American society in a pecuniocratic age? Did Cecil recognize that Art was the closest thing to God's Truth?

When I saw her again late the next morning as I struggled out of slumber, she and Cecil were having coffee. As I joined them at the table with small talk Carol never mentioned her book. Judging from my own experience, I knew that most authors, no matter how exalted, were at least curious about the reader's reaction to their works. Under normal circumstances Carol would have badgered me about what I thought of her novel. But she never mentioned it, at least while Cecil was there. I then assumed then that Cecil didn't know about that part of Carol's artistic life. I decided to wait until she felt ready to discuss it on her own terms. In the next few days, however, I didn't have the chance to talk to her alone.

I spent much of that weekend with Jeanne and Mary Sue. The weather was surprisingly warm for early October and we were able to play on the sand at the beach. Quite a few surfers with their wetsuits on were riding the waves. The pier was crowded with the usual group of fishermen and casual strollers who came out to enjoy the unexpectedly fine weather.

As we became more comfortable with each other's presence my affection for Jeanne was growing stronger, strengthened by my increasing awareness of her intelligence and her fierce sense of selfhood. The years of her hardship in raising Mary Sue alone, while struggling in a pecuniary society with her meager resource, had not dimmed her essentially sunny and optimistic outlook. Mary Sue also became extremely attached to me, and I to her. Jeanne seemed to approve the developing relationship between her daughter and me. More happily, she had received word that her construction company had authorized her use of a company car.

I told Jeanne about Carol and my realization of her artistic and creative talent. I mentioned reading her novel, but did not say anything about her association with the Anthropolitans. I felt that the information should remain private under the circumstances and out of my respect for Carol. But I did tell her that I thought the novel expressed Carol's strong disapproval of her excessively money-rational society. Jeanne agreed that it was excessively attached to a money-philosophy but did not seem to have the kind of intellectually organized disapproval that Carol had articulated in her thought.

Jeanne's view of American society reflected more of her direct experience in life, that something was wrong, rather than as an articulated construction of ideas and institutions. But the two women would have found their feelings about America wholly in agreement with each other's.

Cecil viewed the literally accidental introduction of Jeanne Baker into his friend's life, for whose welfare he thought somewhat responsible, with only passing interest. But he managed to offer me his occasional 'word to the wise' advice about women in general. Carol seemed to like the woman she had never met, yet my enthusiastic description satisfied her as to the woman's character. After all, I was a grownup man with some character-molding encounters with evil forces in the Green Palmers rather early in his life. My own judgment, albeit about a person of the opposite sex, even though always a precarious business, had to be respected.

Early Monday morning I received a call from Judge Roberts' office, reminding me about the 'challenge' case in his court that he had wanted me to come and see. The case, which the parents refused to resolve in one of the commercial courts, thereby docketed at Judge Roberts' government court, was scheduled for two o'clock that afternoon.

I arrived at the courthouse somewhat early, wanting to make sure that I got a good seat because McMiller had reminded me that challenge cases almost always made headlines and were popular with spectators. He said people loved to see the spectacle of parents pitifully fighting to keep their children against the huge machines that wealth could command in its behalf.

Of course, America in 1998 had no public defenders, long ago abolished along with all welfare programs as anti-American. Everyone had to either buy insurance for reasonably competent legal representation or, if too poor to do so, do the best they could with whatever private resources they could muster. It was this reason, as I learned, that the majority of challenge cases, which pitted wealth against poverty, were decided in the challenger's favor.

Not only that, money seemed to have the ability to make *anyone* who had it look good while the opposite was true with the poor. Poverty was not only a source of damned inconveniences, as someone said, but also a damned weight that sank one's moral standing as well.

The American court by then, I learned, had become a place of disputes and settlements primarily for those under TIW's of 50. The affluent Americans, at least with respectable TIW rankings, were well protected with the logger and insurance policies. If caught for violations, they simply paid for their crimes as an honorable way of restitution. It simplified the enormous procedural complications and budgetary expenses.

No longer was the cry of overextended justice heard in the land. It satisfied the civil rightists too, now a small number, who were persuaded that whether poor or wealthy the amount to be paid was always the same. In that sense, the constitutional guarantee of equal justice before the law was deemed now literally perfected in America. Cecil's earlier reference to America as a modest version of 'utopia' seemed to have some validity in reality.

Even a murder, when committed by a wealthy person, could be settled in pecuniary compensation if the family of the victim agreed to the offer from the murderer. In an original landmark case, the court approved the settlement by saying that life had a definite price at the marketplace, and whatever the family deemed a right price for the dead was acceptable to the court. The judge declared that the victim's family, a poor one, was far better served with compensation than with punishing the murderer with imprisonment, a respectable doctor who had killed his nursing assistant with a laser scalpel in a fit of rage.

Following this decision, which was widely regarded as a Solomonesque solution, many poor families of murder victims pursued a financial settlement with the murderer if he happened to be one with a high TIW ranking. "He is already dead, isn't he?" a victim's mother said on TV once. "What good is it going to do us if we send him (the murderer) to an island?"

Most good insurance companies began to underwrite that clause, commonly known as 'death insurance' as opposed to the better-known counterpart life insurance, in their insurance policies for the affluent. Poor murderers, which were always the absolute majority among murderers, however, ended up going to one of the criminal islands.

Paying the government for a crime, when a civil settlement was not involved, was officially hailed as a fine civic duty, as a demonstration of patriotism. When some wealthy stock traders, caught for something called 'inside trading', promised to pay millions of dollars for restitution, although a small portion of their ill-gotten gains, they were hailed as true patriots and were invited to the White House for a photo-op. There the president advised the young Americans to look up to the inside traders as their future role models. On the other hand, those who served time on one of the penal islands, even on partial government subsidies, were subject to community ridicule as social parasites.

'PARASITES ON PARADISE' (a takeoff on 'criminals' paradise') was a common label applied to those non-paying ex-convicts. The paying ex-convicts, on the other hand, were called ex-contributors, although sometimes they were both referred to as ex-cons for short, an unfortunate social practice which always made the ex-contributors protest indignantly.

The county circuit court was divided into three divisions and Judge Roberts presided over Division III which took non-criminal cases that couldn't be resolved in commercial courts. Division I tried personal crimes, and economic crimes, such as contractual violations, went to Division II. With my free time, I roamed the courthouse and learned its inner operations from the secretaries and clerks. A man who looked awfully poor and lost in a modern building obviously alien to him mistook me for a lawyer and asked me if I could give him some free legal advice.

As the trial time neared and the crowd began to gather, I positioned myself so that I could get the best view of the scene. The judge's bench was raised above the floor, with the witness stand on his left and the court clerk on his right. The ubiquitous court stenographer was absent because everything was now recorded on a machine. TV cameras, both commercial and private, were visible everywhere. Aside from the regular commercial TV networks, private citizens were now allowed, for a fee, to bring their own TV cameras to record their favorite trials. In fact, video tapes of sensational trials were some of the more favored home entertainment. The trial of a deranged woman who had detailed murdering her three lovers in succession made the video bestseller list only two months before I arrived in North Carolina, I learned later.

The atmosphere was palpably tense in anticipation. The challenged parents looked frail and scared. The mother, a tired looking woman in her early thirties, must have been an attractive woman once, but hard life had aged her prematurely. The father, a housepainter of little consequence, peered around in the courtroom as if looking for a friendly face. Seated next to them was their lawyer, an elderly gentleman with graying hair and comfortable court presence. He appeared to be the kind of lawyer who was conscientious, and even kind to his clients, but never very successful with his career financially. He studied some papers in front of him and spoke to his clients now and then. The mother glanced at her opposite number across the large mahogany table with obvious timidity and apprehension.

Their opposite numbers, wife and husband and their lawyer, on the other hand, exuded confidence and power and affluence, which were the general privileges of high TIW standings in America and they showed it. The woman, of indeterminate age perhaps because of her makeup and possible cosmetic surgery, was a former college cheerleader at the University of Wilmington. Presently a contract-wife, she was dressed fashionably and looked around the courtroom with her chin jutted high, but gracefully. Her husband, the challenger, a heavyset man of about sixty, was reputed to have a TIW index close to 250, normally a multi-millionaire range.

The couple had seen the parents play with their three-year-old son at a park, liked what they saw and decided to challenge the parents. Their lawyer, a jowly man with an air of arrogance mixed with a sense of personal unhappiness, nervously shuffled his papers. It was rumored that he was one of the high-powered challenge specialists. Contrary to his counterpart, the serene if not overly successful lawyer for the parents, however, he seemed to lack court presence.

Judge Roberts, as he entered his courtroom, looked like a different person, his hair parted more precisely and attired in his elegant black robe. Upon his entrance, the court was ordered to rise and then sit down as the judge took his seat on the raised platform. The clerk inquired if both parties were ready, and both parties said they were.

The judge made a small opening remark for the benefit of the TV cameras which were at the moment hooked up live to their stations.

"The most important question to be decided here today is, therefore," he said looking at some of the cameras. "What is in the best interest of the child, all other things being equal? We have no other issues in court today except what is in the best interest of the child. In other words, which couple could do *more* and *better* for the child in question? Let's proceed, gentlemen."

The first few minutes of the proceedings were spent on the usual legal stuff of checking who was representing whom and where they all resided, etcetera. The challenger's attorney called his man as his first witness. After swearing on the Constitution of the United States, the man gave his name and address.

"Mr. Harris," the lawyer asked. "What is your current Total Individual Worth standing?"

The defense lawyer objected to the question as impertinent, immaterial and irrelevant to the case, and was immediately overruled. He then looked at the couple as if saying, "I tried."

"My TIW as of today is 258," he said proudly.

The crowd, although it had heard of his fortunes, gasped at the high standing, obviously impressed.

"Well," a woman with a small hand-held TV camera not far from me, said. "What a great father he would make!"

Then the lawyer asked him exactly what his TIW consisted of, at which the defense counsel didn't even bother to object. The man proceeded to list all his assets in impressive figures and descriptions. The woman with a hand-held camera gasped at the enormity of the man's wealth.

The lawyer then opened his briefcase and pulled out a sheaf of photographs and documents. He took them to his client on the witness stand and showed them.

"Are these the deeds and photographs of your property, Mr. Harris?"

Mr. Harris, perfunctorily examining them, nodded in agreement.

The lawyer took the sheaf to the clerk and entered them as the challenger's exhibit number one. He gave the defense lawyer a set of copies which the defense lawyer disdainfully pushed to the side. Even the mother, stealing a look at the documents and photographs, looked impressed. If she lost her child, he would be living among all those houses, boats, villas, stocks and bonds, money certificates, ownership papers, quarterly dividends.

The lawyer asked his client how he had made such fortunes.

"I am a venture capitalist," the challenger said proudly.

"What is a venture capitalist, Mr. Harris?"

"I invest cheap and make profits dear with enormously risky ventures," he said. "That's why we are called venture capitalists. We have a great history of contribution to the American economy from the days of the Morgans, the Rockefellers—"

"Thank you, Mr. Harris," his lawyer gently cut him off. "We all recognize the part that venture capitalism has taken to make this great country of ours."

Then the lawyer switched his questions and asked what he, Mr. Harris, would do if he won his challenge and had the child.

With that question, Mr. Harris was instantly transformed from a venture capitalist to a loving father. Beaming with pride and concern, he listed all the opportunities of education, health care, and other 'better things in life' that only a wealthy father was capable of providing for the child. After some more of this demonstration of wealth and love, the witness was declared ready for cross examination by the defense counsel.

"Mr. Harris," said the lawyer for the couple, "have you ever been convicted of child molesting?"

The other lawyer objected. The crowd whispered. The witness looked at the judge for help.

"It's a pertinent question, I suppose," the judge ruled after some deliberation. "Please answer the question."

Mr. Harris said he had never been convicted of child molesting.

"Then were you ever *charged* with child molesting?"

"Sure I was," the man said. "But I paid the victim's family generously and it was dismissed."

"What was the nature of the charge?"

The challenger's lawyer objected and the judge sustained it.

"The witness paid for the settlement," the judge said. "I don't see any relevance."

"Mr. Harris," said the lawyer. "When you took over the Southern Grits Company last September by a fraudulent method, did you know that the owner committed suicide after your takeover?"

The man's lawyer objected that it was irrelevant, immaterial and impertinent. The witness, even before the judge had time to rule, said it was a completely legal takeover and there was nothing fraudulent about it. The judge belatedly admonished the defense lawyer not to raise any more unrelated questions.

"What's the idea?" people around me were saying. "That happens all the time. How else can one get wealthy?"

Apparently, the lawyer sensed the court's disapproval.

"You want to take the boy away from his parents," he said almost whispering, leaning toward the witness. "Have you ever loved anybody in your life but yourself?"

The crowd buzzed and the other lawyer jumped to shout objection. "The question is pointless, your honor," the lawyer said. "The witness has already established his ability to love the child, for which I refer to Exhibit No. 1. Hasn't the witness already demonstrated that by his excellent TIW rank?"

"Objection sustained," the judge ruled. "His ability to love has been established beyond doubt. Proceed."

The defense lawyer said, no more questions. The witness was excused.

"I call Mrs. Harris," the challenger's lawyer said, and the woman almost bounced from her seat as if she couldn't have waited any longer.

She took the stand and was sworn in.

"Mrs. Harris," her lawyer said. "What is your age at this moment?"

"My biological age is forty-eight," she said confidently.

"Has it been certified by medical authorities?"

She said yes. The lawyer went back to his briefcase and took out a document and entered it as challenger's exhibit number two. The defense lawyer took his copy of the document and again pushed to the side only barely glancing at it.

"Your honor, with this medical certificate of her biological age, we wish to establish her physical ability to love the child beyond any shadow of a doubt."

The lawyer then went on with her plans for the child, whereupon the challenger's contract-wife detailed the complete staff devoted to the child. The list of nannies, governesses, chauffeurs and playmates, in three shifts round-the-clock impressed the crowd in the courtroom.

"Give it to her, give it to her," the woman with the hand-held camera was beside herself.

Even Judge Roberts seemed impressed with it. Ho nodded approval. After some more this demonstration of the challenger's ability to love the child, the woman was turned over for cross examination.

The defense counsel rose slowly, feeling the weight of the problem at hand.

"Mrs. Harris," he said. "Your biological age is forty-eight as you stated, and I believe the medical certificate for it. But what is your chronological age?"

The woman hesitates somewhat, but said barely audibly, "fifty-nine."

"I am sorry I didn't hear it and I am sure the judge didn't, either," he said somewhat unmercifully. "Would you say it a little louder?"

The other lawyer shouted objection again. "Your honor, the witness has already established that she is going to have a full round-the-clock staff to care for the boy. Why is the defense counsel raising this age issue?"

"Objection sustained," the judge said. "Besides, who nowadays raise their own children except the very poor?" The judge looked at the couple to emphasize that he meant them by his remark.

"Mrs. Harris," the defense lawyer asked, "why didn't you have your own children when you were younger, much younger in fact?"

The judge frowned at the 'much younger' emphasis but decided to ignore it. Likewise, the other lawyer lifted himself from his seat but, changing his mind, sat down again.

"I was once a cheerleader and keeping my body in good shape was the only way of getting a good contract," she answered.

"With all your money," the defense lawyer said patiently, "why don't you buy one from another couple instead of challenging these poor people? There are plenty of babies for sale on the market. Why this one?"

"I liked the boy when I saw him," she said calmly. "We wanted him then and we want him now."

Chapter Twenty-One

When the defense lawyer said no more questions for the witness, she was dismissed. The challenger's lawyer then proceeded to call the mother as his next witness.

The next thirty minutes or so chronicled the poor and conventionally-married woman's and man's financial woes that had plagued them all their lives. The lawyer cruelly forced the couple to admit on several occasions that they sometimes did not have good clothes for Andrew (the boy's name) and not infrequently could not afford adequate health care. To substantiate his argument, the lawyer produced photographs of the couple's remarkably poor house. After repeatedly making the couple admit that the house was in bad repair, the lawyer laid the photographs side by side with the photographs of the challenger's house. He held some of them up to the TV cameras.

"Is there any comparison, your honor?" he shouted. "In the best interest of the child, would you deny the boy this wonderful house, a mansion by the beach, a villa in Charleston, a boat in Carolina Beach?"

The court crowd chanted "No!" when the lawyer finished his speech. The judge looked at the lawyer disapprovingly as if he were going too far. "You don't have to be so demonstrative about it, counsel," the judge said nicely, however. "We all *know* what's in the best interest of the child."

The defense lawyer was just as resourceful, countering the other side. He had the mother recount the tale of late-night nursing of the boy when he had measles and couldn't afford to stay at the hospital. Through her tears she told how she repaired his clothes so that they would last longer and how she always kept Andrew well clothed, although not always with new ones. Once when the boy was two, he had fallen off his swing set, a set her husband had found at the trash dump and had repainted, and hurt his head, and the mother described how she and her husband had stayed up all night worrying about the boy although her husband had a big day of house-painting the next day.

They had to admit, however, that their joint TIW's had never risen above 45 because the mother mostly did not work, wanting to stay home with Andrew. Both of them promised that the mother would seek more work, now that Andy was old enough for day care.

The couple's testimony was so touching that it almost moved me to tears. But the courtroom crowd seemed almost totally unimpressed by it. The woman with a hand-held camera had not even bothered to record their testimony. Both sides made their final speeches and the judge announced that he wanted to see both parties in his chamber in fifteen minutes before he made his decision on the case. As the court rose, the judge retired to his chamber.

"Why is the trial so short?" I asked a bailiff standing nearby. "Short?" he reacted uncomprehendingly. "What do you mean, short?"

"I thought," I said, feeling like Rip van Winkle, "such trials lasted several days."

"Those days are long gone," he said. "The length of trial now has to accommodate people's attention span. Who wants to watch days and days of trial tapes on TV? Would you? I don't see how they could've tolerated all those long-drawn-out trials."

With that, the bailiff left me. The courtroom crowd was checking their cameras, some stretching, some talking to one another, others trying to guess what the outcome would be. Enterprising bookies were taking bets, which, I later learned, was perfectly legal. The odds were seven to three against the couple getting the judgment, which was roughly the statistical odds in such cases as Dale Flynn had told me.

The bailiff with whom I had been talking a few minutes ago returned to the court and announced, "Is there a Mr. Michael Brown from Laurinville here?"

Surprised, I raised my hand. The bailiff motioned me to join him. "The judge would like to see you in his chamber before the parties get there. He said you would be found in the courtroom."

I followed him to the judge's chamber. I had never seen a judge's chamber before in my life. The bailiff took me straight through an outer office where a young man and a woman, apparently the judge's clerks, were working on a pile of documents on their desks. They paid no attention to us as we passed them.

The judge's inner chamber was decorated and furnished comfortably, more like a living room than a judge's office, apparently well used too.

"Ah, Michael," Judge Roberts called to me as we entered the room, still with his black judicial robe on him. "Come in and sit down. I am glad you came."

I sat on the sofa. The bailiff left, closing the door behind him.

"What do you think?" he asked. "I wanted to talk to you before I saw the parties." He said and glanced at his watch.

"What do you mean what do I think, judge?"

"Do you think I conducted it impartially?" he asked almost conspiratorially.

I said it was hard to tell, given the premises of the case.

"What premises?"

"The speech you made at the beginning," I said, "about the best interest of the child. Or, who could do more and better for the child."

I then told him that as a simple-minded school principal from Laurinville, who had stayed out of the country so long, and therefore unused to the new American way, it was difficult for me to even hazard a guess at his trial because the fundamental assumptions were so radically different. The 'best interest of the child', for example, which was assumed in doing 'more' or 'better', was quite difficult to judge from my own old-fashioned perspective. What was indeed 'best' for the child? Parental love or caretaking by a professional staff? I could have also mentioned that his opening remark could be prejudicial. But in America now it was all very difficult to tell. Judge Roberts nodded sympathetically.

"I am no Solomon," he said with surprising modesty. "But I am going to try a solution that I think would do even King Solomon proud."

"What would that be, Judge?"

"Wait until they get here. I want you to observe how it goes."

In the next few minutes or so, while we were talking about court procedures in general, I could barely contain my curiosity about the judge's new solution. The bailiff returned and announced that the two parties were there. Upon the judge's instruction, they entered his chamber.

Looking at them more closely I realized that the challenger's wife looked much older and the boy's mother much more exhausted. Mother and father sat on the sofa closely together as if they felt they needed each other's support. Both the participants and their lawyers looked at me questioningly. "He is Mr. Michael Brown, a school principal from Laurinville," the judge said. "He is interested in observing our court procedures, so don't mind his presence."

The parties took their eyes away from me and concentrated on the judge.

"The reason I called you in here is this," he said. "Mr. Harris, I know this is a challenge case, not a purchase, so you don't have to agree with me. But how would you like to pay for the child?"

Mr. Harris looked somewhat startled at the judge's remark, and the couple looked at each other as if saying, no.

"Now, calm down and listen to me," the judge said reasonably. "Mrs. Dempsey you are only 29 and in the prime of your life. You can have more children any time you want to. Mrs. Harris here is fif, uh, forty-eight and obviously too advanced in her life to have children, and she likes your boy very much."

So, the mother was much younger than she looked.

"Looking at the whole matter strictly from the best interest of the child," the judge continued. "What the challenger is offering seems irresistible, and you Mr. and Mrs. Dempsey would have to agree on that point. Not many children can have parents like Mr. and Mrs. Harris who can offer the child so much."

"But not love," the mother said suddenly and fiercely as if overcome by her emotion that had made her forget her place. Her husband, seeming more reasonable, held his wife consolingly to calm her down.

"I can love him too," Mrs. Harris said just as fiercely. "The judge is right. You are so young, you can have more children, any time you want to." Then she turned to the judge and said, "how much, judge, how much?"

Being in the inner chamber face to face with the judge, not surrounded by the intimidating paraphernalia of the courtroom, seemed to have made the woman bolder. But there was something pathetic about the older woman's demeanor, and I began to feel sorry for her.

"How much?" she demanded to know. "We'll pay whatever we think is reasonable."

"I have decided," the judge said. "To try a method of settlement that has never been tried before in any American government court. But I believe it's in perfect step with our principle of the marketplace, the oldest and most tried system of fairness known to us."

Both parties looked at the judge with increased attention.

"We are going to have an auction," the judge announced.

"An auction!" everyone, including the lawyers and myself, shouted out in unison.

"Yes, an auction, which is as American as apple pie and motherhood, if you forgive my untimely pun," the judge said bowing to the mother in mock gravity.

"Now," the judge said, explaining the rules of his court. "To arrive at an absolutely fair settlement of this case, I am going to start at what I consider an arbitrary but reasonable amount of compensation, which is one hundred thousand dollars."

The poor couple looked indignant. The challenging couple looked comfortable with the sum.

"Both parties can stop me any time they want at any amount," the judge continued his explanation in a method of settlement tried positively for the first time in human history. "Mr. and Mrs. Harris, you can refuse to raise your bid at any time you think you have reached your limit, that is, whenever you have decided that the price is going beyond the value of the child that you are challenging to possess. Now, Mr. and Mrs. Dempsey, you can refuse any amount offered to you beyond the one hundred-thousand dollars initially offered by Mr. and Mrs. Harris. Either of you can retire to my small room inside at any time, if you need private consultation with each other. If the bid goes up continuously and it is continuously refused, I as the judge of this auction would stop the process when I think it has gone far enough and declare that the case is deadlocked. In that case, I will render my own decision which may or may not be to either party's liking."

He then turned to the two lawyers.

"I know this is highly irregular, but I am going to try a precedent-setting if highly unusual means of settlement. I hope you understand. That's why I decided to deal directly with the couples involved, not through you gentlemen in the usual way. Is that agreeable?"

Both lawyers, somewhat taken aback by the inventiveness of the judge's solution, stated that they would go along if their principals agreed.

That settled, the judge began to conduct his strange Solomon's court.

"Now, Mr. and Mrs. Dempsey, would you agree to give custody of one Andrew Dempsey to Mr. and Mrs. Harris for the sum of one hundred-thousand dollars?"

Without hesitation, both said no. The judge turned to the other couple. "Now, Mr. and Mrs. Harris, your initial offer of one hundred-thousand dollars has been refused. Would you agree to raise the bid?"

"Yes," said Mr. Harris, taking charge since it had to do with money. "We raise it to two hundred-thousand dollars."

The judge turned to the parents. "Now. Mr. and Mrs. Dempsey, the bid has been raised to two hundred-thousand dollars. Would you agree to give up the custody of Andrew for two hundred-thousand dollars?"

Mrs. Dempsey said no. Her husband remained silent.

The challenger seemed to notice a crack in the resolve of the parents. He raised the bid to three hundred-thousand dollars.

Mr. and Mrs. Dempsey looked at each other. The woman swallowed hard and said no. Mr. Dempsey, the housepainter of little consequence, looked somewhat disappointed.

Mr. and Mrs. Harris asked to retire to the separate room to discuss. As the couple retired to discuss their strategy, the housepainter looked at his wife somewhat worried. His wife, however, seemed to hold fast. The judge turned back to me as if saying. "What do you think?" But he looked pleased with the progress of his new invention in the annals of legal precedents.

The challenging couple returned. Mr. Harris' jaws were set firmly as if he had arrived at a resolve.

"Judge," he said, "we raise our bid to five hundred-thousand dollars." He said it in a way that suggested it was their final bid. Perhaps, perhaps not, I couldn't tell. Maybe it was their final bid, maybe it wasn't.

That amount, and the resoluteness in the bidder's demeanor, triggered a serious reaction in the mother, whose joint TIW's had never been above 45, a woman to whom a life of poverty was the curse she had been born with. A half-million dollars was a lot of money to anyone. She faltered for a moment.

"Judge, can we discuss this privately?" the housepainter husband requested, which was granted immediately.

The couple retired to the room where a moment ago the other couple had discussed their strategy. The tension in the room was thick with significance and ambiguity. Would they accept the offer? Would they reject it? Jaws set firmly; Mr. Harris grimly looked at his contract-wife.

Presently Mr. and Mrs. Dempsey returned to the judge's tension-filled chamber.

"Your honor, judge," Mr. Dempsey said in a shaky voice, almost as if ready to cry, "we reject the offer."

Mr. Harris jumped from his seat, shouting "why you dirty—" and went after the housepainter. The lawyers for the two parties, who had not said much during the whole auction, rushed toward their men and separated them.

"Gentlemen, gentlemen," the judged shouted. "Order! Order! I want order in this chamber."

In a matter of a minute, they settled down somewhat, but Mr. Harris was still breathing hard.

"Judge," Mrs. Harris, who had let her husband handle the money matter so far, spoke, "could we retire to the inner office one more time?"

When the judge granted the motion, she dragged her reluctant contract-husband to the room to discuss presumably their final strategy. The air in the chamber, now that the angry man was gone, somewhat returned to normal. Mrs. Dempsey, looking now more determined than ever, intently watched the door to the inner office.

We heard voices raised from the inner office but could not hear the words. Apparently, some heated argument was going on. The housepainter looked at his wife almost pleadingly.

Then all was quite again. A minute or so passed, which seemed like eternity. Finally, the door opened, and the couple returned.

"Your honor," the man said with a booming voice which left no doubt about his determination. "This is absolutely our final offer, and we would like it to be on the record. We offer, absolutely for the final time, one million dol—"

"We accept!" the mother shouted even before the man finished his sentence. "We accept, your honor. We accept." Then she began to weep. The chamber was suddenly quiet except the sound of the weeping mother.

"Well," the judge said somberly. "Then it is this court's ruling that the custody of one Andrew Dempsey is hereby transferred lawfully to the possession of the challenger for the sum of one million dollars. Payment and transfer of said individual shall commence immediately and simultaneously. Case closed."

The judge then instructed the lawyers for some details and, with that done, both parties departed.

There was an audible sigh from both of us at the same time as the parties left his room.

"This is another example that our system of pecuniocracy works," he said, pointing to the door with his chin. "Everyone has his price that we can all agree to."

I looked at the judge in silence.

"Don't you agree with me, Michael?" he said with a slight smile when I didn't answer him immediately.

"I don't know," I said, almost unconsciously. "One would think there is something more important than money—"

"None," the judge said with conviction. "How can there be? What can that be? Love? Patriotism? God? Motherhood? Friendship? Truth?"

"I don't know," I repeated absent-mindedly. "I don't know."

"Tell me, Michael," the judge said softly. "Do you know anyone who would not sell one's loved one, one's country, one's god, one's baby, one's friend, one's truth, if the price were right? Say, a million dollars?"

"But if you live by money, and money alone—"

"—We shall die by money," the judge said quietly. "That, I would leave to the judgment of our posterity."

Chapter Twenty-Two

The courtroom had a nice backyard which almost resembled a small park, still green with well-kept grass and shrubs. Several park benches were placed here and there with aesthetic proportionality in mind.

Dark had started to descend on the backyard, and as I watched from the window in the courtroom, I could see an elderly couple slowly walking toward one of the benches and sitting down just as slowly as they had approached it. The woman opened her sack that she had carried with her and started feeding the birds. The way she proceeded with her feeding efficiently and purposefully, and the way the birds responded with familiarity, made me think that the elderly couple did it all the time, perhaps precisely at that hour.

It was close to six o'clock by the time the mayhem was finally over. The courtroom crowd greeted the news of the settlement, as announced by the clerk on behalf of the judge, with a variety of responses. The odd-makers, bettors and bookies were slightly disappointed at the decision. Some of them started arguing among themselves whether the settlement constituted a 'win' by one party or the other, their argument shaped largely by on which side they placed their bets.

Some said the amount of money made the defendants the clear winners. Their opposite numbers, who were certainly the majority among the spectators, argued that the fact that they, the challenging couple, got the boy, never mind the payment—what's a million bucks to them anyway—meant they, not the defending couple, were the clear winners. The argument eventually materialized as the issue of whether a three-year-old boy with no apparent value intrinsic to his existence was worth that much.

Two men, a minister and a businessman, apparently more combative than the others, were still arguing in the corner on the hallway as the spectators had started drifting away from the courtroom with mixed emotions. Some were obviously upset that the highly anticipated trial produced an anticlimax.

"What's this challenge show coming to?" one such unhappy individual muttered as he was leaving. "I should've stayed home and watched the game show."

Another, more court-experienced spectator worried about the long-term implication of the no-clear-winner decision by the judge.

"Mark my word," a thirtyish woman who claimed that she attended all challenge trials said to no one in particular. "This settlement would make a bad precedent for all other cases to come. Can you imagine watching a game for hours and hours that ends up tied? I can't."

Both this woman and the unhappy man were concerned about the threat to the entertainment value of such cases.

The minister and the businessman, still arguing heatedly in the hallway, were concerned about weightier issues, it seemed.

"Are you saying," the minister, a short, red-faced and gray-haired man of about fifty, said to his companion who was obviously an old acquaintance. "That the boy is worth one million dollars if someone is willing to pay for it?"

"That's right," the businessman replied without hesitation. He was tall and skinny with a crooked bow-tie fastened on a dirty shirt. "It's up to each individual to determine what anyone's value is."

"Do you know, my friend," the minister said, his face getting really red. "That what you are saying is really without any validity, not even marketplace validity?"

"Why not?" his business companion responded.

"For one thing," the minister said, counting with his fingers. "How much does the sperm cost to produce a child, uh, how much?"

Pressed for a quick answer on a thorny issue, the businessman demurred.

"See?" said the minister triumphantly. "You can't answer it. Do you know why? Why, because it costs nothing. Not a thing! Why should anything that costs nothing to produce cost anything?"

"I don't know," said the businessman. "Sometimes it's not easy to get sperm—"

"Ha," said the argumentative minister, "that's a joke. Tell me, my friend, how much sperms have you ever wasted in your life? Can you tell me that? Did you ever miss them, did you? You threw away millions of them, didn't you, here and there and everywhere? In your college dormitory rooms, with your casual encounters, even with your spouse? Waste, waste, and nothing but waste. And now you say one of those millions of wasted sperms is worth one million dollars? Does that make any sense? You tell me."

"What do you think the judge should've done, then?"

"The judge should've awarded the custody to the challenger with ten thousand dollars going to the parents."

"Why ten thousand dollars?"

"For the costs of raising him for the first three years of life. No more, no less."

The tall, skinny man eyed his companion with new admiration.

"You know, Thad," the businessman said. "You should've been a businessman, instead of a preacher."

"Being a preacher is not bad," the minister said. "I have a condo in Florida, my quarterly earnings are up, and my TIW is almost 120."

With that turn of conversation, their attention was suddenly diverted to market speculation, and they drifted away from my view.

I walked out to the backyard but the elderly couple was already gone. I sat where the couple had sat and the bench was still warm with their bodily warmth. The birds flocked to me, expecting a similar show of charity. But I had nothing to give them. They hopped around me uncertainly for a while and then one by one reluctantly flew away.

I stopped at Jeanne's on the way home. Her not having a telephone was such an inconvenience because I couldn't call her ahead.

Mary Sue rushed over, allowing me a big hug. So did her mother.

I described the trial at the county circuit court I had just witnessed, and how I had been privy to the judge's extraordinary auction.

As the story unfolded, Jeanne drew Mary Sue toward her as if it was happening to her and her daughter.

"Never would I let that happen to you," she said fiercely as she held the girl tightly in her arms when I finished the report.

As if to allay her fears I played with Mary Sue hard for about thirty minutes until both of us were exhausted and panting. Still, she wanted to play some more, this time with her stuffed animal friends.

I asked Jeanne if she could manage to take two days off from work on short notice, preferably Wednesday and Thursday. There was a place called Anthropolis that I wanted to visit with her and Mary Sue. It would take at least two full days.

"Anthropolis," she said uncertainly. "I've heard about it a lot."

From what I knew, I said, it was a place worth my looking into. Most visitors went to Disney World, but I wanted to see Anthropolis, I told her. Jeanne was of the opinion that none of her friends had ever visited Anthropolis or known any Anthropolitan as far as she heard. She was more optimistic about the possibility of getting the two days off. She had accumulated enough sick days and the recent automobile accident could be used, if necessary, to persuade her company. She would call me at home the next morning.

I then gently disengaged Mary Sue and left the Baker household, promising to see them the next day.

When I got home, Carol was watching the evening news on TV and Cecil was on the telephone in the kitchen. Carol motioned me to the TV set, pointing to the screen. I sat next to her on the sofa to join her. The TV was turned down low to avoid interfering with Cecil's telephone call.

"His family," Carol whispered, moving her head toward the kitchen. Then pointing to the TV screen once again, she said, "it's about the challenge trial."

The screen was just switching off the court reporter, with the mother's picture in the background, who had been one of the network regulars at the scene. The anchorman, turning from the monitor to face his unseen audience, said that the judge's revolutionary method of settlement was sure to set a precedent for the increasingly frequent challenges.

"We have here with us this evening at WNTV," the anchorman said as the camera showed a well-dressed but terribly uncomfortable looking man sitting next to him, "Professor Showbeck from the University of Wilmington law school faculty specializing in Human Commodities to enlighten us what the decision by Judge Roberts could mean for us in future challenge cases."

Then the anchorman turned to the professor.

"Now, Professor Showbeck," he said. "What does all that mean?"

"What it means is that," the law professor said jerking his head as if it was his way of clearing it for lucid thinking. "It is entirely predictable that cash settlement could accompany court challenges as part of the procedure."

"Meaning—"

"Meaning that it would be a different ball game from now on. Previously challengers never offered cash incentives when they challenged a natural parent."

"Why not?"

"Because cash offers were always made in purchases, not in challenges. But this precedent today opens an entirely new era of baby transfers."

"How is it so, Professor?"

"Well, you see. Up to now, purchased babies and awarded babies were more or less kept separate. Someone offers a price on baby commodities only if they are already on the market. No one can offer any price on any commodity, human or otherwise, unless it is on the market. At least that has been the case so far. But Judge Roberts' decision, which I personally think is a revolutionary, ground-breaking stroke of genius, makes it now possible (there the professor raised his voice and gestured with his hands to emphasize the point) for anyone to try to take over any baby commodities whether they are on the market or not. You simply find a baby you like for any reason whatsoever and challenge the baby's parent or parents along with cash incentives."

"Would that make the challenge a more popular form of baby transfers?"

"Definitely," the professor, finally feeling comfortable, said emphatically. "I expect a dramatic increase in challenges-with-incentives starting tomorrow. It is a classic American tradition of carrot-and-stick. Previously it has been either stick or carrot. Now it is carrot *and* stick. It is this flexibility that makes Judge Roberts' precedent so extraordinary."

"Thank you, Professor Showbeck. Thank you for coming to our studio and enlightening our viewers on this very important issue. Now, turning to other news—"

The TV switched to other items of interest. Carol kept watching it, but my mind was not on other news once the challenge news was over. Then I could hear Cecil still on the telephone, drifting through the partially open folding doors that divided the kitchen and the TV room.

"Yes, Dad," he was saying. "I understand. I sure do. Just hang in there, Dad."

Then he listened some more, repeating, "Yes, Dad, I understand." A couple of times I heard, "Don't worry, Dad."

I had not known about Cecil's family yet and my curiosity was aroused about his relatives. So, I found myself listening with greater curiosity.

"Definitely, I'll be there this weekend. Now, don't forget I am bringing my friend from Laurinville that I'd told you about. Michael Brown is his name. Yes, of course. Love to Mom and Sis. Tell them I'll see them this weekend. Sure, bye."

With that, Cecil finally hung up his telephone. There was a moment or two of silence in the kitchen. Carol seemed totally absorbed in the news, oblivious to her contract-husband. I thought I had allowed Cecil enough time to collect his thoughts from the telephone call. Trouble in the family? I wondered. At any rate, I wanted to discuss the challenge trial case that I had observed and watched on TV a moment ago.

Cecil said a cheerful hello as I entered the kitchen. He was scribbling something on a piece of paper as if writing it down while his memory was fresh. I waited until he was done with his task. Within a few seconds, he finished and looked up. I thought I saw tears in his eyes when he looked at me. Perhaps it was the light.

"It was my dad," he said pointing with his head to the telephone on the wall. "And my mom and baby sister."

Cecil, normally a burly man both in size and mannerism, was surprisingly tender when he mentioned his family members.

"I would be delighted to meet them, Cecil."

"You'll see them this weekend, if you don't have anything else planned," he said. "They want me to bring you with me. They are anxious to see you, of course."

I briefly thought about a weekend with Jeanne Baker and Mary Sue at the beach. But meeting Cecil's family would be the more proper thing to do. I told him that I had nothing planned for the weekend. Cecil was pleased.

"Where do they live, your family?"

"They live in a small town called Elkin, North Carolina. It's a town of about one thousand people or so. I went to high school there, you know."

"Do you see them often enough?"

"Oh, every other weekend or so, if I can. It's about two hours' drive from here on the superhighway. But you know how busy I am. I wish I could see them more often, though."

With that, he stood up and opened one of the kitchen drawers to bring out a photo album of his family. The album was so conveniently located, rather unusual for a family album, that I suspected the McMillers showed it to people often.

In it, there were the usual varieties of family photographs.

"My dad," Cecil said pointing at a photograph which showed a sturdy, weather-beaten man with a farmer's overalls standing next to a silo and an old-fashioned tractor. Part of a barn showed in the photograph. There were other photographs of his father, some with Cecil.

"Dad loves his farm," Cecil said with deep feelings.

His mother, a generous looking woman in her late fifties or so, and his sister who looked to be a late teenager were also in many of the family photographs. Cecil was a totally different man when he was talking about his family, and some of the anecdotes of his childhood were told with obvious affection toward them. It was a surprise to me, for I had always thought Cecil McMiller as a typical American, good or bad, who understood very little of human emotion and cared less about the value of family life and other sentimental aspects of humanity.

It was in a way a pleasant revelation about my friend who had struck me as a slightly overgrown man with the psychic simplicity of a teenager. Obviously, I was wrong about him as there was more to him than met the eye. Perhaps I was right in thinking that I had seen tears in his eyes earlier.

At least in that album, however, there were none of Carol's. I thought either she was in another album, or possibly Carol was absent simply because she was a contract-wife, not a fully accepted member of the family according to American social norms.

My latter guess was given greater credence by two observations that quickly followed. The first observation materialized when I asked Cecil if Carol was coming with us to Elkin.

"No," Cecil said somewhat vaguely. "She doesn't like the country that much. Never been a country girl."

When I looked unpersuaded by the reason he gave, Cecil chuckled in his usual easy manner and said, "Remember, Carol never likes to paint landscapes?"

I decided it was improper for me to delve further into my friend's private affairs, possibly painful ones judged from the repeated assurances that he had been giving his father not to worry. Either the nature of their apparent family concern, or the question of how Carol was involved in it, I didn't have the faintest idea about. Our visit over the weekend might clarify those questions.

The second observation was made when Carol entered the kitchen after she had turned off the TV. Unlike most wives who would never pass up a chance to comment on their family album photos, however, she ignored the scene and proceeded to set up our dinner. The contract-wife paid not the slightest attention to her contract-husband's family pictures, which strengthened my conviction that she and her in-laws, to say the least, were not on friendly terms.

"I am taking Michael to meet my family this weekend," said Cecil, putting the family album away back in the drawer. "They are all excited about it."

"Wonderful," Carol said without looking at us and without apparent enthusiasm. "Do you like the country, Michael?"

I mumbled something about fresh air and farm animals, neither of which had ever been my favorite subjects. But Carol's obviously strained attitude toward her in-laws forced me to say something on behalf of our scheduled visit to the countryside. It was the first time, however, that she was less than her sweet self toward her contract-husband. But there was no meanness in it that I could detect. It was simple indifference, and, Cecil, apparently used to her ways on that particular issue, showed no sign of annoyance or being offended by her demeanor.

Our conversations turned to the challenge case I had witnessed. As I had described my first-hand experience at the scene of the trial our household, to my great relief, once again returned to its normal gaiety.

Chapter Twenty-Three

As she promised Jeanne Baker called me in the morning. She got the next two days off. But she sounded somewhat concerned about visiting Anthropolis.

"I don't know, Michael," she said. "I've heard nothing good about that place."

I assured her that everything would be all right. In fact, I had it on good authority that it was a rather nice place and she would even enjoy the visit after all.

Then I told Carol (Cecil had already left) that I wanted to visit Anthropolis the next two days and that Jeanne and Mary Sue would be coming along. Her reaction to my rather sudden announcement was calm, as though she had already anticipated it. She was somewhat surprised with my decision to take the Bakers along but said she didn't foresee any problems.

To Cecil we would just say that someone I had met at the Fort Fisher Civil War relic invited me to visit another site (say, Hattisburg, Pennsylvania) for a couple of days, which I accepted. I would be back home by late Thursday, however, for our scheduled weekend in the country with his family.

Carol's knowledge of how to get to Anthropolis was impressive, indicating the simple fact that she was a frequent visitor to that forbidden city.

"There is a man named Cornelius who is in charge of day-to-day operation in Anthropolis," she said. "Just ask for him as soon as you get there. He will be expecting you."

She helped me with detailed instruction for the journey, including the conditions of the roads on which we were to travel. Much of it, according to the travel map we had, was covered by superhighways. Some of the old interstates had now been converted to better grades, allowing over 100 miles per hour. But for the last few hours, we would be in no man's land, she cautioned me. If we left early in the morning, she said, we would be at our destination by mid-afternoon. Since a child was involved, there was some extra preparation to consider also.

I spent the rest of the day getting ready for the trip. My evening was spent with Jeanne helping her with her part of the preparation. Mary Sue was delighted when I told her about the trip. Jeanne was still less than sanguine about seeing this city about which no reasonable American she knew had kind words to say. Nevertheless, the simple task of preparing for the road eventually got all of us into a mood of excitement. Advising them to go to bed early because we would have to get up by four in the morning, I returned home to the McMillers.

Cecil showed no particular interest when told that my fictitious Civil War buff invited me to visit him for a couple of days in Hattisburg. He seemed to be quieter than his usual self, preoccupied with his own thoughts. I noticed that this subtle change had started after he got the telephone call from his father the night before. Although he was pretending to be absorbed in the newspaper he was reading, I could sense that it was just a foil to cover up something that was on his mind.

Perhaps it was my own reaction to the knowledge of Carol's involvement with the Anthropolitans, a secret she apparently didn't share with her contract-husband. Having been drawn into this bit of knowledge, and because of my broadening awareness of Carol's unhappy thoughts about her own society as expressed through her short novel, I began to feel instinctively that somehow the whole atmosphere of the house had changed, albeit subtly. Looking back, the change might have started after the memorial service of the drowned student. Cecil, coming home later after a business meeting with Dean Nettor and Jeff and Mutt following the funeral, had seemed slightly absent-minded when he joined us.

Because Cecil had always been a consistently voluble and humorous sort, even this small change in his behavior became noticeable.

Excusing myself relatively earlier because of the early morning departure for Hattisburg, I retired to my room around nine o'clock. It was not easy for me to fall asleep, thinking about the trip ahead to Anthropolis and its inhabitants, and in more bafflement about Cecil McMiller.

Neither of the McMillers saw me leave the next morning. The morning chill of early fall greeted me when I tiptoed out to the car with my overnight bag. The chilly early morning streets and street-lights added eeriness to my uncertain adventure ahead. The city was still sleepy and groggy from the day before.

When I got there, Jeanne and Mary Sue had been ready, Mary Sue still sleeping in her mother's arms. As if we were afraid of being discovered by neighbors, we practically whispered to each other until we were out of the neighborhood and on the main thoroughfare that led us to the superhighway. As meticulously instructed by Carol we followed Superhighway 95 north, which used to be known as Interstate 95, a main artery between New York-Philadelphia-Washington and the vacation spots of the Carolinas and Florida.

To my amazement Jeanne reminded me that she had never been out of North Carolina. She was therefore just as unfamiliar with superhighway travel as her driver from Laurinville. To her, going to Anthropolis, an admittedly strange place with a strange social system unknown to most Americans, was just as adventurous and apprehensive as it was to me. However, she assigned to herself the duty of a map-reader and navigator.

The sun began to emerge, radiating its morning glow, as we approached Richmond, Virginia. Getting hungry because neither of us had eaten, we ordered our breakfast on our mobile phone in the car. Within five minutes or so, we slowed down and came to a stop to pick up our order at an all-purpose service station. A young man with a server's uniform was holding out a box of food with our number written on it, holding the receptor-end of his cashing chip with the other.

This convenient system had been in existence for many years in America, but it was now extended in its range of services and made more efficient than before. We paid for the food with my inserter. The smell of food apparently stimulated Mary Sue, for she immediately woke up and, seeing me and her mother, smiled instantly. She proved to be an excellent traveler. The rest of Superhighway 95 went by fast for us; we were busy entertaining Mary Sue and being entertained by her.

Passing Washington, D.C., we turned onto the old Pennsylvania Turnpike, which had also been converted to a superhighway years ago, and headed west. We drove on the superhighway uneventfully for three more hours until we got to a small town called Tyler about five miles or so north of the superhighway. According to Carol's instruction we were to get off at the US 6 Exit as soon as we saw the Tyler sign. When we got off the highway and turned onto US-6 we immediately realized that US 6 had no longer been open to ordinary American travelers. In fact, there was a sign at the exit from the superhighway that US 6, due to infrequent use by travelers, was no longer under the protection of the federal government and travelers were advised to advance only at their own risk.

I had remembered that America no longer maintained the roads that were not used by enough motorists because they paid their highway taxes only according to the roads they traveled on and how often. Consequently, those highways that were shunned by travelers, for some reason, were naturally dropped from regular maintenance. From this point on, I recalled Carol's instruction, we were in no man's land. We could tell immediately that driving was strenuous because of the poor pavement and the bushes and wild grass that sprang from its many cracks. I was glad that I had the vehicle thoroughly inspected in Wilmington the day before.

"Why do you think people don't travel on this road anymore?" Jeanne asked as if to confirm the suspicion on her mind.

"I suppose we are getting closer to Anthropolis. Americans avoid this road because it leads to nowhere but Anthropolis."

Although the distance between the City of Humanity and the old turnpike was relatively small, the conditions of the road made the going rough and slow, taking many times longer to cover the same distance. We did our best to make our going as pleasant as possible, by telling stories, riddles and jokes, and singing children's songs in which Mary Sue joined us. We made up words with many songs as we sang.

Oddly, we did not see a single vehicle passing us, ahead of us or behind us. The rolling hills and mountains on both sides of the road were not unpleasant to our eyes, but the quiet of nature and the absence of human inhabitation in our surroundings impressed us with desolate authority. To discover that we could move so quickly from the highest level of technological civilization to a sudden wilderness protected only by an island of our automobile was positively unnerving. It was amazing how quickly, within a decade or so, a once fairly civilized region could change into barren land.

We struggled through overgrown plants and cracked pavement, and sometimes fallen rocks and landslides, for three more hours. Mary Sue finally fell asleep and remained so during much of the last part of our journey.

The road suddenly improved as Carol had described and we were obviously getting closer. It was nothing like the superhighway but at least it was free of the maddening interruptions that we had been fighting for the last three hours. We drove for an hour or so on the better road when we saw a sign on the roadside that said, "THE OUTER ZONE OF ANTHROPOLIS."

The sign urged us on for another thirty minutes or so, with an instruction to follow. Seeing the word Anthropolis looming up so large and suddenly, Jeanne reacted as if her heart had fallen down to her feet. I reassured her about the place by the authority of the person who had given us the detailed travel instructions. Sensing a change in our surroundings, Mary Sue woke up from her nap and smiled.

The next thirty minutes or so was heavenly. We were driving through a thick forest which used to be part of the Allegheny National Forest before it was parceled out to the Anthropolitans at a price the federal government couldn't refuse. The outer zone itself, the size of a large city, covered the northeastern corner of the national forest. But the surrounding area, now converted to wilderness due to lack of active use by Americans, served as another protective ring for the City of Humanity to ensure its isolation.

The darkness of the forest that had enveloped us with such comforting enclosure abruptly ended into a panorama of gently sloping hills and farms. Instinctively I stopped the car. The view, suddenly materializing from the dense forest without a warning, was indeed spectacular and took my breath away. Jeanne and Mary Sue looked out the window speechless. Jeanne seemed to be favorably impressed with her first encounter with Anthropolis, which alleviated some of her previous fears of the city. The hills and farms were meticulously maintained and irrigated as if in a picture postcard.

Red barns with white trims and silos stood here and there between hills and farms against the greenery of the vegetation. The early October sun still shone brightly. On one side of the road stood a small sign, almost as an afterthought, that said, "WELCOME TO ANTHROPOLIS." We all got out of our car to get a better view and to stretch. The city itself could be seen about ten miles or so further up from where we stood, surrounded by the ring of its farms.

"You know," I observed. "The Anthropolitans claim to have a utopia here. I don't know about their being a utopia, but I would say it has the makings of a fairy-tale town about it."

"It's so wonderful, isn't it?" she agreed.

While we were exchanging our impressions Mary Sue pointed to the foothill where our road was joined by a smaller road that dissected the farms. "Look, Mommie," she hollered, pulling Jeanne's hand. "People are coming."

Indeed, coming down the hill was a group of people on bicycles. I could see that there were three riders on singles and a pair on a tandem, apparently coming in our direction.

"Hello there," one of the singles said, waving his hand as soon as we got close enough to recognize each other.

Uncertainly we waved back. They looked friendly enough, however. The cyclists got off their bicycles a few yards ahead of us.

"Mr. Brown, isn't it?" the man who had greeted us before, fortyish with an open face, asked.

I said yes, somewhat surprised. He said his name was Nelson and turned to the rest of my party. He squatted down in front of Mary Sue.

"Then you must be Mary Sue," he said as he pulled out a small carved wooden toy that looked like a rabbit. "This little animal came out to welcome you."

As the little girl accepted the gift and was satisfied with the stranger, Nelson stood up to recognize Jeanne. "And this is Mary Sue's mother, Jeanne Baker."

They shook hands.

"How did you know we were coming just now?" I asked after a round of introductions with the rest of Nelson's party, his wife and three children, had been completed.

"One of our friends let us know that you were coming," he said proudly, "but we missed it by a few minutes. We were supposed to have been here to wait for you before you could get here."

Jeanne Baker complimented to the welcoming party on the beauty of the surroundings. As we had guessed Nelson told us that the farms enveloped the entire city forming an outer ring. I told him that I was to ask for a Mr. Cornelius.

"Yes, Mr. Brown," Nelson said, "he is waiting for you. Would you follow us, please?"

We drove the next ten miles or so on the smaller farm road, following the party on bicycles who rode slowly ahead of us, toward the city. The Nelson children looked back from time to time and waved to Mary Sue who responded enthusiastically.

"Well, what do you know?" I said almost to myself, "We just met the Anthropolitans."

"They seem like nice people?" said Jeanne obviously feeling much better about the character of the city and its people she came to see.

I said I was impressed with their openness and friendliness without exaggerating the point. 'Natural' was the term of description that easily came to my mind. The Anthropolitans, if the Nelsons were said to be typical of them, were almost like the friendly townspeople in Laurinville or even some of the citizens I had met in Wilmington. For the most part, Jeanne agreed with my first impression of our hosts.

As we neared the city, we began to see some large buildings on the outer rim of the city, which were obviously factories of some kind because we saw workmen and machines in an organized fashion. We could see more Anthropolitans on bicycles and on foot moving about as soon as we passed the layer of the large structures. They waved and smiled at us without stopping whatever they were doing.

As if to conform to the circular rings that surround the city, the barren zone, the forest, and the farm that formed protective rings, the residential areas were also formed in circular layers with decreasing sizes toward the center of the city. I could almost visualize the whole set up by imagining an archery target in which Anthropolis made up the innermost circle.

Houses on the outskirts of the city were large but as we approached the center the size of the houses got larger. The houses were built, it seemed, with functionality in mind, for they were fairly uniform in design without being identical. However, the increasing sizes toward the center of the city gave them an elusive look of dynamic movement.

We crossed a canal and saw people fishing from their small boats. Some others were rowing about in boats obviously built for speed. There were no motor boats in the water as there were no automobiles on the road as we came in. The bicycle party, apparently coming to the inner core of the city, veered to the right, motioning us to follow them. Up ahead we saw what resembled a row of public buildings, not as imposing as those to which I had been used, but we could tell by their size and design that they were for public conveniences. The Nelsons stopped in front of a building larger than the others and parked their bicycles. We pulled into a spot and parked. Nelson gave us a friendly gesture with his hand that we had come to our destination.

"Welcome to Anthropolis, the City of Humanity, Mr. Brown," he said as we got out.

He pointed to the entrance to the building and said, "Mr. Cornelius is waiting for you inside."

Chapter Twenty-Four

Nelson led us to an office inside the building where two men and one woman were apparently waiting for us. They were dressed like the Nelsons without any sign of distinction except that they were much older.

"Mr. Michael Brown and his party, Cornelius," our guide introduced us as the three stood up to meet us.

"Ah, Mr. Brown, we have been waiting for you," the man with bright white hair and an equally bright white beard said, extending his hand. As we shook hands, he introduced the others as members of the council. There followed a round of introductions.

"This is what we normally call a Council Session, which means we happened to get together for tea," he said gesturing to the other council members to say that we were not interrupting their meeting.

Then Cornelius talked to Mary Sue for a few minutes, almost ignoring us. He finally stood up when he was satisfied that the child was thoroughly comfortable with her new surroundings.

"Nelson, Mr. Brown and his party must be awfully tired," he said. "Would you please show them to their quarters where they can rest for a while? You know how dreadful the effort has to be to get here. I will meet you again in about half an hour or so, to show you, our city. Would that be all right, or would you need more time to rest?"

I said, with approval from Jeanne who was just as anxious, that although we were somewhat tired, we were more anxious to know all about Anthropolis than the rest. Cornelius was pleased.

Nelson took us to a house about a block away, one of the smallest houses on the innermost circle among the rows of houses. Although it was apparently the smallest one, the house was spacious and comfortably furnished.

"We have a few of these units available for guests," Nelson said as we looked around in the house. "But there are no single units for one family in Anthropolis."

"You mean—" I started asking.

"Even the smallest unit has at least two families. We encourage people to live together as a community, rather than as individual units. Not only are there no single-family units here, but also no units for one single individual. All singles must live with other families."

"Why?" asked Jeanne.

"Well, as Cornelius would probably explain it to you later, we believe the desire to be alone away from other people in the community is not very healthy and can corrupt the individual in the end."

Nelson excused himself and went to get our belongings. Within a minute, he returned with our suitcases. He showed how the kitchen worked in case we wanted coffee or juice for Mary Sue, although we would be dining with the Corneliuses while we stayed. After satisfying all our questions about the household Nelson left.

The house had a huge room in the middle which apparently served as a communal hall for all the members of the household because it indeed was spacious enough to accommodate at least fifteen people. A clean and efficient kitchen was built on one end of the large hall. The bedrooms, four on each side, lined up on both sides. All bedrooms opened directly to the large hall. On the two long ends were bathrooms and what looked like storage places. Virtually the whole house was built of wood.

Jeanne and Mary Sue settled into a room and I occupied one next to theirs. I could hear Mary Sue's babble and excited exploration of the interior. She was having a great time running around.

"What do you think, Jeanne," I asked, remembering her resistance to the idea of visiting the city.

"I don't know," she said thoughtfully. "People seem awfully friendly and the place is beautifully kept."

"How about their philosophy of not letting a single-family unit occupy a house by themselves?"

"I think it's a good idea," she agreed quickly, surprising me a bit. "You know, we Americans waste too much space anyway."

She then looked around the house with the keen eye of a woman who had been the head of a household for a long time. "This house would be big enough for three average families to live comfortably together."

I could sense that she was feeling more positive about the Anthropolitans and her previous conception, formed entirely by her own society's prejudice, was being modified by the comforting appearance of the city. Our first impression was that everything about Anthropolis seemed slow and relaxed, an obvious change of pace compared to the hectic urban life of Wilmington or elsewhere.

"Michael," Jeanne looked me in the eye said, "is Carol McMiller one of the so-called Anthropolitan-sympathizers?"

Seeing no reason to deny it, I said she was. Jeanne became thoughtful again.

I told her about Carol's novel and the upcoming visit to Cecil's family in the country. While we were talking about the McMillers who had brought us together and to this strange city, it suddenly occurred to us that the world we had just left was indeed another world. Both physically remote and culturally different from the world both Jeanne and I had inhabited all our lives, Anthropolis seemed nothing like Laurinville or, its nemesis, America. It was a jarring realization. Only Mary Sue, who was happily exploring the comfortable and spacious interior, remained our constant reference point to our former worlds.

There was a knock, and, upon our acknowledgement, Cornelius entered. He inquired if we had found the house to our liking and rested enough. We said we liked the house and had indeed recovered enough to see and hear about Anthropolis. He led us outside. He pointed to an area on the far end of the square where we could see a small park with children playing, and said, "first, let's take the little one to our children's center where she will find a lot of friends and things to do, so that she doesn't have to go around with the grownups all afternoon, right, little one?"

What he referred to as a children's center was indeed a well-maintained park with a fair-size flat building on one side of the park. We could see that there were as many adults as children at the center. As soon as we got there Mary Sue needed no encouragement. She immediately blended into the nearest group of children as if she had known them all her life. There was a great deal of laughter from both children and adults. Cornelius introduced us to a woman who would watch Mary Sue while we were gone. When we left her, Mary Sue hardly bothered to wave to us, she was too busy playing. Jeanne seemed to hesitate a little but accepted the situation as completely wholesome.

"We have five children's centers like this one all over the city," Cornelius said as we walked back toward the square. "But we don't need any more than that because we don't raise children at centers."

"How come?" Jeanne inquired.

"We raise them as our community responsibility," he answered. "You understand we work only about three hours a day here on the average. Which means adult Anthropolitans have plenty of time on their hands."

"Only three hours a day?" Jeanne sounded incredulous and impressed. "Our life here is totally without waste or overindulgence, and three hours is more than enough. In fact, we have been thinking about reducing it further because we have more manpower than we need to produce enough for all our necessities."

"You were saying that adults here have plenty of time in their hands," I reminded him. "What do they do with their time?"

Cornelius smiled. "With plenty of time left from work, we do the most important thing in our community here."

"Which is?"

"We raise children," Cornelius said.

"The whole time?" Jeanne and I said at the same time.

"Virtually the whole time," the Anthropolitan said, somewhat amused.

"Miss Baker, you have a child, what time of the day does she require your care?"

She hesitated. "Well, I suppose all the time." Then she added, "She is but a child."

"Exactly," Cornelius was pleased with her admission. "All children need care all the time. In societies you come from, children don't get round-the-clock care because parents are busy working or tending to other obligations. Work itself takes most of their time, leaving little or no time to be with their children. We have solved that problem by spending all of our time with children whenever we are not at work. In Anthropolis, children get what they need. In America, they don't get enough."

Jeanne was reflecting thoughtfully.

"Of course, we do other things besides raising children," Cornelius said. "It is just that we make it our primary commitment. That's why we don't really need a lot of children's centers because, in a way, they are everywhere there is an adult with a child. What better children's center is there than one in which adults are totally dedicated to children at all times?"

"How do you manage with just three hours of work, Mr. Cornelius?" I asked as it had been on my mind.

"As I mentioned before, Mr. Brown," he said. "If you eliminate waste and overindulgence, you would be surprised how much saving there is to be made. In America, less than twenty-five percent of the labor force produces goods and services to meet the basic needs of the whole population. The rest of them merely get in the way of each other with little or no productive purpose."

"They call it a service economy," I suggested. "It seems to be a world-wide trend among developed economies. People now spend their leisure time being entertained and doing things they like."

"I suppose American society and the rest of the developed world can't stop the trend because either they don't want to or cannot stop it even if it produces nothing but waste and inhuman habits. But it's for them to solve their problem. In Anthropolis we have solved ours. We stopped the economic madness by maintaining a balance and harmony with human nature. All of us have one stomach that cannot be overstuffed. All of us have one body that occupies a certain space and no more. Why break our backs to get more when we cannot possibly enjoy any more than so much?"

"Still, three hours a day seems almost incredible," I reflected.

"Not as incredible as it seems at first, Mr. Brown," Cornelius said. "In America, people work but they work by holding jobs. Here in Anthropolis we work but don't hold jobs. Work is something that has to be done for the survival and comfort of the community. I work three hours a day at a factory myself, as do the other council members. A job, on the other hand, is a source of your income whether there is anything to do in it or not."

"We Anthropolitans work and everything we do in our work contributes to the well-being of all of us. Americans hold jobs but they have no idea how their jobs contribute anything to anyone's well-being but their own. Those 'service jobs' which occupy seventy-five percent of workers mainly serve the jobholders, but hardly anyone else."

We reached the other end of the square from which we could see a huge stadium where people of all ages were engaged in all sorts of sports.

"Here is the fundamental reason why three hours is enough here," continued Cornelius as if he suspected that we weren't convinced of the fact. "Every Anthropolitan worker is a happy and satisfied producer. When he works, the worker is totally dedicated to his work. By doing one's best at work for three hours, the Anthropolitan can be much more productive than an American worker who labors for eight hours with not much to do."

As we watched the people at the stadium, Cornelius explained that the oval-shaped stadium, located at the very center of Anthropolis, was large enough to accommodate all athletic events which took place much of the time. He said that all sports in Anthropolis were 'group' games, there were no sports in which one person won or lost. Winning and losing were bad for community morale, he said. Competition in all sports, mild as it was, was waged at every age level so that everyone participated, not just the young and athletic.

On both short sides of the oval-stadium were two school buildings for children aged five through fifteen in which they studied and lived. Alongside the school stood other public buildings such as the theater, a large library which also doubled as a center for higher learning and research equivalent to the university, city hall where we met Cornelius, a museum, a fire station, a hospital, a concert hall, and a large central warehouse from which supplies were distributed to the smaller outlets in the neighborhood where provisions were made available at all times.

We went near the school buildings, but I didn't see anything that resembled a traditional school with classrooms and playground and so on. Although late for any classes, there were adults and children milling about in all different sizes and with all different tasks.

"We don't have what you might call an educational system," Cornelius said, anticipating my question. "There are no teachers or classes or exams or graduation. We have no one particularly trained to be a teacher because all Anthropolitan adults are teachers. The so-called school is run by volunteers, some of them are parents and others just people who like being with children. Without classes or exams scheduled, our education consists of adults showing children what life is and how it is lived."

We could see through a window a room in which a child was practicing his violin, with an adult sitting next to him.

"Virtually every adult can teach at least one instrument," said Cornelius. "There is no better educational system than one in which every adult in the community is a teacher. Every moment in a child's life, because he is always surrounded by adults, is a moment of education. There is no such thing as school being separated from home. Everywhere and every moment, the child is being educated by adults without the formalities of education."

"How do you teach children of their society's values?" Jeanne asked, as we headed for the library. "Since school doesn't teach them. You don't even have teachers."

"I can see why you would be curious about that point," said Cornelius. "In Anthropolis everyone teaches, and no one teaches. There are no particular values that we write down in a textbook that all children must learn. We teach them by the way adults behave, by example, by demonstrations. Older Anthropolitans teach younger ones by their own conduct. The younger ones do the same for those who are still younger than they are. So, this way, everyone is a teacher and learner at the same time. The very oldest also learn from the young too, because one can always learn more even from children."

Their library, although a busy one, was fairly small, smaller than the one in Laurinville, more so if judged by the standards of the library at the University of Wilmington. The smallness surprised me somewhat and Cornelius read this in my expression.

"Ah ha," the Anthropolitan exclaimed. "You are somewhat disappointed that our library is not very large, aren't you, Mr. Brown?"

I confessed that I had been used to the million-volume university type libraries in America and was expecting a similar size.

'But' Cornelius said without being offended. "Our library has all the great books ever written by every great mind in human history. Obviously, we don't have *every* book ever printed. That would not only be impossible for us, but also undesirable. Many books written and published both in America and elsewhere have little or no value to anyone but their authors, hardly worth the cost of the paper they are printed on. So, why waste the valuable space and money to buy and store them all? All men are created equal, but not all books. On the other hand, we have many copies of a few good books so that people can read them without having to wait in line. For example, Plato's *Republic*, our most popular book, has at least twenty copies, all of them fairly frequently checked out. We have at least ten copies of *Moby Dick, The Old Man and the Sea*, and so on."

"Are they enough, though?" I suggested.

"Of course, they are," he said. "Our science collection is good enough to sustain a community with all its necessary comfort and happiness. Besides, the books we already have are enough for many lifetimes. Even if one does nothing but read every day, one could not possibly read them all. So, why worry about the size of the collection?"

I was not exactly persuaded by his reasoning, but, somewhat at a loss for a better argument, found myself nodding.

Chapter Twenty-Five

"How do people get the money to buy things here?" Jeanne asked as we moved away from the square toward the residential rows.

"We don't have money in Anthropolis," said Cornelius. "No one buys anything and no one sells anything here, Miss Baker. We have a completely self-sufficient economic system so that we don't need money. Our farms grow enough grains and raise enough livestock for the whole population in this city, and our factories produce enough for anything we need here as long as our need is based on the natural necessity of life, not vanity or private desire."

"I understand you don't allow ownership of private property," I said. "How does your system work without that incentive?"

"We don't need that sort of incentive to do our best, Mr. Brown. In American society and to a great extent in other advanced societies, either you pay a man to do certain things he doesn't want to do voluntarily, or you threaten him with violence to do things against his will. They call it a carrot-and-stick approach. But why is it necessary to either seduce a man with money or threaten him to get anything done? The reason for that very deplorable philosophy is rather simple, or so it seems to me: The things you want him to do are not such wonderful things to begin with, so that the worker doesn't see any point or meaning related to the things that he is asked to do."

"The only reason he will do the things he doesn't want to do is if you pay him enough or there is a promise of great material possession as a result, or the dire threat of starvation. Is the man going to be very happy while doing the things he doesn't want to do, or with the material possession that he received as a result of the most unpleasant experience of his life? Can the whole society be a happy place when its entire existence is based on such bad feelings of millions of people?"

Cornelius explained that all factories and processing facilities were located in the outer circle of the city, outside the residential areas. Also on the same row were the workshops for mechanical repairs and hobbies that required heavier and more sophisticated tools.

I learned that the city was dissected by two canals, crossing at right angles, one of which we saw on the way in. There were three roads, the middle one being the highway, between the canals connecting Anthropolis with the outside world, so that altogether twelve small roads and four canals crisscrossed the center of the city. The residential areas occupied the space between the inner and outer circles of public buildings in the fashion of ever-enlarging circles of houses. All the houses faced the center circle. The size of the housing block remained about the same as it spread outward, but the size of the houses changed as we observed earlier.

I asked why the size got larger toward the center of the city.

"The general idea is to encourage people to live together in a household. The larger houses being closer to the events and conveniences of community life, they increase the attractiveness of large-size households and the virtue of mutual tolerance and understanding. Most Anthropolitans prefer to live with other Anthropolitans obviously, and many of the smaller and more private units on the outer circles go practically unoccupied. The kind of struggle for privacy that exists in America is non-existent here."

"No privacy at all?" Jeanne objected.

"I wouldn't say no privacy at all, Miss Baker," said Cornelius smiling. "There is of course the necessity of basic privacy. But we do not place a high premium on the virtues of privacy. As I told you earlier about the virtues of mutual tolerance and understanding, privacy tends to breed selfishness and selfishness tends to breed corruption of the mind. Since we have no commercial business, nobody owning anything anymore than anybody else, we feel no compulsion to be so secretive from each other. We have no reason to think we ought to look better than our neighbors and think we are superior to anyone."

"So, why all that fuss about privacy? We are just comfortable with each other enough not to have to put the blind around us. We don't have to demand honesty from fellow Anthropolitans. Why? Because we don't have any reason to be *dishonest* with each other. What do we gain by hiding something from others and being dishonest in Anthropolis? Absolutely nothing. So, openness and honesty are results of our way of life, not its preconditions. Anyone who lives here would find it awfully difficult not to be open or honest with one another. Not that we are more virtuous than Americans, we just have a different system here."

The late afternoon was unusually warm and even balmy. As we walked through that part of the city, we saw many people painting, reading on the grass, playing ensemble with several musical instruments, strolling, or playing with children. Cornelius always stopped and talked to children whenever we met them on our way. We were obviously strangers, but children and adults alike waved to us and shouted greetings. In the entire residential areas through which we walked we didn't hear one loud scream or see one wild chasing of children. They were all very active but none reckless or unruly.

"We all know one another here," said Cornelius with a tone of great affection. "And we look out for one another."

I mentioned that I hadn't seen any motor vehicles in Anthropolis.

"We have some electrically driven vehicles," he said. "But they are for emergencies. We have one on every block so that everyone can get to it in case of emergency. After use, it is put back there for the next emergency. But we don't use it all the time. We have no reason to rush to anything. No deadlines to meet, no business appointments to attend to, no rush hours. We stagger our work hours all throughout the twenty-four-hour period so that we avoid crowding and congestion in our activities. In fact, Nelson went to work for his three hours right after he left you at the house."

"Do people retire from work?" Jeanne asked.

"Nobody retires from work here," Cornelius said. "Work is so easy and pleasant that most people like to hang around their workplaces. There is no reason for anyone to dread going to work or looking forward to leaving it. We have no weekdays and weekends so clearly divided, weekdays dreadful and weekends wonderful. To us, every day is the same as any other day, we live and work with our fellow Anthropolitans. I know many Americans look forward to weekends because they want to get away from other Americans and dread coming back to work on Monday. None of that here."

"How about holidays, like Christmas?"

"Sorry, no holidays, either," he said, quite amused to be contradicting our expectations. "Why set aside a particular time of the year to give thanks or enjoy each other's fellowship when we do that all the time, all year round? And you wouldn't be surprised to hear that we have no such thing as vacations.

Again, our whole life is one long vacation, if you can conceive of it at all." Jeanne and I were obviously forced into some hard thinking.

"If I may guess," I said after a while. "You don't celebrate birthdays either. Am I right?"

Cornelius burst out laughing, slapping himself on the thigh.

"Well, well, Mr. Brown," he said still smiling. "You are finally catching on. But could you tell me why we wouldn't celebrate birthdays?"

"Simply because you see no reason to set aside a day in the year as a special day for the person wherein everybody recognizes his existence?"

"That explains why no birthday for adults. But what about not having birthday parties for children?" challenged Cornelius.

It was Jeanne's turn. "Because," she said thinking hard. "What can you give your children who have everything? How can you recognize their special day by giving gifts and showing lot of loving when your children are loved at all times, all year round as you say? Isn't that right?"

Cornelius nodded, satisfied. "Now, tell me," he said. "Do you agree with that philosophy?"

We fell silent.

"It would be hard for me," said Jeanne almost to herself. "To skip Mary Sue's birthday next year. But—"

"But?" prodded the Anthropolitan.

"—But if you lived here as an Anthropolitan, I imagine not giving a birthday party for your child would be as natural as giving it if you lived in America."

Cornelius seemed impressed with Jeanne's keen sense of observation and her intuitive struggle to be more objective about Anthropolis, recognizing that her view of the city was heavily colored by her American upbringing.

We returned to the children's center to pick up Mary Sue. She had been playing so hard that she hardly thought about her mother, the woman said. Cornelius said dinner would be served at his household, on the other side of the center circle, and we should come over after we wash up and rest for a while. There was a concert scheduled at the concert hall after dinner, he suggested, if we felt up to it.

We were once again back in our quarters. Jeanne immediately went to task, giving Mary Sue a good bath and changing her. After that, she showered and changed for dinner. I followed suit.

As we walked back to Cornelius' household, Mary Sue was full of tales about her new friends she had made at the center.

"Why aren't we like children?" Jeanne said, obviously inspired by her daughter. "They adjust so easily to new environments, don't they, without prejudices from their past?"

It was a leisurely walk alongside the stadium which was empty as everyone went home for dinner. Suddenly I was overcome by a profound sense of melancholia. It was neither happiness nor sadness, or it was both. It was my reaction to Anthropolis and to America, and thinking about Laurinville, which seemed to be another world. All were so close, yet so far from one another. I stopped and gave Jeanne and Mary Sue a fierce hug. Jeanne seemed to understand my mood and we walked the rest of the way in silence.

The Cornelius household was the same size as our quarters. But there were three families in his household. Beside the Corneliuses, a young couple with a five-year-old boy were introduced as the Murphys, and the other couple closer to Cornelius in age as the Wershows. Since Cornelius had a son with his own family of three children living with them, the household had a total of twelve people from three-months old to sixty-two, with three different family names.

Marge, Cornelius' wife, was having a tough time helping us with their names and ages. But with such varying ages and so many members, the house was surprisingly peaceful and orderly. Virtually everyone helped with the dinner and the table. The older ones, like the Wershows and Cornelius himself, spent their time with the children while we helped the others with their tasks.

"Tell us about your marriage custom," asked Jeanne during our dinner conversation. "How do people get married here?"

Obviously, she was referring to the Murphys and the younger Cornelius since they were closer to her age. The young Anthropolitans looked at each other as if not knowing what to say, and the older ones chuckled. Finally, the task fell on Cornelius once again.

"Nobody marries here in Anthropolis," he said. "None of the young ones here are married."

Jeanne stopped eating, eyeing him as if some more explanation was in order. Of course, I had known the answer from the magazine I had read.

"Marriage is between society and people, and love is between people," Cornelius said, responding to Jeanne's silent prodding. "Marriage as an institution only serves the record-keeping purpose of government bureaus.

Since we have no government here, we need no marriage to satisfy the government. All we care is if the two people love each other, not whether they are married. Why should anyone care if they are 'married' as long as they love each other? Personally, I would consider marriage without love a greater sin than love without marriage."

"This being the case, we can honestly declare that *every* couple in Anthropolis is united because they love each other. Without love, there is no reason why anyone would want to be with anyone and have each other's children. You can force marriage on to a person, but you can't force love. Love has to be true or else it isn't love. A marriage doesn't have to be true, but it will still be a marriage as long as it maintains its institutional form. Of course, we older ones, like ourselves and the Wershows, were traditionally married because Anthropolis didn't exist when we married. We are practically part of the founding generation."

Jeanne seemed to absorb it for a while and we turned to other topics. After dinner, everyone again helped with the dishes and clearing the table. The two younger men washed the dishes whereas their women played with the children. Cornelius, who was one of the second violinists in the orchestra to perform that night, rehearsed his instrument in the corner with Mr. Wershow's helpful critique.

"We don't have a permanent orchestra," he said after the rehearsal was over. "Anyone can be in the orchestra if he wants to. There is no qualification for membership but everyone has to judge oneself whether one is good enough or somebody else is being denied a chance to play. Before every concert program, one of the players is chosen to lead the orchestra without having to be its permanent conductor to terrorize the players. I play in one Haydn symphony in the second half of the program so that I sit in the audience for the first half, and become the player for the second half. Conversely some of those who play in the first half will be the audience for the second half."

"Wouldn't that be confusing?" I inquired.

"No, not really. We just use our good commonsense."

The concert was excellent, and in my opinion the level of the performance was as good as any professional orchestra anywhere. There were several pieces composed by some teenagers, one of whom conducted his own composition, and a violin concerto from Mozart and Symphony No. 2 by Beethoven.

After the intermission, the program continued with a Haydn symphony and concluded with an overture composed by a member of the orchestra. When we returned to the Cornelius household all children, including Mary Sue, who had been left with the older women, were soundly asleep. I carried Mary Sue in my arms, and we walked back to our quarters.

After Jeanne tucked her in, we sat in the family room for a longer while exchanging impressions and opinions about our strange experience. We were tired but still our minds were too stimulated to feel sleepy.

The next day we got up early and, feeling somewhat bolder, walked around on our own. We walked to the foot of the reservoir and watched the early morning fishermen angling for their catch. Every Anthropolitan we met was friendly and helpful without being overly intrusive or inquisitive.

After breakfast at the Cornelius household, again we were given a brief tour of their factories and workshops and some of the public buildings in the inner circle.

"We don't have any bureaucrats here," Cornelius explained when I observed that there were hardly any office workers. "No one ever works here as paper-pushers even for three hours a day. Since our life is organized so simply all our paperwork is done by volunteers, primarily for record-keeping purposes. After all, we still have to deal with one another and with the outside world. But our laws and regulations are so simple that we don't need a large group of workers to push them. Besides, nobody should be a paper pusher anyway. We practically have no government; we don't need one."

"What is your relationship with the United States?" I asked.

"Oh, basically live and let live, close to what Laurinville is to the rest of the United States, I would say," he said. "We are semi-autonomous according to our original agreement. We do some business with them and, obviously, we depend on the United States government for defense because we don't have any armed forces here; we don't even have a police force."

I had so many questions for which I wanted answers. But we didn't have enough time.

"Here is a book I want you to take with you," Cornelius said when I mentioned my further interest in Anthropolis, handing me a sheaf of paper loosely bound into book form. "It's written by one of the sociologists at the University of Wilmington, in fact. Of course, he is long retired, but he wrote it even before we were clearly established as an ongoing system. We drew our practical and intellectual inspirations from this book. You will find it immensely interesting." It was a rather thick tome with a bold title 'REFLECTIONS FROM ANTHROPOLIS' written across the cover. I promised I would return the book as soon as I finished reading it.

Our trip back home itself was uneventful. But both Jeanne and I knew that our views about life had been considerably affected by our visit to the City of Humanity.

On my part, I found the place strongly appealing. I thought I could live in Anthropolis and be happy there. There was a measure of sweet yet well-reasoned simplicity in the City of Humanity that contrasted sharply to the horrid complexity of life in America. I doubted very much that, in spite of its wonderful features, ordinary Americans would find the place attractive enough. Anthropolis and Laurinville seemed to have a closer affinity with each other than either of them with the United States. The City of Humanity would be a good place for Mary Sue or Jeanne's mother, I mused, or perhaps for Jeanne Baker herself. In bold contrast that was sweetly and softly stated, Anthropolis painted a vivid picture of America by its uncompromising rejection of the society to which it owed its existence. For this realization alone, I decided, our trip was a wonderful experience.

Switching my thoughts, thinking ahead to the planned visit to Cecil's family in the country for the coming weekend, I felt something was disturbing me.

But I had no idea then what precisely it was that disturbed me.

Chapter Twenty-Six

"Do you know, Michael," Cecil remarked, "that the family is the first natural human institution ever established?"

He went on to say that the necessity of child dependency on parents made it imperative that mankind must maintain and preserve family life. He mused that his whole adult life would have been impossible without the moral and psychological upbringing he had received from his family.

Cecil McMiller had returned to his normal self once again as soon as we were on the road to Elkin to spend the weekend with his family. He joked and laughed at his own jokes with the kind of uproarious exaggeration to which I had become adjusted.

I argued, for the sake of argument, that the family could easily be replaced by a community, which was in a way a larger family, as demonstrated in the Israeli kibbutz and on the Russian collective farms that I had read about. In those examples (and of Anthropolis, which I didn't mention to Cecil), I suggested, children were raised by other adults who were not related to them by blood.

There were no signs, however, that children brought up thusly had experienced any damaging disadvantages in their later lives. I learned also that many growing up in Boys Town in Ohio proved to be fine upstanding citizens. I was tempted to say that, from what I saw only the day before, the children of Anthropolis were some of the most loved and well-adjusted children that I had ever seen.

"Why is it so important that bloodlines should have monopoly in child-rearing?" I challenged.

"Ah, you haven't seen some of the recent experiments done with the monkeys, have you?" Cecil responded. "According to these experiments, it was proven that the monkey mothers could tell which baby monkeys, although randomly mixed, were their own and gave them love that was very different from what they gave other baby monkeys. Now, how do you explain that?"

I said there might have been some human bias shown by the experimenters, which tended to impose human views upon animal behavior because of their previous expectations.

"We see what we expect to see, you know that, Cecil."

But, in many ways, I was surprised at his tender loyalty to his family in particular and the family institution in general. But I was reminded of our earlier conversations in which he almost ruthlessly defended the rational model of marriage and social structure in America. I felt somehow my sense of continuity was thus violated in the way Cecil expressed his defense of the significance of family life, yet could just as loyally defend the callous money arrangement of his own society in other aspects. Well, every man is allowed some inconsistency in life, I supposed.

"When I was a kid," he recalled one of his anecdotes to entertain me. "We had a baby pig named Humphrey who became like a family pet. He would come into the house and roam around, and even eat our table scraps just like a domesticated animal. I became very attached to Humphrey, but I didn't know Dad had been fattening him up for good smoked hams for the family. Well, one day Dad decided that the pig had grown up enough to be slaughtered. But you know, my poor mom, she was worried sick about little Cecil's reaction. Kid and pig had become such good friends, they thought, God, it was going to be hell to tell the kid that the pig had to be killed."

The situation he was building up was indeed humorous, a rather typical family situation I might have expected in a happy family show on TV in America.

Cecil was in good form, as I was laughing with the anticipation of the punchline. He, teasing me, paused for a while to heighten the effect.

"So, what happened?"

"So, my mom and dad hold a family council, Sis was a baby then. Dad says, you know, Mom, we need the hams for our family. Mom says, but think about poor Cecil. He is gonna die if you tell him you are going to slaughter his pet pig; you know how he and the pig have been so close like brothers." Cecil was always a master of exaggeration and an effective jokester.

"How did you kill pigs in those days?"

"We shot 'em with a rifle. You can't kill 'em with a knife, they squeal like crazy, the whole town can hear it."

He had briefly reverted his speech to his childhood country style.

"So, Mom is very worried, and that upsets Dad, too. Dad, being a very loving and understanding person, says, well, Mom, I am going to have a little talk with the boy about it. I don't know what else I can do."

He paused again to allow me to fully imagine the situation. He was obviously having fun with his narrative.

"I was about eleven or twelve, then. My dad comes to my room where I was playing. Son, he says, I would like to have a little talk with you. So, Dad and I go out to the back of the house and walk up the little hill. Dad and I sit down on the hill, and he says how poor we are and how we need the hams so desperately to feed the family, including the little baby sister. Although you love that pig like your own brother, that pig has to go. Families have to eat."

Then Cecil paused dramatically and looked at me with his devilish grin.

"Oh, Dad!" Cecil suddenly raised his voice like a boy he was portraying in desperate pleading. "Can I shoot Humphrey, please, Dad?"

His punchline was great, and it evoked a howl of laughter from both of us.

"I guess poor Humphrey was not your blood relation," I observed to conclude that episode of his early farm life.

He had some other stories relating to his family. I was anxious to ask him why Carol didn't seem to be part of all this, but kept quiet.

It was late Friday afternoon and the superhighway was somewhat crowded with weekend travelers. But it was a pleasant drive all the way.

We arrived in Elkin at around two o'clock that afternoon. We drove through what constituted the downtown area of Elkin which had one movie house, one department store, and several restaurants among its highlights. It was obvious that Cecil was becoming nostalgic about his old hometown, as he described certain episodes associated with some of those landmarks.

His family lived on a farm several miles to the north of the town. A thick forest covered the whole area between Elkin and his family farm. He explained that a papermill had bought up the whole area for tree-growing business. The company cleared one area at a time for pulp and replenished it with saplings that would take twenty years to grow for another harvest. That papermill forest stretched right up to their backyard fence, Cecil said.

The family house was what I considered a traditional white farmhouse with green trim. Several large trees, including one willow tree hanging low in front, hung over the house. An elderly farmer, whom I recognized as Cecil's father from the photograph album, was working on a truck with the hood raised. Two dogs ran to our car and, as if recognizing Cecil, barked and chased us to the house. A farm that I calculated to be at least several hundred acres stretched to the right of the house, stopping at the papermill forest, but an acre or so immediately around the house was uncultivated, covered with common weeds as if preserved for the dogs to run around in. An old-fashioned tractor was parked against the barn as I had seen in the photograph.

As we pulled in, Cecil's mother and sister, so clearly recognizable from the album, rushed out of the house and stood on the porch waiting for us. We got out and walked toward them. They exchanged wild hugs.

Cecil introduced them to me and me to them, and we exchanged handshakes.

"We heard so much about you," his sister, a late teenager with a ponytail said somewhat bashfully.

"But not anymore than what I've heard about you," I responded, and we had a round of good cheers.

Then we walked to his father who was stoutly ignoring us, concentrating on the matter under the hood. But when we went near him, he got out from under the hood and broke into a big grin. Father and son then proceeded to a hearty hug. I was introduced to his father, and we shook hands. He welcomed me to the farm and hoped that I would have a good weekend with them. He seemed to be the quintessential farmer he was in the photographs, sturdy, shrewd, weather-beaten, wise, frugal, and strong of moral convictions.

He looked so much like a traditional American farmer that I wanted to take pictures of him to show back in Laurinville, calling him 'the Typical American Farmer'. The barn, the silo, the tractor, the dogs, the odds and ends dotting the space around the house were so picturesque that no movie set-decorator could have created a more archetypal rustic farm house.

In fact, that was also true of sister and mother. Sis had a pair of farmer's overalls and a white blouse, and with her pony tail, she radiated the wholesome sense of a farm girl, freshly scrubbed and friendly, not unlike some farm girls I knew in Laurinville. I had no idea what farm girls actually looked like in America, but the way Sis looked could've been straight from any farm catalog

I had seen. His mother, a generous-looking woman, slightly worn out from harsh farm life, was a study in goodwill.

She offered me tea and lemonade, and told me if she could do anything to make my stay more comfortable, not to hesitate to ask her. She was anxious to know what I thought of the United States, and asked me all about my family and life in general in Laurinville. Whatever Cecil had told them about me, they were treating me like a long-lost member of the family.

The house, just like the family that lived in it, seemed comfortable in its arrangement and authentic in its existence, time-tested and standing strong. It was an old structure, but constantly updated and renovated, the latest addition as a concession to modern times, they showed me, being the ceiling fans in the dining room and the family room. Old antique furniture furnished the interior tastefully but functionally. We were put up in Cecil's own room which had the bunk-beds for us, although both of us were slightly over-sized for them. There were all sorts of his childhood memorabilia covering the walls. An open, but screened, window faced the backyard from which a cool autumn breeze gently swept through the room.

The family had not had their lunch, waiting for us to arrive. It was a sumptuous meal in the grand tradition of farm life. Fried chicken, ham, smothered liver, white rice, steamed cabbage, corn on the cob, field peas, potato salad, sweet potato casserole, hot biscuits, pecan pie, lemon pie, and strawberry pie, which was reputed to be Cecil's favorite, were heaped on the table. Our plates were filled several times until we couldn't eat another bite.

All the time, the family exchanged funny stories of Cecil's childhood, some obviously embarrassing, that kept everyone, including me, in constant uproar. I brought out the story of Humphrey the pig, and the retelling of the story made everyone explode with laughter. His father's version was slightly different, not as dramatic as Cecil's, but sounded much more believable.

After lunch, Cecil took me out to show me around. The barn was the most colorful of all the farm relics on the premises, decaying and cumbersome yet with dignity and charm. In one corner was an old remnant of a still which, as Cecil told it, was used by his grand uncle during Prohibition who eventually left them a '32 Dodge which could still be taken out on the highway. Several compartments with unidentifiable but grubby-appearing substances on the floor were sectioned off on one side of the barn, which, Cecil said, was where they used to raise hogs. It was much cheaper nowadays to buy the hams, Cecil said. The smokehouse, which used to be the main instrument of their family food preservation, where presumably Humphrey had met his fate, was practically abandoned. Progress, Cecil lamented, was ruining authentic farm life. There were all sorts of automobile parts strewn about, engines, bumpers, fenders, wheels, doors, dashboards, showing Cecil's early preoccupation with automobiles.

"Hell, I could even build a car out of these parts," he declared. Cecil said the papermill forest was so full of wild animals, especially deer, that the two dogs were practically self-sufficient with the animals they caught and ate. One time they had dragged into the house the leftover bits of a deer they had killed and eaten, which positively horrified his mother.

We spent the evening sitting on the porch. The farm house was so utterly isolated from the nearest highway or neighbors that all we could hear were the insects in the grass and the birds in the forest. Sometimes we heard the howls of wild animals and farm dogs' response with their own howls. Cecil's father, normally a taciturn type, volunteered the information on the difficulty of maintaining a farm his size and operating it in the black.

"The corporate farmers are taking over everything," he said. "And we small independent farmers have a tough time these days."

I asked some polite questions about the state of farmers in America, which had been in decline for many years for their excessive commercialization and so few of them left. But I sensed that Cecil was anxious to steer the conversation away from the topic. I assumed it was a rather painful subject (perhaps the subject of their telephone conversation and the cause of his subsequent mood changes) and did not continue it further.

The quietness of the surroundings on the farm reminded me of the night Jeanne and I spent in Anthropolis. Both the City of Humanity and the farm were an alien existence from the realities of America. Both seemed removed from the hustle and bustle of life, each isolated on its own island of unreality. Anthropolis was like a mirage that had flickered and disappeared. The McMiller farm was like a recreation of a dying past in which farmers worked and lived a happy life, like a ghost trying to come to real life by its sheer effort and stubbornness.

Although I was enjoying the senior McMillers' hospitality and the refreshing country air, I missed Jeanne and her indefatigable daughter. They seemed to be my fragile link to the real world, now becoming stronger in my own sense of reality in this isolated farm house.

I had always had a difficulty in falling asleep in a new environment, and the first night in the country was no exception. I struggled to go to sleep in the lower bunk. Oblivious, Cecil was snoring comfortably in the upper one, totally unconscious to my plight down below. Eventually, I managed to fall asleep, perhaps after counting a thousand sheep.

Then suddenly I woke up. Or, perhaps I had never gone to sleep. It was one of those strange moments in which one cannot tell whether one was asleep or awake.

It was Cecil's father, who was gently shaking his son awake. "Cecil, Cecil," the senior McMiller whispered as if not to disturb the sleeping companion below.

After some effort, Cecil was roused from his sleep. He sat up in his bunk.

"Yes, Dad," Cecil said, still in sleep. "What is it?"

"Shhhh—" cautioned his father. "I want to talk to you."

With some grunting and mumbling Cecil finally got down from his bed. Not to make them feel bad about waking me up, I pretended to be sleeping. Father and son left the room, and in a few seconds, I heard the front door open and shut. But because of the utter quiet of the night, I could hear their footsteps on the gravel driveway, as if they were circling the house. As they came around to my side of the house their voices could be heard through the open window.

Curiosity got the better of me. I had been wanting to know what was bugging my friend and was sure their midnight talk had something to do with that. As I got up and moved toward the open window, I could see the glow of the father's pipe. They were walking down the backyard, coming toward my window on their path. I could hear them somewhat more clearly as they came closer.

Cecil was saying something to his father, almost pleading with him.

"You know, son," the senior McMiller said. "The simple fact is that we need more money, we've been losing money ever since. You say we shouldn't accept business from anybody else, but we've got to survive—"

There was some more pleading from the son. 'Patience' was mentioned two or three times.

"—You have to allow us, son, to—" the word faded, then, "—or else we have to cease to operate this family business."

Father and son did not come around the house again. They had drifted away in the direction of the barn.

Obviously, the family was in deep financial trouble. The father wanted to sell the farm or to turn to another kind of business, to which his son was obviously opposed. Understanding the deep commitment that my friend carried to his family and its farm tradition, I felt sorry for his predicament. Apparently, the pressure had been bearing down on him for some time. I even regretted that I had become privy to their secret family trouble.

I don't remember how long I stayed awake, waiting for my friend to return. But I surprised myself by getting drowsy and, swimming in an endlessly confusing dream of faces and places, I finally fell asleep without seeing Cecil return.

Chapter Twenty-Seven

The next day, which was Saturday, we attended a country fair in progress in the county seat about fifteen miles away. The fair was notable for its overwhelming country flair, cattle and horses among other livestock making up its main highlights. It was largely a dusty and tiresome event, however.

That evening we attended an Octoberfest, a predominantly Germanic festival with live music and a lot of dancing. The McMillers were avid dancers and I was forced into joining the circle for the 'Chicken Dance', but I enjoyed the Viennese waltzes with Sis. The food was great and we stayed on at the fest until close to midnight.

I slept soundly that night and, if father and son had shared another one of their midnight family discussions, I was blissfully unaware of it. All day Saturday, however, neither showed any sign of the distress that had prompted their nocturnal foray.

On Sunday morning before our departure back home, we attended a church service at the suggestion of the senior McMiller. Although neither of us was religious, we agreed to follow the elder's wishes.

Religion by then seemed to have become largely a media spectacle in America, as shown by the Gospel Academy Awards on TV that I had watched. Few old-timers, mostly poor but hearty souls, however, clung to their tradition of backwoods revivals and church congregations.

The church we attended, about two miles or so toward the town of Elkin, was indeed a small church, attended by perhaps less than fifty people. Naturally our presence, two visitors from Wilmington, one a professor, a no mean honor to the country folk, attracted their attention. The faithful strained their necks to look at us all through the service. The pastor, a graying gentleman of about sixty, gave due recognition to our presence as if the others hadn't noticed. He had a fine sing-song voice with which he delivered his sermon of hell and damnation.

The gist of his sermon had to do with the rationalization of religion, especially in reference to the mass media that had revolutionized religion in America. Which somehow reminded me of Carol's novel.

"As a faithful servant of God," the minister declared, "I will never appear on television, nor will I ask my congregation to demean themselves to associate with that sinful instrument of evil."

The point was not exactly clear to me, but at the mention of congregation several faithful chanted "amen."

After the service was over, the minister sought us out.

"Professor McMiller, Professor McMiller," the minister called to us, slithering through his meager crowd to reach us. "Nice for you to have come to our glorious House of God," he said.

Cecil, who had apparently met the minister before, then introduced me and the minister shook my hand heartily.

"Oh, Professor McMiller," cried the minister holding me by the hand and pulling me along with him. "Your friend ought to see our latest addition to the church. It took us three years to complete it, but with the help of the Lord we did it. Now we can really get together to worship the Lord. Come."

I followed the minister to the back of the sanctuary which led us down the stairs to the basement. The basement, directly below the sanctuary, was a good-size room that the minister called "our fellowship meeting place." But it was not the basement that he had wanted to show me. He rushed me through the fellowship meeting place and, crossing the hallway, took me to his prize accomplishment.

"For the glory of the Lord," the minister pronounced. "Our brand-new kitchen!"

It indeed was a kitchen, freshly remodeled and equipped with glittering kitchen appliances. The oven, the refrigerator, the mixer, the microwave, the sink, the cupboard, and even the floor was shiny and new.

"We worked hard for three years to build this kitchen," the minister beamed, "so that we can prepare our Lord's good food here when we have fellowships."

I complimented him on his outstanding accomplishment, which he profusely deferred to the almighty powers of God.

The minister then took me to his office which was situated at the back of the sanctuary. Once we got in it, he closed the door behind him as if we were conspirators.

"I want to show you something," he said as he pulled out a chart. "Our attendance has been steadily rising since I have been here."

It was a graph, the kind that advertisers used on TV to show the trend or effects their merchandise, either going up or going down, in simple lines. The minister's graph showed a faintly recognizable upward movement over a six-month period.

"What do you think?" the minister whispered. "With the Lord's help, our congregation has been growing leaps and bounds."

While I was trying to identify the source of the minister's optimism, as represented in the chart, there was a knock on the door.

Upon the minister's approval a teenage boy stepped in.

"I counted 'em all, pastor," the boy reported.

"How many, how many, Timmy?" the minister asked anxiously.

The boy said forty-six. The minister's jaws dropped.

"Are you sure, Timmy?" he inquired critically.

The boy said, sure, pastor.

"Did you count our visitors too?"

The boy said, yes, he did.

"How about the balcony?" the minister asked. "You know you missed one person last week because he was sitting behind the pillar on the balcony? Remember, Timmy?"

The boy maintained that he had checked the balcony and behind the pillar as well. The minister eyed the chart for a few seconds.

"What the Lord giveth," he said softly to himself, "the Lord taketh away. Blessed be the name of the Lord."

I quietly left his office and joined the McMillers at the front of the church.

On the way home to Wilmington, Cecil was back in his thoughtful mood once again. I became somewhat meditative, too, thinking about the midnight discussion between father and son, and the simple fact that during our whole stay there had been no mention of Carol. The perfect family in every way had acted as if their son's wife, albeit a contract-wife, never existed.

Cecil was silent, watching the road as if he was concentrating on his driving. Once in a while, realizing his silence, he asked me about Jeanne, to which I responded in monosyllables. His silence had discouraged me from talking about her any more than necessary. In fact, the absence of Carol from his family's memories somewhat dampened my wildly favorable impression of them.

We pulled into the horseshoe driveway about four o'clock in the afternoon. Carol was not home, but there was a terse message for me on the kitchen table. It read, "Michael, Urgent. See Jeanne. Carol."

I frowned. Urgent? What could've happened? I wondered. Did Mary Sue get sick from the trip to Anthropolis? Another car accident? Was her mother sick? There were speculations but no answer. Why didn't Carol explain what was wrong? I cursed the absence of a telephone at the Baker household.

In less than fifteen minutes, I was on Sutton. When I approached Jeanne's house, I saw Carol's car parked in front. I parked mine behind hers and walked in without knocking.

Carol and Jeanne had been in deep consultation when I walked in. Seeing me, Jeanne rushed over and hugged me, crying. Apparently, she had been crying for a long time because her eyes were red and swollen.

"What happened?" I inquired, but Jeanne couldn't answer. She just kept crying.

Carol stood up and handed me what looked like a court document, with all the signatures and dotted lines, and so on. It was a "Summons to Appear," issued by the county circuit court. I fumbled with it trying to open it with one hand while holding Jeanne with the other.

"Jeanne has been challenged," Carol said calmly.

"What?" I responded without comprehending.

Jeanne cried louder.

"A man challenged her for the custody of Mary Sue," Carol said.

"That's impossible," I said.

Carol took the document from me and started reading.

MOTION TO CHALLENGE:

In accordance with State Law, etcetera, etcetera, Challenger George Passin, TIW 181, hereby challenges and notifies Defendant Jeanne Baker, TIW 48, for the custody of Mary Sue, female, age two. Challenger is represented by Attorneys at Law Smith, Gates and Borosky, whose address is, etcetera, etcetera...

"Where is Mary Sue?" I asked because I hadn't seen her.

"She is in the back with Mother," Jeanne answered through her crying.

After some prodding, Jeanne regained her composure to answer my questions. "When did you get this summons?"

She said, "Today, delivered by a private courier."

"She called you at home, but I answered the call and came over here," Carol said.

"And who is this man, you know this man?" I inquired.

She nodded.

"Who is he? Why is he doing this to you?"

Jeanne sat down and wiped her face. I was thankful that Carol had been with her.

"I used to work for Passin," Jeanne said. "He is an accountant. I was his secretary."

"Used to work for him?"

"I quit a year ago and went to work for this construction company that I am working for now."

"Why did you quit?"

"Because he bothered me."

"He bothered you?"

Obviously, I wasn't quick to grasp what Jeanne said. She looked at Carol as if asking for help.

"We used to call that 'sexual harassment'," volunteered Carol. "But that charge is no longer taken seriously nowadays because the charged party can pay out of it. Besides, the party that brings the charge almost always has an inferior TIW standing against someone with a superior TIW number. The courts almost always find in favor of higher TIW's, other things being equal. Most women these days either accept money or quit their jobs, and certainly don't think about bringing charges against those men."

"He is challenging you because you quit?"

It was a stupid question, and Jeanne looked at me in agreement.

"He was really after me, but I hated him," Jeanne said as if she still feared and loathed him. "I hated him, I hated everything about him. He was a nasty boss and a cruel man to everyone who worked for him, but especially to women. He ruined a young sweet girl just before I began to work for him and she had to quit, heartbroken, and was later sent to a mental hospital. I was the only woman he couldn't control, he said."

Jeanne recovered some of her strength primarily because of her recollection of the very unpleasant memory about the man.

"When I quit the job and left his office, he swore he would get even with me one of these days," Jeanne said with a shudder.

"But why try it now, after a year? Why not sooner when he was really angry with you?"

"His TIW then was not as good as it is now," Jeanne said. "Recently he won a big account with a corporation and his TIW soared."

"One-eighty-one is pretty tough to beat," Carol said. "That's why that man feels comfortable he can win the challenge."

"He doesn't even love Mary Sue," Jeanne said mournfully. "He loves himself too much. He doesn't care about anybody but himself. I know he will make a very poor father."

"I don't care if he will make the best father in the world," I almost shouted. "He is not going to take Mary Sue, and what's more, he is not going to be her father. Never!"

Then, being reminded of her daughter, Jeanne excused herself and went back to the room to see her.

Taking a deep breath, and somewhat embarrassed by my outburst, I looked at Carol as if asking her what to do about it. She shook her head in a gesture of helplessness.

"Did you see the men posted on the block when you came in?" Carol asked.

I said I was too anxious to notice anyone out there.

"Why, what men?"

Carol explained that the challenger's private guards had been posted to watch the comings and goings of the household.

"The law allows the challenger to 'protect said challenger's interest'. So, most challengers post armed guards to keep the house under twenty-four-hour surveillance just to protect their interest so that their quarry doesn't get away. Thought you might have seen them too."

I peeked out through the window curtain and saw the car that Carol had indicated. She said they would rotate in three or four shifts.

"Isn't that ridiculous, not to mention outrageous, to do that?" I said, furious. "Nobody is going anywhere."

"It serves a psychological purpose as well," said Carol. "This show of force demonstrates the challenger's power, and it unnerves the challenged parents and demoralizes their resolve before the trial. It intimidates them and scares them."

It was indeed absurd and outrageous, and I complained about it loudly.

"How was your weekend in Elkin?" Carol asked, after listening to my angry retorts about unfairness and outrage, as a respite from our present predicament.

I absently said it was great, and the McMillers were wonderful people.

"They are, aren't they?" Carol agreed evenly.

I couldn't tell if she really meant what she was saying. There were so many questions and few answers. The summons from the court said the preliminary trial was set only two weeks away.

"What can she do now?" I asked returning to the subject of Jeanne.

"The traditional way is to get a lawyer and fight it out in court," Carol said. "There is always a chance that she could win, although forty-some against one-eighty-one is tough odds."

"Then?"

"Then prepare for the trial as competently as possible."

"You said the traditional way," I said. "Is there a nontraditional way?"

"You can always run," Carol said calmly. "Some people do it."

"Do they make it?"

"Some do, if they don't mind being fugitives from the law for the rest of their lives."

"What about the guards out there?" I asked.

"What about them?"

"You have to dodge them somehow."

I pushed the curtain to one side to take a look at the guards outside supposedly guarding their employer's interest when I came face to face with a woman standing just outside the window with a strange machine in her hand aimed at the house. We both jumped and stepped back from the window.

"What is it, Michael?" Carol asked.

"I don't know. There is this woman's face—"

There was a knock on the door and I motioned to Carol to indicate that it was probably that woman at the door. She nodded and I opened the door. Standing at the door, very well dressed in a businesslike manner and smiling profusely and somewhat recovered from her fright moments earlier, was indeed the woman. She still held the gadget in her hand.

"Hello, I am a caretaker," she said, holding out her free hand.

I uncertainly shook her hand.

"Your stress level was over 95," said the smiling caretaker, pointing to the machine which, I noticed, had a small meter. "I thought I would stop by and offer our services."

I had no idea what she was talking about and Carol sprang to her feet.

"Thank you very much," she said to the woman. "But we don't need your service at the moment."

"Are you sure?" the woman insisted, holding up the machine. "The stress level was—"

"Yes, we are very sure," Carol assured her, almost pushing the door shut against the woman. "Still, we thank you for your concern."

"If you need anything," the woman managed to produce her business card and hand it to Carol as she retreated through the door, "please contact us. We give—"

"Thank you very much," Carol said firmly and just as firmly pulled the door shut.

"What was all that about?" I asked dumbfounded.

"Oh, they are called caretakers. They offer legal, psychological, emotional, or whatever services people might need. Of course, for a handsome fee."

"How in the world did she know we were in trouble?"

"The stress-o-meter."

"Stress—what?"

"Stress-o-meter, the little gadget she was carrying. The caretakers simply point that thing at the houses as they drive by and if the level registers very high, say 95 as the woman said and I am sure our level *was* that high, they stop by and offer their service. Instead of waiting for clients to come to them, the professional helpers go out and find them. It's a great booming business."

Carol explained further that the machine was so sophisticated that it could tell induced stress, such as induced by TV and carnal passions, from genuine stress, such as that produced at the Baker household. The woman's business card, much larger than the ones I had seen before, had pictures of various stressful situations superimposed by a smiling face, presumably that of the professional caretaker. At the bottom was a motto printed in large block letters:

WE CARE! Apparently attracted by our commotion Jeanne, Mary Sue, and Jeanne's mother came out to the living room. Carol told them about the caretaker woman's uninvited visit.

"They are like vultures," Jeanne's normally unobtrusive mother observed with such a feeling that I was somewhat surprised. "In my younger days, they at least had the decency to give us time to decide what to do first ourselves. Nowadays, they just barge in and offer their so-called services."

"Not that we can afford them, anyway, Mother," Jeanne responded.

By venting our frustration on the caretaker woman some more, all of us soon felt better and regained a sense of resolve concerning the matter at hand.

Carol suggested that she would talk to Cecil about it because, with his friendship with Judge Roberts and some other prominent people, he might know what to do. All was not lost yet. With that assurance, she departed.

Once we were left alone, I was overcome by a strong sense of repugnance. The idea of a man throwing huge sums of money at the poor mother, like teasing a hungry dog with a bone, made me furious. Losing her daughter would be devastating to Jeanne beyond recovery. Losing her man three years ago was terrible enough, now she might lose her daughter.

We sat down and discussed the options. Traditional and nontraditional. "How would you like to live in Anthropolis or even Laurinville?" I said, as the idea had been on my mind for a while. "That means, of course, you would never be able to come back to the United States."

"I thought about that too," she confessed.

The idea was so radical and drastic that we decided not to think about it any further at the moment.

Jeanne promised that she would never let the child out of the house and would keep the house locked at all times, not to open it to anyone not personally known to her. In a materialist society, possession was nine points of the law. As long as we had Mary Sue in our possession, we still had the upper hand.

"Well, we haven't exhausted all the traditional avenues yet," I said. "Cecil McMiller knows a lot of prominent citizens. He should be able to help. After all, he is a successful professor with good connections."

I thus assured Jeanne somewhat and returned to the McMillers to discuss the strategy with Cecil. I passed the man in the car and he eyed me indifferently but with professional ease and confidence. Another man, obviously a partner, stood outside the car smoking languidly.

When I walked into the McMiller household, everything was unusually quiet. Carol was sitting at the kitchen table, staring into space. Something was wrong.

"What's the matter, Carol? Where is Cecil?"

"There is no Cecil," she said, picking up a note from the table and handing it to me. I read the note and it simply said, "Gone to the Center."

"'Gone to the Center,'" I repeated it a couple of times. "What does that mean? What Center? When is he coming home?"

"He is not coming home," Carol said. "At least not for a while." I looked at her uncomprehending.

"What do you mean?"

"Michael, the Center is a psychiatric hospital," Carol said, sighing deeply and hopelessly. "It's called the Recovery Center for mental breakdowns."

It still didn't dawn on me.

"Why?" I asked. "Is he visiting somebody there?"

"No. Cecil admitted himself. He has had a nervous breakdown. This is not the first time, however."

Nervous breakdown! How could it be? Cecil McMiller having a nervous breakdown?

"Yes, Michael," Carol said quietly. "Cecil McMiller had a nervous breakdown and admitted himself at the psychiatric hospital."

I sat there and looked at Carol, not knowing what to say. Carol was absolutely steady with her gaze, meeting mine without wavering.

Then it all came back to me. Of course, it was his family problem. "We need more money," the senior McMiller had pleaded in the pitch-dark of the night. "—or else we have to cease to operate this family business."

Did she notify the family?

She said no.

"Shouldn't we call them immediately?"

Carol said no.

"Why not?" I inquired, somewhat miffed. "Isn't that his family that's the root of all this? I mean financial trouble with the farm?"

I relayed to her some of the conversation I had overheard the night before between father and son, with the conclusion that I felt it was of utmost urgency that we inform the family, forgetting that I was talking to his wife who should know better in such matters, albeit as an outsider.

"He has no family," Carol said.

"What?" I responded stupidly.

"I said Cecil has no family," she said calmly as if she was stating a simple fact that everybody should know.

"I don't understand," I said, really meaning it. "We just came from there this afternoon."

"His family," said Carol of her in-laws, "his father, mother and sister, died in a car accident two years ago."

Something swirled and spun in my head, the world was flat once again. We were in the Middle Ages, and the world had never changed.

"That can't be, that can't be," I finally protested. "I just saw them this—" Then I stopped and uttered: "Oh, my God!"

"Yes, Michael," she said with all her patience. "They are actors."

Chapter Twenty-Eight

It was the Green Palmers all over again. The incredulous was now commonplace. I was tempted to declare flatly and without reservation that the awful truth about Cecil would compare with the most astounding moments of revelation recorded in history, such as hearing that the earth was no longer the center of the universe. But, if the earth was no longer the center of everything, what in the world *was* it? Or, that the divine king had just lost his head to the mob seeking justice on the guillotine; how could the almighty king, son of God, father of men, have his head, along with his queen's, roll into a basket like a common thief? How could that wonderful family on the farm, the loving flesh and blood of mother, father and sister all be fakes, like wound-up dolls, mistaken for real, loving and being loved?

"I want you to see this," Carol said, after I had recovered a semblance of my sanity, and took me to the living room where the TV apparatus was kept. I say apparatus because it was a fine piece of machinery which combined what they called a VCR with all the programs one wanted under one's fingertips, all indexed and numbered in 'compact disks'. With a couple of buttons any program could be recalled instantly on the screen.

Carol proceeded to call up a particular program by pushing some buttons and then typing in the name of the program. It was a soapy family melodrama from Disney World which had gotten into television production, especially family-related shows.

"Watch the next commercial," Carol called my attention to the screen.

I sat there looking at the few seconds of a family, apparently a new version of something called 'Father Loves Best', except in that show the father was not the real one. The family, upon losing its real father to an illness, had accepted an insurance substitute who turned out to be 'better' than the one it had replaced.

Then the break came and the commercial appeared. It showed in slow movement a car pulling up to a beautiful rustic house upon which the visitor, a thirtyish young man, was greeted by the whole family (apparently father, mother, two sisters and three brothers) who rushed out, hugging him, kissing him, and hanging all over him. It was a wonderful moment and visually memorable, smiling faces and tight hugs filling the screen. Sweet, swelling background music matched the magnificent scene of homecoming.

"Are you hungry for real family life?" the voice, gentle and wise with age, said in the background. "Family life you no longer have? Family life you wish you had but never did? Are you lonely without the warmth, support, and love of a family that you once had, you wish you had, or you would like to have? (Then the scene changed to the family praying at their sumptuous meal on the table.)"

"We have the answer. Come to us and spend a week, a month, or even a few days with a family that you can call your own, a family that is exactly like the one in your dream. We have many professionally trained personnel who would be glad to be your father, mother, aunt, grandparents, brothers and sisters—all to your specification. Just describe what you want. What kind of parents, brothers, sisters, or grandparents? Their religious rituals, personal habits and idiosyncrasies in minute detail. Any and all kinds of pets. Send photographs if you have them, which would help us give you a more life-like family. Our professional makeup staff renders it absolutely indistinguishable from the real one. (The family was now looking at the photo album and other memorabilia in the living room.)"

"Many who have tried our service were so satisfied that they return time and time again to re-experience their family life. Life can be richer and more fulfilling with family experience. We offer a special discount for those who have recently lost their loved ones. (The screen showed a variety of faces, apparently satisfied customers with their testimonial.)"

"We are a large family waiting eagerly to serve lonely hearts like you—with warmth, support, and love. Call or write us. We are open 24 hours."

The commercial ended with people getting on the telephone, presumably calling the number to make reservations, some holding a photo in their hands and describing the details in the picture.

Carol turned the set off and I sat there looking at the blank screen.

"We use actors for a lot of things," Carol said. "You know there is nothing very new about it. This is a thriving industry in America."

I recalled Martha Jo's funeral at McDonald's. Also, there was the actor who played Hugh Seago. Those were not too long ago but, with other events following them in rapid succession, I had forgotten all about them. Then my memory raced back to the smiling salesman I met on the plane when I left Laurinville. He said of his charming family as he was showing me their videotape: "This family of mine is costing me an arm and a leg."

I now understood what he meant by that remark. Yes, with their idyllic charm and perfect beauty, his family *must* be costing him a fortune to maintain! It was not too long ago that I left Laurinville but, for all that I have seen and learned in America, it might as well have been another lifetime.

"But," I said miserably, not believing myself, "I never thought that the McMillers on the farm, Cecil's own family—"

"Cecil had an awful time accepting the fact that his family was gone," Carol said. "It was Mutt and Jeff who persuaded him to consider the professional family as a substitute."

"But," I said again. "They were so real, they looked so real. They were—"

"Our professional actors are remarkable with their skill, almost perfect. Can't tell the difference. Most people are satisfied with the results. With Cecil, however, it went one step further."

"How? Why?"

"I suppose some human beings cannot live without being human," Carol said. "I am an artist; I have my own artistic world. And the Anthropolitans whom I strongly support and look to for spiritual sympathy. But Cecil had nothing inside him, especially after his family died. He had nothing to help him deep inside with his agony and with the violence that his society was doing to his sensibilities. He had no external help either, because he was so American in his upbringing, and couldn't find any human group or ideas to identify himself with. He went through several commercial families before he met the current set, thanks to the hard and long search by Mutt and Jeff who arranged the actors for him."

"But what went wrong?"

"Cecil got too attached to his actor-family, and it got to a point where he wanted the 'family' just for himself. But it became very expensive."

Then I remembered the conversation. "You say we shouldn't accept business from anybody else, but we've got to survive—" the father, or the man who acted as father, had said. Then, "—You have to allow us, son, to—" The 'family business' mentioned a couple of times was indeed a business!

"Cecil supported the entire 'family' on the farm, which cost him a great deal of money. He wanted to think of them as his real family, and for nobody else. He couldn't imagine them to be anyone else's family. He crossed that fine line between reality and fantasy, like most people in America."

"Was he having financial trouble?"

"Yes. Cecil had bought the farm and the house in Elkin because it resembled his hometown in Wisconsin where he was born and raised. Remember? Cecil remained after the memorial service for the drowned student to talk business with Mutt and Jeff and Dean Nettor? The actors had complained, through Mutt and Jeff, which had also come to the dean's attention, that they were not getting paid enough and threatened to disband. But Cecil could never accept that possibility."

"Why not go with another family? I mean another group of actors, for heaven's sake?" I felt furious with my friend. "I am sure there are other actors for less money who could play the—"

"Cecil couldn't," Carol said, shaking her head sadly. "He got too attached to his fake family. He couldn't accept anybody else as his father, mother and sister. The ones in Elkin had become just too real."

The telephone conversation in the kitchen, the family photo album, father, mother and sister, the farm, the house, the barn, the dogs, the whole scene flashed through my mind. And how they and Cecil had acted with one another.

"Did he really confuse them with his real family?" I had to ask.

"I would say he did," Carol said. "Perhaps he got to a point where he loved them more than he did his real family. He got very desperate when the complaint and threat to disband came to him through the Mutt and Jeff team, with the dean's knowledge, and went to the farm over the weekend with you to see if he could persuade them to reconsider."

"Obviously he couldn't," I observed.

"Obviously he couldn't," Carol agreed.

Chapter Twenty-Nine

The next morning Carol and I visited the Recovery Center. She was efficient and knowledgeable about the place, which indicated that she had visited the center before. Cecil's wing, which was specially designed for those voluntarily admitted, was separate from the main building which housed more common mental disorders among the lower classes.

The wing in which Cecil was accommodated was incongruously named the 'Wing of Loving', whose sign hung outside the front office. Carol and I registered with the receptionist, a young blonde woman whose smile looked infectiously real. We followed her to the main lobby on the path through a garden. There were incredibly beautiful flowers and shrubs and bushes adorning the garden. But before I could compliment her on the beauty of the garden, the receptionist picked up a flower with a long stem laying on the ground and placed it in the hole in the flowerbed from which it had apparently been extracted. It was an artificial flower, though manufactured with an incredible likeness to the real one.

"We can't maintain a real garden," the receptionist said as if answering me, flashing her infectious smile. "The guests just tear it apart. They are just naughty boys and girls sometimes."

I assumed guest was the formal name given to the self-admitted, and boys and girls a more affectionate and informal reference to them.

The main lobby was divided into what appeared to be a reading room with books and magazines strewn about and a playroom in which I could see half a dozen or so patients busily engaged in woodwork and leather articles. Several workers in white tops were assisting the patients in the playroom as if they were organizing a workshop for weekend hobbyists. The furniture in the reading room suggested home-comfort, very little of it indicating a mental institution.

A lunch and dinner menu was posted on the bulletin board along with the title of a movie to be shown that night. At the bottom of the menu was a note informing the patients that, if the menu was not agreeable, individual orders could be accepted. The movie announcement was accompanied by a note that popcorn and drinks would be served at the movie. The announcement also reminded the residents not to forget to bring their cashing chips.

"We try to make their recovery here as comfortable as possible," the receptionist said noticing that I was reading the announcements on the bulletin board. "After all, they pay for their stay, just like a hotel. This is, as they say, their home away from home."

Carol, with her jaws set firmly, ignored the receptionist as if she was familiar with the woman's nonsense.

Cecil was sitting in the corner of the reading room facing the window. At the sign of someone entering, he turned around and saw us. He was reading a book which he put down on his lap.

"You know," he said without preambles, "the Romans had a good idea about administration."

He pointed to a passage in the book he had been reading, which was indeed about the Roman administration of conquered provinces, his favorite subject of scholarship that had kept him for many hours at the library.

Cecil was in his pajamas, looking somewhat subdued with the recent violent turn of his inner mind, and showing the stubby morning beard as if the turmoil in his mind had dominated his body as well.

His appearance was so different from anything I had seen of him that I had to turn my face away from him to hide the tears swelling in my eyes. He continued on about the Roman administrators.

Carol instinctively looked for and, in his room, found his shaving gear. She immediately started shaving him. Cecil tried to keep talking about the Romans even during the shave.

Carol went back to his room, which was down the hall, one of the three long hallways containing rooms for the residents that spread in three different directions from the main lobby, and brought back some clothes for Cecil. My friend obediently followed Carol's instruction like a child obeying his mother as he put his clothes on, all the while talking to me about the Romans. The shave and the clothes improved his appearance somewhat, but his obedient conduct and his irrelevant babbling about the Romans evoked a terrible sense of pity in me. Then he suddenly realized something and a light of recognition came to his eyes.

"Did you call Father?" he asked Carol. "Did you call him?"

Carol answered that she had.

"What did he say?" Cecil asked urgently. "Was he worried?"

"Yes, he was worried," Carol said. "But I told him not to worry. You would be home pretty soon. Won't you, Cecil?"

"Did you talk to Mom and Sis, too?" Cecil asked without listening to Carol. "Poor Mom and Sis. Poor Dad."

Cecil muttered their names several times more and started sobbing, burying his face in Carol's arms. She patted him on the back like a mother with her little boy. After a minute or so, the sobbing stopped. As if she had been used to the scene of Cecil's breakdown, Carol was efficient but tender with him. I was touched by the efficient yet sweet way she handled Cecil.

After half an hour or so with Cecil we saw his doctor, a heavyset middle-aged man, who told us that he suspected Cecil might have to stay a little longer this time. He had Cecil's previous records of admission and noted that each time his length of stay got longer. He diagnosed his patient's condition as 'acute schizophrenic episode compounded by hallucination'. As soon as the patient calmed down, he would undergo the "therapy," to which Carol seemed to have agreed earlier.

We went through the fake garden and the smiling receptionist once again to get to the parking lot. Carol was quiet much of the way home.

"Why did you marry Cecil?" I asked her the question that had been on my mind.

She was silent for a while.

"I was still struggling for recognition as an artist," she said without hesitation, "with a sick mother. Cecil offered to take care of her with his payment for the difference. Although my TIW was low, Cecil volunteered to offset our differences in TIW's with my talent as an artist. It was a bit complicated calculation to figure out who owed what, but we worked it out and I accepted his offer. Besides, my association with the Anthropolitans needed a foil, and being his contract-wife was a nice, safe position in society."

"Would this—this breakdown make any difference?" I asked, meaning his job at the university and perhaps his situation in his marriage.

"Not really," Carol said. "He has good insurance to cover all his illnesses and lapses from the university. Such breakdowns are so common among the faculty that hardly anyone notices them anymore. For that matter, quite a few others with a relatively high TIW rank tend to use the Recovery Center just for a rest now and then. Mental illness is thought of as nothing more than a common cold."

"What about you and Cecil?" I said. "What would happen?"

She looked ahead as though concentrating on the road.

"Cecil needs me," she said quietly. "I must stay with him. He no longer has his 'family'. I'm the only family he has."

Then she turned to the subject of Jeanne and Mary Sue. I had wanted to talk about them but had not wished to interfere with her acute distress with Cecil's condition at the moment.

"How did Jeanne like Anthropolis?" Carol inquired.

I told her that Jeanne seemed to have been favorably impressed with the city, and that we had briefly discussed the possibility of considering an escape to the City of Humanity. Jeanne had thought the idea feasible. It was a decision with enormous implications. I told Carol that I thought it was the best solution possible under the circumstances.

"But how do we get her and her daughter out of the house, anyway?" I deplored. "With the guards watching them day and night?"

"I have been thinking about a way," Carol said. "But first, Jeanne must decide what she would like to do."

That evening I visited Jeanne. The private guards were still there, fairly bored with their eventless routines, it seemed.

I told her about our visit to see Cecil at the Recovery Center. Jeanne said she had been there too. She had visited the girl who had been driven mad by George Passin.

"But they put her in the main building," Jeanne said, describing it as a less than desirable place because it was basically for those with poor TIW's and the service had left much to be desired.

The recollection of her visit to see the unfortunate girl rekindled her fear of the challenger. She said her mother had taken Mary Sue to the backyard for a few minutes in the afternoon and the guards immediately showed up there, watching them over the hedges that fenced the backyard.

"They are like vultures, waiting for us to die," Jeanne said, furious and fearful. "Mother almost screamed when she saw their faces sticking out from behind the hedges without a warning."

"They are trying to intimidate you and break you down," I observed.

I then told her that Carol and I had discussed the matter and Anthropolis seemed to be the best alternative. The other alternative, the idea of trying to win the case in court, was too fraught with risk against someone like Passin. The afternoon encounter with the private guards had infuriated and unnerved her, which drove her to the idea of Anthropolis with greater force. Jeanne confessed that it looked attractive.

"How about your mother?"

Jeanne said her mother would go anywhere her granddaughter went. Besides, at her age, Anthropolis looked like the kind of place for her. She had been renting the house and the rent was paid up to date, so there was no problem with that issue. Most of the furniture came with the house.

"We like to travel light," she said and smiled sadly.

We fell silent for a minute or so, knowing what the next question would be. We both knew I was the next question. What would *I* do, then? Jeanne looked at me as if the same question had been on her mind.

"I will be with you in Anthropolis as soon as I can," I assured her. "I have some Civil War fort research I had started that I want to finish up at the university. But it won't take too long. In the meantime, I can always come up and see you among the Anthropolitans."

What we would do afterward, after Anthropolis, was left unsaid. Her modesty about our relationship and her unspoken trust in me moved me deeply, and I swore again that Passin was not going to take the little girl away from this mother. The more we talked about the City of Humanity the more the idea seemed to appeal to her. She, in a rare moment of feminine vanity, even joked about how she would look in the smock-like clothes that we had seen worn by the Anthropolitan women.

That brought to the fore the fact that she had been born and reared in North Carolina, and everything she had known all her life was American. She had never been exposed to any foreign culture before in her life, if Anthropolis were excluded from it.

I told her that Anthropolis was after all part of the United States and its people were also Americans, perhaps the best among them.

"Who knows?" I speculated. "Someday, the whole United States might become like Anthropolis."

"Wouldn't that be wonderful?" Jeanne reflected in her unsophisticated but intelligent manner toward such weighty issues of society. "So many people won't have to go to the Recovery Center."

She promised me that she would sleep on the idea, but would make her decision by the next day. She would call me in the morning from work. I played with Mary Sue for the next hour or so, and then returned home.

The private guards apparently noted my coming and going.

Early the next morning Jeanne called me at the McMillers' and told me that she had made up her mind to go to Anthropolis. She said, in her guarded way, that she had decided 'to go there'. She said she would make necessary preparations for the 'travel' immediately. I told her I would see her that evening at her house.

Carol received the news calmly as if she had expected the decision.

"I will make the arrangement," she said in her usual comfortable manner, stressing the word 'arrangement' in a way that implied her unique competence for such a task at her disposal.

Speaking to her about Jeanne's escape from Passin, and watching her remarkable composure toward the event about to take place under her direction, I could not help but admire Carol McMiller. Somehow, I instinctively felt that it was not the first time that such a problem had come to her for resolution. Did her association with the Anthropolitans consist of some sort of underground network?

The next three days or so I rarely saw Carol. She insisted on visiting Cecil alone, and she was gone all afternoons and evenings. When I saw her briefly one night, she informed me that Cecil seemed to be getting better, almost ready for the therapy the doctor had mentioned. Then she went out again.

In the meanwhile, I helped Jeanne by running errands for her. She needed certain articles for Mary Sue, which she could not get without arousing the guards' suspicion. I continued my appearance as her innocent suitor, although I wasn't sure if that had worked on the watchful eyes. However, we made sure that no visible disturbances would be created in the household. Jeanne portrayed herself as the distraught and worried mother who had been challenged by a powerful foe.

On the fourth day, Carol said the plan was ready for Jeanne, to take effect the following Monday. Jeanne said she was ready.

Friday, Saturday and Sunday remained until then.

Chapter Thirty

Carol's plan was simple in conception. But the whole thing evolved around the reality of whether we could fool the watchful eyes of the private guards successfully. As the centerpiece of our plan Carol had obtained a large picnic basket, large enough for a two-year-old to hide in snugly.

I continued to visit Jeanne the next three days and acted as if nothing momentous was happening in our lives. As per our plan, we visited the park and the beach, taking the picnic basket with us. Sometimes we carried food in it, and other times it just contained nothing particular. We wanted to get the guards used to the idea of seeing the basket often enough until there was nothing unusual about it. The first time they saw the basket seemed to shake them visibly, because the taller of the two day-shift men was straining his neck to see what was in the basket. But gradually they lost interest in it, it seemed to us, exactly as we had hoped.

Every morning when I visited the Bakers, the basket faithfully accompanied me as if I was one of the romantic fools from a bygone era. When I was leaving her, I always took it back with me. But whenever I left, I always swung the picnic basket or did something with it to indicate beyond any doubt that there was nothing in it and that the guards knew about it.

Their eagle eyes, at first fiercely watchful, gradually became routine and indifferent. Everything seemed to be working according to our expectations.

The private eyes were nevertheless good watchdogs. They followed us to the park and then to the beach which we frequented every day. The beach was practically deserted by then. The beach season was nearly over and only the hearty surfers riding the waves and the few romantic couples strolling on the beach were seen, cutting a fairly desolate seascape that was once crowded with beachgoers, many of them students from the University.

The two fully-dressed thugs, watching us from a spot near the pier, looked ridiculously conspicuous and out of place. As our beachball bounced in their direction a couple of times, one of them, the shorter one, even tried to hide behind one of the thick wooden pillars under the pier. I thought about giving them a smile, but not wishing to provoke them any more than necessary, refrained from the urge. Often Jeanne and I went over our plans and what we each had to do.

On Monday morning, the weather turned suddenly chilly, the overcast sky ominous with a threat of rain. Carol and I didn't know what to make of the turn in the temperature, but we both hoped it was not a bad omen. If it rained, we speculated, it might not be so fortuitous for our getaway. Before we left the house, Carol and I studied the map thoroughly one more time so that I would be absolutely familiar with our escape route.

By the time we got to Sutton Drive, it had started to drizzle. It was an unpleasant sensation to think about a possible wild chase scene in the rain, although the unpleasantness went both ways.

The faithful guards were on the nearly same spot, half a block or so away from the house, when Carol and I drove up. The instant we showed up they made themselves alert, the shorter man suddenly sitting up from his laid-back position. The other member of the tandem, as if it was his turn on watch, was looking at us with a professionally rehearsed menace.

I turned the car around facing away from the house. Carol and I got out of the car, I carrying the basket. It was another day of uneventful park visiting and beach going, although the weather made both ideas unseemly.

"Do you think they noticed that you didn't go to work today?" Carol whispered to Jeanne as we got inside the house.

Jeanne and her mother were all ready, dressed for traveling light. Mary Sue was blissfully asleep. According to our plan, Jeanne had kept her up late the night before so that she would not interfere inadvertently with our getaway. The household was thick with tension.

"I don't know," said Jeanne. "I hope the last three days off made them forget about today being Monday."

Carol asked Jeanne if she was ready, which was rather unnecessary. But Jeanne assured her that she was. There were several pieces of suitcases lying on the floor close to the door, as testimony to the life of a family which had struggled with a TIW number less than 50 all their lives. It was a melancholy sight. It reminded me of the images of numerous stories and movies where a powerless family was once again planning its escape from powerful evil authorities.

We spent a few more minutes, going over the plan for the final time and making the scene seem more natural to the men outside, before we set out for the day.

"Now," Carol said urgently, looking at her watch. "Let's load up the basket. Get the child."

Jeanne helped me with the basket. Carol was looking at her watch and outside alternately as if the thugs might know what was going on inside.

"Ready," I said, feeling the weight of the basket, which hung somewhat low with its unaccustomed load. I was praying that the bottom wouldn't fall out, not until we got on the road anyway.

"Let's go," Carol said, opening the door.

She and I walked out, casually smiling with each other. I could not help but carry the basket with great care. Swinging it in my usual manner was, on the account of the weight, out of the question.

"Careful, careful," Carol whispered fiercely through her smile as we walked to our car which had been left unlocked.

Through the corner of my eyes, I could see the taller guard, suddenly alerted by the scene. He seemed to have noticed something unusual in the basket, its bottom hanging low to the ground. He elbowed his companion, who had slumped back once again, to a state of full attention.

By then, we were inside the car. I shut the door and started the engine. As I pulled away, passing by their car, the two thugs seemed to be boring with their eyes on us to determine what was afoot with the basket, which was obviously being spirited away. Carol and I maintained our most practiced casualness, my heart pounding, however. The two men seemed to be in a terrible state of indecision.

"Slow and easy, slow and easy," Carol whispered.

I slowly passed the block and saw, just before I made the turn on the next block, that the men got their car started. I could see the smoke belching out of the tailpipe because the vehicle had been parked facing the house.

"There they come," I told Carol who had also seen it because she had been looking back ever since we passed the watch car.

"Push it a little," she instructed, still looking back. "Let's get on the highway as soon as we can."

In my rear-view mirror, I could see the car turn around with a quick savage move, which indicated their redoubtable determination to give chase. Within a few seconds, they were on my tail. They were professionals in the easy and comfortable way they handled their pursuit. There seemed to be no rush in their course of action as if they were certain with what they were doing.

We reached the highway without incident. The chasers made no move to communicate with us. We were almost sure that they were in contact with George Passin, their employer, on the mobile telephone. We kept driving on the highway at the speed that was inconspicuous. We passed at least two highway patrols.

"Would they contact the highway patrol?" I asked.

"Not likely," Carol said. "It is still a civil matter. It doesn't involve the law, not yet anyway."

The drizzle had stopped and the highway was already dry. We had driven for another twenty minutes or so when the chase vehicle, which had been following from a discreet distance, suddenly accelerated as though they had reached an important decision.

"Should I speed up?"

"No," she said. "Just maintain the legal speed."

The legal speed posted on the highway was 75 mph, considerably slower than 95 to 110 mph allowed on the superhighway, but for a driver used to a much slower Laurinville traffic it seemed a high-speed chase.

"How are you doing, Michael?" Carol asked, acknowledging my concern.

I told her I was doing fine. My trip to Anthropolis and back had been a valuable driving experience.

The chase vehicle was suddenly parallel to us on our left. The shorter partner rolled down his window and signaled to us with his hand to slow down. At the same time, he was also shouting the same instruction, which I pretended not to be comprehending.

Then he reached into his breast pocket and pulled out what looked like a document. He held it up with his left hand and pointed to it with the index finger of his right hand, shouting something like 'a court warrant'.

"That's a court warrant all right," observed Carol. "That gives the challenger the right to guard his interest but not the right to stop and search people."

"Would they have weapons," I wondered. "Like guns?"

"They might," Carol said. "But they won't dare use them here. Let's just play innocent bystanders."

The charade went on for a few more minutes, upon which another level of decision seemed to have been reached. They accelerated and managed to get in front of us, all the while the shorter man still signaling for us to slow down or stop. When I pretended to try to change the lane and surge ahead, their vehicle also changed the lane with excellent anticipation and maintained their position ahead of us.

"They are professionals," I said, impressed with their skill.

"Let's see how professional they are," Carol said with mild amusement.

It didn't take too long for the two men to prove they were indeed professionals with their jobs, for they decelerated visibly to the extent that they were forcing me to slow down without actually colliding with us. I had to admire their skill in handling the vehicle to trap their prey.

"Why don't we stop, Michael," Carol suggested as it had become obvious that we had no other choice. "I think we've done our best."

We pulled to the side and came to a gradual stop. The surveillance team immediately joined us by coming to a stop just ahead of us.

"Let's now play indignant bystanders," Carol said. "Let me handle this."

The two men got out of their car and slowly approached us, one on each side like two police officers approaching a speeding driver.

Carol rolled down her window and I did likewise.

"Now, what is this harassment about?" she said with indignation to the shorter man who was coming on her side. "Who are you gentlemen? I want to see your identifications."

The man held up the court paper close to her face as if he wanted no mistake about it. Carol gave it a cursory glance.

"What about it?" she demanded to know. "You have no right to stop us here. We have nothing to do with your court warrant."

"Ma'am," the taller man on my side said to Carol through my window. "We have been watching the object of the court's interest." Then he pointed to the basket that was securely resting on the backseat between two folded blankets. "We would like to see what's in that basket."

"Look here," I intervened, "we are on our way to a nice picnic. There is nothing in it that would be of any interest to you."

"Why don't you let us be the judge of it, sir?" the taller man, who seemed to be the better of the two, said not without some respectfulness in his voice.

"This is absolutely uncalled for," Carol said and she pulled out her pocketbook from which she extracted her driver's license. "I don't know you gentlemen but I know myself. My name is Carol McMiller and my TIW, I will have you know, is over 160. You have no right to treat me like this."

The TIW number impressed the two men somewhat. They looked at each other, then at the TIW number written across the license, then back at each other. They seemed to waver. But the taller man came to a decision.

"Ma'am, you know the court warrant gives us the right to protect the challenger's interest," he told Carol. "The interest is, at least in our opinion, right in the large picnic basket in your backseat. We must see what's in it, and we believe it is within the purview of our rights."

"All right, gentlemen," Carol had come to her decision too. "Then you also know what the consequences would be if you were wrong about it, don't you?"

They looked at each other, then at the basket, then back at each other. "Yes, ma'am, we do," the ringleader said resolutely.

"Very well," Carol said just as resolutely. "I want you to sign this before you do anything."

Carol scribbled something on the pad that she had pulled out of her handbook. It was the now familiar 'bill of satisfaction' form.

"It says you will be responsible for the consequences if you are wrong," Carol handed it to the taller man.

The taller man, as if used to that sort of formality, quickly glanced at the bill and signed it. Carol received it and carefully folded it before she put it in her handbag.

"Michael, let's get out of the car so that these gentlemen can look at the content of the basket," Carol said and we got out.

The two men exchanged glances once again then crawled into our seats. Bending over the back of the front seats, they reached down and cautiously untied the knot that had kept the top closed. Carol and I stood just outside the doors and looked at the two men.

Then the taller man flipped open the top of the basket. It was full of books, which weighed as heavily in the basket as Mary Sue if she had been there. The taller man was instantly immobilized by what he was seeing inside the basket. The shorter man was galvanized into action in behalf of his immobilized colleague. He tore frantically into the first several layers of the books as if Mary Sue could still be found under them. But they found nothing but more layers of books.

They looked at each other, then at the books, then at each other again. Both were red-faced with anger, embarrassment and the realization that they had botched their jobs. They slowly crawled out of the car and faced us.

"We are very sorry," the taller man said stiffly. "I didn't know you ate books for lunch."

"Why, sure," Carol said just as stiffly. "My friend here is a school principal. He eats books for lunch. For that matter so do I."

"Of course," the shorter man said, now quite subdued.

"Don't forget, gentlemen," Carol reminded them as they turned to go back to their vehicle. "That you signed the bill of satisfaction. I also have our conversation on the logger in case you won't remember. You will or your employer will receive *our* court warrant for all the harassment you caused."

"Besides," I shouted to their backs, "I eat books for breakfast and dinner as well in case you didn't know."

The two men slammed the doors and, turning the vehicle sharply around to face the opposite direction, sped away.

Carol and I burst out laughing. We stood on the side of the highway for a few minutes, still laughing, before we got back into the car.

"Where do you think the two detectives are now headed?" I asked.

"To the empty nest," Carol answered. "I don't think they will expect to find anybody at the house. They might have already telephoned another team to rush over there. But all to no avail."

"Nelson and the Bakers should well be on their way by now."

"Nelson knows his way between here and Anthropolis better than anybody," Carol said. "He is avoiding the superhighway in case the road is watched, but he knows all the back roads."

According to our plans, Nelson had been waiting about a block away from the guards as our charade lured them away from the Bakers. As soon as they decided to trail us and left the spot, the Anthropolitan and the Bakers loaded the car and disappeared. The idea was to convince the guards to suspect the content of the basket. It had to be done skillfully so that the suspicion was there without arousing their skepticism about a secondary plot. It worked to perfection.

"For a minute," Carol recalled. "I was afraid the guards might not swallow our bait. You did a great job of carrying the basket just the way you would carry a baby in it."

We turned around and headed home.

"Let's go home and wait for the safe arrival call from our friends in the City of Humanity," Carol said.

The sun suddenly broke through the clouds as we headed back to Wilmington.

Chapter Thirty-One

Late that afternoon a telephone call came to Carol informing her that the Bakers had arrived safely in Anthropolis.

I visited them about a week later, giving the challenger enough time to lose interest in me as a link to his missing prey. But each time I visited them our parting became more difficult for both of us. After my third visit, therefore, I decided to join Jeanne in Anthropolis and enjoy the Anthropolitans who seemed to be truly 'new' Americans. It was while I stayed in Anthropolis that I began the first draft of *Darwin's Progress*, my journey's recollection. I stayed in Anthropolis for three more weeks.

The discerning reader who remembers the beginning of this book knows that Jeanne became my wife. We were 'married' in a simple ceremony conducted by Cornelius for our benefit. But the marriage was duly recognized in Laurinville when we eventually made our way, now with my family, back to my hometown. As soon as we arrived in Laurinville, Mary Sue was formally adopted as my daughter. Jeanne's mother, having made new friends and enjoying the new peaceful environment enormously in her late years, however, decided to remain in Anthropolis. I told her she was always welcome in Laurinville any time, as Jeanne and Mary Sue were welcome, should she decide to come and stay with us.

Cecil McMiller was released from the Recovery Center two weeks later. His memory of the deceased family had been completely removed from his brains by a new therapeutic procedure called 'memory obsolescence'. American medical technology, especially in the field of memory exorcism, seems still unsurpassed. Doctors can pinpoint a particularly disturbing memory source and can remove it with microscopic surgery. The patient recovers from the debility without harming other aspects of life, which is being done on an increasingly massive scale in mental hospitals across the United States. Cecil came home as if nothing else had happened.

Carol in the meanwhile had discharged the actors from service and removed all references to his 'family', including the photo album, from Cecil's presence. Within a week or so, he was well enough to carry out his functions at the university.

A year or so after I had returned to Laurinville, I learned from Carol what had happened to Robert Isaiah Lee, the unhappy philosopher at the University of Wilmington. Upon the expected dismissal from the university, as "his behavior had become increasingly unacceptable to the interest of higher education and to others around him," Lee attempted the most heinous crime in America: He tried to steal his son back from his new parents. He was not very clever about it and was easily caught.

Since such crimes were most severely dealt with in American society, he was sent to one of the 'criminals' paradise' islands where he joined other criminals in their struggle for survival. But the philosopher was not very good at being a prisoner, either, for he tried to escape through the shark-infested waters. However, the authorities were confident that the escapee did not survive. Hearing the grim news and recalling the adventure we had together, I prayed for his tormented soul which had rarely known peace and happiness while he was alive.

Carol McMiller visited Laurinville upon our invitation, bringing some of her artworks with her to be shown our students and townspeople. We discussed my desire to move to Anthropolis someday as Jeanne was all for it, not that life in Laurinville was lacking in anything in particular. I had felt, with my budding career as a writer (after all I had written three books of adventure so far), that Anthropolis was more conducive to my desire to write. She understood.

But I never found out from Carol what happened to God and the Devil in *God's Honest Truth*. I remember stopping her just as she was about to board the bus to the airport on her way back to Wilmington.

"Tell me, Carol," I said. "Did Americans elect the Lord God as their God?"

She smiled that easy smile with which I would always remember the remarkable woman. Then she changed to that faraway look that perhaps only artists and prophets can comprehend. Her smile returned to her face but it was a different smile. It was close to a sorrow of knowing. The engine of the bus roared to take her back to the land of pecuniocracy.

"What do you think?" she shouted above the roar and the bus rolled away.

Two more years passed since I had returned to Laurinville and resumed my duty as principal, when one day I received a letter with no sender's name or address. The postmark was too smudged to tell the place of the letter's origin and the handwriting gave no clue to the identity of the writer. I opened it slowly, seized by a strange sensation of premonition. Inside, there was a small piece of paper with writing on it, and I instantly recognized the writer. On that piece of paper, only the following was written:

I have trodden the winepress alone; and of the people there was none with me: for I will tread them in mine anger and trample them in my fury; and their blood shall be sprinkled upon my garments, and I will stain all my raiment. (Isaiah 63:3)

End of *Darwin's Progress*

Milton Keynes UK
Ingram Content Group UK Ltd.
UKHW022325051024
449173UK00003B/53